The list of suspects

"So there we are," said Detective Chief Inspector Matt MacDermott, the officer in charge of the case. "The murderer is either the factor Archie MacDuff or one of the victim's neighbours. It looks like a stairheid rammy that got out of hand. A plausible scenario in this particular building."

"If you ask me, the factor did it," said Detective Sergeant Madigan.

"You live in a flat, don't you?" said MacDermott.

"You know I do. It's all I can afford since the wife kicked me out."

"It isn't managed by MacDuff & Son by any chance?"

"No, but all those bastards are the same. They've been getting away with murder for years. It's time one of them was held accountable."

"Somehow I don't think your case against young MacDuff would stand up in court," said MacDermott. "Not without a little more evidence. But we can be sure of one thing. If it wasn't him, it was someone who was still in the building at seven o'clock this morning. So the murderer's name is somewhere on this piece of paper."

They looked together at the list.

"Did any of them have a motive?" asked Madigan

"We're talking about Walter Bain," said MacDermott. "*The* Walter Bain. Did any of them *not* have a motive?"

By the Same Author

Close Quarters

Angus McAllister

Matador
9 Priory Business Park,
Wistow Road, Kibworth Beauchamp,
Leicestershire. LE8 0RX
Tel: 0116 279 2299
Email: books@troubador.co.uk
Web: www.troubador.co.uk/matador
Twitter: @matadorbooks

ISBN 978 1788036 689

British Library Cataloguing in Publication Data.
A catalogue record for this book is available from the British Library.

Printed and bound in the UK by TJ International, Padstow, Cornwall
Typeset in 11pt Minion Pro by Troubador Publishing Ltd, Leicester, UK

Matador is an imprint of Troubador Publishing Ltd

Contents

Tenement life

During the 19th century the word "close", which had originally referred to the back court or enclosed space behind a group of tenements, came to mean the common passage within the building, running from the street to the back court. To the tenement dweller, the close was much more than simply the common entrance. The fact that it was clean showed that the tenement's inhabitants were decent, respectable folk… In wealthier areas, tenement closes were often tiled and were known as "wally closes"…

Every tenement had a strict rota for stair cleaning… There was no worse judgement on neighbours than that they failed to clean the stairs… Stairs were swept daily, and cleaned at least weekly with a scrubbing brush and water, then wiped with a clean damp cloth. Doormats were shaken outside and banisters cleaned with a special brush. Door brasses — bell, handle and letterbox - and banister knobs were polished until they shone.

The National Trust for Scotland, *The Tenement House* (2016)

PROLOGUE: THE BODY IN THE LIVING ROOM

August 2000

Walter Bain was dead. He lay face down on his living room floor, his bald head burst open, the thick pile of the carpet soaked in his blood. He was dressed in pyjamas, dressing gown and carpet slippers, a complete bedroom outfit from Marks & Spencer. Beside him lay a cast-iron poker with a brass handle. Its thick tip, which had square edges and looked like a solid, elongated arrowhead, was covered in blood and looked easily capable of having inflicted the injuries. Its companions, a shovel, brush and tongs, were still on their stand beside the empty space where the murder weapon had hung. Until now, the purpose of the set had been entirely ornamental, the gas-fuelled imitation coal fire having no use for such antique implements.

The flat in which Walter Bain had lived for the last thirty-five years, and in which he had now died, was on the second floor of an old tenement building at Number 13 Oldberry Road, Glasgow. It was only a short distance from Byres Road, at the heart of the city's west end. It had four storeys and contained seven flats and a shop.

Although more than a hundred years old, the building looked good for its age and seemed to have benefited more than most from the grant-aided refurbishment that had swept the city clean in the 1980s. Its brownstone had been transformed into bright red sandstone, its chimney heads rebuilt, its old slate roof (noted mainly for its sieve-like qualities) replaced with a new one of tiles. Where there had once been an untidy cluster of television aerials, there was now a single mast, attached to an amplifier in the loft and serving all of the flats. Metal pins had strengthened the back wall in those places where it had begun to sag. The back court was particularly nice: its close-cropped drying green, a new red-painted metal pole at each corner, was surrounded by concrete slabs in an ornamental layout, and the old washhouse, redundant in an age of launderettes and washing machines, had been converted into a smart bin shelter.

Much of the same had been done to the building's neighbours. However, alone among them, Number 13 could boast an additional improvement: the small garden area in front of the ground floor flat was separated from the pavement by a new parapet wall topped by a low iron railing. A matching metal gate, together with the security door at the close mouth, acted as a disincentive to unwelcome visitors. All of the surrounding buildings had an old, crumbling wall, still bearing the stumps of the original railings, removed sixty years earlier to make into weapons for fighting the Germans. The new wall at Number 13 might have been even more impressive had it extended for the full length of the building; instead it continued in a right angle along the far side of the short path leading to the building's entrance, leaving an open, paved area in front of the shop.

The murder was reported to the police just after 7 am by a telephone call from the victim's wife. By mid-afternoon, most of the preliminary work was done and a number of facts established:

1. The victim had probably died between midnight and 4 am. The results of a post-mortem, which might give a more precise estimate, were still awaited.
2. The likely cause of death was a number of heavy blows to the back of the head, which had fractured the skull and caused a fatal brain haemorrhage. The poker found lying beside the body was almost certainly the murder weapon.
3. According to Mrs Bain, she and her husband had gone to bed together around 11 pm. At some subsequent stage, she thought she remembered the doorbell being rung persistently and her husband going to answer it. However, she had taken a sleeping tablet before going to bed and this memory was very vague. She had got up around 7 am and found the body, shortly before phoning the police.
4. The door of the shop was guarded by a security camera, whose field of view incidentally included the front door of the building. The entire night had been recorded on a timed videotape. Between 11 pm and 7 am it showed only one person leaving the building, a young man in his twenties. He had later been identified as Archie MacDuff, junior partner of MacDuff & Son, House Factors and Property Agents, who managed

the building on behalf of its various owners. He had entered the building at 11.35 pm, along with one of the residents. A number of other people had entered the building between 10 pm and 4 am, all residents.

5. Painters were presently working in the building, redecorating the close and stairwell. Their operations had left a film of dust in the back close, so that anyone leaving during the night by the back door would have left footprints. There were no such prints.

"So there we are," said Detective Chief Inspector Matt MacDermott, the officer in charge of the case. "The murderer is either Archie MacDuff or one of the victim's neighbours. It looks like a stairheid rammy that got out of hand. A plausible scenario in this particular building."

"If you ask me, the factor did it," said Detective Sergeant Madigan.

"You live in a flat, don't you?" said MacDermott.

"You know I do. It's all I can afford since the wife kicked me out."

"It isn't managed by MacDuff & Son by any chance?"

"No, but all those bastards are the same. They've been getting away with murder for years. It's time one of them was held accountable."

"Somehow I don't think your case against young MacDuff would stand up in court," said MacDermott. "Not without a little more evidence. But we can be sure of one thing. If it wasn't him, it was someone who was still in the building at seven o'clock this morning. So the murderer's name is somewhere on this piece of paper."

They looked together at the list of names:

1. William Briggs, comic-book dealer, owner-occupier of Flat 0/1.
2. Henrietta Quayle, retired teacher, owner-occupier of Flat 1/1.
3. George Anderson, university lecturer, joint owner-occupier of Flat 1/2.
4. Catherine Anderson, teacher, wife of George and joint owner-occupier of Flat 1/2.
5. Agnes Bain, widow of the victim, owner-occupier of Flat 2/1.
6. Anthony Miller, insurance clerk, tenant of Flat 2/2.
7. James McKelvie, student, tenant of Flat 2/2.
8. Gus Mackinnon, solicitor, owner-occupier of Flat 3/1.
9. Jenny Martin, student, tenant of Flat 3/2.
10. Joe Robinson, student, tenant of Flat 3/2.
11. Angela Murray, student, tenant of Flat 3/2.
12. Archie MacDuff, property agent, visitor to Flat 3/2.

A third tenant of Flat 2/2 had moved out the previous day and could therefore be ruled out. So could the shopkeeper and his family, who didn't live in the building. They had also discounted the two children of George and Catherine Anderson, Eddie (5) and Rita (4), on the ground that neither was strong enough to have applied the fatal blows and would have needed to stand on a chair to do so. It was also doubtful whether Rita could have reached high enough to ring the Bain doorbell.

"Any more daft ideas?" asked MacDermott, having put Madigan right on these points. "Just so we can get them out of the way?"

"Since you mention it," said Madigan, "can you be absolutely sure the killer isn't someone else, someone who left the building by another way?"

"You mean by a window? Not by one on the landing, they're all stuck with paint. And not from one of the flats, unless one of the residents is protecting somebody."

"From Bain's flat, maybe?"

"You mean the killer did the deed, then climbed out the kitchen window and shinned down a drainpipe? I don't think there's any evidence of that, but I suppose we could check. He also might have got in and out from the adjoining building via the loft. The point is, why would he bother? Even if he knew about the security camera at the front, he could still have left by the back door. If he saw he was leaving footprints, he could have obliterated them behind him. No, for the time being, I think we can assume he's one of those on our list."

"Or she is."

"Yes. Giving up on the factor, are you?"

"It would be great if it was him. But I suppose we've got to consider all of the possibilities. Did any of them have a motive?"

"We're talking about Walter Bain," said MacDermott. "*The* Walter Bain. Did any of them *not* have a motive?"

1. THE NEW TENANTS

August 2000
Jenny Martin, Flat 3/2

Jenny Martin never actually met Walter Bain, as she and her flatmates only moved into the building on the day before he was found dead. However, he did succeed in making his presence known, and before the day was over Jenny had heard so much about him that she felt she knew him quite well.

Since the flat had been let to them furnished, it was not a full-scale removal and Joe hired a small van for the day to transport their personal effects, as well as a few items of furniture that had sentimental value, or were necessary to supplement their landlord's minimalist approach. Jenny brought a bedside table and a couple of extra chairs for the living room, Angela an antique dressing table inherited from her grandmother and a couple of extra chairs for the kitchen. Bringing the dressing table required an extra trip from her parents' house in Cumbernauld, but Angela was keen to finally move it into a house of the right age and with enough space to accommodate it properly. Jenny didn't mind. She and Angela shared a somewhat old-fashioned outlook, unusual in girls of their age; it was one of the reasons why they had become such good friends. Joe grumbled a bit about the extra trip, but it was only for show. It was a pity that the landlord's cheap fittings detracted somewhat from the dressing table's new setting.

Joe owned the best stereo system of the three and they installed this in the living room. They also hired a TV and video recorder. The landlord had emphasised the fact that there was a communal TV aerial, providing perfect reception on all channels, though he had not gone so far as to provide an actual TV set in order to prove the point. He had made so much of this that they were expecting some satellite or cable facility, but all it provided were the five terrestrial channels. They unanimously agreed, for the sake of their studies, that this would be enough.

They received their first indication of other life in the building while bringing in the dressing table. It needed all three of them to carry it, and they had to lay it down on the pavement for a moment in order to open the iron gate at the end of the front path. While Joe was doing this, Jenny happened to look up and noticed that, in two separate flats – the one on the first floor, above the shop, and the one above that again – someone was looking at them out of the living room window. The first figure drew back quickly as soon as Jenny looked in her direction, and she only got a brief glimpse of a thin, grey-haired woman. The man in the second-floor flat stayed where he was, staring fixedly down at them. Jenny couldn't make out much detail, but she could see that he was bald, wore glasses, and looked below average height. He was probably in late middle age, but it was difficult to be sure.

"We're being given the once-over," she said.

Joe and Angela looked up and Joe gave a friendly wave. The man didn't move or respond in any way. "Be like that," said Joe. "Come on," he said to the girls, "we'd better get this thing up the stairs."

They had to stop again at the end of the path to open the security door, and then set the table down again in the close while the door closed behind them. The walls on the close and stairwell were tiled to shoulder level; the tiles were of a dark-green pattern, and the plaster above them, and on the ceiling, was painted a lighter green. The close and stairwell were in the process of being redecorated, but the front close had already been completed and the paint was dry. In the back close, a painter – a young man in overalls that might once have been white – was applying distemper to the walls; in that part of the building, it seemed, the quality of decoration was to be a little lower. Just inside the close, stuck above the tiles on the newly-painted wall, there was a hand-printed notice, wrapped in polythene. Angela read it aloud:

DID YOU CLOSE THE FRONT GATE?

"Did I fuck!" said Joe, and the girls laughed.

The painter looked up. "You didnae shut the gate?" he said. "You're for it, pal."

"How do you mean?"

"You'll find out," said the painter, and laughed.

They didn't pursue this any further, but continued with the tricky job of carrying the dressing table up the stairs to the top floor. At the first floor, another painter – this one middle-aged – stopped work and took his stepladder out of the way to let them pass. He shook his head. "Did I hear you say you didnae shut the gate? Oh dear!"

They didn't feel like discussing it further at that moment. "Aye, right," said Joe, and they carried on up the stairs.

Eventually the table was in place in Angela and Joe's room; this was the larger of the two bedrooms and faced the front of the building. As they paused for breath, deciding what to do next, Jenny took a look out of the window.

"I don't believe it," she said.

"What?"

"A woman just came out of the close, shut the gate, then went back in again."

"Who was it?"

"I'm not sure. It looked like that old dear on the first floor."

"For God's sake!" said Joe. "I'd have closed it on the way back out."

The dressing table had been the last item to be moved. They had a cup of tea and rested for a little while, then Joe left to return the van to the hire company. He set off down the stairs whistling loudly, to make sure the neighbours would know that someone was leaving. Jenny and Angela watched at the living room window, certain that he was also being watched from elsewhere in the building. When he got to the front gate, he stood for a moment or two, holding the gate wide open and grinning up at them. Then he closed it behind him with a flourish and walked over to the van.

10

"Typical Joe," said Angela. "We're hardly in the door and he's started to wind up the neighbours."

"It's beginning to look as if some of them are a bit peculiar," said Jenny.

"Well, we are in the west end."

It wasn't long before Jenny's theory was further confirmed. They were busy hanging pictures, replacing the landlord's tasteless choice with their own prints, when they heard the letterbox rattle. Jenny went out and returned with a sealed envelope and a large sheet of thick paper, rolled up like a scroll. She opened the scroll. It was a page from an old calendar: on one side the month of June in the previous year was set out below a coloured photograph of Glencoe; on the other there was a handwritten list:

September 1	Stairs
September 15	Stairs
September 29	Stairs & Close
October 13	Stairs

And so on, at fortnightly intervals, for the rest of the year. On most of the list only the stairs were mentioned, until just after Christmas when the close made a reappearance.

Jenny opened the envelope and brought out several sheets of paper, this time computer-printed:

The accompanying list shows the rota for cleaning of the common parts. Your responsibility is for the two flights of stairs and two landings between the second and top floors. This responsibility is shared with Mr Mackinnon, the owner of Flat

3/1, who sadly tends to be very neglectful of his duties. The stairs should be carefully swept and then washed with warm water and detergent. The addition of a little disinfectant can contribute to a wholesome and hygienic atmosphere in the common area. Pine fragrance, which can be purchased at a reasonable price from Woolworths in Byres Road, is very suitable, but this is only a suggestion. The tiles should be wiped with a damp cloth and the metal support of the banister, whose intricate corners can be a haven for dirt, carefully dusted. The wooden top of the banister and its metal studs should be polished.

All windows, including the one on the landing, should be washed every six weeks, or more often if desired. Dirty windows detract from the smart appearance of a building. It is fortunate that Mr Mackinnon lives on the top floor, as this renders the disgraceful condition of his windows less noticeable at street level.

As Mr Briggs is the only ground-floor resident, the remaining residents take a turn of cleaning the close on alternate weeks. The back court, with the exception of the drying green, should be swept with a stiff brush at this time.

I will notify you when it is your turn to cut the grass. I have custody of the communal lawnmower, which can be uplifted from my house. Your day for using the green is Tuesday.

Your wheelie bin is number seven from the left, which you will see has been inscribed with the number of your flat. You should transport it to the front of the building every Monday night (or before 7 am on Tuesday morning if you prefer) to be emptied by the council, thereafter returning the empty bin to the bin shelter as soon as possible. It detracts from the smart appearance of the building to have wheelie bins cluttering the pavement for a prolonged period.

You should refrain from making excessive noise at all times, and particularly after 11 pm. This is a family building in which the residents strive to maintain the highest standards. Unfortunately, we have not always found tenants to be the most co-operative in this respect. Owner-occupiers (with the exception of Mr Mackinnon) have higher standards, as they have a financial stake in the building. Hoping that you will be the proverbial exception that proves the rule.

Yours faithfully

Your neighbour

Walter Bain (Flat 2/1)

They had just finished reading this for the second time when they heard the letterbox again. This time they found a leaflet advertising a jumble sale that had taken place several weeks before. They looked at it in puzzlement for a moment, before noticing the handwritten note on the back:

You should always shut the front gate after you, as leaving it open will annoy Mr Bain. If any visitors are leaving your flat in late evening, they should remove their shoes and refrain from talking while descending the stairs, as sounds are amplified by the stairwell and any noise will annoy Mr Bain.

Yours truly

Henrietta Quayle (Flat 1/1)

The writing was in old-fashioned copperplate and covered every inch of the small slip of paper.

They showed these communications to Joe when he returned. "Jesus Christ!" he said. "Who *is* this guy?"

"Baldy Bain," said Jenny. "That must have been him we saw at the window."

"And she must be the old dear in the flat below him," said Angela. "Lucky her."

"I know the west end's full of nutters," said Joe. "But why do they all have to be up our close?"

"I see our turn of the stairs starts next week," said Jenny. "You'd think we could wait till the painters are finished."

They forgot about their neighbours for the time being and got on with their work. By 8.30 they decided that the flat was looking good and that they had earned a drink. Their new home was only a few minutes' walk from all of the pubs on Byres Road. It remained to be seen whether or not this would prove to be a good thing.

Jenny was twenty-one years old and about to enter her final year of a law degree at Glasgow University. Angela was one of her classmates and they had been friends since first year. Angela was the same age as Jenny. Joe was a final-year accountant and he and Angela had been together for two years now. He was twenty-five, having spent a few years in work before returning to education. Until now the girls had continued to live with their parents, Jenny in Hamilton and Angela in Cumbernauld. Both had found it reasonably easy to commute, but felt that living locally would benefit their studies in their final year. It would also be handy for late-night socialising, though of course they planned to keep that to a minimum in the immediate future.

Joe had lived in the west end for several years, and had moved out of a bedsit to join the others in their new flat. The three of them got on well together, and Joe and Angela didn't seem to mind the idea of having Jenny living with them. As for Jenny, sharing with a couple meant that they could split the rent three ways while still keeping the living room free for communal use.

During her three years at university Jenny had fallen in love with the west end. She had never come across anywhere else quite like it, either within or outside Glasgow. The proximity of Glasgow University was only part of the reason. A mere hundred yards or so beyond the north end of Byres Road was the headquarters of BBC Scotland, and its south end was almost adjacent to the city's Western Infirmary. In addition to all that, Byres Road bordered, or was near to, several residential areas: working-class Partick and Maryhill were on the south and north respectively, middle-class Hyndland and Kelvinside somewhere in between. All of these elements were enough to create an odd mix of people, which in turn attracted misfits from other parts of the city and beyond. In the west end the excesses of youth were carried on into adulthood and middle age, and even longer for those who could last the pace.

The Centurion, where the three friends were now headed, was Jenny's favourite pub in Byres Road. It stood almost at the midway point of that long thoroughfare and was the least specialised of the many pubs in the area. Other bars could be chosen depending on whether you wanted to meet, at various stages of alcoholism and degeneracy, actors, academics, students, writers, gangsters, young people, older people, young business people, older business people, unemployed, retired, working-class or middle-class people, blacks, whites, Marxists, capitalists, gays, nurses, junkies, posers of every age, class and persuasion, or any of the other minority groups that together made up the area's peculiar majority. In The Centurion you got a little of everything, along with a few other people who were less easy to classify.

It was on the ground floor of an old tenement building that had been refurbished a few years earlier. The pub had also been given a modest facelift at some point, but that had failed to bring about the change in clientele that the owner had probably hoped for. Its interior design remained undistinguished. The customers provided its character.

After a couple of years trying out the more usual student locations, Jenny and her friends had settled in The Centurion as their main headquarters; Joe, who was already a regular, had introduced them to it. As well as its own quota of students, it had so much more to offer besides.

When Jenny, Joe and Angela arrived the bar was well filled but not overcrowded, about normal for a Thursday. The ageing sociologists, the alcoholic gangsters and the defunct lawyers were all there, though the old men on Death Row – a single line of seats along the passage leading to the Gents' toilet – had already finished their quarter gills and left for the night: lunchtime and early evening was their time, weariness and increased traffic in their corner having by now persuaded them to head for home.

The regulars had been given these titles by Joe's friend Danny Boyd, who was sitting with Andy Sloan and Cathie Anderson at their usual table. Jenny and Angela now joined them while Joe got up the drinks. Danny and Andy were both in their forties and looked like hippie survivors from the 1970s. Danny's red hair was now shorter than it once had been, a style that harmonised better with his receding hairline. Andy still had all of his hair, though it was now greying; it too was now kept to a reasonable length, probably to placate the bus company which employed him as a driver. Danny worked for the council parks department, and when he wasn't at work or in The Centurion he was an avid reader and a more educated conversationalist than any student Jenny had ever met. Andy was divorced and Danny, so far as Jenny knew, had never been married.

Cathie was in the pub less often than the others and Jenny had only met her a couple of times before. She was a large woman in her early thirties, who worked part-time as a primary school teacher.

"Is that you moved in?" asked Danny.

"Yes," said Jenny. "We've been at it all day. Thought we deserved a drink."

"I don't need an excuse," said Danny. "Where's your flat again?"

"Oldberry Road. Number 13."

"You're joking," said Cathie. "That's where I live. First floor. You must be the new tenants on the top floor?"

"That's right," said Jenny. "It's a small world."

"You were there before," said Danny. "At the party."

"What party?"

"*The* party. Coupla months ago. You musta been there. Every cunt in the world was."

"Tell me about it," said Cathie. "It was in the other tenanted flat, right above us. My kids were up half the night."

"*That* party?" said Jenny. "Bloody hell. I couldn't have told you where it was. I don't remember much about it. It was just after our exams finished." She turned to Angela. "*You* were there."

"Was I? Yes, I think I was. Joe too."

"Did you hear that Joe? That party a couple of months back? It was in our building."

"What party?" Joe handed the girls their drinks. "You don't mean *that* party?" He laughed. "Mr Bain must have been pleased. I wonder whose turn of the stairs it was that week?"

The girls laughed. Danny looked at them. "Am I missin' something?"

"Take a look at this," said Jenny. She brought Bain's code of practice from her pocket and handed it to Danny. He began to read it with Andy looking on.

Cathie only glanced at it briefly. "Is he still using that thing?" she said. "George translated it into English for him shortly after we moved in, before we joined the club and fell out with him. That bastard couldn't write a bookie's line, or a dirty joke on a toilet wall."

"Is that one of your specialities?" asked Danny.

"Fuck off. That must be about eight years ago. We haven't been providing him with any new copies, so he must be photocopying it. Next thing we know he'll be getting the factor to divide the cost among the rest of us as a common charge."

Jenny thought that she must be joking, but she seemed serious. Danny and Andy continued reading. "Fucksake," said Danny when he was halfway down the first page.

"Christ," said Andy.

This continued to be their refrain, at half-page intervals, until they reached the end. Danny went back to the beginning and began to read it again.

"Typical Bain," he said. "The man's aff his heid."

"You can say that again," said Cathie.

"You know him?" asked Jenny.

"Heard about him," said Danny. "Everybody has. Mainly from Cathie and from Gus. Especially from Gus."

"From Gus?" asked Jenny, glancing across at the defunct lawyers' table, where the gang of four sat, at various stages of intoxication. "You mean Gus Mackinnon? Don't tell me he's one of our neighbours too?"

"Top floor," said Cathie. "Flat opposite you. Did you not notice that he got a special mention in Bain's manifesto?"

"We never made the connection," said Joe. "Bloody hell. Are all of our neighbours in here tonight?"

"That's the lot," said Cathie.

"Anyway," said Danny. "What's the man on about? Naebody does their turn of the stairs in Glasgow."

"Speak for yourself," said Cathie.

"Naebody does their turn of the stairs in Glasgow," Danny repeated. "I've never washed a stair in my life. How about you, Andy?"

"Never. In your close, you just sweep the dirt under the nearest junkie."

"That's no' fair," said Danny.

"Aye it is. Danny keeps findin' corpses in the close."

"That's no' true." Danny took a quick gulp from his pint, choked, and began a fit of coughing. The others looked on in concern, but he recovered in a moment or two, his train of thought unbroken. "That's no' true at all. It only happened once."

"I remember you told me," said Joe.

"That's awful," said Angela. "What did you do?"

"I stepped over him."

"You didn't!"

"I thought he was just sleepin'. Anyway, naebody washes the stairs in Glasgow. What about you, Joe?"

"Not me. Never."

"That won't change," said Angela. "It'll be left up to Jenny and me."

"Don't be daft," said Danny. "Naebody else does it. What about you, Ted?" he asked one of the sociologists, who had just left the next table to go up to the bar.

"What's that?"

"Do you ever do your turn of the stairs?"

"Never."

"Never at all?"

"Never at all."

"Why's that?" asked Jenny.

"I live in a bungalow."

"You're a traitor to your class," said Danny.

The sociologist laughed and went on his way to the bar. "No he's not," said Andy. "He's middle-class. They all live in bungalows."

"You're middle-class, Jenny. Do you live in a bungalow?"

"I live in a tenement. As of today."

"I mean before that."

"My parents live in a semi-detached. But we once lived in a tenement. And my mother used to wash the stairs."

"She must have had middle-class pretensions, even then. Anyway, that was Hamilton, this is Glasgow."

"Christ, Danny, how about changing the subject?" said Joe. But Danny was on a roll. "What about you, Jack?"

"What about me?" said the barman, who had arrived to wipe the table and gather empty glasses.

"You live in Partick. Do you ever wash the stairs?"

"Never."

"See, I told you."

"We all chip in and pay a woman to do it."

"I don't believe it, I'm surrounded by the bourgeoisie."

"Absolutely," said Jack. "I used to live in a south side semi. I'm an eccentric millionaire." Jack was a mature student in his early thirties. He was their favourite barman.

"You mean your wife nabbed the hoose after you split up?"

"You got it in one," said Jack. "Now I've got to clean up after bastards like you." He moved on to the next table.

"Let me get this straight," said Joe. "You're asserting your working-class roots by being a clatty bastard? If we all had dirty closes it would bring on the revolution?"

"Don't be daft. I'm just makin' a point."

"I think you've made it. How long have you been in here?"

"No' long enough. What do you say, Gus?"

This was directed to one of the defunct lawyers, who had left his table and was passing on the way to the toilet. He was a big man with an unsteady gait, which made him look a little like Boris Karloff as Frankenstein's monster, minus the bolt in the neck. The walk was probably the temporary result of intoxication, though few in The Centurion had ever had a chance to test this theory.

"What?" said Gus. He looked a little more defunct than usual and held on to their table for support, which shook a little under his weight. "Hello Danny. Hello Cathie. Oh, hello Jenny."

"Hi Gus."

"You live in a tenement?"

"That's right. Close quarters." He laughed. "You'd better believe it."

"Do you ever dae your turn of the stairs?"

"Do I fu—" He stopped, looking at the girls a little shamefacedly. "Never."

"Not at all?"

"Never ever. Never at all. I'd sooner have all my toenails pulled out." As he resumed his journey to the toilet, it looked as if this might have happened already.

"Looks like our stairs will only get cleaned once a fortnight," said Jenny.

"He's in a bad way," said Joe.

"It's the drink," said Danny.

"You think so? No, I can't see it. It's definitely not the drink."

"Fuck off."

"You can call me a snob," said Angela, "but —"

"You're a snob."

"But I'm not too keen on him and his pals. I don't think it's the best way to start our legal careers, associating with the likes of them."

"Don't be daft," said Jenny. "Do you think the Law Society's got spies in here?"

"Probably."

"Uch, Gus is all right," said Danny. "He's no' like the others. I've a lot of time for Gus. He did me a big favour once."

Jenny stopped Gus when he was passing on the way back. "Did you hear that, Gus?" she said. "We're neighbours."

"What?" Gus leaned on their table again. "Oh, hello Jenny."

"You live at 13 Oldberry Road, don't you? Top floor?"

"That's right. How did you —?"

"We're your new neighbours. Joe, Angela and me. We've just moved into the flat opposite you."

Gus stared at them while this registered. Then he said, "Oh no! You haven't! Tell me it's not true."

"What's the matter, aren't we good enough for you?"

"What? Don't be daft. Oh Christ, don't tell me you've moved in there."

"Why, what's wrong with it?"

"Have you got all night?"

"He means Walter Bain," said Cathie. "Who else?"

"It's time somebody sorted out that bastard once and for all," said Gus. "The way he's treated that poor boy downstairs is the last straw. Just because he held a party. OK, it may have got a wee bit out of hand."

"Just a bit," said Cathie. "But it wasn't Tony's fault. He's just a little naïve. He didn't realise that in this area you hold a party at your peril. Especially if you're just round the corner from all the pubs. George and I don't hold it against him, and we had more cause to complain than anybody else. But Bain won't leave it alone."

"It's time somebody topped the bastard," said Gus. "I'll do it tonight. I've been putting it off for too long."

"You're right," said Cathie. "It's high time somebody offed him. The whole building would be on your side. He ruined Billy Briggs, now he's ruined young Tony, he's terrorised Henrietta Quayle for decades. He almost reduced my George to a nervous wreck when we first moved in. And as for what he did to you…"

"Absolutely," said Gus. "So that's agreed. I'll do it tonight."

"You're too pissed," said Cathie. "Leave it to George and me. We'd only need to leave the kids a couple of minutes. Nobody would believe that we left them at all. It would give us an alibi."

"Maybe the whole close could do it together," said

Danny. "Like in that Agatha Christie film, *Murder on the Orient Express.*"

Jenny was finding the situation increasingly surreal. Gus was pissed, of course, but Cathie seemed quite sober and quite serious. Maybe it was just a ploy on her part to stop Gus from doing something stupid. "Surely Bain can't be that bad?" she said.

"Oh yes he can," said Gus. He looked for somewhere to sit down, but all the seats at the table were occupied. "Come on over to my table and I'll tell you all about it."

Intrigued, Jenny lifted her drink and got up to follow him. "I won't join you," said Cathie. "I don't like some of the company you keep."

"Good decision," said Danny. "Your jaiket's still on a shaky nail in here. You don't want to give Aitken the slightest excuse."

"See if I care," said Cathie. "But it's time I got back up the road. I was on my own with the kids all day while George was at work. I just needed to get out of the house for a bit."

She finished her drink and got up to leave. Joe and Angela decided to stay where they were, but Jenny accompanied Gus back to the table where his friends were sitting. She wanted to ask him what Cathie and Danny had been talking about, but realised that this might not be tactful in front of the new company.

There were four "defunct lawyers": Gus, Bob Waddell, Norrie Spence and Ernie Dunlop. The term "defunct" referred to their status within the legal profession, but in the case of two of them it could have described their physical condition as well. They were all in their fifties and had known each other since they were at university together.

She had met them all before, but her information about their history derived mainly from Danny, who could be relied upon for an endless supply of knowledge and gossip about all of the pub's regulars. They themselves tended to be more reticent about their past transgressions. Gus was different from the others, in the sense that he was still a lawyer: he was still entitled to practise, should he ever sort himself out enough to set up in business, or find someone willing to employ him. Neither seemed very likely at the moment. The others had achieved their present status with a push from the Law Society and, in Norrie's case, after a few years in jail. Both Norrie and Ernie had been struck off for allowing their clients' money to become mingled with their own, the difference being that in Ernie's case it had happened accidentally, whereas Norrie's had been a case of deliberate fraud. Ernie, in fact, was still working in the law. He was employed as an unqualified assistant in a firm of solicitors who got the benefit of his legal skills (apparently quite substantial when he wasn't handling money) at a bargain rate.

Bob Waddell was the most recent addition to the group. "The trouble wi' Bob," Danny had said, "was that he thought he could manage a legal practice as if he was runnin' a stall at the Barras. It got tae the stage that so many of his clients were complainin' tae the Law Society that he had to keep stoppin' work on his other cases tae explain himself tae the Law Society, so then the other clients would complain tae the Law Society and he'd have to think up a story about them, and so on. Eventually he was spendin' all his time helpin' the Law Society wi' their enquiries and gettin' nae other work done. Neither were the Law Society, so they decided it would be a lot easier all round just tae strike him aff." Thus had the legal career and professional reputation of Bob Waddell been snuffed from existence.

Jenny suspected that Danny's account contained more than a little element of exaggeration. Nevertheless, Bob Waddell was the member of the group that she liked least. He was the only one who showed any bitterness, who still seemed resentful about what had happened. Maybe this was because he'd had less time to get used to it, but Jenny also sensed an arrogance in the man, an inability to acknowledge that any of his problems might have been his own fault. Apart from Gus, he was the one who drank most heavily and who was seen most often. Ernie and Norrie, though they were long-term Centurion regulars, still had day jobs and were only occasional drinkers, but when all of the group happened to be in the bar at the same time, they congregated together in their own little colony of professional outcasts.

Jenny didn't share Angela's reservations about associating with the defunct lawyers. She didn't think it would do her future career any harm to observe, at first hand, some object lessons on how it could end in disaster. All the same, she didn't think she would ever ask any of them for a reference.

Norrie and Ernie greeted her warmly and moved along the bench seat to make room for her. Bob was a little more reserved; maybe, with her career in front of her, Jenny reminded him too much of what he had lost.

27

Gus resumed his seat at the other side of the table. "Guess what," he said. "Jenny and her pals have just moved into the flat beside me, across the landing."

"What? You're joking!"

"At 13 Oldberry Road?"

"Oh dear, oh dear!" said Norrie. "Did you buy it or just rent it?"

"We're just tenants."

"That's not so bad then. You can get out of the lease. We'll advise you."

"What's the problem?" asked Jenny, becoming increasingly alarmed. "Is Gus that bad a neighbour?"

"Bad enough," said Ernie. "He'll never do his turn of the stairs."

"I've already gathered that."

"I've already told you what the problem is," said Gus. His voice was still a little slurred, but he seemed to have sobered up a little, rendered eloquent by passion. "I'll tell you again what the problem is in two words, no three words. Walter Fucking Bain. Pardon the French, Jenny."

Although the lawyers swore as much as anyone else, they always apologised if it happened in the presence of a woman. Jenny was uncertain whether this old-fashioned courtesy was a characteristic of their former profession or of their age group. "I've already heard from him," she said.

She gave Bain's instruction sheet to Gus, remembering too late that it contained several disparaging references to him. However, this didn't seem to bother or surprise him. He read it surprisingly quickly for someone in his condition and passed it on to the others. It failed to evoke the same degree of astonishment as it had at the other table, but there were a few chuckles of recognition.

"We've all seen this before," said Ernie. "He's been handing this thing out for years. But he's right, you know. Gus's windows are a fucking disgrace. Sorry, Jenny."

"It saves me buying curtains," said Gus. "Anyway, the bloody things won't open."

"But it's not his fault," said Ernie. "You see before you a broken man, a once-eminent lawyer ruined by drink and the premature onset of old age. Now in the case of some of us, you might argue that our troubles were brought on by ourselves…"

"Speak for yourself," said Bob Waddell.

"But in Gus's case, his Nemesis came from elsewhere, though from within the very building you all occupy. In other words, a certain neighbour whose name has already cropped up."

Gus seemed to have found nothing to disagree with in this analysis. "I'll kill that cunt," he said. "Sorry, Jenny. So help me, but I'm going to top the bastard."

"You've been saying that every night for years," said Norrie.

"This time I mean it. I'll swing for him."

"They've abolished capital punishment."

"So what's stopping me? I've neglected my duty and now he's starting on the younger generation. What he's doing to that boy downstairs is the last straw."

"What's he doing to him?" asked Jenny.

"He's having him evicted. Him and his flatmates. In fact, I think this is their last night. They're moving out tomorrow."

"But how can he do that?" asked Jenny. "What's it got to do with him?"

"You don't know the man's methods. He'll have phoned the boy's landlord a hundred times a day, inflicting brain damage, until he gave in."

Jenny found this a little difficult to believe, but the others seemed to find it plausible.

"So if I kill him tonight, maybe I can stop the eviction. The whole close will thank me."

"So I've gathered," said Jenny.

Gus continued in a similar vein, becoming a little repetitive. Jenny only got a confused impression of the reasons for his own grudge against Bain, though a lot of it seemed to involve sandblasting, reroofing and other refurbishment work on the tenement during the 1980s. There also seemed to be something else, something more recent and more serious, but she couldn't get a clear idea about what it was. Gus's fixation about Bain was even more obsessive than Danny's earlier one about stair cleaning.

After listening to him for some time, Jenny decided that it was time to rejoin her friends. Her drink was finished and the others, whose pace had slowed over the long course of the evening, didn't seem to have noticed. But before she got round to moving there was a new development. A young man came into the pub, walking past them on his way to the bar.

"There's young Archie MacDuff," said Ernie.

Gus, who had his back to the bar, turned round. "So it is. Archie!"

He finally managed to attract the newcomer's attention, after he had bought his drink and turned round.

Gus waved him over. At first he seemed a little reluctant to join them, until he saw Jenny. Then he came over and stood beside their table.

"Jenny, I'd like you to meet Archie MacDuff. Archie, this is Jenny … What's your second name again?"

"Martin."

"Jenny Martin." Jenny and Archie shook hands. "Grab a chair and sit down," said Gus.

Archie borrowed an empty chair from the next table. The others moved along and he set it down opposite Jenny. Jenny got the impression that he had only joined the company because of her, and wished that she'd been quicker making her escape. It would be rude to run away now. Then Ernie offered to buy her a drink, and she was reconciled to staying on a little longer.

Not that there appeared to be all that much wrong with young Archie. He looked about 25 at the most, carried a smart leather briefcase and wore a new business suit which was just a little too big for him, adding to his slightly gauche and vulnerable air. Jenny might have found him quite appealing, except that he matched the rest of the table in drunkenness. His short hair was a little ruffled and his tie loosened. He seemed to be on his way home from the office, having taken the slow, tourist route along Byres Road.

"Are you on your own, Archie?" asked Norrie.

"No," said Archie. "Oh no. There's a whole team of us." He looked around the bar, failing to recognise anyone. "Well there was."

"Never mind," said Gus. "I wanted you to meet Jenny. She's studying law up the road." He waved along the bar, in the rough direction of Glasgow University.

31

"Is that right?" said Archie. His interest in Jenny seemed to grow. He paused, and said a little self-consciously, "I'm in real estate."

The ex-lawyers burst out laughing in unison. "You mean unreal estate," said Ernie. "This is the west end."

"He's a factor," said Bob. "A house factor." He sounded as if he were referring to some inferior form of life.

"Don't hold it against him," said Norrie. "He's just a daft boy."

"We're estate agents as well," said Archie, sounding a little aggrieved.

"There you are," said Ernie. "I told you he was respectable."

"If you only asked me over to insult me…" said Archie, half-rising to his feet.

"Sit down, son," said Gus. "Don't listen to them. I wanted you to meet Jenny. Not to chat her up, to tell her something she needs to know. She's just moved into 13 Oldberry Road."

Archie looked horrified. "Oh no! You haven't!"

"She has indeed. Archie's firm manages our building," he said to Jenny. "At least they call it management. Sorry son, I'm only kidding."

Jenny already knew that The Centurion was the epicentre of the west end, but tonight it had surpassed itself. First two of her neighbours and now the factor. On the other hand, Archie seemed to have been in every other pub in the area, so maybe that made it less of a coincidence. "13 Oldberry Road," he said. "The close from Hell!"

"We've just been talking about Satan himself," said Gus.

"Walter Bain?" said Archie. "I'm going to kill that bastard!"

"No, no," said Gus. "We've already sorted that out. *I'm* going to kill him."

"What have you got against him?" asked Jenny.

"What have I got against him?" asked Archie incredulously. "What have I got against him? He's a bastard! He drove my father to an early grave."

"Your father's still alive," said Ernie.

"If he goes before his time, it'll be down to Bain. My dad's a broken man because of him."

Bain the breaker of men, thought Jenny. This was ridiculous, even by Centurion standards.

"Dad's completely allergic to the man," continued Archie. "He won't even let you mention his name. He won't have anything more to do with 13 Oldberry Road. So guess who's left to deal with it? It's driven me to drink!"

"But surely he can't force you to manage the property," said Jenny. "Why don't you give it up?"

"Are you kidding? You don't know the man. He won't let us. He's been through every other factor in Glasgow."

"MacDuff & Son were the last on his list," said Bob, a little nastily. "I wonder why?"

"Who the fuck are you to talk?" said Archie, rising to the bait at last. "At least we're still in business."

"Calm down, boys," said Gus. "Let's concentrate on the real enemy."

Archie took a drink from his pint and was quiet for a moment. "I've been thinking about it a lot recently," he said eventually, "and there's only one thing to be done. I'm going to kill him."

Gus and his friends didn't seem to find Archie's outlook in the least extravagant. "You can't do that, son," said Gus. "I won't let you make the sacrifice. You've got a long and promising career in front of you as a daft boy. I've got nothing to lose. I'll do it." He drank the last drops from his whisky glass and the final inch of beer from his half-pint. "I'm away to do it right now."

Nobody made any effort to stop him, either because they didn't believe he was serious or because they hoped he was. He got up from his chair with an effort and began to walk unsteadily towards the toilet.

"Maybe I should see him up the road," said Jenny.

"Don't be daft," said Norrie. "Sit down and finish your drink."

"But will he get home all right?"

"He has every other night for the last twenty years," said Ernie.

A few minutes later Gus came out of the toilet and made for the door. Jack the barman helped him on his way and saw him outside. When Jack returned, Jenny waved him over.

"Is he all right?"

"Safely across the road," said Jack, "and moving more or less in the right direction. He keeps going on about wanting to kill somebody. Do you know anything about that?"

Jenny laughed. "Just a little."

Archie sighed. "If only he meant it. It'll be left up to me, you wait and see. As my father always says, 'If I want a job done right, I've got to do it myself.'" He seemed unaware that he was betraying MacDuff Senior's opinion of his son's competence. Then, as if he'd been given the baton in a relay race, he took over from Gus, resuming the older man's monologue on the subject of Walter Bain.

The defunct lawyers listened tolerantly, appearing to relish the new exposition of their friend's obsession, told from a different perspective. Or maybe they were just too drunk to bother. Jenny felt trapped. When Archie offered to buy her a drink, she accepted, just to get him away from the table.

"You'll be looking for a new flat now?" said Norrie.

"It's a bit late to move out tonight," said Ernie. "You'll be able to get a new place tomorrow."

"I don't believe this," said Jenny. "First Gus and now him. Are they both mad? Can Bain really be as bad as all that?"

"Yes to both," said Ernie.

"The boy's not mad," said Bob. "You need to have a brain for that."

There was a break in the conversation while they all enjoyed the silence caused by Archie's absence. Jenny was now wishing that she'd stayed with her flatmates. Not just because she was bored, but mainly because she'd come into the pub still excited and optimistic about her new home. Now she felt depressed about it. The adventure had gone sour. Could one neighbour really have such an effect? Maybe upon other owner-occupiers, but surely tenants didn't need to bother about him? Or did they? After listening to Gus and Archie she was beginning to think she'd be sharing the building with a monster. When the bogey man came to your door, would he back off just because you flashed your rent book in his face?

Archie brought the drinks back to the table and sat down. "Do you know how many times Bain phoned me today?"

"Yes, you told us."

"Ten times!"

"No," said Ernie, "you only told us five times."

"No, the number of times he *phoned* me. Ten times. My secretary kept telling him I wasn't in but he wouldn't listen. He'd just go on and on and on and on and on and on until she gave up and put him through. It's not her fault. She's a nice woman, she doesn't deserve it. If she hangs up on him, he just phones back. She can't put him through to my father, it would give him a bad turn just hearing the man's name. She can't leave the phone off the hook. You can't do that, not when you're in business. You can't have a factor that doesn't answer the phone."

"Why not?" said Bob. "The city's full of them."

"And do you know why he was phoning? Just to make sure Tony Miller's definitely moving out tomorrow. He's desperate to get him out of the building. All because he held a party."

"Not *a* party," said Jenny. "*The* party."

"I've told him it's got nothing to do with me, it's up to Tony's landlord, but of course he's been on to him as well. He wants both of us phoning the landlord, making his life a misery, just to make sure he gets the message. He wants to catch him in a pincer movement." Archie raised his hands to illustrate this, and smiled, as if Walter Bain's throat was between his outstretched fingers.

By now last orders had been announced, and when closing time followed for once it came as a relief to

Jenny. Except that Archie seemed to have attached himself to her. "Where is it you live again?" she asked him. A little unsubtle, but Archie was in no condition to notice this.

"Bearsden. But I can't ask you back. My folks are there."

"That's not quite what I meant," said Jenny. "How are you getting home?"

"I'll take a taxi. Unless you can give me a bed."

"We don't have a spare one. We'll get you a taxi."

There was a queue in the Ladies' toilet and when she arrived in the street Archie was talking to Danny and the others. She'd introduced him in the hope of sharing the burden, but now wondered if it had been a mistake.

"What did you say your name was?" Archie was saying to Danny.

"Danny."

"No, your second name."

"Boyd."

"That's what I thought you said." Archie giggled drunkenly. "Danny Boyd. I like that." He began to sing to Danny. "Oh Danny Boyd —"

"GET TAE FUCK!"

"What's the matter with him?"

"I think he's heard it before."

Jenny decided it was time to find a taxi. As usual, there were plenty of hackney cabs going up and down Byres Road, but they were all taken. For several minutes she looked in vain for the yellow light of a vacant one, but it was the wrong time of night. Archie had reattached himself to her and was making no effort to find a taxi for himself. She could easily abandon him, but he seemed in no condition to manage on his own.

"They're all full," she said.

"What are?"

"The taxis."

"Oh," said Archie. "I could always come back to your place."

"What for?"

"To phone a taxi."

Jenny thought about it. Why not? Joe and Angela would be there. "All right. Just to phone a taxi."

"Unless you've got drink in the house."

"No, we've got no drink. None at all. We've just moved in." She noticed that Joe was holding a carry-out bag and hoped that Archie hadn't seen it.

Danny came over to her. "We're goin' doon tae my place for a blaw. You up for it?"

"No," she said. "I don't think I'll bother."

"You sure?"

"Yes."

"I'm going back to Jeanie's to phone a taxi," said Archie.

"OK," said Danny. "See you later."

Too late she saw Joe and Angela begin to follow him down the road, leaving her alone with Archie. Joe even winked at her, the bastard.

"What did he mean, going for a blaw?"

"To smoke dope."

"Oh. I'm not into that."

"Neither am I," said Jenny. "They say it can start you on fags."

Archie took a draw on his cigarette, the remark lost on him.

Jenny had a last look for the yellow beacon that signalled a vacant hackney, but no reprieve came. "Come on," she said. "Let's go."

As they started on their way, Archie tried to put his arm around her and she lifted it off again. Then she realised that he needed the support and gave in.

"I like you, Jeanie," he said. "You're nice."

Far too nice, thought Jenny. *That's my problem.* "It's Jenny," she said.

"What?"

"My name's Jenny."

"Oh. Sorry Jeanie, I mean Jenny."

He began a reprise of the Walter Bain monologue, a selection of unedited highlights. Jenny didn't mind too much: it was better than drunken advances. Then, about halfway through their journey, he suddenly stopped.

"I've just realised. We're going to 13 Oldberry Road."

"So?"

"I can't go there. That's where Bain is."

For Christ's sake, thought Jenny. *Of course that's where Bain is. Why else have I been listening to all this shite?* But she was too nice to say it out loud. "What's the matter, you're not afraid of him are you?"

"Am I fuck! Sorry, Jeanie. Of course I'm not afraid of him." His tone carried little conviction.

"Anyway, he'll be in bed by now."

"How do you know?"

"He sounds like the type. Or do you think he's got the place bugged?"

"I've thought about that," said Archie, with complete seriousness. "But Gus says no. He says that if Bain had wanted the place bugged he'd have gone to the factor – that's us – and asked us to get estimates, so that we could pick the cheapest and charge it to everybody in the close as a common repair."

Jenny laughed. From all she had heard about Bain, this sounded plausible. Gus had surely been joking – she *hoped* he had – but Archie obviously believed him. Anyway, Archie had now overcome his impulse to run off – why on earth had she talked him out of it? – and they proceeded on their way.

When they arrived at 13 Oldberry Road the building was in darkness. Everyone had gone to bed, or had still to come home. Or maybe some of them lived mainly in the kitchen. The front gate was wide open, but Jenny closed it carefully behind them. As they approached the security door, Archie put his finger to his lips. "Sh!"

He is *afraid of Bain*, thought Jenny. Or had he set his mind on killing the man in his sleep?

She unlocked the security door, pushed it open, then jumped back in fright. The door swung shut again.

"What's the matter?"

"There's a body in the close!" Surely this only happened in Danny's neighbourhood, down in Partick? Were the dead junkies creeping north? Then she realised what she'd seen and opened the door again.

Gus was lying halfway down the close, asleep, his back against the tiles, his long legs blocking the passage. Vomit had dribbled from his chin, down the front of his shirt, on to the stone floor. She tried to shake him awake, while trying to keep clear of the vomit. "Gus! Gus, wake up! You can't sleep here."

Gus didn't stir. "Sh!" said Archie, pointing up the stairs. Jenny shook Gus more vigorously, but this time keeping her voice in a whisper.

Gus opened his eyes and looked at her blearily. "Goany kill the cunt," he muttered.

"Come on Gus, you've got to get up." But Gus had shut his eyes again. Jenny tried to pull him to his feet, but in spite of all her efforts he hardly moved. In his present state, he comprised 16 stones of inert matter. "Give me a hand, Archie."

Archie tried, but in his condition it only made matters worse. They got Gus halfway to his feet, then all of them collapsed in a heap. Some of the vomit rubbed off on Jenny.

"Leave him," said Archie. "He'll be all right."

"We can't leave him here."

"It happens all the time. Bain told me. He wants to have Gus evicted."

"How can he do that? He's an owner-occupier."

"Sh!" Archie whispered. "You don't know the man."

But though she had yet to meet him, Jenny was beginning to feel that she did know Bain. Reluctantly, she realised that she had no option but to leave Gus where he was. They would never be able to get him up to the top floor. She checked that he was sitting upright, breathing normally, unlikely to choke, then she and Archie carried on upstairs. At Archie's insistence they went on tiptoes, his finger continually to his lips as he exhorted her to silence, particularly when passing Bain's door on the second floor. For a would-be assassin, he seemed remarkably timid.

Once they were in the flat, out of earshot of the neighbours, he grew more confident and his thoughts returned to murder. With difficulty, Jenny managed to get him to shut up while she phoned for a taxi. She tried four numbers: three of them rang out, and the fourth could promise nothing within the next forty-five minutes. She told them not to bother. It didn't seem to worry Archie, who appeared to be quite happy where he was.

"Have you got anything to drink?" he asked.

"No."

"I had to go out for a drink tonight. That man drove me to it. Do you know how many times he phoned me today?"

"Yes, you told me."

But of course he told her again and continued in the same vein. "Don't bother with the taxi," he said. "I'll just go down and ring the bastard's doorbell until he gets out of bed, and when he answers the door I'll grab him by the throat and – and I'll wring his neck." He laughed. "Get it? I'll ring the doorbell, then I'll wring his neck."

"Hilarious," said Jenny. "Would you like a coffee?"

"Yes, please."

She thought this would give her a break from his company, but he followed her through to the kitchen, talking all the time. She hated people who did that. Eventually they were back in the living room with the coffees, Archie's flow unabated. His homicidal agenda, fuelled by the proximity of his intended victim, was growing in strength and conviction.

Eventually Jenny couldn't take much more and excused herself to go to the toilet. With any luck Archie wouldn't try to follow her there. She lingered as long as she could, washed her face, combed her hair, brushed her teeth, reapplied her make-up. Not for Archie's benefit – definitely not for that – but to fill time and combat the fatigue that was gradually overcoming her. When she left the toilet there was no sign of Archie – she had half expected him to be waiting outside the door – so she went into the kitchen and tidied up a little, then went to her bedroom and did the same.

Finally, reluctantly, she went back to the living room. It was with mixed feelings that she found him sprawled across the sofa, asleep. Should she try again for a taxi? To hell with it. Joe and Angela could deal with him. She took his shoes off and pulled his feet up, putting a cushion under his head. He turned and settled himself more comfortably without waking up.

Jenny went back to her bedroom and before long was fast asleep in bed.

She was wakened by the sound of Joe and Angela arriving home. She was first jolted out of sleep by the slamming of the storm door, followed by the slightly less noisy closing of the inner door.

"Sh! You'll wake Jenny."

"You think she got lucky?"

This was followed by a bout of giggling. Jenny switched on the bedside light and looked at her clock radio. Ten past four. The giggling was continuing, right outside her door. Every so often it would die down, there would be a hushing competition, then it would start up again. There was no point in trying to get back to sleep for the moment. Jenny got out of bed, put on her dressing gown and slippers and opened the door. Joe and Angela were propping each other up in the middle of the hall, paralysed by the prospect of deciding which room to go into.

"Hi Jenny. Sorry, did we wake you?"

"Where's your boyfriend?"

This set them off again. "He's not my —" Jenny broke off. What was the point?

She put her finger to her lips and pointed towards the living room, then walked over and opened the door carefully. The sofa was empty. She quickly checked the rest of the flat. He was gone. At least one of her problems was solved.

"He was on the couch. He seems to have left."

"Done a runner, has he?"

"You must have tired him out."

This of course was also extremely amusing. When they paused for breath, Jenny said, "Is Gus still lying in the close?"

"What?"

"Did you see Gus in the close?"

"Gas in the close?" said Joe. "I didn't smell anything. Just as well I didn't light a fag."

Jenny waited impatiently through their next period of incapacity. People in their condition could be really tiresome if you hadn't been getting high along with them. Never mind, she'd get her revenge in the morning. Surely they couldn't have failed to notice Gus if he'd still been lying there? Or had they flown right over him, oblivious?

"Someone's been sick in the close," said Angela.

"Just as well it's not our turn to clean it," said Joe.

They were off again. At least her question was answered. If they'd noticed his spoor, they couldn't have overlooked the man himself. "See you in the morning," said Jenny abruptly and left them to it.

She awoke again just after nine. By 9.30 she had showered and dressed and had begun to make breakfast when the doorbell rang. She went through to the hall, opened the inner door and storm door, swinging the latter right back until it was flush with the wall.

Two casually-dressed young men stood on the landing, one about Joe's age, the other a little older. The older one flashed a card in front of her. "Detective Sergeant Madigan," he said. "This is Detective Constable Thomson."

"Oh."

"Can we come in?"

"Of course."

She stood back and let them pass, shutting the inner door behind them. She led them through to the living room. "What's it about?" A ludicrous theory occurred to her and was immediately dismissed.

"All in good time, Miss. Do you live alone here?"

"No, I've got two flatmates. They're still asleep."

"Late night, was it?" Madigan was smirking.

"Yes. That's not a crime is it?" Wrong thing to say. Why was she being defensive?

"No, not at all. Not by itself. If you could just give me some details we'll let your friends lie on for the moment."

At Madigan's prompting she gave him their names and other particulars, and an estimate of when they had all arrived home the previous night. She was able to give a fairly accurate one, explaining how she'd been wakened by Joe and Angela's arrival.

"You say you arrived home about 11.30. Actually, it was nearer 11.40, but that's not bad. Did you come home alone?"

Jenny felt her face redden. What was going on? "No," she said. "I didn't."

"That's right. Can you tell us who the young man was?"

In other words, did she know him or was he just an anonymous, one-night stand? Madigan seemed to have a knack of being offensive without actually saying anything that could be the subject of a complaint. Jenny gave him Archie's name. "He's the factor," she said. "He's a partner in the firm that manages the building. MacDuff & Son, I think they're called."

"Really?" Madigan seemed to find this of particular interest. "I'll need to keep a note of that firm's name. A factor who provides his services in the middle of the night?" Jenny didn't like the meaning he seemed to read into the word "services". "That must be a first. Do you know when he left? He has left, I take it?"

"Yes. I don't know exactly when. He was gone when Joe and Angela came back. When I went to bed, he was sleeping on the sofa here, the one you're sitting on."

"Is that so?" Madigan and his companion looked at each other. "Well, that seems to fit."

"I don't want to be rude, but do you mind telling me what this is all about?"

The policemen exchanged glances again. "I don't see why not," said Madigan, as if he were making a great concession. "Since two of you are lawyers, we'd better keep on your right side. We're here because there's been a murder in the building."

"*What*?"

"A Mr Bain, who lived on the floor below. Did you know him well?"

"I've never met him. We only moved in yesterday."

"Of course. For someone who didn't know him, you seem rather upset."

"Someone's been murdered, for God's sake. Practically next door."

"Yes, of course," said Madigan. "It must be a shock. Well, we'll try to get through this as quickly and painlessly as possible. Have you got a VCR?"

"What?"

"A video cassette recorder."

"Yes." She pointed to it, underneath the television.

"Good. Mind if we use it?"

"No, of course not. Why?"

"You'll see in a moment." Jenny noticed that Constable Thomson had a videotape in his hand. "Meanwhile, you'd better give your friends their first alarm call. We'll need to speak to them in a moment."

Jenny went through to Joe and Angela's room. She knocked on the door first, but this precaution proved superfluous. They looked set to remain unconscious for the rest of the morning, if left to it. She did her best to waken them and tell them what was happening, then returned to the living room.

Madigan and Thomson were looking at the television, at a slightly blurred image. It took Jenny a moment or two to identify it. In the foreground was a side view of the shop on the ground floor, but the rest of the building's frontage had been caught in the background, including the security door on the close and the path leading up to it. Madigan restarted the tape, which had been paused at a single frame. White numbering at the foot of the picture showed the time of the recording. It was just after 11.39. Jenny saw herself come up the path, with Archie's arm around her. Somehow they both looked equally drunk. She saw herself unlock the front door, partially open it, then start back.

"Just as well you were telling us the truth, eh?" said Madigan. "Something seemed to give you a fright there."

"Gus Mackinnon. The man across the landing. He was sleeping in the close."

"That must be the gentleman who arrived about an hour before you. He did look a little unsteady. Was it him who was sick in the close?"

"Yes."

"I see. Did you help him upstairs?"

"We couldn't move him. He had gone by the time Angela and Joe came home."

"So he made it upstairs sometime between 11.40 and 4 am. Probably took him all that time." Madigan fast-forwarded the tape to 3.10 am. The front door opened and Archie came out. He looked a little steadier than before, but not much. "Exit the super-factor," said Madigan.

"He's left the front gate open. Did he not see the notice in the close?"

Angela came into the room, followed by Joe shortly afterwards. Jenny's mention of police and the murder had aroused them more quickly than would otherwise have been possible, but they looked rough. They'd managed to get dressed, or maybe they had slept in their clothes. Jenny introduced them to the policemen and they sat down just in time to see the recording of their return to the building at 3.58 am. How did it take them so long to get upstairs, Jenny wondered?

It became apparent in a moment. Jenny was relieved to see that their performance considerably outclassed that of Archie and her. The front gate gave Joe the pretext for an impromptu comedy act, a silent movie routine that was overacted and which greatly outstayed its welcome: he displayed shock and astonishment at finding the gate open, held his head in despair, resolutely made sure the gate was closed and the catch fastened. His audience of one, at any rate, was appreciative. They held each other, shaking in silent laughter, for what seemed an interminable time. Then they began to kiss, and that took even longer. Finally they set their befuddled minds to the insuperable task of unlocking and opening the security door before the show was finally over.

"Didn't realise you'd become movie stars, did you?" said Madigan. "Must have been a good night."

"Great," said Joe.

"I won't ask you what you were on," said Madigan. "Seeing as we've got more serious matters to deal with.

Anyway, that's enough for now. We may be back later. Don't flee the country."

Jenny accompanied the policemen to the front door. "Your friend the dosser," Madigan said. "You said he lives opposite?"

"That's right."

"We tried him first but we couldn't raise him. Hardly surprising, I suppose. If you happen to see him, tell him we'll be back up, after we've been to the other flats."

"OK."

She returned to the living room. Joe had gone back to bed. Angela looked as if she would like to do the same, if only she could summon the energy. "We'll all be murdered in our beds," she said.

"By the look of you, they'd be doing you a favour." Jenny looked up a number in the telephone directory, then lifted the telephone receiver.

"Who are you calling?" Angela asked.

"Gus."

"Who?"

"Our neighbour, across the landing."

The possible significance of this managed to penetrate Angela's mental cloud. "Do you think that's a good idea?"

"I don't know." Why was she phoning Gus? To warn him? She told herself it was only to check that he was all right. She was aware that she had failed to say anything to the police about having been in Gus's company the previous evening, about his repeated threats to kill the victim. About Archie having made similar threats. Did that mean she was already compromised? But she couldn't really believe that either of them had been serious or, when she'd last seen them, physically capable of the deed.

On the other hand, each of them had subsequently slept off some of their drunkenness. If Gus had recovered sufficiently to climb six flights of stairs, he was probably also capable of committing a murder on the way up.

She tried Gus's number. It rang out for a while, then an answering machine switched on. In the recording, Gus sounded more coherent than on the previous evening, though perhaps not entirely sober:

"This is Gus Mackinnon. If you're selling double glazing, fitted kitchens, life insurance, or anything else, or if you're Walter Bain, you can FUCK OFF! Otherwise you may leave a message after the tone."

"What's the joke?" Angela asked.

"Gus's answering machine."

Angela wasn't sufficiently motivated to enquire further and Jenny didn't bother to enlighten her. She waited for a moment or two, wondering what to do, then made up her mind.

"I'd better check if he's all right," she said. Angela didn't comment.

Jenny went out to the landing and rang Gus's doorbell, having first looked down the stairwell and listened for any sign of police presence. There was none. The two detectives would be in one of the other flats, out of earshot.

She waited for a few moments then rang the bell again. She was about to try for a third time when she heard the inner door open. The storm door opened a fraction and

Gus's head appeared. He looked terrible: bloodshot eyes, grey hair unkempt, unshaven. It was funny how designer stubble was attractive in a younger man, but just made an older one look dirty and untidy. It took him a moment to recognise her.

"Jenny! What are you doing here?"

"I'm your new neighbour, remember?"

This also produced a delayed reaction. "Yes, of course," he said eventually. "I remember. Sorry Jenny, I had a rough night."

"I know. I was there. I wanted to check if you were all right."

"That's nice of you. I was asleep, till some bastard tried to get me on the phone."

"Sorry Gus, that was me. Something's happened, I need to speak to you. Can I come in?"

"Of course," he said. He pulled the storm door back and she followed him into the house. It wasn't long before she understood his reluctance to admit her. He had obviously slept in his clothes, having removed only his jacket and shoes. He hadn't put on the hall light and the only illumination came from the half-open doors to the kitchen and back bedroom. Jenny had expected the house to be a mirror image of her own, but noticed that the layout was different. The sole pieces of furniture in the hall were a telephone table and a large wooden bookcase; Jenny noticed in passing that many of the books were law books, some of them old hardbacks. Two plastic rubbish bags, both full, lay by the wall, adding their own contribution to the musty odour that pervaded the house, and a pile of empty cardboard boxes blocked the entrance to the front bedroom. Nothing had been dusted for a long time and the carpet badly needed vacuuming.

"Sorry about the state of the place."

"Don't worry about it."

He took her into the living room, which had a derelict, unoccupied appearance; presumably it was the least embarrassing room to show a guest and Jenny tried not to think about what the kitchen and back bedroom must be like. It was sparingly furnished: an old three-piece suite, another bookcase, glass-fronted this time, and a wooden dining table with four upright chairs. The table sat in the bay window, its top covered with an untidy heap of books and papers that looked as if they hadn't been touched for some time. A gas fire, that also had an unused look, was fitted into an old-fashioned fireplace, and assorted rubbish littered the mantelpiece. The units of an expensive hi-fi system, also dust-covered, were stacked in a black metal rack, several classical LPs lying on the floor nearby; the large loudspeakers faced the sofa, one on top of a wooden record cabinet, the other on the floor. The daylight was muted by what looked like several years' accumulation of dirt on the windows, but at least he had been joking about his lack of curtains: two long, velvet drapes hung at the windows, permanently drawn back. They were quite nice curtains, and would have been even nicer after a visit to the dry cleaners.

"Have a seat," said Gus. "Just throw that stuff on the floor."

"Thanks." Jenny cleared a pile of old magazines and several polythene bags from an armchair. She resisted the temptation to dust the seat with her hand before sitting down.

"Sorry about the mess. The man downstairs reported me to the Sanitary."

"Who?"

"The Environmental Health."

"Good God. What happened?"

"They went through the motions." Gus chuckled. "No pun intended. They weren't really interested, but they had to do something to get Bain off their back."

Well he's off their back now, thought Jenny, wondering how she would raise the subject.

"My daughter helps me out," he continued. "She does my washing. She sometimes has a go at tidying up, but she doesn't know where to start. She's a good girl, studying to be a doctor. You remind me of her, Jenny."

Oh God, thought Jenny. *Time to get on with the main business.* "I thought I'd better let you know. The police have been up looking for you. They'll be back soon."

"Looking for me?"

"They've been talking to everyone in the building. There's been a murder."

"A *murder*?" There was a pause while Gus tried to take this in. Then something seemed to occur to him and he looked at Jenny hopefully. "It wasn't Bain by any chance? Tell me that Bain's been murdered. Please!"

"As a matter of fact, it was him."

"You're joking."

"I wish I was." Jenny paused. "I don't quite know how to put this, Gus. But last night, in the pub. You said you were going back to kill Bain."

"Did I?"

"About a hundred times. Maybe more."

"Christ! Did you tell the police that?"

"No."

"You should have. You'll get into trouble."

"Not half as much as you. You didn't do it, did you? I doubt if you were capable."

"I can't remember," said Gus. "I can't remember much at all."

"You were sleeping in the close when I got home. I tried to get you up, but you wouldn't budge. Do you remember waking up, going upstairs?"

Gus shook his head. "To tell you the truth, that's happened before. Hang on, something's coming back. Christ, no it can't be."

"What?"

"I've got a vague memory of ringing his doorbell, getting the bastard out of bed. Or maybe that was another night. Or maybe it was a dream."

"You'd better not tell me any more," said Jenny. "If it makes you feel any better, you're not the only one in the frame. Archie MacDuff came back with me last night. To phone a taxi," she added quickly. "He fell asleep on the couch, left in the middle of the night."

But there was none of the innuendo that she'd got from Madigan. Gus merely looked concerned. "Young Archie? That's right, he was in the pub, wasn't he?"

"You introduced me to him. And he kept threatening to kill Bain as well."

"Oh no," said Gus. "You say he was in the building last night? He's got nearly as much motive as me. The stories I could tell you!"

"You have told me. So has he."

"Well that does it. We can't let the boy go down. I'll confess to it."

"Don't be bloody stupid. He was as drunk as you. Neither of you was capable."

"Some of the worst crimes of passion were committed through drink," said Gus. "I can't believe it, I did it at last." He noticed Jenny's look of alarm. "Don't worry, I'll keep my mouth shut, unless it looks as if they're going to pin it on Archie."

"You mean you think you might have done it?"

"Who knows? Who cares?" He laughed. "It's just beginning to sink in. Bain's dead. I don't normally speak ill of the departed, but in his case I'm delighted to make an exception. The new millennium dawns at last!"

He stood up. Colour had returned to his face and he was noticeably more animated, as if the news of his neighbour's demise had acted like a vitamin shot. "You say the police are coming back? You'd better get back over to your own flat, Jenny, we can't let them find you here."

"You're right," she said. "What are you going to do?"

"I'll have a wash and shave," said Gus. "Put on some clean clothes." He laughed again. "If I've got time, I might even tidy up a bit. Can't have the cops thinking I keep a dirty house!"

2. A FRESH START

Summer 1981
Gus Mackinnon, Flat 3/1

It had been an eventful year so far. Unemployment was at its highest post-war level and there had been riots in a number of English cities. Assassination attempts had been made upon the US President and the Pope, and an unemployed 17-year-old youth had fired six blank shots at the Queen during the Trooping the Colour ceremony. IRA hunger strikers were dying in Belfast's Maze prison. The Polish trade union Solidarity was locked in a struggle with the country's communist government. On the positive side, America had launched its first space shuttle, the Yorkshire Ripper and the killer of John Lennon had both been convicted and sentenced, and Prince Charles was to marry Lady Diana Spencer on 29th July. For those remaining unmoved by any of this, there was the Rubik's Cube, a puzzle comprising a number of variously coloured smaller cubes which could be arranged into 3 billion possible combinations, only one of them correct. In Scotland alone, 30,000 people had bought a cube and been driven mad by it, though in the west end of Glasgow it was difficult to tell.

To Gus Mackinnon, all of the above took second place to a more personal disaster. At the beginning of the year, he and his wife Joyce had separated after ten years of marriage. Now she was suing him for divorce. Since the separation he had rented a furnished flat, but he had now decided that it was time to put his living arrangements on a more permanent basis. When he saw the advert for the Oldberry Road flat, he had already viewed a number of flats and made two unsuccessful offers.

He almost missed the advert, which had been placed privately by the owner rather than through an estate agent. It said that the flat was in Hyndland, a high-class residential area to the west of Byres Road. In fact it wasn't nearly far enough west to deserve this distinction. At this point in his life Gus was less alive to the convenience of living within easy walking distance of the Byres Road pubs. But he decided to have a look at the flat anyway.

He arranged to view it at 6 pm, left the office early and found that he had time for a quick pint in The Centurion before his appointment. It was a Thursday evening, and the usual early evening crowd had half-filled the bar. There was a scattering of students who thought themselves too mature for the Queen Margaret Union or the Beer Bar and who found The Centurion an acceptable halfway house on the road to adulthood. At the other end of the age divide, the Brigadier and the Brothers Grimm sat in single file, guarding their whiskies and the path to the Gents. Three sociologists from the university were having an argument about whether Solidarity or the communist government was the true voice of the Polish people; on the face of it, Solidarity had the better claim, but the support of the Pope made it politically suspect. Gus only caught a fragment of the discussion as he passed their table, but it had been going on for months and he had now put together most of it.

Various business people, fresh from their west end offices, stood or sat at the counter, trying to distance themselves from the rest of the clientele. Among them was Norrie Spence whom Gus joined, at the same time nodding across the bar to Danny Boyd. Danny often drank with the sociologists, but tonight was with a man Gus didn't know; he looked familiar, however, a west end face, part of the human background furniture of the area's incestuous social scene.

"Hi Gus," said Norrie, putting aside the *Glasgow Herald* crossword "Want a pint?"

Gus brought over a vacant stool and sat beside him. "I'm only in for one. I'm viewing a flat at six."

"No problem," said Norrie, waving over the barman. "I'll add it to the list. Where's the flat?"

"Oldberry Road. The advert said it was in Hyndland."

"Cheeky. It's in Partick, isn't it?"

"Or Dowanhill maybe," said Gus. "Hyndland's definitely stretching it a bit. It's just round the corner in fact."

The barman brought over the drink and Norrie paid for it. "Cheers," said Gus.

"Cheers."

Gus took a long drink from his pint and some of the day's stress began to wash away. For a few moments he said nothing, but enjoyed being away from the end of a phone, having no one competing for his attention. Norrie understood this and returned to his crossword.

"How's it goin', Gus," said Danny Boyd, who had just come up to the bar. His drinking companion, Gus noticed, had just gone out the front door.

"Hi Danny," said Gus. "Want a pint?"

"Naw, it's OK," said Danny. "I've just ordered one. Thanks anyway."

Danny was unemployed, but he never cadged drinks. How did he manage it, Gus wondered? He was able to survive without spending his day continually in overdrive, taking incessant phone calls, meeting clients, supervising staff, doing a continual juggling act with several dozen transactions, all requiring his individual and immediate attention. When he took a drink it was for recreation, not to ease the tension that had quickly built up in the morning, remaining constant all day; it was a prelude to a free evening, not a necessary dose of medication before going home with a briefcase full of title deeds and other documents which required a period of sustained concentration impossible in the office. Of course, Danny didn't have to pay for a wife and two children who lived in a villa in the suburbs, while still having to take on a second mortgage in order to find a bed for himself. It seemed like a much simpler life.

A life, Gus realised, with its own, quite different pressures. How did you achieve a balance between the two extremes? On the face of it, Norrie seemed to have succeeded. If he was working harder than Gus, incurring even more stress, it didn't show. And it wasn't because he had settled for a more modest lifestyle. He was the same age as Gus and, like him, was a partner in a firm of solicitors. By Gus's reckoning Norrie shouldn't have been earning any more than him. And yet, not only did he also support an ex-wife and two children, but he had remarried, started a new family and was occupying, not a modest flat, but a villa in North Kelvinside.

"You got your invitation yet?" Danny asked.

"Invitation?"

"Tae the royal weddin'."

"No," said Gus. "It must have been sent to my old address. I've been meaning to ask the wife about it, but she isn't talking to me."

"Bloody parasites," said Danny.

"That's not fair, I'm supposed to support my family."

"Naw, I mean Charlie an' his bird. Why the fuck should we support them?"

"Why the fuck should we support you, pal?" said Norrie, when Danny had returned to his seat. Norrie never spoke to Danny and had remained with his newspaper while Danny was at the counter.

"Uch, Danny's all right. Live and let live."

"You shouldn't offer him drink."

"He never accepts it."

"But he never seems to go dry. If he spent some of his money on a haircut, he might be able to get a job."

"Him and two and a half million others. If it was that easy, I'd buy a share in a barber's shop." Gus quickly finished his drink and stood up. "Anyway, I'd better get over and see this flat. Thanks for the pint."

It took him only a few minutes to walk to Oldberry Road. When he turned off Byres Road, he passed from a busy thoroughfare, filled with people, traffic, shops and pubs into a residential area. The traffic noise faded a little as he walked away from the main road, between long blocks of old tenement flats. One of the nice things about the west end was that it had remained mostly untouched while elsewhere so much of the old city had been obliterated by redevelopment. Dumbarton Road, which cut through the centre of Partick at a right angle to Byres Road, was like a time capsule, a sort of urban national park preserving a portion of the old Glasgow that had been bulldozed away elsewhere. On the ground floors of its unbroken line of tenements, not only were all basic human needs catered for, from alcohol to curry, but you would also find all sorts of funny little shops that you'd never see in a modern shopping centre. As you moved northwards, parallel to Byres Road, the housing became grander, the flats bigger, tenements eventually giving way to terraces, though many of the latter were subdivided for occupancy by students and other itinerants.

Gus was now in an area about halfway up this uncertain social ladder. Number 13 Oldberry Road was a four-storey block of flats, at the end of a long block, uniform in design. It stood at the junction of two roads, and there was a small grocer's shop on the ground floor. It would have been built, Gus estimated, towards the end of the nineteenth century and its red sandstone was now darkened by a hundred years' accumulation of grime. Otherwise it looked good. The small garden in front of the only ground-floor flat was well maintained, the green-tiled close and stairwell clean. A wally close where people did their turn of the stairs. On his way up to the top floor, he looked out of the stairwell window to inspect the back yard. The grass was cut short, though the concrete surround was cracked in places and there was a derelict washhouse. Four aluminium dustbins, dirty and battered, sat in a small brick shelter.

He reached the top floor flat he was looking for and rang the bell. The storm door was open, and both it and the inner door looked in need of painting, in contrast to the bright frontage of the flat opposite. He heard footsteps within the flat and the inner door opened. He immediately recognised the man who opened it. He was Danny Boyd's drinking companion from The Centurion, the reason for his early departure now apparent.

He looked about 30 – perhaps a year or two younger than Gus – and was casually dressed in jeans, trainers and an open-necked shirt. His dark hair was long, though not quite as long as Danny's.

"Mr Welsh?"

"That's right. You must be Mr Mackinnon. Come on in."

Gus followed him into the hall. "Do I know you from somewhere?" Welsh asked.

"I just saw you in The Centurion. You were drinking with Danny Boyd."

"That's right. You know Danny?"

"Oh aye."

"Small world, eh man?"

He showed Gus round the flat. It looked as if he lived on his own: at least there was no one else in evidence, and the place had the feel of a house that had lacked a woman's touch for some time. Welsh appeared to sleep in the back bedroom, which contained a king-size bed and a large, old-fashioned wardrobe, but although the front bedroom did contain a bed, it seemed mainly to be used as a box room. There were gas fires in the kitchen and living room and a gas cooker in the kitchen. Welsh had obviously tidied up prior to the viewing, but nothing could disguise the generally shabby condition of the flat. The decoration was old, the furniture older, and there were none of the modern features – like double glazing, central heating or a fitted kitchen – that you would take for granted in a modern property.

On the other hand, the place had potential. The rooms were large, the ceilings high. The living room had a large bay window and ornate cornicing on the ceiling. The old-fashioned fireplaces had been retained and the doors had the original wood panelling, though Gus suspected that this had resulted from indolence rather than any conservationist instinct. It looked like the sort of flat that would go on the market after the death of an old person who had lived in it all his or her life. Gus discovered later that Welsh had bought it in exactly these circumstances, thereafter showing a talent for inertia beyond his years.

Welsh said very little while Gus was looking round. He seemed very relaxed, showing none of the eagerness to impress that sellers often displayed.

"What's included in the sale?" Gus asked.

"I'm not with you, man."

"What fittings are you leaving behind? The gas fires?"

"I hadn't thought about it. Yes, I suppose so."

"The cooker?"

"Definitely."

"Carpets and curtains?"

"They're not up to much, but sure, you can have them."

He's right, Gus thought, *they definitely aren't up to much.* But if he did end up buying the place, they would provide him with some sort of start, and he wouldn't have to renew everything right away.

"What about entry?"

Welsh seemed uncertain. "Whenever you like. I've already got somewhere else to live. Just give me a week or so to get organised."

"OK," Gus said. "I'll give it some thought. If I'm interested, you'll hear from me soon. Who's your lawyer?"

"Waddell & Co."

"Bob Waddell?"

"That's right. You know him?"

"Oh aye. I'm a lawyer myself."

"Is that so? Better watch what I say."

"I wouldn't worry about it."

He didn't look worried. He didn't look as if he had ever been worried in his life. "I'm going back to The Centurion. Fancy a pint?"

"Why not?" said Gus. "I expect Danny will still be there."

When they left, Welsh locked the storm door with an ancient iron key, 6 inches long. It looked like the key to a dungeon rather than a flat. He kept it separate from his other keys, and when he put it in the pocket of his jeans it made an obvious bulge.

As they were walking down the street, Gus said, "What are the neighbours like?"

"Oh, they're all right. I never see them."

"I thought I saw someone looking out of a window at us."

"I didn't notice."

Later, Gus would wonder whether Welsh had sounded evasive. However, at the time he seemed as casual as he had been about everything else.

When they arrived back at The Centurion, Norrie, who had a family to return to, had gone. Danny was sitting in the same position as before, the level of his pint – which might or might not have been the same one – a few inches lower. A couple, Andy and Sarah, whom Gus knew only slightly, had joined him. They greeted the newcomers in unison.

"Hello Gus."

"Hello Toby."

"Didnae know you two knew each other," said Danny.

"We've just met," said Gus. "I was up viewing his flat."

Gus went up to the bar and bought a drink for Toby Welsh and himself. The others declined his offer.

"You buyin' a place?" asked Danny when Gus returned to the table.

"'Fraid so. Looks as though the wife and I won't be getting back together."

"That's a shame," said Danny. "I'm really sorry to hear that, Gus."

"One of these things."

"So where's the fancy woman?" asked Andy.

"There's no fancy woman," said Gus. "Or rather, she's called a legal practice."

They nodded, but didn't comment further. Gus could see that they didn't really understand. To them, a lawyer was someone of impossible wealth. The west end, and The Centurion in particular, might contain an egalitarian social mix, much less rigidly classified than elsewhere, but there were times when tact was required. People who were unemployed or in low-paid jobs didn't want to hear complaints from a solicitor about his stressful day. Gus decided that it would be better to drop the subject.

The conversation turned to the royal wedding, which seemed to be Danny's *idée fixe* for the day, perhaps for the whole month. "It's bad enough that half the country's signin' on, without all that shite as well. It really gets up my nose."

"Bad scene, man," said Toby. "You'd be better off with a snort of coke."

"Aye, right," said Danny. "I mean, if I was a taxpayer I'd object to my money bein' spent on that pair. What do you think, Gus?"

"I don't really care," said Gus. He didn't, nor, unlike Norrie, did he care about whether it was spent on Danny or his friends. None of that figured high among his current concerns. "At least he's marrying a commoner."

"Is he fuck, her faither's an earl."

"I thought she had a job," said Gus, who had paid very little attention to the story of the developing royal romance. It had been a difficult issue to ignore recently, but he had succeeded well.

"That job's just a hobby. Stolen fae some worker that really needs it."

"She's a nice-looking chick," said Toby.

"Oh, don't get me wrang," said Danny. "I'd gie her one if she was stuck."

"I can't see her ever bein' that stuck," said Sarah.

"Fuck off. What do you think, Andy?"

"I'm sayin' nothin'."

This, with variations, made up the conversation for some time. Toby Welsh contributed as much as anyone else, though Gus felt he was learning very little about the man. Then he offered to buy Gus a drink, though without making the same offer to the others. Gus accepted and Toby went up to the bar.

"You really goany buy his hoose?" asked Danny.

"Maybe. I haven't made my mind up."

"Watch him. He thinks he's a fly man."

"What does he do?"

"As little as possible. Or, tae put it another way, anybody he can."

"I'll make sure I get a good lawyer."

"Anyway," said Danny, "I wouldnae offer too much for his flat. He's been tryin' tae sell it for ages, but he's no' had a nibble."

"Why's he selling?"

"He needs the money."

Toby returned with the drinks and Gus was prevented from learning more. The conversation refocused on the wedding.

Half an hour later he left for home. The others were all still there and looked settled for the evening. He bought himself a Chinese takeaway and headed back towards the two-room furnished flat, part of a subdivided terrace house, that he presently occupied.

Gus had arranged to get a loan from a building society with which he did regular business. When he phoned them to arrange a survey, he persuaded them to appoint a particular surveyor who was known to him, one he knew he could trust. At the same time he sent his secretary to the Mitchell Library to check back issues of the *Glasgow Herald*. This confirmed what Danny had said. The flat had been advertised every week for the last five weeks.

Why was it taking so long to sell? West end flats usually sold quickly: if Gus hadn't already known that, his earlier, unsuccessful offers for other flats would have confirmed it.

There were a number of possible reasons, not all of them sinister. The housing market was sluggish during the summer, and that was a time when the aggressive sales techniques of an estate agent could be useful, when selling privately could be a false economy. Many potential buyers would have been put off by the amount of work the house needed. And Gus suspected that Toby Welsh was asking for too high a price; he felt sure that some property investors, amateur and professional, would have been sniffing around, but possibly hadn't offered enough to take care of Toby's financial problems.

Of course Toby's solicitor should have been able to advise him on a better approach. But Gus knew his solicitor and was not surprised.

The survey report took unusually long to arrive, but when it eventually came it confirmed his instinct. The property was sound and the asking price too high. The reason for the delay was the difficulty the surveyor had experienced in finding the owner at home. Gus wished that he had given the surveyor the names of a few Byres Road pubs to look in; that might have speeded things up a little.

By now he had decided that he wanted the flat; his lease was due to end in a month, he didn't want to have to renew it, and he was too busy at work to devote any more time to house-hunting. He sent a formal offer to Waddell & Co to buy the flat at £1,000 below the asking price. The offer included a clause providing that the price would include the gas cooker and fires and all carpets and curtains. He also inserted a four-day time limit for acceptance, hoping that a deadline might focus Toby's mind; from what he had seen, his mind might be in need of focus.

On the day before the expiry of the time limit he had still received no reply. He went into The Centurion for a pint on the way home and told Norrie about it.

"Who's his lawyer?" Norrie asked.

"Bob Waddell."

"For fuck's sake."

"Exactly."

"So," said Norrie, "abandon all thoughts of conspiracy. Simple incompetence is the explanation."

"Still, it seems a bit of a coincidence that Bob should be acting for him."

"Not really, from what you tell me about the seller. You know how Bob finds business. He does a pub crawl of Byres Road, hoovering up clients."

"You're right. I'll phone the bugger in the morning. I can always extend the deadline if I have to."

But he was given an opportunity for earlier action a few minutes later when Toby Welsh entered the bar. Gus waved to him and he came over. "Did your lawyer get my offer?" Gus asked him.

"What offer?"

"I sent an offer to your lawyer. It expires at noon tomorrow. I might be able to extend it if you're interested."

"How much did you offer?"

Gus told him. Toby seemed a little disappointed, but didn't comment further. "Mr Waddell seems to be a wee bit careless," he said. "Is that typical?"

Norrie laughed. For the first time a hint of alarm showed through Toby's normal nonchalance.

"I can't comment on that," said Gus.

"He'll remember to send you his bill," said Norrie. "I wouldn't worry about that."

This didn't seem to give Toby much reassurance. "I'll give him a ring in the morning," he said, and went over to join some other people whom Gus didn't know.

"I should report you to the Law Society," said Norrie. "Dealing with the other side's client behind his lawyer's back."

"Fuck off," said Gus. "Anyway, I was wearing my buyer's hat, not my lawyer's one. And I doubt if Bob Waddell even knows how to spell 'professional etiquette'."

"I can't argue with that."

Next morning he managed to get through to Bob Waddell on the third attempt; it seemed that Toby Welsh had found him in Tennents Bar the night before and instructed him to accept Gus's offer. Gus got the impression that Bob had already forgotten about this by the time he phoned, but the call managed to evoke a response and a written acceptance of Gus's offer, agreeing to all of its conditions, was hand-delivered before noon. It contained several typing errors, but made enough sense to be legally binding, and Bob had remembered to sign it.

Gus relaxed, for a short time at least. His house hunting was over.

The day of the royal wedding arrived, 700 million people across the world (who presumably disagreed with Danny Boyd) watched it on TV, and the newlyweds sailed off on the royal yacht for their honeymoon. The west end and the rest of the planet found new obsessions to fix upon. In Gus's case, they remained much the same as before.

The agreed date of entry for his new flat was three weeks after the conclusion of the contract, which was a little tight. Gus managed to get the conveyancing transaction settled in time by hounding Bob Waddell through every stage, having letters delivered rather than posted, even doing some of the work that should have been the responsibility of the seller's solicitor. On the morning of the date of entry, he went personally to Bob's office to hand over his cheque and collect the title deeds and keys, a time-consuming service that would never have been afforded to a mere client.

Bob's office was in the west end, not far from that of Norrie. He had a one-man practice and he took on all kinds of legal business: conveyancing, executries, civil and criminal court work, anything sufficiently legal in nature to justify the issue of a fee note. He displayed the versatility conferred by incompetence: if you were sure to bungle everything you did, there was no need to specialise.

It was some time since Gus had visited Bob's office, but it was as he remembered it. Everything was for show:

flashy business sign, brightly painted rooms, luxurious carpets, hardly a piece of paper to be seen on the desks of Bob or any of his staff. All the mess had been swept under the carpet, or rather into some back room that constituted a fire hazard. There were several people in the waiting room, some of them looking bored, others angry, none of them happy about Gus being able to jump the queue.

"You've been a bit pushy about this one," said Bob. "You're worse than the bloody Law Society."

"For Christ's sake, Bob. This is my own house."

Bob waited impatiently while Gus carefully inspected all of the documents, not only to check that they were in order, but also to make sure they were the right ones. "Don't you trust me?" said Bob.

"Of course I do, Bob," said Gus, hoping that he sounded sincere. "I just like to do things properly, you know that."

"Waste of time, if you ask me," said Bob, finally accepting Gus's cheque and handing over the keys. Gus knew that they were the right keys: one small Yale and one solid iron giant. "What's that for?" Bob asked. "Has it got an outside lavy?"

Gus laughed. "I don't think there are many of those around any longer, Bob. Otherwise I'm sure you'd be selling them as starter flats."

"Fuck off."

"It's for the storm door. I should be able to repel all boarders."

Since he was in the area, he would have liked to check out the flat right away, but he was already late for another appointment and went straight back to his own office. His trip to the west end had left him behind with his work and it was nearly 7.30 before he managed to finish up for the day. He made straight for Oldberry Road, for once managing to bypass The Centurion.

As he was unlocking the storm door – turning the big key required some strength of wrist – he heard a door open on the floor below him. He paused for a moment but there was no further sound; no one came upstairs, or went downstairs, nor did the door close again. He decided to ignore it: if one of his new neighbours wanted to meet him, he could show himself first. He swung the storm door back and used the Yale key to open the inner door.

The first thing he noticed after entering the hall was that he was standing on bare floorboards. There was also a faint smell of gas, so he put his cigarettes and lighter back in his pocket. The light was dim and it took him a moment or two to find the light switch. He operated the switch but nothing happened. Toby must have switched off the power at the mains, a good idea. But then his eyes adjusted to the gloom and he noticed a simpler explanation: a bare light fitting, with no shade and no bulb.

It took him only a few minutes to confirm that the house had been stripped bare. There were no carpets, no curtains, no bulbs or shades. The gas fires and cooker were gone. Everything detachable, plus a few things that shouldn't have been, had been taken away.

Gus walked from room to room several times, trying to collect his thoughts. Then he realised that there was little more that he could do that night. He made sure that all of the gas taps were turned off and decided to open a few windows, to air the place a little. Most of them remained stuck or jammed shut, but he managed to open those in the bathroom and back bedroom by a few inches. He found the gas and electricity meters in the hall cupboard; high on the wall a small window, bisected vertically by a single iron bar, looked out upon the landing, admitting just enough light to see by. He decided against using his cigarette lighter for further illumination. He turned off the main electricity switch and checked the tap beside the gas meter. It appeared to be turned off.

Alone among his confused thoughts there was one fact of which he was sure. He needed a drink. He was less certain about whether or not he wanted to run into Toby Welsh.

He pulled the inner door shut and locked the storm door. As the big key turned noisily in the lock, he heard a door open on the landing below. It was as if both doors operated in tandem, one locking and the other opening by a single turn of the key.

Gus went downstairs. A man was standing in the vestibule of the house immediately below his. "Good evening," Gus said.

The man didn't return the pleasantry. "Have you bought the flat upstairs?" he asked. He had a mild manner of speaking, but it sounded a little like an accusation. He was a smallish man, almost completely bald, and wore glasses with thick plastic rims. He also wore carpet slippers and a woollen cardigan with most of the buttons fastened. His age was difficult to determine, but he was possibly in his forties; he looked like the type who acquired a middle-aged look early in life, thereafter remaining identical for the next 40 years or so.

"That's right," said Gus, extending his hand. "I'm Gus Mackinnon."

The man shook his hand, a little reluctantly it seemed to Gus, and his grip was weak. "Walter Bain. Gus, you said. Is that short for Angus or Fergus?"

"Neither."

Gus wondered if Bain was going to invite him into his house, but he seemed content to carry on the conversation on the landing. He was still regarding Gus suspiciously. "Do you know the fellow who lived up there before you?"

"I just bought the flat from him."

"I mean, did you know him before you bought the flat?"

"No, I answered an advert in the paper."

"I thought I saw you and him going down the road together."

"We've got friends in common. Why, is there a problem?"

"No, oh no. I just wondered if you were friends, that's all."

"No," said Gus, "and I don't think we ever will be." Bain still seemed reluctant to believe him. Gus quickly told him about the stripping of the flat. He needed to tell someone, and this man was keeping him away from The Centurion.

Bain appeared unmoved by the story. "These things belonged to him, didn't they?"

Gus decided against giving him a lecture on the law of contract and the legal principles relating to heritable fixtures. "He was supposed to leave them. Anyway, taking all the light bulbs, is that not a bit much?"

"I don't know," said Bain. "Light bulbs cost a lot of money these days."

"Do they? I suppose I'm about to find out."

"Oh yes," said Bain. "He wasn't a very good neighbour, you know. I was always having to phone the police about him. It cost me a fortune in phone calls."

"The police? What did he do?"

"The noise he made! The people he invited back! This is a family building, you know. I hope you realise that."

"I think I'm reasonably well house-trained," said Gus, a little irritated. It seemed that his guilt was to be presumed until he could prove otherwise. "Anyway, I think I'd better be —"

"What is it you do?" Bain asked.

"I'm a solicitor."

Bain's manner changed immediately. The air of suspicion was gone and he smiled at Gus. "A solicitor? Is that so?"

"Yes. What do you do?"

"I work for an insurance company. A solicitor, eh? That could be very useful."

He didn't elaborate upon this, but Gus began to have forebodings. Like most lawyers – as well as doctors, accountants and many other professional people – he tended to be reluctant to admit his calling, as this normally earmarked him as a recipient of boring confidences and a source of free advice. "Well," he said, "it's time I was —"

But Bain would not let him go. "Are you married?"

"I'm getting divorced. That's why I bought the flat."

"Yes, there's a lot of divorce about these days." Bain spoke as if it was a type of disease. "Mrs Bain and I have been married for 15 years."

"Very nice. I think I should —"

"Yes, as I said, this is a family building. We've lived here since we got married. I came from Paisley originally."

"Is that so?"

"Yes." Bain chuckled, as if he had admitted to a rakish past. He wasn't just a bald, middle-aged bore, he had once lived in Paisley! "Do you mind if I ask you a personal question?"

"What?" What was Bain going to ask him about? His sex life? That could be answered very quickly.

"How much did you pay for your flat?"

None of your bloody business, Gus thought. But to say so would not be a good start to neighbourly relations. Anyway, it was a matter of public record for anyone who took the trouble to look it up. "Fifteen thousand pounds," he said.

Bain looked delighted. "Fifteen thousand pounds! Is that so?"

"That was the price."

"So my house must be worth at least the same. It's identical to yours, you see."

"Is it really?"

"Exactly the same. Do you know what mine cost? Have a guess."

"I've no idea."

"Go on, have a try."

Gus's thirst was now intense and this was not helping his mood. "Twenty-four pounds seven shillings and sixpence," he said.

Bain seemed uncertain how to react, though he was obviously irked at having his surprise spoiled. "No, it wasn't *that* cheap," he said. "I paid two thousand pounds. What do you think of that? Two thousand to fifteen thousand in 15 years. Not a bad investment, eh?"

"Great," said Gus. "Look, I don't want to be rude, but I really have to go."

"All right," said Bain. "When are you moving in?"

"I'm not sure. A week, ten days maybe." That, at least, was when he had to be out of his present flat. Would he be ready to move in upstairs by then? Maybe if he bought an airbed and a paraffin stove...

"I'll need to let you know about your turn of the stairs. About cutting the grass and all that. I'll leave you a note."

"Fine," said Gus. Never mind about sleeping on bare floorboards, as long as the stairs were clean. Unbelievably, Bain was actually going back into his house and closing the door. "'Bye," said Gus.

Then, as Bain's door closed he heard one open downstairs. It was like a domino effect, running down one side of the building. Thank God there was a shop on the ground floor.

A woman was waiting for him on the next landing, in the doorway of the house below Bain. She regarded Gus anxiously as he came downstairs. He discovered later that this was her permanent expression: the source of her anxiety was existence itself, not any specific aspect of it. She was thin, of medium height and, like Bain, her age was difficult to guess. She was at least in her forties, Gus estimated. She wore a long, old-fashioned skirt and high-necked blouse and her greying hair was tied in a bun.

"Good evening," he said. "I'm Gus Mackinnon. I've just bought the flat on the top floor."

She lightly grasped his extended hand, letting it go again immediately, as if it had given her an electric shock. "Thank God!" she said. "I've been praying for a miracle!"

"Sorry?"

Something seemed to occur to her and the worried expression was replaced by one of horror. "Oh!" she said. "I didn't… I mean…"

"What's the matter?"

"I should have asked you…Did you know Mr Welsh before you bought the flat?"

"No, I answered an advert in the paper."

"He isn't a friend of yours? I thought I saw you and him go down the road together."

"We've got friends in common. He's *definitely* not a friend of mine."

He had said this with enough sincerity to convince her. "Thank God!" she said again. She fidgeted continually as she spoke, shifting her weight from one foot to the other, extending her arms alternately back and forward, as if she was dancing to an inaudible rock band or badly needed to go to the toilet. "I can't believe he's gone at last. That man is *evil*."

This seemed like an exaggeration, though Gus was generally receptive to the proposition. "Really?"

"The *people* he took up there! The *women*! The *orgies*!"

"Orgies?"

"You wouldn't believe it, Mr Mackinnon. Do you know what I think?" She lowered her voice to a whisper. "I think he was running a – a *brothel*." The last word was almost inaudible.

"Is that so?" Gus laughed. "I seem to arrive everywhere too late." She looked startled and became suspicious again. "I'm only joking."

"I thought Mr Bain would never be able to get rid of him. He kept phoning the police. He was always getting me to phone as well. The trouble was, he phoned too often and the police stopped taking any notice. When they called, that man Welsh would just ask them in for a drink. It became a regular stop for them. That's the police for you. Nothing but bribery and corruption."

An interesting image was forming in Gus's mind. The local constables, weary from treading the west end streets at night, nipping up to Oldberry Road for a drink and a bit of nookie. He hoped they wouldn't want to continue the tradition. "You don't need to tell me about the police. I'm a lawyer."

"Is that so? Are you really? I used to be a history teacher, but I've retired now."

She didn't seem quite old enough for retirement, but Gus tactfully made no comment. As they continued to chat he thought he was going to be invited into her house, but like Bain she seemed to prefer to conduct her conversations on the landing. Perhaps she had still to be finally convinced that he was not an agent of his evil predecessor.

He finally managed to break away without being impolite. He went straight to The Centurion.

The brothel-keeping incarnation of evil was drinking with a group of people at one of the tables. Gus went over to him. "Can I have a word?"

"Hullo there, man. Sure, have a seat."

"Can I speak to you in private?"

Welsh followed him over to the counter, looking sincerely puzzled. "What's the matter, man?"

"I got the keys of the flat today."

"Great. Does that mean I'll get my money soon?"

"I don't know. Probably."

"Magic." He laughed. "Is that the big key in your pocket or are you just pleased to see me?"

"Very funny," said Gus. "What the hell do you think you're playing at? You've taken everything away. The cooker, the fires, the carpets, the curtains. You agreed to leave them."

"Did I? I can't remember."

"It's part of the contract."

"I don't know anything about that. You'll have to ask my lawyer. He said it was all right to take that stuff."

"Did he?"

"Sure. I mean I needed the bread, I had to sell what I could. I was hoping to get a higher price for the pad, you know. Calm down, man. Do you want a pint?"

How many second-hand light bulbs equalled the price of a pint? "No thanks," said Gus. "You say Bob Waddell told you it was all right to take the stuff?"

"That's right. You can ask him yourself. I saw him in The Aragon about twenty minutes ago."

"I'll do just that," said Gus. He left the pub and crossed over to The Aragon.

Bob Waddell was still there, drinking with an old man whose face looked vaguely familiar to Gus. Bob was probably trying to talk him into making a will, or into replacing a valid existing one with an ambiguous substitute. He excused himself and joined Gus at the counter, with the ease of one who regularly has to keep new clients at arms length from irascible former ones.

"What's the problem?" he asked, as soon as several drunks and the high level of background noise had insulated them from the old man.

Gus told him. "He claims you said it was all right to remove the stuff."

"No I didn't."

"He says otherwise."

"He's a lying little shite. Anyway, what's the problem? None of these things were fixtures."

"Yes they were. The fires were, anyway. That's not the point. My offer included them and you accepted it. Without reading it, obviously."

"Calm down, Gus. Don't get your knickers in a twist. Do you want a pint?"

"No," said Gus, though he did want one.

"Why worry about it? There's nothing you can do. He'll have sold the stuff by now."

"You could give me a refund. A couple of hundred pounds, say."

"Fuck off. The transaction's settled."

"I could sue him."

"So sue him. I'll represent him. I'll get a fee whether he wins or loses. Come on Gus, why bother? Have a pint."

"Fuck off," said Gus, and went back to The Centurion.

He separated Toby Welsh from his friends again. "I saw Bob Waddell. He denies saying you could take the stuff."

"What? He's lying, man. That's what he told me. I'm sorry, Gus. This is a bad scene. I don't want any aggro."

"Neither do I." One of them was certainly lying, but Gus wasn't sure which. "Would you be willing to take a couple of hundred off the price?"

"Can't do it. I've got debts. Be reasonable, you got the place cheap."

Gus thought about it. He *had* bought the place at a good price, and in his own way had employed a certain amount of cunning in order to achieve it. He too had benefited from the incompetence of Toby's lawyer. And the stuff was all rubbish, which he would have replaced as soon as he could. And he was tired, and he was thirsty, and there was only an hour left until closing time.

"Come on, man," said Toby. "Be cool. Do you want a pint?"

"Why not?" said Gus.

3. SOME FOLK WILL COMPLAIN ABOUT ANYTHING

Winter 1981
Gus Mackinnon, Flat 3/1

The normally busy junction at the top of Byres Road was deserted and Gus was able to cross Great Western Road without any problem; only the occasional vehicle had passed him during the walk from his house and there were even fewer pedestrians. It was what he would have expected at 8.30 on a Sunday morning, though he had never checked it out before. It wasn't the way he usually endured his weekend hangover.

He passed through the gates into the Botanic Gardens and his pace quickened. Somehow he would find what he needed here, though he hoped it wouldn't be in the bushes. It was a clear, dry morning and in other circumstances Gus might have enjoyed the weather. The frosty panes of the Kibble Palace and of the larger glasshouse barely reflected the first light of dawn; the grass was also coated with frost, the flowerbeds barren and the path was hard under his feet. It was milder than it had been, but still cold enough.

He thought of trying the door of the Kibble Palace, but he knew that it and the other glasshouse would be closed. The idea of al fresco relief, in tropical warmth under a banana tree, was just a fantasy. It was probably also a criminal offence: he would have to ask a lawyer about that. Then he saw what he was looking for, over to the right, its back to the boundary wall with Queen Margaret Drive.

He quickened his step, trying not to become too hopeful; he had already been disappointed when he found the other place closed. Then, as he drew nearer, he saw that the doors were open and he almost broke into a run.

He went into the Gents and entered the nearest cubicle. It was clean and there was a lock on the door, though the latter was not essential at this particular moment. There was also paper and so he would not need the tissues he had brought with him specially. He hung his padded anorak behind the door, shivering as he lowered his trousers and sat down. The seat was cold on his backside and for a moment his body resisted. But his need was too great and soon his bowels were emptying.

It was too cold to hang about for long, but after he had finished he allowed himself a moment or two to relax. Behind him, he heard a vehicle drive up Queen Margaret Drive; across the road, in the headquarters of BBC Scotland, a lonely staff would be transmitting early morning radio and TV programmes, for those interested in that sort of thing. But Gus had his own communication to make; the medium was more modest, but the message profound. He brought out the felt-tipped pen, now an indispensable item among his portable effects, and found an empty space among the usual pathetic scribblings on the plaster wall. In black, bold capitals he wrote:

WALTER BAIN IS A CUNT

This was now to be found in lavatories throughout the west end. He had given much thought to the wording: adjectives like "miserable", "useless" and "selfish" had been considered and rejected, as only depicting particular aspects of the man's character. The plain statement was more comprehensive in scope and had more impact. It had depth and resonance. Soon all of Glasgow would know.

How had it come to this, shivering in a cold toilet, in a deserted park, early on a Sunday morning? Only a couple of days earlier he had spent a miserable Christmas, and an equally rotten New Year awaited him later in the week. Yet only a fortnight before he had thought that his life was beginning to improve...

Before leaving the flat, Gus checked that everything was in order. The new gas fires in the living room and kitchen were both on, and also the electric convector in the hall. It was not a time to worry about gas and electricity bills. All the inside doors were ajar, so that the warm air could circulate, particularly in the bathroom; leaving on its electric fan heater would have been too much of an extravagance, though he had put it on for a while earlier, as a small extra boost to the general temperature. He also made sure that all curtains in the house were closed, for the sake of whatever minimal insulation that would provide.

The house was looking good. In the few months since he'd moved in - a camper in an echoing enclosure - a transformation had taken place. It had cost a lot, but not as much as it might have. The flat had been completely redecorated: the old woodwork cleaned and varnished, the walls covered by woodchip paper and emulsion paint, variety being added by prints of paintings rather than vulgar wallpaper patterns. The redecoration had been done cheaply through a business contact. His brother-in-law Sam – his sister's husband, family contacts through Joyce being cut off – worked for a large carpet manufacturer and had provided all his carpets at wholesale prices, even laying them himself. Through his own contacts, Sam had also been able to get him curtains and much of his furniture at a discount. And all the light sockets were now fitted with bulbs, some of them even having shades. For these Gus had paid the full retail price. This had also been the case with the replacement cooker and fires. Though now he was beginning to wish that he had gone to the even greater expense of installing central heating.

He had brought with him very little to build upon. Virtually all of the family effects accumulated during ten years of marriage had been left with Joyce and the children. He had escaped with his hi-fi system and record collection, which Joyce had been glad to be rid of, and two large bookcases, since he had been the family's main book owner.

He put on a padded anorak, scarf, fur hat and gloves before opening the door. It was 9.30, he had finished his homework and there would be at least an hour's drinking left, after allowing at least half an hour to complete the obstacle course in the stairway.

As a prelude to this, he found two notes, handwritten on scraps of paper, lying in the vestibule between the inner and outer doors; he had kept the storm door closed to help keep the heat in. He looked at the first note:

You must keep heat in the house at all times for the sake of burst pipes and would you turn down your radiogram as this is a family building.
Walter Bain (Flat 2/1)

He turned to the second note:

I hope you are keeping your house well heated, as there is a great danger from burst pipes in this weather. Please excuse me for mentioning this, but any water penetration would greatly annoy Mr Bain.
HQ (Flat 1/1)
PS: There have been more burglaries in the area. The criminals think that the cold has lulled us into a false sense of security.

Gus was about to crumple up the notes, then changed his mind and put them in his pocket to show in the pub. Anything for a laugh. Bain's note had annoyed him, though not because it seemed to encourage the bursting of pipes rather than the opposite. Gus was proud of his hi-fi system, whose separate components had originated in Germany, Japan, Switzerland and even Britain, and to see this expensive international collaboration described as a radiogram was almost as insulting as the suggestion that moderate helpings of Mozart and Beethoven could corrupt the young.

Although he was well wrapped up, he felt the cold hit him as soon as he entered the landing; even within the house it was there in the background, pushing through the feeble barrier provided by his heaters. He turned the big key in the door, yet again wishing that he had got round to oiling the lock, so that he would not send such a loud signal down the stairwell; he had added extra locks to both doors, but had kept the original one as much out of tradition as for security.

He got safely past the first hurdle, Bain's storm door, shut like his own against the cold. As he started down the next flight of stairs the prospect of fitting in an extra pint arose, then abated as he heard Henrietta Quayle's storm door creak open.

"Hello."

"Hello."

"Dreadful weather, isn't it?"

"Awful."

"Are you going out?"

"Yes."

She stopped short of asking him where he was going at this time of night, though he was sure that was what she really wanted to know. She probably thought he was going to seek out Toby Welsh and a few of his friends to bring them back for an orgy, just to warm everyone up. He decided to leave her wondering. She had retreated back to the inner doorway, trying to catch some heat from the house, clutching a shawl around her, the shivering adding a new dimension to her fidgeting. Apparently he still wasn't considered safe enough to be asked in; maybe he never would be.

"Well, I'd better not keep you out here," he said.

"Did you get my note?"

"Yes. Don't worry, I've left all my heating on."

"Are you sure?"

"Positive."

"It's really important to keep as much heat in the building as possible. The plumbing is really old. We could get burst pipes."

"Yes, I know."

"Mr Bain would be very annoyed if any water got into his house."

"I'd be very annoyed if any got into mine."

"Last night was the coldest since 1973. And they say there's even worse to come."

"I can believe it. Don't worry, I've done everything I can think of."

But worrying was her permanent condition. The weather was only her current pretext. Underlying that was the biggest spectre of all: the wrath of Walter Bain. Along with the ongoing conspiracy among Glasgow criminals to murder her in her bed in the course of stealing her modest possessions.

At least this time he was permitted an early escape when the cold forced her back indoors. He made his way to The Centurion like an Arctic explorer heading for the Pole, taking short steps to avoid slipping on the ice.

A wave of heat hit him as soon as he entered the bar. He knew that this was only in contrast to the temperature outside and that the effect would not last. The inadequate central heating had been supplemented by a couple of paraffin heaters, their smell adding to the impression that he had entered some outpost in the wilderness, but he noticed that most of the customers still had their coats on. He also noticed that they were enjoying the privilege of a rare evening appearance by Aitken, the pub's owner. He was leaning on the counter chatting to a customer, letting the other barman do all the work, ignoring Danny Boyd who was standing a few feet away waiting to be served. Aitken was probably not much older than Gus, but his conservative appearance and manner made him seem older.

"Yes sir, what can I get you?"

Gus seldom came in during the day and Aitken hardly knew him, apart from the fact that he was a lawyer and had the right type of haircut; any type of haircut at all would probably have given him preference over Danny.

"I think this man's before me," said Gus.

"Oh," said Aitken, appearing to see Danny for the first time. "What would you like, sir?" he asked, the last word heavily laced with sarcasm. Danny told him and he walked slowly away to pour the pint.

"Cheers, Gus."

"No problem, Danny."

Aitken took so long to get Danny's drink that the other barman became free and Gus got served first after all. "That cunt's no' real," said Danny, keeping his eye on Aitken, who had passed a nearby beer tap to seek out one at the other end of the bar. "He'll serve me slops if he can get aff wi' it."

"He certainly isn't trying to break any speed records."

92

"The Advanced Fuckin' Passenger Train would be faster."

"I wouldn't go that far."

"I just gie him the Neanderthal look, darin' him tae lift the slop tray. It usually works." Aitken had finished pouring the pint and Danny, having mesmerised him into maintaining its purity, turned back to Gus. "The bastard would like to bar me, but I'm no' goany give him an excuse."

"Quite right."

"He's a wanker."

"If you're looking for an argument you'll need to change the subject."

"A complete tosser. You can tell by his name."

"How's that?" asked Gus. "I can't remember his first name."

"Dick."

A mouthful of beer entered Gus's windpipe, and his face grew red as he attempted to laugh and cough at the same time. The pub owner returned with Danny's pint, having stopped on the way back to talk to another customer, and glared at them.

Danny gave him a handful of change. "I think that's right."

Aitken went off, carefully counting the coins before putting them in the till. Then he sought out a respectable customer upon whom he could confer his wisdom. Gus was now abandoned, his credentials having proved deceptive. By their friends do ye know them.

"You all right, man?" asked Danny, as Gus finished spluttering and took another drink.

"Fine. You shouldn't come out with things like that when I've got beer in my mouth."

"I'm sittin' over there, if you'd like tae join us."

Gus looked at the table Danny had indicated, where three sociologists were engaged in debate. "No offence, Danny, but I'm not in the mood for Marxist analysis. It's already enough like bloody Siberia in here."

"It's your loss," said Danny. "Your fascist pals are sittin' over there." This wasn't said nastily and Gus didn't take it that way. Gus tried to avoid getting into political arguments with Danny. He was far better read than Gus and could back up all his assertions with references to Marx. Gus was no more convinced by this than he would have been by a Christian fundamentalist quoting the Book of Revelation, but it still left him at a disadvantage in debates.

He went over to join Norrie Spence and Ernie Dunlop. It was unusual to see them together. Norrie generally favoured the quick pint at teatime, while Ernie preferred something similar just before closing time. Gus, who had acquired both habits, saw each of them regularly, but usually separately.

"What was the big joke?" asked Ernie.

Gus told him. Ernie laughed, but Norrie seemed to be in a morose mood. He was also drunk, his five o'clock session having apparently been extended. Ernie's arrival seemed to be more recent, and he looked relieved when Gus appeared.

"Some weather," said Gus. "You manage to get here without falling on your arse?" Ernie lived in Hyndland, where Byres Road was at a safe distance, but still a handy enough target for an evening stroll. When the weather was normal, at any rate.

"Just about. Don't know about the way back, though."

Gus turned to Norrie. "Don't usually see you here this late. You OK?"

"Great," said Norrie, with heavy sarcasm. "Great. Never better."

"What's the matter?"

"Don't ask." Norrie got to his feet unsteadily and went to the toilet.

"What's wrong with him?"

"He's like the Advanced Passenger Train," said Ernie.

"How do you mean?"

"Fucked."

"That bad? What's the problem?"

"I don't know." Gus got the impression that Ernie felt he had said too much and was now retracting. "He won't say what it is, but something's definitely bugging him."

"Is everything OK at home?"

"As far as I know."

"I don't know how he does it. Keeping two families."

"You make him sound like a Mormon."

"Not quite. He pays for two, but only gets to live with one. I couldn't afford that. Could you afford that?"

"Who knows?" said Ernie. "Money comes in, the bills get paid. I don't concern myself with such trivia." Like Bob Waddell, Ernie ran a one-man business, but that was the only resemblance between them. Bob's care with his finances was matched only by his disregard for his clients. With Ernie it was the other way about.

"I mean, we're all in the same game," said Gus. "I find the extra mortgage bad enough, without taking on an extra set of wife and weans as well. And he never seems to get stressed. He's always so bloody laid back."

"Not tonight, he isn't," said Ernie. "How's the flat doing anyway?" he added, changing the subject as Norrie rejoined them.

"Taking shape," said Gus. "Though I'm still not too sure about the neighbours." He brought out the two notes and handed them to Ernie. Ernie chuckled as he read them and passed them to Norrie, who looked at them briefly without their contents seeming to register.

"Who's this guy Bain?" asked Ernie.

"Don't start me. He thinks he owns the building."

"There's always one. In a building with eight flats, it's a statistical certainty."

"Seven flats. But Bain goes beyond that. You could say that the political and economic conditions of the 1930s nurtured fascism, but that only explains Mussolini and Franco. Hitler was something else."

"Bloody hell, Gus. You been talking to the sociologists?"

"Christ, no. I just like to extend my interests a bit beyond the law."

"There's no accounting for taste." Ernie glanced at Norrie, but he was looking gloomily down at his drink, content to stay out of the conversation. "Anyway, this is the west end. The odd one out's bound to be a lulu."

"I wouldn't mind so much if he didn't live directly below me. If I put my hi-fi above the lowest level, he starts banging on the ceiling. It's not as if I bother him late at night: when I go back after the pub, I always use earphones."

"You can't please some folk. They'll complain about anything."

Gus was accustomed, from the days of his marriage, to using restraint while listening to music. But in the flat he had rented prior to buying his new one, he'd had to endure the constant hammering of loud rock music through the thin walls of the converted terrace house. He had retaliated with counter-blasts of Tchaikovsky and Wagner. It had almost been worth putting up with all that shite from next door, just to be able to turn up the volume with a clear conscience.

"That bastard would have the mice wearing carpet slippers."

"You got mice?"

"I was speaking metaphorically."

"You're getting far too intellectual, Gus. You're a lawyer, you're supposed to be a Philistine. Let's change the conversation to something we both know about. Let's talk about why British Rail is allowed to spend £37 million of taxpayers' money on a high-speed train that couldn't go down to the shops without breaking down. Better still, let's talk about the law."

"I didn't realise you knew anything about that."

"Fuck off. How are things in the office?"

"Shite."

They talked shop for a while. Norrie occasionally joined in, but stayed mainly out of it. His mood didn't improve. When last orders were called, Gus supplemented the pints by buying himself a whisky to ward off the cold.

They saw Norrie into a taxi, then Gus walked home, sharing the journey with Ernie for a short part of the way. The drink provided a slight, but only slight, barrier against the cold. When he got back to Oldberry Road, it was quiet in the close and stairwell; it was probably past bedtime for the Bain and Quayle households. There were other people in the building, of course, but Gus hadn't seen much of them in the few months since he'd moved in.

It was good to go into a house that was already warm, an expensive luxury that he could get used to. He shed his outer clothes and went through to the kitchen to put on the kettle. He made himself a cup of tea and had taken it through to the living room when the doorbell rang. Christ, not again.

He was tempted to ignore it, but they would have seen that his living room light was on. If they rang again, Bain would be banging on the ceiling. He went through to the hall and opened the inner and outer doors.

A group of long-haired youths, with full carrier bags, stood on the landing. Then Gus noticed that some of them were women.

"Is Toby in, man?"

"Sorry, he doesn't live here any more."

"We just thought we'd come up for a wee drink an' a blaw."

"I can see that, but he's not here."

"We couldnae just come in anyway?"

"I'm afraid not. I've got an early start tomorrow."

"OK man. No sweat. It's cool."

It's more than that, thought Gus as he shut the doors again. *It's bloody freezing*. This had been happening several times a month since he had moved in, though recently it had been tailing off a little. Was it always the same people? Surely not, or the message would have got through by now. Though it was difficult to be sure.

Had Toby Welsh really been keeping a brothel, or had there just been a surfeit of visits like this? It was looking as if he had just been a handy and accommodating impromptu host for members of the local hippie community who felt like moving on somewhere new at closing time. By now, Henrietta Quayle must have thought that Gus was continuing the tradition, though probably it was too late for her to be maintaining her post at the window. At least Walter Bain should have been glad to get an upstairs neighbour whose behaviour was more moderate, but some people were never satisfied.

Later, as he lay alone on his new, king-sized bed – he was by nature an optimist – he could almost hear the ghosts of past orgasms echo round the cornicing. Maybe next time he would ask the buggers in. If Bain was going to complain anyway...

The freeze persisted and grew worse over the weekend. The weather was blamed for a series of fatal accidents on the roads; these, and the broken bones of pedestrians who slipped on the ice, were keeping the hospital casualty units busy. At Glasgow Airport planes were being cancelled or delayed because of ice on the runway. On its third day of operation, the Advanced Passenger Train broke down yet again leaving 200 passengers stranded at Preston, and British Rail cancelled its next scheduled runs. Even in London, Big Ben had stopped as a result of the wintry conditions. All but five of the major football fixtures in Scotland were cancelled, and widespread hardship was being suffered by the elderly, by the disabled and, after several days without horse racing, by the bookies.

At first Gus seemed to have escaped any personal consequences from this breakdown of civilisation. He was not a football fan or a betting man and had no rail or air journeys planned. Since he didn't believe that drinking and driving should be mixed, he very seldom used his car; as his city-centre office was only a few stops away on the subway, this was not much of an inconvenience. And The Centurion was still open; Aitken had at least managed to keep enough heat in the place to stop the beer from freezing.

Gus had kept his heating on full, night and day, and it had seemed to pay off. Water still ran from the cold taps when he turned them on, and it continued to drain away successfully from the sink, bath and washbasin. And at first his toilet was working normally.

The problem first occurred on Sunday morning. He had done nothing more exciting the previous evening than go back to the pub, where the extra weekend customers had provided a welcome mutual body warmth. On the way home he had bought a takeaway curry, as a further slight insurance against hypothermia. He let the beer pass through him in the course of the night without flushing the toilet; Walter Bain had demanded, in a number of his regular notes, that Gus should not flush it after 11 pm, as the sound was liable to disturb the sleep of the Bain family during the quiet of the night. Still hoping that the man might be contained by appeasement, Gus had complied.

100

Bain probably deserved a break after having Toby Welsh as a neighbour.

At 9 am, when the curry had the usual effect, he was left with no choice. Being a Sunday morning, it was still quiet, but he reckoned that the Bains would be early risers and could cope with the disturbance of a flushing toilet. Then, when he operated the flush, his bowel contents refused to go away, but instead rose halfway up the bowl along with the water level. He poured in several kettlefuls of boiling water, but it only brought the level up slightly higher. He added half a bottle of bleach, then shut the toilet lid for the time being.

He phoned several plumbers on Monday morning, beginning with the firm that the factors normally used for common repairs in the building. On the basis of his description they all made the same diagnosis. The soil pipe, which ran down the exterior of the building and was unaffected by the heating inside, had frozen. There was no point in a visit. Nothing could be done. The problem would sort itself out with the thaw, provided that there hadn't been a burst.

He got through the next few days by pissing in a basin and pouring it, with helpings of bleach, down the kitchen sink. He did his best to train his guts to operate while he was in the office or in the pub, though he did manage to use the toilet at home a couple more times before the level of foulness got too high. The weather grew slightly milder and it started to snow. A thaw began, slight but definite.

On Wednesday evening he arrived home from the office, via The Centurion, around seven o'clock. When he opened the storm door, he found about a dozen

101

notes in Bain's handwriting scattered over the floor of the vestibule. He could hear the phone ringing inside. He gathered up the notes and went into the house. He was barely in the door when the phone stopped ringing. He saw that the notes seemed to be more hysterical in tone than usual, half of them written in red ink, with a liberal use of block capitals and exclamation marks. The words "toilet", "sewage" and "plumber" seemed to recur regularly. He had taken the notes into the living room to read them properly when the doorbell rang, then rang again, and again.

"For God's sake!" Gus muttered as he returned to the hall and the doorbell continued to ring.

Walter Bain was at the door. "Don't flush your toilet, you can't flush your toilet."

"I haven't flushed it since Sunday. The soil pipe's frozen."

"It's burst. It's coming through my ceiling."

"The soil pipe?"

"No, no, your – ah – sewage." Bain obviously had to force himself to use such a vulgar word. But this was an emergency, and he had risen to the occasion. "Didn't you get my notes?"

"Most of them. I think there was one missing."

"*What?*"

Gus sighed. "I'm just in. I was about to read them when you rang the doorbell."

"I've been trying to phone you. You didn't answer."

"As I said, I'm just in."

"You'll need to phone a plumber."

"I've already tried."

"So have I. You'll need to keep trying. You can't flush your toilet. Whatever you do, you can't flush it."

"I told you, I haven't flushed it since Sunday."

Bain looked at him suspiciously. "I hope you haven't been putting – ah – urine down the kitchen drains?"

"Good God! I'd never dream of it!"

"I hope not. This is a family building. We try to keep up the highest standards. You can't do that sort of thing."

"Don't worry, I've bought a ball of string."

This was either too subtle or too risqué for Bain. He looked at Gus uncertainly. "You can't flush your toilet."

"I won't. Do you think I could have a look in your bathroom, see what the problem is?"

"Oh no, I can't let you do that. Why do you want to do that?"

"I'll need to explain the situation to the plumber. He won't come out unless I can convince him that it's an emergency. I'll have a better chance of doing that if I know exactly what's happened."

Bain still seemed unconvinced, but agreed to cooperate. Probably he thought that a continued refusal might make Gus flush his toilet out of spite. Gus followed him downstairs, mildly interested in the fact that he would be seeing inside the Bain house at last.

He found himself in an alternate, bad-taste version of his own flat. The architecture was identical, the décor quite different. The wallpaper was furry and its pattern competed in volume with that of the carpet. The lampshade matched them in style if not in colour. The old woodwork on the doors had gone, either covered or replaced by flat hardboard, then painted lilac and fitted with plastic handles. A mirror with an ornate gilt frame hung on the far wall, beneath it the only piece of furniture, a modern telephone table. The bathroom was partly tiled with red-patterned tiles, and the wood surround was painted red, the plaster above it pink. There were furry mats in front of the bath and WC.

Gus had expected a burst ceiling and a bathroom sprayed with a mix of plaster and the Mackinnon bowel contents. Or maybe a sewage-drenched family member. But at first he could see nothing unusual at all, until Bain drew his attention to a small, discoloured patch on the corner of the ceiling beside the window. The patch was no more than a couple of inches in diameter and, as Gus watched, a small drip formed in its centre and fell into a basin which had been squeezed between the side of the toilet bowl and the far wall. The basin contained a small puddle of water with a yellowish tinge.

"It doesn't seem too bad so far," said Gus.

"*What*?" said Bain. "Are you *joking*? If you flush your toilet, goodness knows what'll happen."

"But I won't flush it."

"The ceiling could come down."

"I know, I won't flush it. The toilet, that is."

"You'll need to get a plumber."

"That's a good idea. I'll do that."

"They're very busy just now."

"Is that so?"

"But you'll just have to keep trying. I'll do the same."

"That's very good of you."

After his initial reluctance to let Gus into his house, Bain now wouldn't let him leave. Gus gradually fought his way to the front door, parrying Bain's repetitive demands with multiple reassurances. All this time Mrs Bain stood in the background, glaring at Gus in silent support for her husband.

Back in his own flat, Gus immediately checked the toilet. If the pipe had thawed, the worst of the threat might have safely drained away. But it was still there, the level not noticeably lower. The thaw had been partial, probably confined to the section of pipe within the building, where the leak had occurred. The pipe was possibly ready to split further, maybe needing only the extra weight of water from Gus's cistern to crack it completely open. If he could only know exactly when Bain would be sitting on his own toilet seat, Gus could unload it all on top of him with a turn of the wrist. Maybe if he were to bore a peephole in the floor…

Why had the pipe only frozen below Gus's house? Why was there still a clear passage from Bain's flat to the sewer? Probably because the more regular flushing of the toilet had prevented the ice from forming, whereas in Gus's section of pipe it had been given a free hand, while he was at work or in the pub, or showing consideration to his downstairs neighbours during the night. Had they shown a similar consideration to Henrietta Quayle? He doubted it.

At least he had been given a subject of conversation for the pub. When he went back later that evening he told Ernie all about it and showed him the notes.

"You should keep an album of them," said Ernie. "You could even arrange them into an anthology and get them published."

"The bugger would claim half the royalties."

"That's true. But it would still be worthwhile. You'd have to be selective, of course; they're a bit repetitive."

"Just a wee bit."

"And you'd have to decide how to classify them. The best Malapropisms, the best grammatical howlers, the most subtly patronising and insulting… Or should it be according to subject matter: plumbing, noise nuisance, turn of the stairs or whatever?"

"We could have a best seller here. It would be just compensation for all the grief the bastard gives me."

"You can't entirely blame him. Think of him, sitting there on the pan, the Shite of Damocles poised above his head…"

Gus spluttered. "Not when I'm drinking, please."

"You brought up the subject."

"I know. I'm sorry, let's change it. Have you seen any more of Norrie?"

"Since when?"

"Since we saw him in here last week, pissed and suicidal. He hasn't been showing for his usual teatime session."

"I haven't seen him," said Ernie. "But I'm not usually in at tea time. I prefer having my tea. My wife likes it that way too."

As before, Gus got the impression that Ernie knew more than he was admitting. Yet he generally saw less of Norrie than Gus did. What was the source of his information, if he had any?

He telephoned the factor's plumber from work the next morning. It took him several attempts.

"Are you the neighbour of that man Bain?" asked the harassed woman he finally got through to.

"Yes."

"He's been on the phone all morning." It was still only 10.30. "Will you tell him to stop pestering us? We're inundated with work as it is."

"I know, I'm sorry."

"I've told him we can't do anything until the pipe's completely thawed. But he won't listen. He just keeps saying he wants to speak to the boss. But he's out like the rest of the men, working round the clock."

"I know how you feel, but if there's —"

"Mr Craig says I should just tell him to – he says he won't come at all if he keeps getting pestered like this."

"But I'm the one that's being inconvenienced."

"I can't help that."

Gus sighed. "I know. Do what you can. I'd be very grateful."

He tried the factor and got a similar reaction. Bain had already been there, continuously. At the factor's suggestion, he decided to try another plumber, and began to work his way through the list in the Yellow Pages. Bain seemed to have beaten him to all of them, raising hackles, preparing an antagonistic reception for him. How could the man be on the phone to so many people simultaneously? Eventually Gus couldn't afford to take any more time off his work and gave up for the time being. How did Bain manage it? Was he at home, accumulating a huge phone bill? More probably he was at work, misusing the time and resources of his employers.

That evening Gus sent him a carefully worded, tactful note, suggesting that his efforts might be counter-productive. The only result was to provoke a hysterical visit and an increased number of follow-up notes. The situation was not helped when Bain demanded to inspect Gus's toilet and actually saw what had accumulated above him.

The position remained much the same until the weekend, when the freeze returned with increased intensity. On Friday night, Gus went to the pub early, carrying with him Bain's latest communication:

> You must wire up your toilet handle with wire in case of accidental flushing when inebrated.

"What you goany dae?" asked Danny.

"It's Friday night. I'm going to get inebrated out my skull."

"Are you goany wire up your toilet handle?"

"Maybe, but definitely not with wire."

"What else can you wire it up with?"

"That's a good point. I never thought of that."

"Fuck off. I don't suppose it's very easy gettin' hold of a plumber the now."

"You suppose right. Have you heard the one about the plumber who married a commoner?"

"Anyway," said Danny, "why's the man gettin' so uptight? Just because your shites are comin' through his ceilin'?"

"That seems to be it."

"Some folk'll complain about anythin'."

"If you ask me," said Toby Welsh, "it couldn't have happened to a better guy."

"No argument there," said Gus.

"But what's his problem?" asked Danny. "I mean, I don't suppose they were exactly well-formed turds by the time they made it through."

"They didn't even start out that way."

"For God's *sake*!" said Sarah. "Can we not talk about something else?"

"Sorry, Sarah," said Gus. "I'm afraid it's becoming something of an obsession with me."

"See thae modern liberated women?" said Danny. "You can talk about sex a' day and they'll no' bat an eyelid. But if you mention bowel movements they go mental. It's the last taboo."

"I don't believe this," said Sarah.

"If there's a taboo, you've got tae break it," said Danny. "That's the story of human progress. You break taboos. That's what I do anyway."

"Let me see if I've got this right," said Andy. "You're goany bring on the revolution by talkin' about shite?"

"I think the word 'about' is superfluous," said Gus.

"Fuck off."

"Anyway," said Gus, turning to Toby. "What about you? You might have warned me about Bain."

"Come on man, that's business. I was trying to sell the place, not put you off."

"How did you get on with him?"

"How do you think? I just ignored him, it's the only way. If you fart after nine at night the man's going to complain. You might as well give him something to complain about. Just do what you like, that's what I did."

"So I gather. I still have buggers up looking for you every other night."

"Sorry man, I know a lot of people. If they brought a carry-out or a wee bit of grass, I just let them in."

"Too right," said Danny.

"Though I must admit, it was getting a bit regular. The word got round. A few strangers were beginning to show."

"I don't know how you could tell the difference," said Gus. "They all look the same to me. They all look fucking strange. Sorry, Sarah."

"It's all right to use the 'f' word," said Sarah. "Just give the toilet stories a rest."

"Hey, this could be the start of a new artistic scene," said Danny. "We could call it 'The Bowel Movement'."

"Fuck off!"

"Henrietta Quayle thought you were running a brothel," Gus said to Toby.

"Wish I had been, man. I could have done with the bread."

"I'm sure she thinks I'm still doing the same."

"That woman's off her nut. I'm telling you man, she's on a drug-free trip."

About half an hour before closing time, Gus went into the only cubicle in the Gents, to see if he could hurry along his natural processes. There was no lock on the door, but he had long legs and was able to keep it shut with his foot. While meeting with partial success, he passed the time by looking at the graffiti.

His favourite was written on a block of wood that had been fitted as a replacement window sill. It was cut roughly, put in crooked and had been left unpainted. It looked as if Aitken – even in Glasgow's Wild West it couldn't have been the work of a professional – had used an axe instead of a saw and a brick instead of a hammer. It had now been in that condition for several years. The message said:

SOME FUCKIN JOINER

Inspired, Gus wrote up his Walter Bain declaration, after spending some time getting the wording right. His biro dried up several times on the vertical surface before he was finished. He would need to find a more suitable pen for the rest of his campaign.

The situation remained the same well into the New Year, during which time Bain's notes kept Gus's waste bin regularly filled. The students in the flat opposite let him use their toilet, though he tried not to bother them early in the morning or late at night. He didn't even try asking Bain for the use of his, feeling sure what the answer would be; in any case, he didn't want to be the one sitting down there if the pipe finally gave.

But it didn't. The inconvenience to Bain remained minimal, while for Gus the opposite was the case. No one would have realised this from the attitude of Bain, who continued to hold Gus solely responsible for a situation that was beyond his control. Gus finally got hold of a plumber late in January; Bain's continuing intervention, he reckoned, had delayed the visit by at least a fortnight. By that time a great deal of urine had flowed down the kitchen sink, though even Bain had known better than to push him on that one.

4. THE FACTOR FACTOR

Spring 1982
Gus Mackinnon, Flat 3/1

"Who are you going to vote for?" asked Gus

"I don't vote," said Danny. "Wastea bloody time. What about you?"

"Pastor Jack Glass. No Pope in Glasgow, that's what I say."

"I thought you were an atheist."

"Aye, but am I a Proddie atheist or a Catholic atheist?"

"Fuck off. Though if you ask me, it's a waste of perfectly good trees. Cuttin' them doon just for him."

"Especially since he'll never get near Bellahouston Park."

"How's that?"

"They'll shoot down his helicopter when it passes over Ibrox."

"It would be the first time thae morons ever came in useful."

"I didn't know you were a Celtic supporter."

"Fuck off. Anyway, who you really goany vote for?"

"Probably Roy Jenkins. Aye all right, don't say it."

"Jesus Christ, Gus. He's a carpet-bagger."

"According to some."

"He's a traitor."

"Traitor to whom?"

"Tae the workin' classes. Anyway, he was never a real socialist. He doesnae give a damn about the Hillhead punters. All he wants is a seat in Parliament so he can lead his traitorous party."

"I'm not going to argue with you, Danny. I've had a hard day."

"But why the hell do you want to vote for Woy? He cannae even speak English."

"Not like you?"

"Fuck off."

"His English is excellent. He just has a slight pronunciation difficulty. One his political opponents are inclined to exaggerate."

"He cannae pronounce his Rs."

"Why would he want to pronounce his arse?"

"Because he fuckin' talks out of it!"

It was the week of the Hillhead by-election and the west end was in carnival mood. Eight candidates were in a scuffle over the last Tory seat in Glasgow, pared down to a 2,000 majority at the 1979 General Election. The serious contenders were the Tories, Labour, the Scottish Nationalists and the recently formed Social Democratic Party (in alliance with the Liberals); the last of these had sent a heavyweight, the Right Honourable Roy Harris Jenkins, a former Labour cabinet minister and co-founder of the breakaway party. These big four were grappling with one another to win over what was described as the best-educated electorate in the country.

Some of those who knew the area better felt that it was more typified by the fringe candidates, who were decorating the campaign like gaudy butterflies before their brief political lives came to an end on polling day. The most conventional of these was the Ecology Party candidate; she shared the bottom half of the hustings with a fake Roy Jenkins, who claimed prior ownership of the Social Democratic Party's name and had changed his own name by deed poll in an attempt to win the seat by fraud; Pastor Jack Glass, seeking support for his Protestant Crusade against the forthcoming Papal visit; and Lieutenant-Commander William Boaks who represented (or perhaps comprised) the Public Safety Democratic Monarchist White Resident Party.

"At least there's one thing we'll agree about," said Gus. "This campaign's getting to be a real nuisance."

"Aye, you're right there."

The bellow of a loudspeaker van was heard in the distance, escalated as it drew nearer, then slowly faded again. From where they sat you had to concentrate to make out which party it belonged to. Gus didn't bother making the effort.

"Where's your pal these days?" Danny asked.

"Who?"

"The other lawyer. He used to be in here every day at tea-time."

"You mean Norrie Spence?"

"Is that his name? I havenae seen him for months."

"Neither have I. He seems to have stopped coming in." Gus wondered if he should say more. It wasn't a secret after all. But there would soon be enough gossip without him helping to spread it. "I suppose I'd better think about getting up to this meeting."

"When is it?"

"Seven o'clock. I'd better make a move soon."

"What's it about?"

"Christ knows. Here's the note he sent me."

This proved sufficient to confirm the change of subject. Danny looked at the note:

There will be a meetting of 13 Oldberry Road Glasgow owners of flats and shop at 7pm Tuesday the 23rd March 1982 in the undersined flat with the factor Mr MacDuff to discuss close affairs with refreshments so you must attend and oblige.
Walter Bain (Flat 2/1)

"Close affairs? Who you been shaggin'?"

"Who knows? I'd had refreshments at the time."

"At least he's got some bevy in."

"Don't be daft. He means a cup of tea and a biscuit."

"Mind your language."

"Exactly. And knowing Bain, he'll get the factor to divide the cost among all the owners as a common charge."

"You're kiddin'!"

"He comes from Paisley."

"You're not kiddin'."

"Do you know he sent me a bill for having his bathroom ceiling replastered and painted? Because of a wee mark the size of a beer mat."

"I hope you wiped your arse wi' it."

"I paid it."

"For God's sake, man!"

"I know. But you don't know him. He never lets go. He just keeps on and on and on and on and on at you, until you do what he wants just for a bit of peace. He's driving me to drink."

"At least that's one thing in his favour."

"No it isn't. He's driving me nuts. I don't know how to deal with him."

"I'll tell you how tae deal wi' him. It's the easiest thing in the world. It couldnae be more simple."

"You've got to tell me. What is it?"

"Just tell him tae fuck off."

Gus left the pub at ten to seven. He hadn't yet eaten, but could pick up a takeaway later if Bain's hospitality proved inadequate, as it probably would. Back in the street, the noise of the election campaign returned to full volume. He wondered if Bain had complained about it. Who would he complain to? His MP? The last one was dead and the new one wouldn't be in place for another couple of days. But he wouldn't let a little thing like that stop him.

When he turned off Byres Road, a Tory loudspeaker van followed him round the corner, as if it were targeting him exclusively, in a final attempt to cling on to its party's slender majority. Then it drove past him and the noise gradually subsided. It would soon be over, thank God. At least some colour was being added to the drab frontages of the tenements by the election posters in the windows. In this area they were mainly for Labour and the Scottish Nationalists, the Social Democrat logo being seen less often and the Tory one hardly at all. It would be unsafe, of course, to predict the outcome of the election from this; in Hyndland, the arrangement of window colours would be quite different.

In 13 Oldberry Road, each of the tenanted flats had a Labour poster, but there were no others. Gus had thought about getting an SDP one, but hadn't got round to it. It was a couple of minutes to seven when he arrived home. He hung up his coat and left his briefcase in the living room, first removing the file for his purchase of the flat, which he'd brought home with him from the office; it contained his notes on the title deed conditions, which might come in useful at the meeting. Then he used the toilet – a recently restored luxury which he still enjoyed – combed his hair and brushed his teeth; he would have more credibility as a solicitor if the smell of drink from his breath was minimised. It was just before five past seven when he arrived at Walter Bain's front door.

"You're late."

"Sorry, I was held up at work."

"Held up? You mean by robbers?"

"No, by work."

But that wasn't a good enough reason. Probably the other one wouldn't have been either. "You'd better come in."

"Thanks very much."

"Make sure you wipe your feet."

Gus gave the mat a prolonged rubbing with the soles of his shoes, hoping he'd wear a hole in it. "Am I the last to arrive?"

"No."

Gus had seen Bain's hall before, but now entered his living room for the first time. It was a nightmare doppelganger of his own living room, directly above. The furniture probably dated from the 1960s, at the nadir of post-war taste; it should have been falling apart by now, but was in unexpectedly good condition. The original fireplace was gone, replaced by one from a less elegant period. On the walls there was a retrospective exhibition of prints from Boots the Chemist. And as the flat lacked its own garden in which to place gnomes, the Bains had compensated by filling the room with small ornaments in a similar style.

Several dining room chairs, still unoccupied, had been interspersed between the three-piece suite to form a wide circle round the fireplace. The only other people in the room were Mrs Bain, Henrietta Quayle and a man whom Gus guessed was the factor. He wore a business suit and was about Gus's age. Bain didn't bother to introduce him.

Gus sat down on the settee, beside the factor; Bain hadn't offered him a seat, but he assumed it was all right. Bain sat on one of the dining chairs. This gave him slightly more stature than the others, as befitted the chairman.

"Are we expecting any others?" Gus asked.

"I sent everybody a note."

"Including Mr Singh?"

"Yes. He's the Pakistani who owns the shop," Bain explained to the factor.

"He's Sikh," said Gus.

"Is he? I saw him in the street earlier and he looked all right."

"No, I mean he's not from Pakistan, he's from India. He's a Sikh."

"Oh."

No one spoke for a moment or two. "I'll be glad when this election's over," said Gus eventually.

"I just hope the new MP's better than the last one," said Bain. "I could never get him to do anything."

Gus didn't know what the previous MP had died of, but was now forming a theory. The silence resumed, occasionally broken by small talk. Neither of the women said anything. In the case of Henrietta Quayle, Gus guessed, it was because she was terrified of Bain. Mrs Bain, on the other hand, was displaying the usual silent support for her husband; like Mrs Micawber, her defining characteristic appeared to be support for her husband.

By 7.15 there had been no further arrivals. "I don't think anyone else is coming," said Gus.

"We'd better start," said Bain.

"Can we do that? There are only three flats represented."

"I think Mr MacDuff can speak for the owners of the tenanted flats. I suggested he should get their authority."

The factor nodded. Gus wondered how often Bain had made the suggestion to him.

"So," said Bain. "That means five flats are represented. I think that gives us a forum."

"Yes, and it gives us a majority as well."

Bain regarded Gus uncertainly for a moment, then let it drop as he assumed his chairman's role. He cleared his throat and consulted the notebook on his knee. "I called this meeting for three reasons mainly. First of all I wanted to talk about the tenanted flats. This is a family building with high standards, and having crowds of students in the close subtracts from that."

"When are they in the close?"

"Second, I'm concerned about the number of repairs we've had to pay for recently. And last, I wanted us to meet Mr MacDuff who's just taken over as factor. As you know, the previous factors, Peacock & Pettigrew, were unable to keep on acting for us because of reorganisation."

As far as Gus knew, Peacock & Pettigrew still undertook factoring business. Probably they had just wanted to reorganise Walter Bain out of their lives.

"Personally, I was glad to see the back of them," continued Bain. "They charged us all £50 a year. I don't know what they did with the money."

"Did they go on many foreign holidays?" asked Gus.

"What? I don't know. We only had them for a year. Before that it was Biggar, Boyce & Bailey, and before that Harper & Glen, or was it MacSporran & Co.? And then there was Cassidy & Kydd."

"I know them," said Gus. "They call them Butch Cassidy and the Sundance Kid."

Four faces looked at him blankly.

"Because they're the biggest gang of cowboys in the city."

The expression of the Bains remained unchanged. The factor covered his mouth suddenly and coughed. Henrietta Quayle's expression intensified from foreboding to terror.

"Mr Mackinnon likes to amuse us," said Bain, looking unamused. "Anyway, as I was saying, Peacock & Pettigrew resigned and they recommended Mr MacDuff. Are they friends of yours, Mr MacDuff?"

"No."

"Oh, well we're hoping you'll be an improvement on the others, Mr MacDuff. It wouldn't be hard. So that's three things on the agenda, the tenant factor, the repairs factor and…" He hesitated, but it was now too late to stop. "And – ah – the factor factor."

There was a brief silence. "I don't think we need to discuss that," said Gus. "I'm sure we're all happy to welcome Mr MacDuff to the fold." There was no response. "So what repairs are you talking about?"

"I'm glad you mentioned it," said Bain. "If you look at the last half-yearly bill, you'll see five accounts from slaters. *Five accounts.* It comes to nearly £20 each."

"That's right," said Gus. "The roof was leaking. I was getting rain in. So was the other top flat."

"*I* wasn't getting rain in," said Bain. "Were you getting rain in, Miss Quayle?" Henrietta Quayle promptly shook her head.

"That's because I put a bucket under the drip. Maybe I should get Mr MacDuff to divide up the price of that. It cost me £2 from Woolworths."

"You can't do that."

"I won't insist on it. On the other hand, maintaining the roof's a common repair. There's no doubt about that. It's in the title deeds."

"I don't know about that. We'd need to get a legal opinion."

"I'm a lawyer."

"Yes, but you're not independent. We need a second legal opinion."

"For God's sake, that would cost more than repairing the roof. All you need to do is ask the factor. Tell him, Mr MacDuff."

So far the factor had seemed determined to remain neutral. "I'm afraid Mr Mackinnon's right," he said after a moment's hesitation. "It is a common repair. The roof serves the whole building."

"It doesn't serve me."

"What if there was no roof?" said Gus. "You'd get rain in then all right."

This degree of speculation seemed beyond Bain's imagination and he remained unconvinced. However, he realised that he wasn't going to win this particular argument. "All right," he said. "Let's suppose, just for the sake of argument, that what you say is true. Why did the slater have to come five times? Why didn't he repair the roof properly the first time?"

"Oh he did. But where do you think he got the slates from? This building is a hundred years old. They don't build them with slate roofs any more."

"I don't understand."

"Have you ever seen a slater go up on a roof carrying slates? I haven't. Neither has anyone else. They just move them around. If I complain too much, they'll shift the leak to the flat across the landing. Or pinch slates from the building next door. Am I right, Mr MacDuff?"

But the factor wasn't going to support him on that one. Like his predecessors before him, he probably received backhanders from all their contractors, including the slater. "I think that's a slight exaggeration," he said.

"We've never had bills like that before," said Bain.

Probably not, Gus thought. Toby Welsh would just have left a bucket under the leak, rather than do anything as energetic as phoning the factor. Maybe he even had the right idea. At least he could have kept the bucket in the same place, rather than having to move it to a new spot after every visit from the slater. "There's only one way to deal with this situation," he said.

"What's that?"

"Get a new roof. Reroof the building."

This reduced Bain to silence for a moment, then he said, "But that would cost hun– That would cost thou– I'm not getting any rain in. Why should I —?"

"We could apply to the council for a 90 per cent repairs grant," said Gus. "We'd only have to pay a tenth of the cost, and that would be divided eight ways. There would be no more slaters' bills."

"But —"

"The factor could submit the application on behalf of us all. Isn't that right, Mr MacDuff?"

For the first time the factor's interest seemed to have been captured, as he viewed the prospect of some real commission, well beyond his modest management fee, commission that was not only substantial but legal. "Yes," he said. "I've already submitted applications on behalf of a number of properties."

"There you are," said Gus. "It's already happening, all over the city. It would add to the value of all our houses."

"Would it?"

"Yes." The factor nodded his agreement. "We'd be better doing it now," continued Gus. "If we don't, it'll have to be done in a few years' time. The grants may be reduced by then, or stopped entirely."

"I don't know," said Bain. "I'm not getting any rain in."

"You should think about it," said MacDuff. "A lot of buildings are getting it done. You might think about renewing the chimney-heads at the same time."

"There are also environmental grants available," said Gus. "For stone-cleaning, sprucing up the back courts, all sorts of things. You could add thousands to the value of your flat at the council's expense."

"You mean at the ratepayers' expense?"

"Yes, but you'll have to pay rates anyway. You might as well get some of it back."

"But we'd still have to pay part of it."

"A small part. Split eight ways."

"I don't know."

"You could always get a second mortgage."

"*What*? You mean borrow *money*?"

"Not all that much," said Gus. "What do you think, Miss Quayle?"

Henrietta Quayle, who had been engaged in an armchair version of her fidgeting routine, jerked to a halt, appalled that she was being asked to speak. She opened her mouth, looked at Bain, then shut it again. Finally she said, "I - I don't know."

"Maybe we should forget about the other things for now," said the factor, "and just think about the roof."

"But I'm not getting any rain in," said Bain.

The discussion continued to circle round the topic for a while, as Gus and the factor tried to divert Bain from his short-term selfish interests by appealing to his long-term selfish interests. Finally, having failed to reach a conclusion, they moved on to the next topic. Gus and the factor did their best to convince Bain that there was no legal way to prevent the owners of the tenanted flats from letting their properties to students. Bain remained unconvinced but was eventually reduced to temporary silence. Gus finally made his escape just after nine o'clock; the tea and biscuits had failed to appear, probably withheld by Bain as retribution for not getting his own way.

Back in his flat, he replaced the papers he had taken with him in his briefcase and used the toilet. He was about to leave for the pub – too late now for any homework – when a note came through his letterbox.

It was from Henrietta Quayle. Although he was in the hall when the note arrived, she had already gone back down the stairs by the time he picked it up:

You shouldn't provoke Mr Bain the way you do.
You don't know what he's like.
Henrietta Quayle (Flat 1/1)
PS: I agree with you about the roof. Maybe the rest
of us could club together and pay Mr Bain's share?

Gus reread the note to make sure that he had understood it properly, then put it in his pocket before leaving the flat. He still hadn't eaten and, after closing time, headed for the nearest fish and chip shop. Danny accompanied him down Byres Road. On the way, they noticed an election message, spray-painted on a gable end:

WOY IS A RANKER

"See, what did I tell ye?"

"It does have a certain elegance. It almost inspires me to add a contribution of my own."

"About Woy?"

"No, about Walter Bain."

"Why don't ye?"

"Damn it, I've left my spray gun in my other jacket."

Polling Day came and went. Roy Jenkins, despite his speech handicap, confounded the opinion polls and vindicated the bookies by winning the seat comfortably. The west end returned to its normal level of madness.

Gus's proposal to renew the roof had mainly been intended to provoke Bain, but by the end of the meeting he had found himself convinced by his own arguments. It really would be a good idea to take full advantage of council grants and have the building refurbished. The factor should be able to do the bulk of the work. And he was sure he had already gone some way towards convincing Bain: the idea of boosting his private investment from the public purse, Gus was sure, had struck a chord deep within the man's soul. He only needed to be given the right nudge.

The solution came to Gus a few nights later when walking back home from the pub; his brain, still stimulated by the drink, but without the distraction of being engaged in conversation, was in a freewheeling and creative mode. The scheme would need careful planning, but the idea was simple.

So powerful was the concept that it survived into the next day's sobriety. By then he doubted its wisdom, but his enthusiasm returned in the evening, growing incrementally with each pint. For several days his commitment to the project waxed and waned, following a similar pattern. But there was nothing he could do while the weather remained dry.

About ten days after the election it began to rain heavily and the time for a decision arrived. Gus left for work in the morning, having first emptied and cleaned the plastic bucket before replacing it under the large drip that fell steadily from the living room ceiling.

It continued to rain steadily all day. As he left the office at 5.30 Gus realised that it might be some time before he would get so good an opportunity. He would have to go home right away and put his plan into action. Unfortunately his route from the subway station required only a slight diversion in order to take him to the front door of The Centurion. But after supplementing his first pint with a couple of whiskies, his resolve came back.

As he left the pub at twenty past six it was still raining. When he arrived in front of the close a few minutes later, he checked that neither Bain nor Henrietta Quayle were on window duty, then tiptoed up the stairs. His only setback was when he turned the big key in the lock of the storm door, sending the usual echoing signal down the stairwell. With any luck, Bain would fail to notice it; he had no reason, as yet, to be on the alert.

The drip was still falling and the bucket was a quarter full of dirty water. For the moment he left it where it was, fetched a claw hammer, and began to ease out the tacks of the fitted carpet in the corner of the room nearest the leak. Moving the bucket and a coffee table out of the way, he then pulled back the corner of the carpet and underfelt until the drip was falling on to bare floorboards. He put the bucket back in place and sat the table on the corner of the lifted carpet to prevent it from rolling back.

There wasn't enough water in the bucket. He could fill it up with tapwater, but would it seem credible that such a large bucket had filled in the course of the day? Probably not. He found a small saucepan in the kitchen, filled it almost to the brim from the tap, and put it in place of the bucket. It was only after he had emptied the bucket into the kitchen sink that he realised his mistake. The water in the saucepan was too clean: it had to look as if it had filtered through a crumbling roof and filthy attic. What could he put in it? Instant coffee? No, Bain would think he was getting sewage again. Dirt from his hoover bag? But it contained too much insoluble fluff. He went back to the kitchen, quickly swept the vinyl-covered floor (it badly needed cleaning), removing the larger items of rubbish before taking the shovel through to the living room. He emptied the dirt into the saucepan, stirring it well in with a wooden spoon. Then he put his coat back on and fetched his umbrella, ready for a quick escape.

Finally he filled his kettle, returned to the living room and topped up the saucepan until it overflowed on to the floorboards. Then he examined his handiwork sceptically. The overspill continued with each drip, but only by a very small amount. To hell with it. He moved the saucepan to the side and emptied the kettle on to the floorboards at the spot where the drip was now falling. Then he returned the kettle to the kitchen and fled from the house.

He closed both the inner and storm doors quietly, leaving the latter secured by the mortice only, not risking the noise of the big key. He tiptoed quickly down the stairs. Then, after checking that the window surveillance had not been resumed, he hurried off through the rain to enjoy a slow pint.

When he returned around eight o'clock the rain had stopped and Bain was at the window. He met Gus on the second floor landing. "Where have you been? I've been phoning you. I've been leaving notes."

"I was working late. What's the problem?"

"What's the *problem*? There's water coming through my ceiling."

"Yes, it's been some day. The rain's hardly stopped. Never mind, it's off now."

"But why is it coming into my house?"

"I don't know. I left a bucket under the drip. It must have filled up and overflowed."

"Have you been drinking?"

"I had a quick one on the way home. Why, what's that got to do with it?"

"The rain's been coming through my ceiling."

"I was only in the pub for half an hour. If I'd come straight home it wouldn't have made any difference."

"But I'm not on the top floor. It shouldn't come into my house."

"Don't worry, Walter. I'm sure it's easily sorted. I'll check it out and let you know."

But Bain was following him up the stairs, and remained at his heels as he opened the doors and entered the house, stepping over the heap of hysterical confetti on the vestibule. Damn it. Had the rain been off long enough for the last drip to have completed its journey through the roof and ceiling? If Bain saw that the saucepan had been moved away from the leak… Why couldn't the bugger have given him a couple of minutes start to get into the house and adjust his props? But, thank God, the drip had stopped and all that could be seen was a rolled-back carpet and a small, water-filled saucepan sitting on wet floorboards.

"That's not a bucket. That's a saucepan."

"That's right, I remember now. I needed the bucket to wash the stairs. I meant to put it back."

"Why's your carpet been lifted?"

"It got wet and I wanted to give it a chance to dry. I'm sorry, I should have left it down as blotting paper for the rainwater."

"And that's only a small saucepan. No wonder it filled up."

"It's the only size I've got. I usually just cook for myself. I don't give many dinner parties."

"Don't you have anything else? A basin, maybe?"

"Yes, I've got a basin. I sometimes need it to wash the dishes."

"But we can't have this. There's water coming into my house. First your soil pipe and now rainwater. We can't have this. It's never happened before."

"I'm sorry if I haven't been a model neighbour like Mr Welsh." Bain looked at him sharply but Gus had kept his face deadpan. "Look, Walter, I'm sorry about what's happened. Have a seat for a moment and I'll get the bucket back." He lifted the saucepan and carried it from the room. He had to hold it steadily to avoid spilling water on the floor and he could feel Bain's eyes on him all of the way. He returned with the empty bucket and put it in place on the damp floorboards.

"We can't have this," said Bain. "If any more rain gets through it'll mark my ceiling."

"I know." Gus pointed upwards, where the leak had caused discolouration and a small bulge in the plaster. "I can show you a few other places like that. And I had the whole place redecorated when I moved in."

But Bain wasn't interested in Gus's decoration, only his own. "You'll need to get the slaters back."

"If you think it'll do any good. They'll probably just do more damage, clumping about the roof in their tackety boots. But I'll get on to the factor tomorrow."

"It'll need to get sorted."

"Of course it will. But don't worry, I'll put the carpet back and make sure the bucket stays in place. I can buy another one for the stairs. Mind you, there could be a problem when I go on holiday. I was thinking of going away for the Glasgow Fair."

"You're going away for a *fortnight*?"

"But you never know, we might get decent weather for once. I could always leave you my key, so you could come up and empty the bucket."

"But this is ridiculous!"

"I know. That's the trouble with these old buildings, Walter. You can't keep mending them with sticking plaster. The whole roof structure's probably rotten. And that's not all. The wiring for my lights is all in the loft, and I'm sure it's pretty dodgy because I've had a few electric shocks. God knows when it was last renewed. I doubt if Toby Welsh or the old man before him did anything about it."

"What's that got to do with it?"

"Think about it. Rainwater hitting a piece of exposed wiring. It could set the building on fire."

"*What*? You'll need to have that wiring seen to! We can't - we can't have—"

"I'm planning to have it done. Though I don't really see the point while the roof's still leaking. I hope your flat's insured."

At last Bain was reduced to silence and soon Gus was able to lead him quietly from the house. He had been hoping to give Bain the necessary nudge. It had been more like a hefty boot on the backside.

It was time to return to the pub. Before, he had been trying to summon the nerve to put his plan into action. Now, he was ready to celebrate.

5. A DAY IN THE LIFE

Wednesday 13 October, 1982
Gus Mackinnon, Flat 3/1

7.10 am

"I don't think we can finish the roof just yet," said the workman. "Not without Mr Bain's permission."

"But the council's good for the money," said Gus. "They've approved the grant."

"You can't trust politicians. What if the grant gets cancelled? Mr Bain would have to pay all of his own share. We can't have that." The workman was English and spoke as if he had been educated at Oxford or Cambridge. He was sitting at the piano in Gus's living room playing a Mozart piano sonata. None of this surprised Gus, though he noted with admiration how deftly, with his feet encased in such large boots, the workman was able to operate the sustaining pedal.

"But we can't go on for ever with a tarpaulin for a roof."

"You won't have to," said the workman, executing a brilliant semiquaver run as he spoke. "We're taking the tarpaulin away next week. We need it for another job."

"But that would leave us with no roof at all."

"Yes, but the ceiling will still be there. And the weather's been quite dry for the time of year."

"It doesn't look that way to me," said Gus, pointing to a corner near the window, where a small waterfall poured from the ceiling into a large tin bath. It was wonderful what you could still buy in Woolworths.

"You'd better make sure that gets emptied," said the workman. "We can't have any rain getting into Mr Bain's house. It could damage his antique furniture and ruin his valuable paintings. We can't have that."

"I'll buy a bigger bath. And a few groundsheets to spread over the carpet."

The sonata's slow movement came on and Gus allowed it to capture his full attention. How could so many things be wrong in a world that contained such beauty? There was no other sound in the background, apart from birdsong. It had been a great idea to move into the back bedroom; merely shifting his bed across the hall had transported him, for a little while each morning, from the town into the country, the songs of thrushes and robins replacing the diesel engines of double-decker buses. The birds harmonised much better with the music from his clock radio.

At 7.25 he managed to sit up in bed and light a cigarette. This set off a bout of coughing, a herald of the tribulations during his conscious hours. He had a slight headache, his mouth felt dry and sticky, and the fatigue that pervaded his body seemed more appropriate for someone about to fall asleep rather than one who had just wakened up. It felt like a normal morning.

A few moments later, still smoking, he got up, went through to the toilet and then to the kitchen, where he filled and plugged in the kettle. He switched on the radio which, like the one in the bedroom, was already tuned to Radio 3. The sonata ended and the announcer, speaking in the voice of the workman, introduced the next piece. Gus opened the door of the fridge and received a pleasant surprise. He could feel himself smile for the first time since regaining consciousness. Sitting there, sharing the near-empty shelves with a tub of margarene and an opened carton of milk, was an unopened can of Coca-Cola. He must have bought a second can along with his takeaway the previous evening – had it been a fish supper or a kebab? – just to keep in the fridge for the morning. What wonderful foresight! He opened the can and sat down at the kitchen table, alternating between his cigarette and long draughts from the can. When the kettle boiled he made himself a mug of instant coffee deciding, after smelling the milk carton, to have it black with plenty of sugar.

He fetched his shoes from the bedroom so that he could be cleaning them while finishing his coffee. In the morning, every second had to be utilised. He had to keep on the move or he'd never get out of the house. Somehow his shoes had become caked with mud. How had that happened? The short journey home from Byres Road didn't take him through a field at any point. He removed the mud with a stiff brush, then used a softer one to apply a coating of polish. Leaving the polish to soak in, he carried the radio and the half-full coffee mug through to the bathroom where he shaved, showered and, after gulping down the last of the coffee, brushed his teeth thoroughly. The toothpaste had the strongest mint flavour he'd been able to find; this was designed, together with the smell of aftershave, to mask any lingering odours from the previous evening.

There was also mud on his suit, along the bottom of the trousers. He left it hanging over the back of the chair and brought another suit from the wardrobe, along with one of the newly-laundered shirts which he'd picked up the previous day. The radio was still on, but for some time now his mind had been preoccupied by tasks that awaited him in the office.

Only when he was ready to leave did he go through to the living room to open the curtains and pick up his briefcase. There was no piano there, of course, but at least the place was dry. Actually, the room in his dream had been the living room of the house he had formerly shared with Joyce and the children, though there was no piano there either.

He left the house at twenty-five to nine. He had hoped to make it to the subway before the rush hour, but now he would be right in the middle of it.

11.05 am

Gus finished dictating the last letter and put down the tape machine. Then he sat back in his chair, allowing himself a moment to relax. He had finished dealing with his mail and half of the morning was left. He would have liked a cigarette, but the staff weren't allowed to smoke and he had to show an example. What next? A client was coming to see him at 11.30 and several urgent tasks competed for the period until then. He looked at his notebook and his notes from the half-dozen calls that had interrupted his dictation. Some of them required follow-up calls. First, he would have to get the mail moving. He called through his secretary and gave her the tape, along with the bundle of mail. "Thanks, June. Would you mind bringing me a coffee?"

"Of course, Mr Mackinnon."

Gus would have preferred to be on first name terms, but his senior partner, Donald Murray, insisted on more formality between partners and staff. He looked at his notebook and was about to lift the telephone receiver when it beat him to it by ringing first.

"Your wife's on the phone, Mr Mackinnon."

"I don't have a wife. Sorry Margaret, put her through."

"Gus?"

"Hello Joyce. How are you?"

"Oh, not so bad. Yourself?"

"Oh I'm fine."

"And the kids?"

"Great. That's why I'm phoning. Are you still OK for Saturday?"

"Of course. When do you want me to pick them up? Eleven o'clock?"

"Could you make it ten? It's just that —"

"Sure. No problem. Ten it is."

"Will you be driving?"

"Of course. Why? What? Oh, I see. You know I don't drink and drive."

"Do you do much driving these days?"

"Joyce, we don't need to be sparring partners any more."

"I know. I'm sorry. Old habits and all that. It's just that – I mean, ten isn't too early is it?"

"Don't worry, I'll have a quiet Friday night. Ten pints at the most."

"Gus, that's not funny."

"Aye, OK. Joyce, you know I take my responsibilities seriously. That's half my problem."

"You're right. I'm sorry. Where were you thinking of going with them?"

"I thought I'd take them for a pint. Introduce them to some Byres Road wildlife."

"Gus, that's —"

"Not funny. Aye, all right. I was going to take them to the pictures. If I'm picking them up early we can go for an ice cream or something. I'll take them to the University Café, they like it."

"Good. Gus, have you seen this morning's *Herald*?"

"Only a glance. Why?"

"There's a piece about Norrie Spence. On page four."

"I didn't see it. Has his case come up?"

"He got five years. You knew about it?"

"Oh aye. Five *years*? Christ!"

"You never said anything about it."

"I'm very discreet. I'm a solicitor."

"I couldn't believe it. I still can't. When you say you knew about it — ?"

"I knew he'd been charged. I knew the Law Society had struck him off. I didn't know anything before that. Mind you, I wondered how he managed to keep two families going in such style. I thought he must know something I didn't about the legal game. In a way, I suppose he did."

"I think I prefer your methods. How's the flat going, by the way?"

"Oh, fine. We've almost got a roof again. And I still haven't murdered the man downstairs."

"What's that about the man downstairs?"

"Some time when you've got a day to spare I could tell you all about it. But I wouldn't advise it. Look, Joyce, I'll need to get on. This'll no' get the wean a new frock."

"She's well enough dressed. They both are."

"It's just a saying."

"I know that. I just mean… We're doing all right. You can afford to slow down a bit."

"Thanks. I don't know if the job'll let me. Anyway, I'll see you on Saturday."

"OK then. 'Bye Gus. Take care."

"You too. 'Bye."

Gus replaced the receiver and sat still for a moment. He could feel his heart speeding and his hand trembled. He wanted a drink, or at least a cigarette. Instead he finished off the coffee his secretary June had brought in during the telephone call. Brown, with one sugar, exactly how he liked it. At least the office milk hadn't gone off. Why did he get so nervous when he spoke to his ex-wife? At one time he'd felt more relaxed in her company than with anyone else he'd ever known. At least the hostility had died down to no more than the occasional piece of sniping. After another year, who knew what might be possible? Maybe they could even get back together again. Could it happen? Probably not.

His copy of the *Glasgow Herald* was lying on the corner of his desk. He'd managed to read some of the front page on the subway, but once in the office he'd only had time for a quick glance at the death notices. That, of course, was work, an essential daily discipline. He had to see if any of his clients had died, particularly any who might have left a will in the firm's custody.

He opened the paper and found the article Joyce had referred to:

SOLICITOR SENTENCED TO FIVE YEARS

Former solicitor Norman Howard Spence was sentenced to five years' imprisonment at Glasgow High Court yesterday for obtaining more than half a million pounds by fraud and embezzlement. Spence (38), not content with stealing more than £250,000 which he held on behalf of clients, doubled his money by obtaining mortgages for non-existent properties from several building societies. Spence was tried in Glasgow Sheriff Court, but remitted to the High Court for sentence by Sheriff Walter Wheaton, who felt his maximum sentencing power of two years to be inadequate for this case. Agreeing with him, Lord Kelvin sentenced Spence to five years. "This was the grossest breach of trust," he said, "a betrayal both of the people he represented and of the honourable profession whose reputation he has sullied. There have been too many cases like this recently and they must be treated with the utmost severity."

Earlier this year, Spence was struck off the roll of solicitors by the Law Society of Scotland. His former partners in the firm of Meadows, Mackay

& Spence have undertaken to repay the money in full.

Gus read the article twice, and then the phone rang again.

"A Mr Honeyman to see you, Mr Mackinnon."

"He's early. OK, Margaret, ask him to have a seat for a moment."

Honeyman? What was he again? A conveyancing transaction? No, an executry. He must have an appointment for some reason. Gus fetched Honeyman's file from the cabinet and took it back to his desk, quickly flicking through the most recent items. By the time the client was admitted, Gus would be fully briefed, ready to inspire the confidence expected from a professional adviser.

2.25 pm

"Can you spare a moment, Gus?"

"Of course, Donald. Sit down. I'll get these letters back to you later, June."

"Fine, Mr Mackinnon."

"How are things, Gus? Still busy?"

"What does it look like?"

"Yes, it never stops, never stops. Did you have a good lunch?"

"I just got in a sandwich."

"You should take a break, Gus. Why do you think we close the office for an hour?"

"It's the only time during the day when I get any peace."

"I know what you mean. I've just had lunch with Adrian Shepherd."

"Oh, how is he?"

"Fine. He's just had a summons for speeding. I said I'd pass it on to you."

"Of course. No problem."

"I know we don't do much court work these days, but Adrian's business is worth a lot of money to us. We can't have him going elsewhere."

"Absolutely. Don't worry, it doesn't exactly need Perry Mason."

"Quite. It's good if we can keep our hand in. You know what they say. A lawyer without a court practice is like a lion without his teeth."

"If he'd been arrested for murder, it would be another matter."

"If he'd been arrested for murder, I'd be less interested in keeping him as a client. Talking about criminals, did you read about young Spence?"

"Yes. I see he got five years."

"Good thing too. I don't know what's wrong with this new generation of lawyers. They've got no standards. Present company excepted, of course. In my day, if you were reported to the Law Society even once in your entire career, it was a shameful stain on your reputation. Now there are all these new firms springing up like weeds, batting off complaints daily as if they were going for a century at Lords. Spence is a friend of yours, isn't he?"

"I know him. I haven't seen him since this business first came out. He's been avoiding his usual haunts."

"Well, he'll be avoiding them for a little bit longer now. I take it you'll be happy to leave it at that?"

"I won't be trotting up to the Bar L to see him, if that's what you mean. Or sending him a cake with a file in it."

"Good, good. He's let the side down very badly. Very badly. We can't be seen to associate with people like that."

"Absolutely."

"I'm glad that's understood. Gus, I wanted to have a word with you. You don't seem your usual self lately. Not since you and Joyce split up. Are you looking after yourself properly?"

"I'm getting by."

"I worry about you. You don't look well."

"I'm OK."

"You should try to slow down a bit. And maybe go a little more easy on… Well, that's none of my business."

"You don't need to worry."

"Just the same, it wouldn't do any harm if you tried to say "no" occasionally. Anyway, I'd better let you get on. Oh, and I told Adrian he could come in and see you tomorrow. I hope that's OK."

"No."

"What?"

"Just a joke, Donald."

5.05 pm

"Is that everything, Mr Mackinnon?"

"Yes June, off you go."

"Thanks. Mr. Mackinnon, are you all right?"

143

"Yes, yes of course. Why?"

"I just thought you looked a bit… I don't know."

"I'm feeling a little tired. It's been some day."

"You're right there. Do you know how many letters I typed? Thirty-seven!"

"If you had time to count them, you can't have enough to do. Only kidding, June. Don't panic."

"Well, I'll get off then."

"Sure. I won't be long myself. I just need to tidy up my desk a bit and decide what to put in my briefcase. The subway should have quietened down by then."

"Goodnight, Mr Mackinnon."

"Goodnight, June. See you tomorrow."

6.20 pm

"Can I have a wee word, Gus?"

"Sure, Danny. What is it?"

"Could we speak in private? It's a bit personal."

"Of course. There's a space over there, at the end of the bar. I'll see you in a minute, Bob. I'm just going to have a word with Danny."

"Sure."

"Thanks, Gus."

"No problem, Danny."

"I'm sorry tae take you away from your friend."

"I don't know if I'd call him a friend. Anyway, what can I do for you?"

"I'm lookin' for a wee bit advice."

"Carry on."

144

"I doano what tae do. The whole thing's drivin' me crazy."

"Well, maybe I can help. What is it?"

"You know how I moved intae a new place the other month?"

"I remember you mentioning it."

"I had to move fae the last place. The landlord wanted everybody oot."

"You probably had rights. Anyway it's too late now."

"The new place is no' up tae much, just another mouldy bedsit. But it'll dae all right."

"So what's the problem?"

"You know how my rent's paid by the social?"

"Yes, well, I sort of assumed that."

"Well, I cannae get them tae pay any money for it. They've paid nothin' since I moved in and there's three months owin'."

"But surely you're entitled to get it paid?"

"Oh aye, they don't deny that. They just cannae seem to get my new address intae their system. I've lost counta the number of bloody forms I've filled in."

"So what's their story?"

"Well, you know how the council have taken over the social security payments? If I speak tae somebody at the council, they say the social have still tae clear it. If I take it up wi' the social, they say it's oot their hands and I should see the council. They keep passin' me back and forward. It's drivin' me daft."

"I get the picture."

"If I try to phone either of them… Well, first of all I've got tae find a phone box that's no' been vandalised. Then, it doesnae matter whether it's the council or the social, they keep me hangin' on till my money runs oot."

"Bloody hell."

"If I go there, it doesnae matter which one of them it is, they keep me waitin' for hours. Then I get landed wi' a different cunt fae the last time, one that knows nothin' about it. It's been goin' on like this for months. I'm goin' aff my heid."

"I'm not surprised. You should have told me before, Danny."

"I didnae like tae. I know you think I'm a bit of a waster."

"Danny!"

"I know you probably think I don't want tae work. It's no' that easy right now."

"I know that. Danny, you don't need to tell me this."

"I used tae have a job. I've applied for plenty, well no' so much lately. You get discouraged after a while."

"It doesn't matter."

"It probably looks to you as if I think I know it all. But that's just a front. Tae tell you the truth, I've no' got much confidence."

"Danny, all this is neither here nor there. What matters is getting you sorted out. We need to put a bomb under the bastards."

"How do you do that?"

"I can write to both of them. You'd be amazed at the magic a lawyer's letter can work."

"I cannae pay you anythin'."

"Behave yourself. I'll have a word with your landlords too, see if I can keep them sweet. Who are they?"

"The Premium Property Company. They operate through a firm called Cassidy & Kydd."

"For God's sake!"

"Sorry?"

"I know them. They're probably getting paid the rent already and don't realise it. That would require some kind of book-keeping system. The good news is that they'll never evict you. That would require something resembling efficiency."

"Aye, maybe, but I don't want tae —"

"It's all right, we'll get it sorted out. You know, there might be a better way. I can write the letters, no problem at all, but do you know what would really do it?"

"What?"

"Go and see your MP."

"What? You mean Woy?"

"Have you got another MP? You're still in the Hillhead constituency, aren't you?"

"Aye. Aye, I think so. But I cannae dae that. Go tae Woy Jenkins? For fuck's sake!"

"Why not? That's what he's there for. He's your representative, whether you voted for him or not. Walter Bain, my downstairs neighbour, he's been to see him seven times."

"What about?"

"Christ knows. Probably about the stone cleaning. Or the repairs to the back wall. Or the back court. Or the communal TV aerial. Or the new wall and railings."

"What wall and railings?"

"The ones he wants at the front of the building, at the ratepayers' expense. Never mind that nobody else gets them. Or it could be about something else entirely. Maybe he thinks his rates bill is five pence too high. Who knows? Sorry Danny, I'm getting distracted."

"It's OK. You really think Woy would see me?"

"Of course he will. He holds regular surgeries. And there's a general election coming soon, so he needs to be seen to be doing his job. He'll be worried in case the Tories get back in, after Mrs Thatcher's glorious victory in the Falklands."

"Don't start me!"

"Aye, all right. Look, you'd better give me some details and I'll get things moving tomorrow. I'll write to the Social Security and the council and I'll speak to the landlords. But I think you should go and see Roy as well. I can write to him too, or give you a note to take along with you."

"Gus, I really appreciate this."

"It's no problem, Danny. I have the technology."

7.45 pm

"Would you like another cup of tea, Mr Mackinnon?"

"No thanks. I'd better be getting upstairs." Gus patted his briefcase. "I've got work home with me. As usual."

"You work very hard, Mr Mackinnon."

"You can call me Gus."

"Oh no, I couldn't do that, Mr Mackinnon."

I suppose not, Gus thought. *After all, this is the first time she's asked me into her house. We can't be on first name terms just yet. That would be moving far too quickly on a first date.*

"Well, that's up to you, Miss Quayle."

"You remind me of Mr Johnstone who used to live in the opposite flat. He was an accountant and he worked very hard too. He died very suddenly of a heart attack a couple of years ago. It was a terrible shock. He wasn't much older than you."

"Thanks a lot, Miss Quayle. That cheers me up no end."

"Oh, I didn't mean... Oh, I'm sorry, I never ..."

"Don't worry about it, Miss Quayle. You know I like my little joke."

"That was a terrible thing to say. I didn't... You know..."

"I know. Don't worry, I can take care of myself."

"I can't believe some of the things you say to Mr Bain," she said, casting a wary glance at the ceiling. They had already, at her insistence, been speaking in quiet tones. Now her voice was barely above a whisper. Though in this case her paranoia was probably justified. Bain probably had his ear to the floor at that very moment. "You shouldn't provoke him the way you do."

"Why not? Considering what he puts us both through, I think we're due a little fun."

"Sh! He'll hear you! You're a terrible man, Mr Mackinnon. But I think it's wonderful what you're doing to have the building improved. I don't know how you talked Mr Bain round."

"I don't think you want to know about that, Miss Quayle."

"But I worry about the scaffolding being up all the time. Anyone could climb up in the middle of the night. None of our homes are safe."

"It's just something we have to put up with. Don't worry, it won't happen."

"Do you think so?"

"Or if it does, maybe they'll pick the man upstairs. If there's any justice."

She gave a nervous giggle. "Oh, that's terrible, Mr Mackinnon. But you're right." Her voice had dropped until it was barely audible. "He's an *awful* man. You don't know what I've had to put up with over the years."

"I think I have an idea. Anyway, I'd better be going. Thanks for the tea. I like your house."

"Do you really? It hasn't been modernised, like Mr Bain's."

"You mean it hasn't been vandalised?"

"Oh Mr Mackinnon! Keep your voice down!"

Gus was being entirely sincere. Like Bain's flat, Henrietta's Quayle's was of course identical in structure to his own. It gave him an impression of what his own flat must have been like before the years of neglect on the part of Toby Welsh and his aged predecessor. The antique wooden furniture, even the carpets and curtains, looked as old as the house itself, but lovingly cared for and preserved. A slight musty smell, flavoured with mothballs and furniture wax, reminded him of visits to his grandmother's house as a boy. A modern TV set and an electric fire fitted into the original fireplace seemed a little out of place by contrast.

Gus already knew that there was no gas in her house:

this was another of her many phobias. It was a constant source of anxiety to her that most of the other flats were supplied with this deadly fuel, and she constantly imagined that she smelled gas leaks. This obsession was as long standing as those about Bain and burglars, and had easily survived the transition from coal gas to natural gas, the dread of poisoning easily replaced by a terror of explosions.

He managed to take his leave and began to tiptoe up the stairs. He badly needed to visit the toilet, having thought it would be unduly presumptuous of him, on his first ever visit, to ask Henrietta Quayle for the use of her facilities. But her door had barely closed behind him when he heard one opening on the landing above. How did the bugger do it? Telepathy? Hidden cameras or microphones? Some ancient faculty born to the people of Paisley, which the rest of the human race had evolved out of?

"Hello Gus. I thought that was you."

"Hello Walter. If it's all the same, I'm in a bit of a hurry."

"I wanted a word about the environmental grant. It'll only take a minute."

Gus sighed and braced himself, hoping that he wouldn't end up having to wash the stairs early that week. Since the improvement work had begun, it was impossible to get past Bain's door. It really was too bad when you could no longer go straight up the stairs, unimpeded, to your own house.

He wondered how dangerous it would be to climb up the scaffolding.

Gus put the portable dictating machine down on the coffee table, beside the bundle of folded title deeds and the piece of pink ribbon that had tied them together. He looked again at the open deed on his lap and the archaic words he had been reading:

> Which steading of ground is part and portion of ALL and HAILL the farm and lands of Auchenclachan, with the houses biggings yards mosses muirs meadows coals coal heughs and hail parts privileges pendicles and pertinents whatsoever thereof lying in the said Parish of Kilmacraftie and County of Lanark, sometime belonging to Mrs Wilhelmina Winifred Williams or Wilkie, Lipton Lane, Lanark and now to the Superiors; But these presents are granted and the said steading of ground is disponed in feu with and under the whole burdens, stipulations, conditions, declarations and others following, videlicet: (First)...

Normally he skimmed through such documents, quickly picking out the important parts with a skill born of long practice. Now he reread the passage slowly, almost, it seemed, reading the words for the first time, the familiar phraseology now alien and puzzling, as if he were seeing it through the eyes of a layman. Maybe the public's mistrust of lawyers was well founded. Readers of that day's papers certainly wouldn't have been persuaded to the contrary. Gus picked up the dictating machine again, winding back the tape a short way to check where he had left off. His headache hadn't abated, despite the aspirins he'd swallowed earlier, and the coffee had failed to ward off the fatigue that seemed to permeate his entire body. He looked again at the document in front of him, but the words still refused to make sense. In a way, it seemed miraculous that he had ever thought they did. He ought really to set the work aside until tomorrow, he had already done a full day's work, he was entitled to a rest. But the transaction was due to be settled the following week and he was already behind with it. He shut his eyes for a moment, trying to clear his head, regain his focus. Then he put aside the document and tape machine, got up and put on the television. A few minutes distraction to rest his brain, then back to work.

He returned to the sofa and vacuously watched a quiz show that happened to be on. A few minutes later he felt his eyelids begin to droop.

10.20 pm

"Gus! Over here!"

"Susan! I didn't expect to see you here."

"I hope it's a pleasant surprise."

"Definitely. What have you done with Ernie?"

"For once he's the one at home watching the kids. This is my friend Sandra. We had her over for dinner. Why don't you join us? Sandra, this is Gus Mackinnon, the friend of Ernie's I told you about."

"Pleased to meet you, Sandra."

"You too, Gus."

"Ernie said I might find you here. I expected you a bit earlier."

"I'm usually in before this. I fell asleep in front of the television."

"And almost missed the pub? You're losing your touch, Gus."

"I know. A disaster, barely averted. It wasn't just the TV that did it. I was examining some title deeds. You know, if the Law Society had any enterprise in them, they would market these things as a new, drug-free aid to slumber."

"You work too hard, Gus."

"Don't we all?"

"Sandra and I wanted to find out what this place looked like. To see where Ernie keeps disappearing to. I can't say I'm particularly impressed."

"There you are. And you thought we were out enjoying ourselves!"

"Quite. I suppose you saw today's paper. About Norrie Spence."

"Yes. As a matter of fact, Joyce was the first to tell me about it. She hadn't known anything about it in advance and it came as a bit of a shock."

"How is Joyce?"

"Fine. We seem to be talking to each other, bar the occasional sniping."

"You'll be telling me next that you're getting back together again."

"I wouldn't go that far."

"You should compare notes with Sandra here. She's recently been divorced as well."

"I'm sorry to hear that, Sandra. I know how you feel."

"Thanks Gus. Maybe we should get together some time, cry on each other's shoulders?"

"You know Sandra, I might just take you up on that."

11.55 pm

Gus lay in bed, still awake, as the fish supper in his stomach tried to soak up the two pints he'd managed to fit in before closing time. He'd been tempted to make up for lost time by adding a double whisky, but the presence of the two women had deterred him. And now the sleep which had so easily overtaken him earlier in the evening was eluding him.

He would need to get some rest. It had been a hard day, though no worse than usual and probably no worse than the one to follow.

And yet for some reason he was in an optimistic mood. Maybe it had something to do with the telephone number he had just written in his diary. The number of Susan's friend Sandra.

6. THE BUGBANE CURSE

Autumn 1999
Billy Briggs, Flat 0/1

After a long period during which nothing much happened to Billy Briggs, three things occurred that changed his life completely: his business partnership broke up, his Uncle Arthur died, and he met his daughter for the first time.

Until then, Billy had not been particularly discontented with his life. Many people might have found it boring to sit around in a shop all day, but Billy received frequent visits from people who shared his passion. Once in a while one of them even bought something. And during the quiet periods he was able to read comics, his favourite activity for as long as he could remember.

Unfortunately, there were too many of these quiet periods, which was not good for business. "We can't go on like this, man," his partner Robbie had said. "We're barely making enough to cover the rent and rates."

"What do you suggest?"

"I'll have to buy you out and run the place myself."

"Run the place yourself? How long do you think you'd last, sitting around here all day?"

"I wouldn't have to. We're already closed on Mondays. Lesley could spell me on her days off. And you know as well as I do that there are plenty of schoolkids who can help out at weekends. All they need is a little pocket money, and the right to read as many comics as they like, as long as they don't damage the stock."

"Fair enough," said Billy, "so why don't *I* buy *you* out?"

"Have you got any money?"

"No, have you?"

"A little. More than you, I think. I've been taking some advice. I don't think your share's worth all that much. Half the cost of the stock I take over and something for goodwill. I would think five grand in total should about cover it."

"Oh do you? Have you got five grand?"

"Not quite. I was thinking I could pay it up gradually."

"I see."

"Anyway, think it over. We need to do something. If you have a better idea, let me know."

But Billy couldn't think of an alternative. He knew something had to be done. If Robbie hadn't come up with a proposal, Billy would have drifted on until they hit the rocks. He knew action was required, but taking the initiative wasn't his strong point. So, after a little grumbling, he went along with Robbie's proposal.

It seemed that Robbie had already seen a lawyer, and very soon he had the papers ready for Billy to sign. It was only then that Billy discovered the sting in the tail. "It says here that I can't open another comic shop in Glasgow."

"That's right. Why, do you want to open another shop?"

"Not right now, obviously. I don't have the money. But in the future, who knows?"

"The restriction's only for five years. The lawyer says it's standard in agreements like this. It wouldn't do if I paid you for goodwill and you opened a rival shop across the street."

"It doesn't say across the street. It says the whole of Glasgow."

"Ours is a specialist market. Another shop in Glasgow would hurt the business. So would one just outside Glasgow, but I couldn't stop you from doing that. You could open a shop in Hamilton if you wanted."

"Why on earth would I want to open a shop in *Hamilton*?"

"It's just an example. You could make it Clarkston, if you preferred. Or Paisley."

"Now you're *really* taking the piss."

But again it was a token protest. He couldn't possibly afford to open another shop on the money he was getting for his share of the business. Even if Robbie paid him all of it at once, it wouldn't be enough.

By the time Uncle Arthur had died, leaving Billy his house and all of his money, it was too late. The deal was already concluded.

Billy felt a little guilty about his inheritance. He hadn't been particularly close to Uncle Arthur. They didn't have much in common, as Uncle Arthur hadn't been interested in comics. Apart from the summons to hospital just before his uncle's death, he hadn't seen Uncle Arthur for at least two years. That had been at the funeral of Billy's father, when Uncle Arthur, who was a bachelor, emotionally declared that Billy was now his only surviving relative and that they would need to keep in touch. Billy had been quite moved by this at the time and had expected Uncle Arthur to show up at the shop sometime. But he never appeared.

As on so many other occasions in his life, Billy now regretted having left it to someone else to take the initiative. He arranged Uncle Arthur's funeral and took on the job of executor without any expectation of reward for this final small courtesy. But Uncle Arthur's will, which was five years old and hadn't been changed since, left everything to Billy's father, and Billy inherited by default.

There wasn't much money, only a few thousand after the lawyers had been paid off. It came, nevertheless, just in time to save him from having to claim unemployment benefit, after the initial meagre payment from his former partner ran out. He could of course have signed on as unemployed immediately on his retirement from the partnership, but he hadn't got round to it. As long as he had some money, it was easier to wait and see if something would turn up. And it did.

The real windfall was Uncle Arthur's flat. The mortgage had been paid off some years before, and Billy now owned the flat outright. It was a two bedroom flat, in a refurbished tenement, just off Byres Road, in Glasgow's west end. It occurred to him that, if he sold it, he could survive on the proceeds for some time. On the other hand, the security of having his own place was an attractive prospect. And as long as he had some cash in hand there was no need to make a final decision. He told himself that the wisest course would be to leave the rented flat that he shared with several other people and move into his new property. It was also the easiest course, so it was the one he took.

Then he had another idea. He looked out the contract for the sale of his share in the business and read it carefully. All it said was that he couldn't open another shop. It said nothing about mail order trading from home, using the internet. He already had a computer, and now he had cash to buy stock and a spare bedroom in which to store it. By his standards, he reached a decision fairly quickly.

He had only been in operation for about a month when his ex-wife called him.

"Billy?"

"Yes."

"At last! The trouble I've had getting hold of you. Have you been trying to hide from me? You did a good job."

"Uh, what is it that you —?"

"Don't you recognise my voice? It's been a while, I know, but —"

"Arlene?"

"Bingo!"

After all these years, it only took a few words for him to be back on the defensive. It didn't sound as if she had changed. "How are you?"

"Oh, I'm fine. You sound the same as ever. Anyway, this isn't just a social call."

"Oh?"

"Don't sound so suspicious. The reason I'm phoning is that Alison would like to meet you."

"What?"

"Alison would like to meet you. She's your daughter, remember?"

"Of course I remember. You took me by surprise. I didn't think she knew anything about me."

"She didn't, not until recently. We always thought we should tell her the truth when she was old enough. She needed a little time to get used to the idea, but now she wants to meet you. It's quite natural."

"What age is she now? Fourteen?"

"Well done, you can count. I hear you've started your own business. These arithmetical skills should be a help."

"I see you haven't changed."

"I'm a little older, and even wiser. Well, do you want to meet her?"

"Of course I do. It's just that…"

"What?"

"I didn't think you'd want me to see her."

"I don't think I could stop her, now that she knows. I don't see any point in trying. Anyway, I'm sure the pair of you will get on."

"You think so?"

"You're about the same mental age. Maybe she's a little more mature."

Billy was extremely nervous before the meeting. He wasn't sure whether this was due to the prospect of meeting his daughter or of seeing his ex-wife again. But after the initial introduction he soon began to relax. During the telephone call, he got the impression that Arlene had resumed hostilities at the point where they had broken off so many years before. But in front of Alison she behaved quite differently. She seemed genuinely prepared to let Alison make up her own mind about her father. She even seemed friendly, though Billy wasn't fooled by that.

They met on a Saturday morning, in a tearoom near the city centre. During his time at the shop this would have been Billy's busiest time of the week, but now he could work more flexibly. He noticed in passing the changes in Arlene. She had put on a little weight, though not much. She was still an attractive woman. The main change was in her style of dress, which was now much more conservative, more middle class. She was casually attired, but would have looked more at home in a golf club than at the comic convention where he had first met her. What age would she be now? A year younger than him, which would make her 35. She could have passed for older. No one said that of him, he thought smugly, though his hair was now slightly thinner and cut a little shorter to compensate.

But Alison was the main centre of his attention. She was delightful. She was a pretty girl, of medium height and build, with little of the awkwardness and none of the skin blemishes so common in adolescents. She had inherited her father's blonde hair. At first she was a little reserved, but her shyness soon passed. She seemed a good-humoured and easy-going youngster, with a charming smile and ready laugh, characteristics which, though Billy didn't know it, had prevented her mother from ever forgetting who her real father was. She was excited at meeting Billy, and seemed to find his account of how he earned his living of absorbing interest.

At her age, of course, this was perfectly natural. Arlene had once had similar interests; otherwise their short-lived relationship would never have occurred. Unlike men, women never seemed able to sustain their youthful enthusiasms into adulthood.

But Alison was still unspoiled. The meeting was judged by all to be a success and it was agreed that Alison could visit her father from time to time after school hours. As long, of course, as her mother was kept informed of her movements.

It wasn't long before the arrangement came into effect. Less than a week had passed before he met Alison again.

At first he failed to recognise his daughter. When he opened the door at five o'clock the following Thursday, the two figures on his doorstep looked as if they had stepped from the pages of *Vampire Millenium*, the graphic novel he had just been reading. Unruly black hair, gaudily painted faces adorned with metal, tight, colourful tops that stopped short of metal-ringed navels, skirts that reminded him of the curtain pelmets he had inherited from Uncle Arthur, except that they were a little shorter.

"Hi Dad. This is my pal Shona."

"Alison? Good God!"

"Can we come in?"

"I think you'd better." *Before the neighbours see you,* he thought. He hadn't yet got to know his neighbours very well, but they seemed like a nosy bunch. Just as well this was the west end of Glasgow, whose residents were accustomed to unusual phenomena. "What have you done to your hair?"

"It's a wig, silly."

"And when did you get that tattoo?"

"Don't panic, it's just a transfer. Well, Dad, what do you think of my gear?"

Billy tried to think of something tactful, but his imagination failed him. "What does your mother say?"

"You must be joking. Mum would kill me. I've left my school uniform at Shona's. I'll change back before I go home."

The girls looked admiringly round his hall. Billy hadn't had the time or the spare cash to redecorate, and the dark varnished woodwork, the patterned wallpaper and the fitted carpet had survived from Uncle Arthur's day. However, the framed prints had now gone and the walls were almost entirely covered by posters of comic heroes and villains, along with sympathetic associates from the worlds of fantasy, horror and science fiction. Behind the front door, ready to jump on visitors, lurked Boris Karloff as Frankenstein's monster. On opposite walls, Superman and Batman averted disasters and caught villains. At the far end Captain Tornado faced his arch enemy, Professor Cranium. And above them, attached to the ceiling with blue tack, Spider-Man crawled towards the light which, enclosed in its Green Lantern lampshade, cast a sinister pall over the whole room.

The Invisible Man was probably there as well, though it was difficult to be sure.

The living room presented a similar blend of traditional old and garish new, the wallpaper almost obliterated by posters. Uncle Arthur's velvet curtains had been retained, preserving a respectable facade for the benefit of passers-by outside. However, most of his furniture had been sold or jettisoned, apart from a settee, a few upright chairs and a large wooden table in the middle of the floor supporting several racks of comics. Two filing cabinets (part of the pay-off from his former partner) had been added and also a desk with a computer. Apart from that, every available space was filled by comics: in bookcases, on metal racks, in boxes stacked on the floor.

Despite the above, the room was as clean and tidy as its contents would allow. Billy was not slovenly by nature, and a collector of antique furniture could not have bestowed more love upon his treasures than Billy did upon his comics. Those not entirely enclosed in containers were wrapped in clear plastic envelopes, and all had been stowed carefully and tidily. Every surface was kept dusted, and what remained visible of the carpet was regularly vacuumed. Even the windows had recently been washed, and so had the white lace curtains, which admitted the light while providing the privacy necessary for a ground-floor apartment. In the small front garden, the grass had been cut and the borders weeded. Billy was not keen to draw attention to himself or his business, except in cyberspace and specialist literature. He was not trying to attract passing trade. He was unsure of the legality of running a business from his house, nor did he want his former partner Robbie to be able to accuse him of having opened a shop. Since the other half of the ground floor was already a shop, he thought it safest to preserve a residential appearance.

In his care of the flat's external appearance, he had surpassed Uncle Arthur himself, in his latter days at least.

When he first received the keys, he had found an illiterate note behind the door from a man upstairs called Bain, suggesting that the windows and front garden required attention. He had resented this unnecessary reminder.

"This is a *really cool* place," said Alison, when they had reached the living room.

Shona was similarly impressed. "I've never seen a house like this before."

"I'm sure that's true. Does your mother know you're here?" he asked his daughter.

"Oh yes, she said we could come here for our tea."

Their tea? Did he have any food in the house? Never mind, there was a chip shop round the corner.

"What's the matter, Dad? You're not scared of Mum are you?"

"Well, yes. I suppose I am."

Both of the girls laughed. "Don't worry Dad," said Alison. "By the time I get home, I'll be a demure little schoolgirl again. I'll even get back in time to do my homework. I won't get you into trouble." She laughed again, obviously delighted by her surroundings.

Now that he was becoming a little more used to his daughter's outlandish appearance, Billy had to admit that she and her friend blended in quite well with the décor of his flat.

"This is a *really cool* place," Alison said again. "Mum wouldn't even let me do out my *bedroom* like this."

"I'm sure she wouldn't. I like to think I'm still young at heart."

"Mum says the reason you split up was that she grew up and you didn't."

"I suppose that's another way of looking at it."

"I didn't even know you *existed* until a few months ago. I thought Adam was my real father. Why did you never keep in touch?"

This seemed too much like private family business. Billy looked across at Shona, who had picked up his copy of *Vampire Millenium* and seemed absorbed.

"Don't worry about Shona," said Alison. "She's my best friend. We tell each other everything." Shona smiled up in acknowledgement; Billy almost expected her to have vampire fangs, but she hadn't gone that far.

"You were still a baby when your mother and I split up, and it wasn't long after that before she met Adam. We thought it would be better for you to think of him as your father, until you were old enough to understand." And Arlene didn't demand any money for childcare, he could have added, though that didn't seem tactful.

"It wasn't because I didn't love you," he added awkwardly. "We just thought it was the best thing for you." Or rather, Arlene had thought that, and Billy had gone along with it.

Alison seemed to accept his explanation quite happily. Presumably it confirmed the account she'd already received from her mother. Arlene didn't seem to have tried to turn his daughter against him. This surprised him, and he felt grateful to his former wife, an unusual sensation.

"It's funny having two dads," said Alison. "I used to call Adam Dad, but now I call him Adam. *You're* Dad."

Billy was moved. "That's nice. I like that. Doesn't Adam mind?"

"He's OK about it. He always knew I'd meet you one day. And I've got a young brother and sister. He's still *their* dad."

"What's Adam like?"

"Oh, he's all right. He's a bit old-fashioned, like Mum. He's not cool like you."

"You mean, unlike me, he's grown up?"

Alison laughed again. It was a delightful laugh, which betrayed the little girl behind the disguise.

The girls stayed for about an hour, chatting, looking round the flat and reading comics. Then he took them down to the University Café for their tea. Fortunately, they both had coats, which they had been carrying on their arrival. He now insisted that they both put them on, fully buttoned up. At first he felt a little self-conscious in public with them, but it soon wore off. The more he talked with them, the more they just seemed like teenagers rather than aliens.

As they were leaving the flat, Alison said. "I really like it here. Can we come again?"

"Of course you can. As long as your mother knows where you are."

"Definitely, don't worry about that. Can we bring some other friends? Your flat's a magic place to hang out."

"Uh… yes, I suppose so."

"Great!"

As they were leaving the building, he happened to turn round and noticed that they were being observed from two different flats upstairs. The watcher on the first floor quickly withdrew before Billy could get a proper look, but on the second floor, a bald man with glasses continued to stare fixedly down at them.

The girls returned the following week, with a couple more friends, and from then on the visits became more frequent, the company larger. Some boys joined the group. When the October school break came, they were there almost every day. Fancy dress remained obligatory, but beneath the fearsome appearance their accents gave them away. They were nice, middle-class kids from Hyndland and North Kelvinside, the west end's more well-to-do areas, having the mildest of revolts against their adult mentors. They were back home well before bedtime, with the paintwork scrubbed off, the metalwork detached from their unpierced flesh, the clothing kept in holdalls or hidden in the houses of the more liberal or less observant parents. Billy found he was having to keep his kitchen better stocked with food, though many of them brought their own.

He wondered if he should check out the situation with Arlene, but the dressing-up seemed like an innocent enough secret and he didn't want to spoil their fun. Besides, he reasoned that Arlene would be in touch quickly enough if she thought anything was wrong.

He also quickly learned the wisdom of keeping his more valuable comics locked away or stored in the bedrooms, which he kept out of bounds. His visitors were not like the kids who had helped out at the shop. The latter were often loners – fat, bespectacled, spotty, or combinations of all three – who had retreated into the world of comics from an unpleasant reality, and treated these coloured-paper talismans with the same reverence as Billy and other adult enthusiasts. They were also a little older than Alison and her friends. They could be relied upon to carefully read any number of comics, without in the least affecting their sale value. But this new group were different.

Billy learned this early on when he mildly remonstrated with one of the boys, who was roughly folding back the pages of a comic with one grubby hand, while holding in the other a can of Coca-cola that looked on the point of spilling over the pages.

"Be careful with that."

"Why? It's only a comic."

"Do you know how much it's worth?"

The boy looked at the cover. "15 cents, it says here."

"That's a first issue of *The Slime Fiend*. It ran for only seven issues between 1972 and 1973. I could sell that for about £400. A complete set could go for about ten or twenty times that."

The boy quickly dropped the comic on to the table. "Jesus Christ!"

Billy was almost as offended by this as by the desecration of the comic. "I hope you don't use that kind of language at home."

"I'm sorry, Mr Briggs."

Alison quickly came to her father's defence. "You should show more respect, Johnny Craig. My dad earns his living selling these."

After that, she helped him to police the comic reading: hands had to be washed in advance, food and drink kept at a safe distance, pages could not be bent back or turned down at the edges, everything had to be put back exactly where it was found. They all submitted to Alison's authority without complaint; she was their means of admission, after all.

All the same, from then on Billy kept his more valuable comics well out of the way. He laid out a few cheap decoys: *Rod Lightning*, *Creatures of the Mist*, *The Psychic Avenger* and other rubbish like that. He also forbade them access to his computer. This was not difficult, as computers weren't a novelty to them; still, he didn't want any of them seeking out dubious websites that were inaccessible at home or at school.

He enjoyed getting to know Alison and he enjoyed the general company. He related well to kids of that age, probably for the reason his ex-wife would have given. One or two of them even began to show an interest in becoming serious comic collectors. Billy had been worried in case he would feel lonely after leaving the shop and moving into a house on his own. That was not proving to be a problem.

He had other visitors too. He had hoped to keep his customers at arm's length, but it was inevitable that those who lived locally would want to come in person to browse. At first his identity was hidden behind a new trade name and telephone number, and an anonymous e-mail address, but many of the personal callers were also customers at the shop and word soon got back to his former partner. Robbie lost no time in phoning him.

"Hey Bishop, what's going on, man? I hear you're back in business. You're not supposed to open another shop."

"I haven't. I'm operating from home."

"Come on, it's the same thing."

"No it isn't. Read the contract, the one your lawyer drew up. It says 'shop'. Anyway, I'm selling by mail order. Most of my customers are outside Glasgow."

"Not all of them."

"The ones who come here are after rare issues. You didn't want them, remember? You let me keep them as part payment of my share. What do you expect me to do with them?"

"Read them, same as you always did."

"Be reasonable, Robbie. You're not interested in second-hand issues. You only want to sell new comics. Commercial stuff: *Chip Silicon*, *The Silver Crescent* and all that crap. Trashy plastic figures, media spin-offs. You can have all that to yourself. I'm catering for the top end of the market, and most of it's outside Glasgow. We're not really in competition with each other."

Robbie sounded unconvinced, but didn't seem disposed to take it further.

In fact, Billy hadn't been completely honest with his former partner. It was true that his Glasgow callers were mostly after rare issues, and that these remained the bedrock of his mail order business. It wasn't his main purpose to sell the latest issues of *Superman* and *Batman* and other comics that could easily be picked up over the counter in any city or town of a reasonable size. All the same, he found he was receiving orders for these from more remote locations, and since working from home enabled him to fulfil such orders at a competitive price, he saw no reason not to do so. He had to eat, after all.

Contrary to the beliefs of his former partners (marital and business), Billy did have some business ability. He knew his subject and he knew his market. In the past Robbie had provided the business acumen and Billy the specialist expertise, but some of the former had rubbed off on Billy over the years. His methods were simple. He operated from one bank account in which he had put all of his meagre capital and in which he deposited his takings. From the same account he lifted the money he needed for day-to-day living. By business standards his overheads were modest – council tax, electricity, telephone etcetera – and these he paid monthly by standing order or direct debit, in order to avoid any sudden, large bills. After a few months, he noticed that the balance in his account was remaining static, and even showed the occasional modest increase, which he could use to buy stock. To Billy this meant success. He was surviving financially.

Inevitably, the customers sometimes called when Alison and her friends were in residence. There was not much interaction between them. The customers tended to be grown-up versions (in stature, at least) of the kids who helped out at the shop. When pursuing their quests, it was a normal experience to have to wade through hordes of adolescents, and they hardly noticed their existence. For their part, the kids either ignored the other callers or looked upon them with disdain. Those who had begun to develop a serious interest in comics even began to regard the visitors as a timely warning as to where such an activity could lead if taken to obsessive lengths.

"Who *are* these guys?" Alison asked her father (the visitors were mostly male). "Is that what reading comics can do to you?"

"Comics are the effect, not the cause," said Billy.

"What do you mean?"

"They're not geeks because they read comics. They read comics because they're geeks."

"Oh," said Alison. "Why don't they get a *life*? At least *you're* not a geek."

"Thanks."

It was true that Billy was a little more personable than some of his customers. His arrested development was not so apparent on the surface. Unlike many of them, he even occasionally had relationships with women, though (as with Alison's mother) they tended to be short-lived.

But, apart from that, was he any better than the geeks? What kind of life did he have, apart from comics? Until lately, not much. But now he had a daughter. Because of that his life was much richer.

Henrietta Quayle was worried. She was always worried – that was how her brain was constructed – but this time the feeling was more intense than usual.

The subject of her concern was the new occupant of the ground floor flat. She knew very little about him, that was the problem. In such a situation, her imagination generally filled in the gaps. And the paranoid nature of her imagination meant that the explanations it came up with were seldom comforting.

For more than thirty years, the ground floor flat had been occupied by Arthur Briggs. Apart from her and Walter Bain, no one had lived in the building longer. She and Briggs hadn't exactly been friends but, unlike Bain, he had been a pleasant enough and uncontroversial neighbour. He had even gone out of his way to help her on one occasion when it had been badly needed. He had never become involved with the affairs of the building; or, to look at it another way, he had had as little as possible to do with Walter Bain. He never went to any of the meetings called by Bain, or became involved with the refurbishment of the building, though he had always paid his share of the cost without complaint. For most of his time in the building he had taken his turn of washing the close, his windows were regularly cleaned (very important on the ground floor), and his small front garden had been kept tidy.

When his health started to decline, he had begun to neglect these duties. To Henrietta, this was understandable, but not to Walter Bain. To him there was no excuse for avoiding communal chores, not illness or even death. When Arthur became ill, decades of good behaviour were promptly forgotten. Only his present transgressions were relevant. In his usual fashion, Walter put regular reminders through Arthur's letterbox and, in his usual fashion, Arthur ignored them. Throughout the entire period of his residence in the building Arthur had ignored Walter Bain; presumably, once he was dying, he saw no reason to change this.

Henrietta missed the new occupant's arrival. This was unfortunate, since you could learn a lot about people from observing what came out of the removal van. Later, she saw some of Arthur's furniture being taken away in a van, and wasn't sure what to think. The new occupant didn't change the name on his front door, or at the front entrance. Did that mean he was a relative? The flat had never been up for sale, she was sure of that.

At first the signs were good. The new neighbour washed the close when it was his turn and, a few days later, Henrietta met him when she left the building to go to the shops. He was in the front garden, washing the outside of his living room window. He was a young man, quite tall. He had light blond hair, quite long, though not long enough to cover his single gold earring. He was dressed casually, in T-shirt, jeans and trainers.

A little hesitantly, she said, "Good morning."

He turned round. The first thing she noticed was the motto on his T-shirt, which read "Children of the Night", in black, Gothic letters. What could that mean? It seemed ominous.

His ready smile was a little reassuring. "Good morning," he said. He now seemed a little older: in his thirties, maybe, rather than his twenties.

"I… I'm Henrietta Quayle. I live upstairs."

He brought a tissue from his pocket, wiped his hand dry and extended it, stepping across the narrow garden. "Pleased to meet you. I'm Billy Briggs."

Henrietta shook his hand briefly. "Oh. Were you related to Arthur Briggs?"

"He was my uncle."

"He was a nice man. We were neighbours for more than thirty years. I was sorry when he died."

"Thanks. We weren't really all that close. But I was his nearest surviving relative, so he left me his flat."

A memory came back to Henrietta of a fair-haired boy, in the company of his parents, whom she'd occasionally seen visit Arthur many years before. She couldn't remember having encountered him as an adult, until now.

"What is it you do, Mr Briggs?" This seemed more tactful than, "Why are you at home at eleven o'clock on a weekday morning?"

"Billy. Nothing, at the moment. I used to be in business."

He didn't say what that was, and she couldn't quite bring herself to ask him. Why was he no longer in business? Had Arthur left him a fortune? He had never seemed all that rich.

Billy didn't seem disposed to chat further. For want of anything else to say, Henrietta said, "Mr Bain will be pleased to see that you've washed the windows."

Billy frowned slightly. "I'm not doing it to please Mr Bain. I'd have done it anyway, so his note was quite unnecessary."

"I'm sorry, I didn't mean …"

Billy smiled again. "It's all right. You can tell him I'll be attending to the garden shortly. On the other hand, don't bother. I'll keep it as a surprise."

For the time being, Henrietta was reassured. Then the visitors began to arrive at his flat. Soon they increased in numbers and frequency. When she passed the front door of the ground floor flat, loud, brash pop music could be heard from within.

The appearance of the visitors was not encouraging. She remembered the motto on Billy's T-shirt and his vagueness about his business interests, and this fuelled her imagination.

What could she do? Who could she talk to? At one time she might have confided in Gus Mackinnon, but now she suspected that he would just laugh at her, even if she could catch him sober. She visited the Andersons and told them her suspicions, but they were sceptical. They *had* heard the music – they were in the flat directly above

177

– but it was never played late at night, and they didn't feel disposed to complain. As they spent much less time than Henrietta looking out of the window, they had seen nothing that bothered them.

With extreme reluctance, Henrietta realised that there was only one course left to her. Normally, she would never have contacted Walter Bain; she saw far too much of the man as it was, without being the one to initiate contact. All of her instincts were firmly against it, but a desperate situation required desperate measures.

So she wrote Walter Bain a note.

Even before his daughter's appearance, Billy's social life was less restricted than some might have thought. Although the comic universe might seem to outsiders to be a minority sub-culture, it was one that extended across the Western world and beyond. It was an international movement – dominated, admittedly, by the products of the North American continent – but international just the same. And it was wrong to think of it as a movement exclusively for juveniles, or adults of a juvenile disposition. It extended far beyond the worlds of fantasy, horror or the supernormal: there was much more to it than larger-than-life heroes (and heroines) taking on grotesque and powerful villains. There was also Archie, Jughead and Veronica continuing their sixty-year sojourn at high school. There were explicitly "adult" comics, though that generally meant adolescent. There was also political satire, social comment, philosophical speculation, adaptations of classic novels, many sub-cultures within the sub-culture. After all, as Billy often pointed out, pictures could be art, words could be art, so why should a combination of the two be denied that status as a matter of principle? In any field, 95 per cent or more of what appeared was rubbish. You judged painting, sculpture, music, literature, theatre and cinema by their best products, and so it should be with comics.

Billy believed all of this, and his evangelical arguments were quite sincere. Just the same, he still had a secret preference for superheroes and villains, and for the monsters that threatened humankind from space or from within a surreal, alternative Earth. The least subtle products from a few decades before had acquired stature with time, had become historical documents, their intrinsic value boosted by period charm and limited availability. And in modern times, writers like Alan Moore or Clive Dangerfield had shown that this bedrock of the American comic book could be subverted, taken in new directions, its genre boundaries burst open and transcended.

Within the international comics community Billy was something of a minor authority, a well-known fan who was consulted for his expertise, asked to settle arguments. He often attended comic conventions in different parts of the United Kingdom and occasionally, when money allowed, in the United States. On the days when the kids didn't appear at his house, or after they had left, his evenings were spent in internet chat rooms or exchanging e-mails. He also had a circle of local friends, all comic enthusiasts, whom he visited, or who visited him.

One of the latter, Gordon Williamson, had for some time been trying to involve Billy in a new project, an adult comic set in Glasgow, reflecting Glasgow culture and humour. Several attempts at this had been made in the past, but most had been fairly short-lived or had died in infancy. Most, in Billy's opinion, had aspired to adulthood in a most infantile way, trying to do for Glasgow what *Viz* had done for Newcastle. This was not something Billy felt his home city should necessarily be grateful for. So far Gordon had appeared to be trying for something similar, except that he seemed determined to be doubly offensive by extending his so-called satire into the honourable superhero tradition. Billy had no objection to his beloved genre being subverted in an intelligent way, but so far Gordon's ideas for a west of Scotland super-anti-hero – *Fancyman*, *Fatman*, *Middenman*, *Captain Cludgie* – had failed to inspire him. As had *Shug Ugly, the Clyde Sludge Monster*. And a vampire hunter called Patrick Cross, or a graphic novel called *Last Exit to Salcoats* were just daft.

Billy had been in his new business for about a couple of months when Gordon called personally to promote his latest idea. The Bishop wasn't taking his e-mails seriously enough, so a face-to-face pitch was required. As he pressed Billy's button at the security door, he heard the noise from the ground floor flat. What was going on? Had the man gone mad?

He heard an electronic crackle and a high-pitched voice said, "Hello?"

"I'm looking for Billy Briggs."

"OK". Before he could give his name, the entry system buzzed and he was admitted to the close. A minute later, Billy opened his front door.

"Hi Gordon."

"Hello Bishop. What's going on? Have you started some kind of punk commune? Your members seem a bit under-age."

"My daughter's here with her friends."

"I didn't know you had a daughter."

"Well, you do now."

He followed Billy through the hall into the living room, noticing the décor only in passing. None of it surprised him. He expected nothing less of the Bishop.

"THIS IS MY DAUGHTER ALISON. GORDON WILLIAMSON."

"HI THERE."

"PLEASED TO MEET YOU. JESUS, BISHOP, WHAT A DIN. WHAT *IS* THAT SHITE?"

"MIND YOUR LANGUAGE. COME THROUGH TO THE KITCHEN."

They crossed the hall, closing two doors between them and the noise. Alison, Shona and a couple of others followed them, curious about the newcomer. He didn't seem like one of the geeks. Like Billy, he looked superficially normal.

"They don't like my music," said Billy. "They bring their own CDs."

"I was worried. What *is* that stuff?"

"That's Doctor Caligari," said one of the boys, in an injured tone.

"It's time he was back in his cabinet, son. An honourable name dragged in the gutter, eh Bishop?"

The boy shook his head. These guys had seemed a little better than your normal adults, but not when it came to music. "Why do they call you the Bishop, Mr Briggs?" he asked.

Alison and Shona burst out laughing. "What *planet* are you on, Jimmy Green?" Alison asked.

Having been put down from all directions, Jimmy returned to the living room. The other boy followed him. Still curious, Alison and Shona remained.

It was a large kitchen, much the same as Uncle Arthur had left it, apart from a few posters. It was the only room in which every available crevice had not been used to store comics, which did not mix well with the emanations from a cooker and washing machine. The exception was Uncle Arthur's old sideboard, which sat in a bed recess at the opposite end of the room from these appliances. Its drawers and the cupboard beneath were ideal for flat storage of larger comics. Here there was a complete set of *2000 AD* and an unbroken run of *The Eagle*, from its first issue until 1960. So far they had seemed uncontaminated, but Billy was thinking of moving the sideboard into the hall.

Mundane kitchen items like cutlery had been dumped in a box in the food cupboard, apart from a single knife, fork, desert spoon and teaspoon in the drip tray beside the sink. A minimal supply of plates was stacked beside them.

On top of the sideboard, Uncle Arthur's fruit bowl had been replaced by a large, green-ceramic bust of the Mekon, its bony face under the huge skull glaring malevolently at the room's occupants.

"Anyway," said Billy. "What can I do for you, Gordon?"

"I want to sound you out on my latest notion. It's my best yet. I've done a script for the whole first episode."

"Gordon wants to start an adult comic, set in Glasgow," Billy explained to the girls.

"Great!" said Alison. "Can we hear it?"

"Go on, *please*," said Shona.

"It's an *adult c*omic," Billy warned.

"It's not *that* adult," said Gordon, keen for a more appreciative audience than his friend. "I don't think they'll be corrupted."

"Go on Dad, you're such a *prude*. We can handle it."

"OK, but if it gets too hairy, I'm stopping it."

They sat round the kitchen table. Gordon opened his script and began to read: "Title: *The Adventures of Flyman*. Opening blurb: Forget Batman, forget Spider-Man, it's Glasgow's own *Flyman*."

The girls chuckled. Encouraged, Gordon carried on: "Second blurb: With his top pair of hands he will embrace you as a friend, while the bottom pair is rifling through your pockets."

The girls laughed again. Billy sighed. The last thing the man needed was encouragement.

Inspired by the audience response, Gordon's performance became more animated. "First frame, top panel: The Horseshit Bar, somewhere in Glasgow."

The girls sniggered and Billy tutted.

"A group of friends are enjoying a quiet refreshment.

"Picture: Four young men sitting at a table, drinking pints. One of them has just pulled his drink away in time from a passer-by who is being sick. In the background, three men are having a fight beside the bar. At another table, a man is trying to get his girlfriend drunk.

"First man: I really enjoy havin' a quiet refreshment.

"Second man: Aye, it's a really civilised way to spend a Saturday afternoon.

"Man with girl: Dae ye fancy me yet?

"Girl: Naw, get us another Special Brew."

"Right, that's it," said Billy. "We've heard enough."

"No, Dad," said Alison. "This is great stuff. We want to hear the rest."

"Please, Mr Briggs," said Shona.

Gordon was as keen to perform as his audience was to listen. Billy gave up. He hoped Arlene would never hear about this and began to prepare his defence.

The story continued in a similar vein. In the next frame, there is a close-up of one of the friends, an angelic-looking young man, well dressed, with short, fair hair. "Meet Johnny Straight, model citizen," says the caption. "Quiet and clean living, apart from the occasional wee civilised refreshment. Perfect father and faithful husband. The man who makes 'Mother's Pride' more than just a loaf of bread."

There is a bulge in Johnny's cheek. An arrow points to the bulge, bearing the caption: "Unmelted butter".

But Johnny has an incredible secret. Whenever confronted by any moral or financial pressure, dark and hidden forces are unleashed within his metabolism, and a strange transformation occurs. "Whose round is it?" asks one of his friends, and another replies, "I think it's Johnny's." Johnny is now in a condition of obvious distress, with bizarre noises coming from his body – URK! CRACK! GURGLE! CREEK! – as he makes a bolt for the toilet. "I'll get one up in a minute, lads," he says. "Got to go to the bog first". In the next frame two men in the toilet look up startled at the peculiar noises – SNAP! WHEECH! POP! SKITE! CREEARRK! OOOARRARGH! – coming from the cubicle.

Billy was shaking his head. Alison and Shona were squealing with delight, Gordon's vocalisation of each noise bringing on a new attack of giggles.

Johnny Straight has transformed into Flyman, who now emerges from the cubicle. Flyman is a small, misshapen man, dressed in black, with a balding head and bulging eyes. Two single hairs sprout from his forehead, like small antennae. He has two pairs of arms, six limbs in all. The two men at the urinal look round, astonished. With his bottom left hand, Flyman surreptitiously lifts a wallet from the back pocket of one of them.

Flyman returns to the table of the three friends, who regard him with collective dismay. "Christ, it's Flyman." "Aw naw!" "I'm no' here." "Hullo boys," says Flyman, "whose round is it?" In the background, the fighters at the bar are now having a friendly sing-song; the girl is leaning over her boyfriend, who is slumped over the table, unconscious with drink. "I love ye, Willie!" she says.

"It's Johnny Straight's round," says one of the friends. "He's just gone oot the door," says Flyman. "He's no' well. I'd get them up, but I've left my money in my other trousers." "Is that the ones wi' the pockets doon tae the ankles?" asks the second of the friends. Flyman points to the third friend, who is trying to hide under the table. "How about you, Jimmy? I seem tae remember I bought you a pint in 1992. Or was it 1985?" "Fuck!" says Jimmy.

Yet again, Billy expressed his disapproval, but was ignored.

The rest proceeds along the same lines. Ten ponced pints later, Flyman is leaving the pub, jingling the change in his pocket, singing, "Fly me to the mugs." He helps a blind man across the road, relieving him of his clothes on the way over. At the other side, the blind man, now naked, thanks Flyman, while commenting that the weather seems suddenly to have got much colder. Later, Flyman realises that he must hurry home, no expense spared, and buys a half fare on the bus to Drumwheechle, claiming that he is big for his age. It seems he has a hidden weakness: he must return to his own lavatory before closing time. Back at Johnny Straight's house, he climbs up a drainpipe on the back wall to the toilet window. Johnny's wife, hearing the noises from the toilet – GOO-AR! WHEECH! CRACK! – reflects that it is time he gave up curries. Changed back, Johnny rejoins his wife, who is worried whether he may have spent too much money. "Don't worry," he says. The last frame shows the angelic Johnny, now with a halo above his head, hugging his wife and clutching a bundle of banknotes. "I think we'll be able to feed the weans this week," he says. Behind him, the shadow of Flyman lurks.

Gordon closed his script. The girls burst into delighted applause. Gordon turned to the expert. "Well?"

"It's a bit better than your previous efforts," said Billy.

"Oh, don't be so stuffy, Dad!" said Alison. "It's brilliant."

"Magic," said Shona. "Are you going to draw it yourself?"

"I can't draw," said Gordon. "I thought my cousin John could probably do it."

"He probably could," said Billy. "Hang on a minute." He left the room and returned a moment later with a thick, well-worn paperback. "You need to be careful," he said. "You can think you've got a new idea, and then find it's been used before." He consulted the book. "There was an American superhero called *The Fly*. He appeared in three different runs: 31 issues from 1961 to 1965, 9 issues from 1983 to 1984, and 17 issues, with one annual, from 1991 to 1992."

"I know that one. It's not the same."

"Oh, and there's a *Fly Man*."

"I don't believe it!"

"Variation of *The Fly*: 8 issues from 1965 to 1966. Not highly regarded."

"That's well in the past. I don't suppose it played on the double meaning of the word "fly?"'

"I doubt it. Legally, I'd say you're in the clear."

Alison seemed torn between irritation at her father's pedantry and admiration of his expertise.

"Well, I think it's super," she said. "I think you should go ahead. I'll definitely buy it."

"So will I," said Shona.

"There you are," said Billy. "Your adult material definitely appeals to the adults."

Walter Bain didn't normally pay much attention to what Henrietta Quayle said. He had very little regard for her opinions. However, though he wouldn't have called her a good neighbour – that was not a concept he recognised – in the hierarchy of bad neighbours she was probably the least offensive. She was afraid of him and was more or less under his control. If all of his neighbours had been like her, his work would have been a lot easier: the work of managing a building that kept up proper standards of family decency, that preserved and enhanced the value of his investment.

Nominally, it was the factor who maintained the building but, like all of his kind, he was completely hopeless. The current one was even worse than those who had preceded him. No, the real manager of the building was Walter Bain, who continually struggled to maintain the highest tenemental values on behalf of the small community of residents. You'd expect them to be grateful, but all he ever got was indifference, rudeness and lack of cooperation.

He looked again at the note Henrietta Quayle had put through his letterbox:

Dear Mr Bain
I am sorry to bother you, but I think something is going on in the ground floor flat. Have you seen the visitors: strange men and brazen young girls? Have you heard the music they play? I fear the very worst. We are back to the days of that dreadful man Welsh who used to live on the top floor. Twice in the same building; it is really beyond belief!
I apologise again for troubling you, but I think maybe we should be concerned.
Yours,
Henrietta Quayle.

The stupid woman could be completely wrong, of course. But he had seen some of the evidence himself. The offending activity often continued after he had returned from work. He had certainly heard the music. Not from his own house, which was two floors up on the other side of the building, or he would certainly have complained earlier. It was not like the noise inflicted upon him by that drunkard upstairs. Still, you could hear it clearly in the close, and it followed you some way up the stairs. You could even hear it in the street, if there wasn't a bus passing.

It made no difference to him that the music from above consisted of orchestral pieces by Beethoven and Mozart and that the sounds from the ground floor were of popular music from the hit parade. He was not particularly aware of the distinction. It was all noise. What mattered was how loud it was and where you could hear it from. Heavy rock was superior to Beethoven, simply by reason of its distance from the Bain household.

The ground-floor visitors were another matter. He had seen some of them himself. Not only young girls but young boys too. If Henrietta Quayle was right, then it was worse than even she could have imagined.

He showed the note to his wife Agnes. "What do you think of that?"

"What about it?"

"Haven't you seen the people coming in and out of the ground-floor flat?"

"Now and then."

"Hasn't it bothered you?"

"No."

"Haven't you wondered what's going on?"

"No."

"You're in the house more often than I am. Haven't you seen anything?"

"I don't stand looking out the window all the time. I've got other things to do."

Walter Bain sighed. Once he could have relied upon his wife as his strongest supporter. These days she seemed to be losing interest. He often felt that he stood alone against every other resident, that the building's crumbling moral structure rested entirely upon his ageing shoulders.

Someone more sensitive than him to the feelings of other people might have wondered more about his wife's change of attitude, might have been more curious about the reason for it and concerned for her welfare. But Walter Bain was not that type of person, even when it concerned a close member of his family.

What should he do? It was six o'clock. There was no evidence that his wife was near to having the evening meal ready. At one time it would have been waiting for him when he got home. "I think I'll go downstairs and have a word with him."

"Please yourself."

He had never actually met the new ground floor resident. He had seen him from the window. He had sent him instructive notes, though he had not received the courtesy of a reply from the man. Certainly, Briggs – if that was his name – had washed the close and followed Walter's other suggestions, but that could just be a cover. It was time to introduce himself in person. On what pretext? He would think of one.

The music could be heard in the distance as soon as he left his flat and it grew louder as he descended the stairs. On reaching the front door of the bottom flat, he knocked loudly and rattled the letterbox, to make sure he could be heard inside. After a moment or two, the door opened and the noise grew even louder.

The appearance of the girl who answered the door took him by surprise and at first he couldn't think of anything to say. Previously, he had only seen the visitors from a distance. He now got a close view of unruly hair streaked with different colours, heavy and garish make-up, a flimsy top exposing too much flesh above and below, matching metal rings in nose and navel, a skirt that hardly existed. What age was she? Far too young, that was certain.

She glared at him. "Yes?"

"Is – is this where Mr Briggs lives?"

"Yes. Are you here on business?"

"No. No, I'm not!" He could think of nothing to add. "Never mind," he said. He heard the door bang behind him as he fled upstairs.

There was now no doubt. As soon as he was back in his flat, he phoned the police. As usual, they didn't seem interested. They were almost as bad as the factor. What did he pay his taxes for?

Several days and a number of calls later, he got through to a Sergeant Barnes. He was new to Walter and, unlike his colleagues, listened to his story sympathetically. The next day, he called to take statements from Walter and Henrietta Quayle. He was a young man, who still seemed to have some of the energy and enthusiasm for his job that was so lacking in the others.

The day after that, the police raided the ground-floor flat.

"Well, Barnes," said Detective Chief Inspector Matt MacDermott, "this is a fine mess you've got us into."

"Yes sir."

"You promised me a paedophile ring. What do we

have? A bunch of schoolkids hanging out at a comic shop."

"It wasn't a shop, sir, it —"

"Shut up, Barnes. A teenager visiting her father and bringing along a few pals."

"Yes sir."

"And who do these pals turn out to be? Not just any bunch of kids. Oh no. They're all pupils of Glasgow Academy which, in case you don't know, is one of the poshest private schools in the city. A list of their parents reads like a local *Who's Who*. Do you know who the Briggs girl's stepfather is? Adam MacEwan, the MP."

"I know that now, sir."

"But now it's too late, isn't it? Now, we're all in the shit, thanks to you. Barnes, remind me again, what put you on to this case? What was your source of information?"

"A phone call from one of the neighbours."

"From Walter Bain?"

"Yes sir."

"And you'd never heard of him?"

"No sir."

"Barnes, how long have you been with us?"

"Only two months, sir."

"A whole two months and you'd never heard of Walter Bain? That's like the Pope saying he's never heard of the Virgin Mary. Bain phones us on average two or three times a week. He's always complaining about some stairheid rammy or other. That man could start a riot in an empty close."

"Yes sir." Barnes could have pointed out that the Chief Inspector was mixing his metaphors, or his floor levels at least. He decided that the time was not appropriate. He could also have reminded his boss that he had given the operation his blessing, though now that he thought of it, the name "Walter Bain" might not have been mentioned.

"Did nobody try to warn you about Bain? None of your junior colleagues?"

"Uh, they may have said something."

"But you didn't listen. You wanted the glory of uncovering a paedophile ring, an under-age brothel operating right under our noses."

"With all due respect, sir. We watched the property for more than half a day. It did look suspicious. You should have seen the way the girls were dressed."

"I did. And now, for the first time, so have their parents. I think they're going to be grounded for quite a while."

"And the men who called there. Very peculiar."

"Sad bastards who collect rare comics. I doubt if they even noticed that the kids were there."

"Sheriff Bunyan was happy to sign the search warrant, sir."

"That was before he knew his daughter would be lifted in the raid. Along with what? Remind me what you found in the flat. Any porn, child or adult?"

"No sir."

"Any drugs?"

"No sir."

"What about the pills in the aspirin bottle?"

"They were – uh – aspirin, sir."

"Cunningly concealed in the bathroom cabinet, I suppose. No, there were no drugs. No smack, no ecstasy, no coke, apart from the stuff manufactured by the Coca-Cola company. Not even the remains of a joint. Not even any cigarettes. From what I hear, he wouldn't allow smoking in his house and didn't own an ashtray. He thinks it's bad for his health and, even worse, bad for his comics. Oh, and we forgot to mention alcohol. Was he turning the kids into under-age drinkers?"

"There was no alcohol, sir."

"Not that we could do him for having a bottle of whisky in his cupboard, if there was no evidence that he was giving it to the kids. So what *did* you find in his flat?"

"Comics, sir."

"Nothing else?"

"A bed, kitchen appliances, a few chairs, some other sticks of furniture, and —"

"Comics? Lots and lots of comics?"

"Yes sir. And a computer. We took that away."

"What's on it?"

"We're still examining the hard disc. He'd bookmarked a few websites."

"Kiddie porn? No, let me guess. Comic publishers."

"Something like that."

"You won't find anything, Barnes. You'd better carry on and finish the job, but you'll find nothing, I'm sure of it."

"I think you're right, sir. But what about his T-shirt?"

"What T-shirt?"

"One of the other neighbours, a Miss Quayle, told us Briggs wore a T-shirt that said, 'Children of the Night'."

"Children of the Night?"

"That's right, sir."

Detective Chief Inspector Matt MacDermott gave a deep sigh and stared at his younger colleague. It might have made Barnes feel even more uncomfortable, had that been possible. "Barnes?" he said eventually.

"Yes sir?"

"What university did you go to again?"

"The University of Edinburgh."

"You know Barnes, I have a modern outlook. I don't really object to fast-track graduates in the police force. Even when, like you, they have no common sense. I just wish the education they gave you was a little more relevant. You'd have been better going to one of the new universities and taking film studies."

"I don't understand, sir."

"'Children of the Night'. It's a quote from Bela Lugosi in *Dracula*. Referring, if I remember correctly, to the wolves that howled in the forest around his castle. Even I knew that."

"Oh."

"I expect it also crops up in some comic or other. You're getting desperate, Barnes. William Briggs is innocent. He's the most innocent man who ever walked the face of the Earth."

"Yes sir."

"Barnes?"

"Yes sir?"

"You're an idiot."

"Yes sir."

"God!" said MacDermott. "What a cock-up! I just hope nobody leaks it to the press."

But somebody did. It was too good a story.

Billy Briggs may have been innocent, but in the eyes of his ex-wife Arlene and the other parents he might as well have been guilty. The scandal of having to pick up their children from the police station, the way their children were dressed, were quite enough. Until then, even Billy had not realised quite how distinguished were the parents of his young visitors. He had known that Adam MacEwan was an MP, of course, but Shona had never mentioned that her father was a sheriff.

"I'm sorry, Dad," said Alison tearfully as her mother took her away. "It wasn't your fault."

But that was a minority opinion. Next day, the breaking of the story did nothing to change that:

POLICE RAID COMIC SHOP

Judge's daughter arrested for reading *Superman*

Yesterday evening Glasgow police swooped upon a flat in the city's west end, hoping to crack a local paedophile ring. What did they find? Under age sex? Drug-fuelled orgies?

No. Not even a 14-year-old smoking an illicit cigarette. They discovered a bunch of posh kids reading *Superman* and *Batman* and taking coke – by that, of course, we mean drinking the popular beverage known as Coca-Cola.

Billy Briggs (36) is a comic dealer who runs his business from home. From time to time his daughter Alison, who lives with her mother and stepfather, local MP Adam MacEwan, drops in with some of her friends. They read comics. They listen to pop music. They consume soft drinks and packets of crisps. They dress a little more casually than their stuffy, middle-class parents would normally allow.

Oh, and there's also the odd visit from a few ageing nerds, looking for rare back issues of *Spider-Man*.

All very innocent? Not according to Billy's dotty neighbours who thought something much more sinister was going on. Not according to the police, who were daft enough to believe these fantasies.

Last night, red-faced officers were…

And so on, in papers local and national, on TV and radio. It wasn't long before Arlene was on the phone, completing the demolition job she had begun the night before. He didn't really mind the abuse – it was quite like old times – except that she now confirmed what he'd already suspected would be the case. Alison's visits were to stop. For the foreseeable future.

At least the publicity might be good for his business. But even that hope faded, as his new fame brought about other consequences. He received a letter from Robbie's solicitor, warning him that his business was in breach of their agreement. The council planning department wrote, advising him that he had no permission to run a business from home.

And, a fortnight after the raid, he returned home after a local comic mart to discover that he had been burgled. All the comics were gone, not only his stock, but his personal collection, built up over a lifetime. They had also taken his computer, now returned by the police, and his hi-fi system.

There was also a note from Walter Bain, complaining that the "removal men" had broken the security door and had left the front gate open.

After the police had left, Billy sat on one of the chairs the burglars had thoughtfully left him and brooded. The police had been sympathetic – no doubt still embarrassed by their previous encounter – but couldn't offer much hope. Clearly, Billy had been targeted. The newspapers had drawn the attention of specialist thieves to the address where a valuable comic collection could be found; before that, Billy had only been locatable by phone and e mail, and the phone book only listed Uncle Arthur, not the company name Billy traded under. The thieves must also have known about the comic mart and that Billy was certain to attend it. The police didn't have a specialist unit for comics, but maybe Billy himself might have some idea who was behind it?

But he didn't. There was not even any certainty that the thieves were local. To those familiar with the comic market, Billy's collection would have been worth driving a distance for.

At least, the police concluded, you'll have a good insurance claim.

The insurance. He had renewed Uncle Arthur's contents policy, mainly because the insurance company had pestered him about it. He had intended to get the value of his comics appraised and have them specifically included in the policy, but he hadn't got round to it.

The flat felt empty and dismal without his comics. The

posters, which the burglars had also kindly left behind, only served to remind him of his loss. The place felt doubly empty without Alison and her friends. Especially without Alison.

What now? He didn't even have a TV to watch. He'd never had one, though if he had, no doubt the burglars would have taken it as a bonus. He could go upstairs and launch a savage physical attack upon Walter Bain. But that would only get him into more trouble, though it was something he didn't rule out for later, once he'd had time to plan it properly.

Instead he did something quite uncharacteristic. He left the flat, securing the front door as best he could – what did it matter now? He walked down to Byres Road and went into a pub. He was not a drinking man, but there were times, like the present one, when it seemed like an appropriate response. He bought himself a pint of beer and looked around. At one of the tables, he recognised one of his neighbours and walked over.

"Do you mind if I join you?" Three middle-aged men looked up at him. "I'm Billy Briggs, your neighbour."

"Not *the* Billy Briggs?"

"Owner of the comic book bordello?"

Billy winced. Some of the headlines still hurt.

"Sit down, son," said Gus Mackinnon. He was showing the effects of alcohol a little more than the others, but seemed particularly sympathetic. "Tell us your story. Tell us how Walter Bain shafted you."

Billy sat down among them. "What makes you think he had anything to do with it?"

"Didn't he?"

"Yes. It was all his fault."

"Of course it was. It always is."

Billy hadn't met Gus Mackinnon before, not properly. He had seen him leaving the building often enough, and a couple of times he had found him sleeping in the close and had propped him against the wall, making sure his breathing was unimpaired. This had not been enough to cause Gus to remember Billy, but as soon as he realised who he was, he and his friends became receptive listeners. Billy told them the whole story, including the burglary.

"Well, I wouldn't bother about the planning department," said Gus. "Walter Bain will have been phoning them on a daily basis. They only wrote to you so that they could send him a copy and get him off their backs."

"How can you know that?"

"I know Walter Bain."

"And the letter from your partner's solicitor," said one of the others, the man called Ernie. "That's probably just a try-on. He probably can't touch you if you're working from home. Depends on the wording of your contract, of course."

"But how do —"

"We're lawyers, son," said Gus. "Used to be, anyway. Some of us still are. Take our word for it, you can still carry on your business. I'm sure of it."

"What with?"

"Well, that's a point. You were a bit silly about the insurance, Billy."

"Bloody stupid!" said Bob Waddell.

"We all make mistakes," said Ernie, looking pointedly at the previous speaker.

"Anyway, none of that's important," said Billy. "I'll never see Alison again, that's what *really* matters."

"You'll never see who again?"

"Alison. My daughter. I'd only just met her and now she's gone for ever. I'll never see her again."

"What age did you say she was?" asked Ernie.

"Fourteen."

"I wouldn't worry," said Gus. "In a couple of years she'll be old enough to see whoever she wants. My guess is she'll be back long before then. I expect you add a little glamour to her middle-class existence."

"I hope you're right," said Billy. "I'm sorry. I'm not usually like this."

"It's all right. It's quite understandable." Gus shook his head. "Another victim falls foul of the Bain curse." He turned to his friends. "Haven't I told you about that man?"

"You've told us."

"Once or twice."

"Has he done something to you?" asked Billy.

"Has he? Have you got all night?"

"You know," said Billy. "I don't usually talk like this. But that man Bain, he's – he's a bastard."

"No he isn't."

"What?"

"Remember, we're lawyers. We define things precisely. We can provide you with the correct technical expression."

"What's that?"

"He's a fucking cunt," said Gus. "That's the legal definition."

Billy was a little surprised at hearing such language

from a lawyer. In the circumstances, however, it seemed appropriate. Maybe the law was a more interesting subject than he'd realised.

Billy only stayed for a couple of drinks before making his way home. He could understand how someone might be driven to alcoholism by living near Walter Bain, but that was not his way. Just the same, his meeting with Gus and the other lawyers left him a little more optimistic. They had given him some good advice. As well as reassuring him that he would not be prevented from continuing with his business, they had provided him with some ideas about his insurance claim. Uncle Arthur's insurance would probably not pay out for a valuable comic collection, but it would cover a modest claim for the sort of item you would expect in a normal household. Billy hadn't had a TV, video recorder, or lots of other things the insurance company would expect in a standard claim. He could claim for these and maybe get enough for a new computer and hi-fi – which the insurance would probably cover – and spend the rest on comics. And he still had money in the bank. And the comics he had bought at the mart that afternoon.

But Alison was still gone. She might be back, but not for some time. He needed to do something to vent his frustration. He remembered his friend Gordon's idea for a Glasgow comic. His last idea had been quite good. Maybe Billy could make a contribution of his own. The drinks and the night air put his brain into creative mode. An idea began to form.

There were some comics that were based, not on fantasy, but upon the real experiences of the writers.

Until recently, Billy's life had been comics, leaving little scope for an external input of realism. But now he had something to write about. And he didn't need to abandon fantasy entirely.

Back home, he looked out a writing pad and pen, inexpensive items the burglars had been happy to leave behind. He had already worked out the main and secondary titles:

THE CURSE OF BUGBANE
The red sandstone menace

As the ideas rushed in, he wrote quickly to get them all on paper. When he got his new computer, he could type it out with the proper layout:

First frame: In a large northern city, there was a community of people who lived in lovely, red caves. Picture showing a row of bright-red tenements, their windows sparkling in the sun. In one of these caves lived young Sandy Stone, a happy fellow who was always holding parties for the local pixies and elves. Picture of Sandy, a youth with bright red hair, and a group of elves and pixies singing and dancing in his cave. A balloon shows the words of their song:

Pixies are wee
Elves are wee
But we're just as happy
As we can be.

But in a nearby cave, there lurked an evil goblin called Bugbane, who was jealous of all these happy creatures. Close-up picture of Bugbane. He has a large, bald head, bulging eyes and an evil smile that reveals rotting teeth, dripping with venomous saliva. Bugbane's speech balloon: "They won't be happy for long!"

Billy continued to write. He was beginning to feel a little better.

7. COLLAGE

1982 – 1992
Gus Mackinnon, Flat 3/1

1982

Note from Gus Mackinnon to Walter Bain
Dear Walter
Sorry you were unable to get me in. It's because I was out.

I spoke to Mr Snow, the aerial man. He's sorry he hasn't been able to get back to you, but he assures me that he got all 17 of your phone messages.

As I suspected, the reason we can't get Channel 4 on our new communal aerial is that we're tuned to the Darvel transmitter. It gives us better reception than Blackhill, but won't transmit Channel 4 until some time next year. As you suggested, I asked Mr Snow about a rebate, but he won't budge. Legally, we don't have a claim.

You should take comfort in the knowledge that you're not missing anything you'd want to let into a family building. This new channel seems to contain nothing but bad language and explicit sex — they say that soap opera *Brookside* is little better than pornography.

The other day I caught a glimpse of their dreadful quiz show *Countdown*. I don't think *that* will last.
Your neighbour
GM

1983

Note from Walter Bain to Gus Mackinnon
Have you seen the factor's bill? How can my share of
electricity for the commune ariel come to £7-43 a quarter?
You told me it would be peenuts.
WB

*Letter from Gus Mackinnon to MacDuff & Co, Property
Agents & House Factors*
Dear Mr MacDuff
13 Oldberry Road
I enclose a copy of a letter I have sent today to the South
of Scotland Electricity Board. I think it is self-explanatory.

I also enclose a cheque for £52 in respect of the
electricity bill. I will pay your factor's account when you
have sent me an amended version.
Yours sincerely
Gus Mackinnon

*Letter from Gus Mackinnon to South of Scotland Electricity
Board*
Dear Sirs
13 Oldberry Road, Glasgow
Electricity supply for communal TV aerial
Your ref: BF/ID
I refer to previous correspondence and telephone calls on
this matter.

You may recollect that we recently had a communal
TV aerial fitted at the above address, and that this is
powered by an unmetered supply, for which you charge

us £10 per year. Since I arranged for this on behalf of the building, you thereafter sent me the first bill of £10. I paid this for the sake of convenience, but asked you to send any future bills to our factors MacDuff & Co for their attention.

It now seems that, in an overenthusiastic application of this principle, you have sent the domestic electricity bill for my flat to the factors. Mr MacDuff has obligingly paid this and has now apportioned it among the owners as a common charge.

While I have no objection to this, and would even consider it an incentive to abandon my gas fires and cooker in favour of their electrical equivalents, I find that my neighbours are less enthusiastic about the arrangement.

Would you please amend your electronic records so that my domestic bills are sent directly to me once again?
Yours faithfully
Gus Mackinnon

Letter from MacDuff & Co to Gus Mackinnon
Dear Mr Mackinnon
13 Oldberry Road: electricity accounts
Thank you for your letter with enclosures.

Please accept my apologies for this mix-up. I can't think how it happened, but suspect that the many telephone calls we receive from Mr Bain may have contributed to the confusion.
Yours sincerely
Angus MacDuff
MacDuff & Co

Note from Walter Bain to Gus Mackinnon
I saw a strange lady leave the building this morning. Is she a friend of yours?
WB

Note from Gus Mackinnon to Walter Bain
Dear Walter
You will need to be more specific. This area is full of strange people, male and female, though few of the latter are noted for ladylike qualities.

A lady friend of mine did leave the building this morning, but she is not in the least bit strange.
GM

Note from Gus Mackinnon to Henrietta Quayle
Dear Henrietta
There's no need to worry. The lady in question isn't a burglar, but a friend of mine.

So far she hasn't murdered me in my bed, or anywhere else.
Gus

Note from Walter Bain to Gus Mackinnon
I never get you in. We need to talk about repairs as noise and dust from sandblasting is quiet apaling.
WB

Note from Gus Mackinnon to Walter Bain
Sorry you missed me. I've been working late a lot recently.

I don't think there's anything much we need to discuss.

I'm dealing with it all from the office and everything's under control.

Stone-cleaning a building is a messy business and a certain amount of dust and noise is inevitable, especially if you opt for the cheapest method, as you insisted. Take comfort that it is only temporary, and think of the poor Arabs in the desert who have to endure sandstorms all year round throughout their lives.

By the way, I think they're going to give us the wall and railing. Maybe you should stop phoning the council in case it causes them to change their minds.

GM

Letter from Gus Mackinnon to MacDuff & Co
Dear Mr MacDuff

Thanks for your letter. As far as I can see, the environmental work is proceeding satisfactorily. The bin shelter is complete and the repairs to the back wall are under way.

I note that the council has agreed to the new parapet wall and railing at the front. It will look rather odd, being the only one on the block, but try telling that to you know who. I expect the council consider that giving us the wall and railing is a more efficient use of their resources than continuing to deal with twenty calls a day from the man. If Mrs Thatcher's privatisation of British Telecom is proving successful, it must be largely due to Walter Bain.

I've been managing to avoid him lately. Fortunately, he hasn't been able to get my office number out of me or find out the name of my firm in order to look the number up. Please don't give it to him.

I realise that you are not so lucky. I suppose it wouldn't

be very good for your business to move your office and go ex-directory.

Yours sincerely

Gus Mackinnon

Note from Gus Mackinnon to Henrietta Quayle

Dear Henrietta

Thanks for your note. There's no need to be concerned. I'm perfectly well and haven't been lying dead behind my front door.

For the sake of my sanity I've been going to some lengths to avoid our mutual friend WB. In fact I've been in most evenings, for some of the time anyway. In order to avoid the sentinel at the window, I don't come down Oldberry Road any more, but approach the building from the back. If I keep close to the back wall, he can't see me from his kitchen window. If I tiptoe up and down the stairs and open and close my front doors quietly he can't hear me. This is much easier now that I have oiled the locks and stopped using the big one on the storm door. I have also taken to wearing rubber-soled shoes, of the type known in my youth as "brothel creepers" – please excuse the risqué expression.

To those observing from the front of the building, I always appear to be out because I sleep in the back bedroom and am now living in the kitchen. I have moved my TV there, though I have to keep the sound very low. It is connected to the communal aerial point in the living room by a 30-foot extension cable I bought in Woolworths. Sometimes I sneak through to the front room to listen to my hi-fi on earphones in the dark.

If you want to speak to me on the phone, all you need to do is let it ring three times, hang up, then dial again immediately. In this way, I'll know that it isn't Walter and I will answer. All my friends and office colleagues now use this code. I have to speak very quietly, of course. I'm sure Walter has heard these interrupted rings, but he's too thick to work out what's happening.

Needless to say, all of the above is confidential. I suppose he'll catch me eventually, but it can't be helped. Climbing up the scaffolding would be dangerous, especially after an evening's refreshment, and so would using a rope ladder. That would in any case be impractical, since there's no one in my house to pull it up after me or let it down on my return.

By the way, the environmental work and repairs are all under control. Thanks to Mr Bain's great influence with the council, we are going to get a new parapet wall and railing.
Yours
Gus

1984

Letter from Sandra McFadyen to Gus Mackinnon
Dear Gus
This is a very hard letter to write.

You're right that I've been putting off seeing you lately. I'm a terrible coward and I'm sorry that I've had to put this in a letter.

You're a lovely man and I'm very fond of you. We had some good times together for quite a while.

I know you work very hard and that your job is extremely stressful. I also know, from Ernie and others, that you are very good at it. However, and I hope you'll forgive me for saying this, it's clear that you rely too much on drink to see you through the rough patches. In the long run this can only lead to disaster. Something similar happened with my ex-husband, though he's much less of a gentleman than you've always been.

For a while I was vain enough to think that I'd managed to change you. Other people said how much better you were looking. But recently, I think you'll agree, there's been something of a deterioration.

As you know, I'm still fragile from one disastrous relationship. I think it's best that we should call it a day before we become any more deeply involved.

I'm sorry again to have to put this in a letter. But, to be honest, it's been difficult lately to catch you sober enough to have a serious conversation.

I wish you nothing but the very best for the future. I really hope you can sort yourself out. There aren't many real gentlemen like you left, and you deserve a much better life.

Yours, with great affection
Sandra

Letter from Gus Mackinnon to MacDuff & Co
Dear Mr MacDuff
13 Oldberry Road: Electricity supply for communal aerial
I enclose the annual bill of £10 for the above, which the Electricity Board have once more sent directly to me. Could you please deal with it? I've told Mr Bain that

his share of £1.43 is likely to be included in your next common charges account. I believe he is saving up for it in his Paisley piggy bank.

Yours sincerely

Gus Mackinnon

1985

Note from Walter Bain to Gus Mackinnon

There is peculier sounds through the wall from next door. I think these men are having an unatural relationship outragous in a family building.

WB

Note from Gus Mackinnon to Walter Bain

Dear Walter

I can't think what you mean. Can you be referring to those excellent gentlemen tenants who fortnightly put the owner-occupiers to shame, filling the building from loft to close with the smell of fresh pine?

Noises in the wall sound to me like a poltergeist. I've also heard that the narrowest of cavities in these old buildings provides little in the way of deterrence to a determined rat.

Your neighbour

GM

Note from Gus Mackinnon to B. McIntyre and S. Bonomy

Dear Bob and Stuart

I don't want to be intrusive, but you might want to consider moving to the back bedroom. In this way you can take advantage of the building's architectural design in order to place a stairwell between you and the Bain family residence. As a bonus, you will awake to the dawn chorus instead of the Number 44 to Knightswood.

Your neighbour

Gus Mackinnon (Flat 3/1)

1987

Letter from Donald Murray, Murray & Mackinnon, Solicitors, to Gus Mackinnon

Dear Gus

This letter is to confirm what we agreed at our meeting yesterday.

You are a fine lawyer and were a great asset to the firm for many years. I am extremely sorry that the continuing deterioration in your work and your conduct has reached such a stage that we have to part company. Lunchtime drinking and unexplained absences are bad enough, but the volume of your work has declined along with its quality. We have never been reported to the Law Society before and this is something that cannot be allowed to happen again.

Our firm is a small one and there is no room for passengers. Young Forbes is now doing most of your work and is shaping up well as partnership material.

I am glad that you have agreed to settle this amicably and that I will not have to invoke the terms of our partnership agreement. Once your share of the business has been independently valued I will prepare the necessary papers for you to sign. As we agreed, there will be an immediate lump sum, and the rest will be paid by instalments over a period of years. I think this arrangement will be best for you as well as for us.

Now that Joyce has remarried and your children are growing up, this should give you some degree of financial independence. I hope you take advantage of it and try to improve your situation.

I'm sorry that it has come to this. Take care of yourself.

Yours

Donald

Draft letter from Gus Mackinnon to Donald Murray (not sent)

Dear Donald

When you say the firm has no room for passengers, you smug, ungrateful old bastard, what you mean is that it has no room for any passengers apart from you. If the strain has begun to show on me, it's because I've borne you on my back for more years than I can remember. You'd think I would be due a bit of gratitude, but no, once your packhorse has served his purpose, it's off to the knackers yard with him, and bring in a new one.

It's always the same with bastards like you who inherited the family business. You wouldn't last a day without someone like me to wipe your arse for you.

At least young Forbes's ready tongue should serve both of you well in this respect. If he ever becomes half as good at being a lawyer, then you might stand a chance of survival. But I doubt it.

I hope you're able to keep up the payments. I intend to get all my share if I have to bring you down in the process. I have an enduring thirst which I intend to maintain in its accustomed style.

You are the Walter Bain of the legal profession, you useless, hypocritical old cunt. That's the worst insult I can think of.

Fuck off

Gus

Letter from Gus Mackinnon to Donald Murray (final version, actually sent)

Dear Donald

Thanks for your letter. I look forward to receiving the formal papers for signature in early course.

I expect to have my room cleared within the next few days. I'll also leave a note on the current state of my transactions. I trust it's all right if I get Moira to help me?

Yours sincerely

Gus

1988

Note from Walter Bain to Gus Mackinnon

You must stop playing your radiogram late at night this is causing a disgraceful nuisance which you must stop. If it does'nt stop I will take legal action and oblige

Walter Bain (Flat 2/1)

216

Note from Gus Mackinnon to Walter Bain
Dear Walter

I had a few friends back last night for drinks. Sorry if this bothered you. I realise it was a bit late, but I couldn't bring them back earlier, as the pubs were still open.

Incidentally, it's a bit naughty of you to refer to my expensive hi-fi system as a radiogram. A "radiogram" would have been much less audible.

The two policemen you sent up were very nice chaps. They stayed for a while and had a drink. It seems that you are well known down at the station, and we had a great time exchanging stories. As you may have noticed, one of them is very fond of the music of Wagner.

You know, what with all the friends I have down at the pub, I'm not at all lonely, but it's still very thoughtful of you to arrange for so many people to visit my flat. The environmental health inspector was particularly charming.
Your neighbour
Gus Mackinnon
P.S. I can recommend a good lawyer if you want one.

1992

Note from Walter Bain to all owners
There will be a meetting of all close owners at 7.30 in Flat 2/1 on Wedensday 7th Octobar 1992 to discuss close affairs and oblige. Mr MacDuff the factor will be pressent. The new securty door is on the agenda.
Walter Bain (Flat 2/1)

Note from Gus Mackinnon to Walter Bain
Dear Walter

I'm only a part owner of the close, but presume I qualify for attendance by my ownership of Flat 3/1.

I would submit my apologies for the meeting, but in fact I will not be in the least bit sorry to spend my evening in the pub instead.

I am happy to agree to the fitting of a security door. It will be one more obstacle for me to overcome on my way home at night, but I recognise that it is for the common good. I'm sure I can rely on you to drive a hard bargain with Mr MacDuff.

Your neighbour

Gus Mackinnon

P.S. I wouldn't put the security door on the agenda. It would be much better at the end of the close.

8. MORE EFFORT REQUIRED

Autumn 1992
George Anderson, Flat 1/2

Monday 24th August 1992

This is the first entry in my new diary.

I'm writing it on the computer that Cathie bought me for my birthday. It's the best present I've ever been given. Only Cathie could have had the wonderful judgement to know so well what I needed. It makes writing so much easier, much more so than on my old portable typewriter. It has liberated me.

So who am I? Why do I want to keep a diary?

My name is George McCallum Anderson. I am 25 years old. I was born, brought up and educated in Edinburgh. Like me, my parents are academics. My father is a historian and my mother is a philosopher. Being of a rebellious nature, I rejected both of their callings and studied English literature.[1] After achieving a first-class honours degree at Edinburgh University, I obtained a post as a research student at Glasgow University, where I recently completed my PhD. I have now obtained a lecturing appointment at the new University of Strathkelvin. It doesn't have the

---

1   This is intended to be ironic

status of Edinburgh or Glasgow, or even of Strathclyde, but lecturing jobs are hard to come by. Strathkelvin's English department is new, the Arts not having figured prominently during its past incarnation as a technical college. I will be in at the beginning. I will be a part of any greatness that may develop.[2]

It was after I moved to Glasgow that I met Cathie. Not right away: I've been here for three years, but I only met Cathie earlier this year. Things have moved quickly between us.

I've never been very good at getting to know women. I didn't really get to know Cathie. She got to know me.[3] I met her in the Queen Margaret Students' Union, where I went for a drink with Roger Williams, one of my university colleagues. I said I thought I was getting too old to drink in a students' union, but Roger said this was nonsense. He is two years older than me and beginning to lose his hair, so I took him at his word. Cathie was sitting at the next table with some other girls and she began talking to us. At first I thought she was a student, but it turned out that she is a primary school teacher.

At the end of the evening, she asked me out. Soon we were going steady and now we're living together.

Previously, we were both living in rented flats. When Cathie suggested that we should live together, I gave up mine and moved in with her. Her flat is not much more than a bedsit, but it has its own kitchen and bathroom. Now that I've got the job at Strathkelvin, Cathie has suggested that we buy a flat together. I agreed and proposed we should get

---

2   This is not intended to be ironic, though it is perhaps a little optimistic

3   This is not a complaint.

married, but she said no, one step at a time, we should wait until we're sure. I'm already sure, but she knows best.

Why do I want to keep a diary? Because I want to record the day-to-day occurrences in my life.

Cathie is saying that I should finish up and come to bed. I don't seem to have got very far, but she knows best.

After all, I can't let writing about my life get in the way of actually living it. Otherwise, there would be nothing to write about.[4]

Tuesday 25th August 1992

Why do I want to keep a record of my life? That is easy. Because I want to be a writer.

Correction, because I *am* a writer. So far, not one who has been very successful or prolific, or able to earn a living by his art. But I know what I am. I've known it since I first learned to read. For most of my life it has been the only thing about which I've been completely certain. Now that I've found Cathie, I've acquired another certainty.

So far my published output amounts to a couple of academic articles. Several more are due to appear soon, based upon the material of my PhD. But as yet I've had no fiction published, not that I have written much, or submitted much for publication. The same is true of poetry, though I don't want to be a poet. The novel is the thing. The novel embraces all of life.

Unfortunately, a novel embracing all of my life would not be very long.

---

4   Lurking somewhere here is a paradox.

Keeping a diary will achieve several things. It will give me practice at writing. It will provide a permanent record of my life's minutiae, which would otherwise fade or become distorted with time. My day-to-day existence may not be rich in novelistic material, but what there is will remain available and accumulate over the years.

Cathie has also suggested that I should use the diary to practise writing in a style that is less academic and more accessible to the general public. I have been trying to do this. When I showed her yesterday's entry, she said that I'd succeeded very well, apart from the footnotes. She is right. No more footnotes.

She also said I'd been very nice about her, no doubt because I knew she would be reading my diary. I protested that I'd written nothing but the truth, and I make the same declaration here. Though I suppose that proves nothing, since I know she'll read this entry too.

I think she's teasing me.

I'll have to cut this entry short. We're going out to view some flats. I'll report back on this in my next entry.

Friday 28th August 1992

Three days since my last entry! My resolve to write up the diary every day didn't last very long.

The trouble is that it's very time consuming. If it's intended to give me practice at writing, it would be self-defeating to dash off my entries in a hurried or slipshod fashion.

Maybe a daily entry isn't necessary. Even my absent-minded brain can recall details of my experiences for several days at a time, even up to a week. And I've taken to carrying a small notebook in my pocket, in which I can quickly make jottings to aid my memory.

As the reader will have guessed, the intervening time has been used up in flat hunting, so far with little success. We've decided that we must remain in the west end of Glasgow, where we met and where we're presently living. This will be reasonably handy for Cathie's school, which is further west, in Anniesland, as well as for Strathkelvin University, which is nearer the city centre. Also, the west end is the only place to live. That is Cathie's opinion, and also mine. The west end is a colourful place where academics and other eccentrics can find easy camouflage within the lunatic undergrowth.

Unfortunately, there are many people who share our opinion and the competition for houses is high. So are the prices.

Over the last few days, we have viewed a number of flats. Most of them were unsuitable: too small, too expensive, too near Byres Road, too far from Byres Road, requiring too much work. Finally, last night we found one for which we want to submit an offer. It is in Downside Road, which joins Byres Road on its western side, about halfway down. The flat is far enough along to be free of traffic noise from Byres Road, but is still only a few minutes' walk from the subway and the main bus routes. It is on the top floor of an old tenement building that has been refurbished and stone-cleaned, like many in this area. It has been modernised, though not in an obtrusive fashion, and is in good enough condition to move into without much work.

It is also barely affordable, if you take into account our combined salaries, our modest savings and the prospect of several years austerity.

We have already been in touch with a building society to arrange a mortgage. Now, as a matter of urgency, we need to find a solicitor to submit an offer on our behalf. Cathie doesn't have one. My parents do, but the firm is in Edinburgh. We could ask around our friends, but we don't have time.

"To hell with it," said Cathie. "It's a simple enough job. We'll get someone from the Yellow Pages."

We reasoned that other people will have used this method and that the names at the top of the alphabet might be overused. So we started at the bottom. We quickly came upon a firm that is situated locally: Waddell & Co.

We telephoned them earlier today and have an appointment with Mr Waddell on Monday.

Monday 31st August 1992

This afternoon I had a meeting with the English department at Strathkelvin University. To be more accurate, I had a meeting with the only other English lecturer. Nor is it quite true to call us a department. The English lecturers belong to the Social Science School, an eclectic mix of sociologists, psychologists, social workers, economists, philosophers and lawyers, as well as the English teachers and a few others less easy to classify in terms of recognised subject areas. However, the dominant elements seem to be the sociologists and the psychologists, both by virtue of their numbers and their degree of influence. There is apparently an ongoing demarcation dispute between the Social Science and Business Schools regarding the proper home of the economists and the lawyers; for some time there has been a stalemate on this issue, and at present each school contains one economist and one lawyer each. However, the Business School apparently has no ambitions to extend into the realms of philosophy or English, and our monopoly of these disciplines remains unchallenged.

I seem to be entering an academic environment radically different from those I've been familiar with at the universities of Edinburgh and Glasgow.

This contrast is exemplified by Ken Ramsay, my fellow English lecturer. I am acquainted with many English lecturers from the years of my extended education, but none like Ken Ramsay. He is a scruffy little man in his forties with untidy, thinning hair, an unkempt beard and a pot belly. When I met him he wore jeans and an old jersey bearing the traces of several recent meals. When I was interviewed for the job I'd been surprised by the absence from the panel of anyone from my own discipline, but I'm less surprised now.

Officially, I don't finish at Glasgow University until the end of September but, apart from marking a few resit papers, my duties there have ended. When Ken phoned me to arrange a meeting, I was glad of the opportunity to find out more about my new job, as well as to get some respite from flat hunting.

We met in early afternoon in the staff coffee lounge. I thought we would later move on to his room, but we didn't. The lounge is on the top floor of the main university building, a square, six-storey, redbrick heap, built sometime in the 1930s. It looks like an old mill or warehouse but was, I'm told, custom built for the purpose of education. It was previously known as Woodside College. It is at the top of one of Glasgow's many hills, and from the window of the staff lounge one is afforded an excellent view of the city centre, a landscape of fine Victorian architecture scarred by high-rise blocks, concrete flyovers and gap sites. (Not that Edinburgh can claim any great superiority: climb to the top of Arthur's Seat and you will quickly see that the city's historic centre is also under siege by the vandals).[5] I understand that from the other side of our building – where the top floor offices of the university management are afforded a more congenial, westward view – a glint of the River Kelvin can be seen in the far distance, a gift to those hard-pressed in the search for a new name to accompany the new university status. Whether this sighting is with or without the aid of binoculars I'm not sure. Of course the same river flows by only a few hundred yards from the much more impressive, Victorian-built walls of Glasgow University's main building, but they don't need a new name.

"Pleased to meet you," said Ken, as we shook hands. "It's high time we had another English lecturer. Makes a change from bloody leftie sociologists." He was rather roughly spoken, in keeping with his appearance if not his calling.

5   Earlier on I'd have made this a footnote, but I now see that, with the use of brackets, it can easily be incorporated within the main— Oops!

I had many questions to ask him. I'd learned a little from the papers accompanying the application form and a bit more at the interview, though I'd been too nervous to remember all of the questions I'd wanted to ask. Top of my list, now that it had been confirmed that there were only two of us, was how we could be expected to run an English degree with these numbers.

"You must be fuckin' joking," said Ken. "Maybe we'll offer an English degree some day. But don't hold your breath. English is only a minor element in courses taken by students majoring in other subjects. Eventually, if it's popular enough, we might be able to take on more staff and take part in more modules. English could even become part of a joint degree. Or maybe that was a fuckin' pig that just flew past the window."

Ken explained that Strathkelvin University would be operating on a modular system. Instead of the traditional university session, the year is divided into two semesters; this is similar, I believe, to the system used in America. A fresh set of modules is studied in the second half of the academic year, and there are final exams at the end of each semester. Degrees are able to contain more variety, each element being offered in a compact, student-friendly, bite-sized component.

As a result, instead of forgetting everything they've learned at the end of each year – after two years in the case of honours candidates – students will be able to effect this mental clearance on a half-yearly basis. A much more efficient system, obviously.

This last observation didn't originate from Ken, but has been added by me. Already my enthusiasm is being tempered by cynicism. When I told Cathie about it, she said she always thought that a module was a kind of spaceship that landed on the moon, and that a semester was something you wore under your shirt. She had to explain the second part of the joke to me, but I've resisted the urge to make it the subject of a footnote.

Anyway, the idea is that the modular structure, when employed in a university, can free courses from a strict, programmatic discipline. Those small components of knowledge and understanding, like a child's building blocks, can be assembled into a near infinite variety of combinations, in some or even all of which English will have the chance to find a modest foothold. Ken listed some examples, based upon existing and proposed modules: they included Urban Studies with English, Social Psychology with English, Dialectical Materialism with English, the Semiology of the Class System with English, Historical Determinism with English, the Philosophy of Sociological Anthropology with English... the list was almost endless.

I was beginning to detect a theme emerging, but I said nothing for the time being.

In most cases, the intrusion of English into these modules doesn't reflect the actual situation, but is merely wishful thinking on Ken's part, a contrived attempt to justify the doubling of our numbers. He explained that he's scheduled to contribute to a new module to be called 'Capitalist Infrastructure and the Rise of the Detective Novel'.

"What has capitalist infrastructure got to do with the rise of the detective novel?" I asked.

"Christ knows," he said. "I'll just be lecturing on the detective novel. It'll be up to the sociologists to add the Marxist shite."

I said nothing, unable to think of a suitable response. It occurred to me that he had strayed into the realm of political comment, knowing nothing about my own views. Marxists are not uncommon in the academic community (though they have been under siege since the Thatcher era). As it happens, however, like my parents, I am a left-of-centre liberal, equally despised by extremists at each end of the political spectrum. Cathie is a Labour supporter, but her views are much more grounded than those of any Marxist I've met.

"Anyway," he continued, "if you want, you can offer a module on the subject of your PhD. Two modules if you like. What was it on again?"

"Amos MacKerrel."

"Never heard of him."

"You and just about everyone else on the planet. Most of his books are out of print. You know what it's like, trying to come up with an original topic for a thesis."

"Oh aye," he said, though I suspect that he doesn't.

"He was a nineteenth-century Scottish science fiction writer."

"Science fiction? Nineteenth century?"

"Well, that's something of a conceit on my part, in order to attract attention. It would be more accurate to say that he belongs in a long Scottish tradition of fantastic literature, seen in writers like Hogg, Stevenson, MacDonald or Lindsay. I've tried to trace this line into modern times, with writers like Alasdair Gray, Iain Banks or Magnus Brown. It's my contention that—"

"Aye all right," said Ken.

I was beginning to notice a certain abstracted expression that I've seen in others when I go into any detail on this subject. The only time I've come near to falling out with Cathie was when I got her to read my masterwork. She only did so very reluctantly, and for a long time afterwards would say very little about it. Finally, when pressed after a few drinks, she told me she thought it was "a load of shite".

I admire Cathie's forthright nature, but there are times when it can be very hurtful.

"This Amos…"

"MacKerrel."

"What did he write?"

"His best-known novel is *Omega 13*."

"That sounds like science fiction."

"It's from the Ancient Greek alphabet."

"Aye, I know that. What I mean, was he a Marxist?"

"I don't think so. No, definitely not. Does it matter?"

"Not really. Nobody else'll ever read him. Maybe one or two students, if you're nice to them. Not even them if you give them good enough lecture notes. It's just that I think our Dean, Billy Trotwood, wanted to sound you out about Marxism at your interview. But he wouldn't dare with the Principal there. The Principal wanted to make sure that we didn't appoint a Marxist. He thinks we teach too much Marxism."

At the time of my interview I'd been too nervous to detect any of these undercurrents within the interview panel. From what Ken now told me, and from what I already knew about the recent transformation of colleges into new universities, I began to gain some insight into the background to this apparent tension within the university's management. Most of the Scottish colleges (and those elsewhere in the UK, I believe) offer only sub-degree courses and until recently were under the control of the local authorities. In Scotland, most of the councils are Labour-run. However, those colleges which became universities – Glasgow, Paisley, Napier, Dundee, Robert Gordon and others – already offered degree courses and were directly answerable to central government. This meant that they were under the (supposedly loose) control of the Scottish Office which, since 1979, has meant the Tory government in Westminster. However, when the job of Dean of the Social Science School fell vacant a few years earlier, the predominant element within that school had somehow managed to stay below the Scottish Office's radar and appoint Professor William Trotwood, a prominent Marxist academic, to the post.

"When the Secretary of State found out they'd appointed this commie bastard right under his nose," said Ken, "he nearly burst a fuckin' blood vessel. But there was nothing he could do about it."

Nevertheless, possibly exceeding his legal powers to some extent, the Secretary of State had done his best to shut this particularly annoying stable door, to put at least some of the genie back in the bottle. Professor Trotwood's wings had been clipped at an early stage, and his expansion plans for his new department were cancelled. And then, shortly afterwards, the previous principal, who

231

had been too weak or too lazy to stand up to the empire-building ambitions of the Social Science School, was due to retire and be replaced by a successor suitably qualified to oversee the transformation of Woodside College into a new university. Seeing his opportunity, the Secretary of State (allegedly) made sure that the new appointment was to his liking. "He gave the job to one of his pals," said Ken. "Bobby Gray, who was the principal of Morningside College in Edinburgh."

I felt sure that it couldn't have been quite as blatant as this. Probably much of this is speculation on Ken's part. Or am I being naïve?

We chatted for several hours before parting company and I took the subway back to Byres Road. I'd been given much food for thought. At least my duties don't appear to be very onerous. Under the watchful eye of the new Principal, a revised social science degree, appropriate to our new university status, is presently under construction. It will take several years for this degree to come fully on stream as the first intake of students progresses through the course. Initially, my work will involve a limited amount of teaching, but I'll also be involved in the preparation of new modules, to be taught in future years. I should have time for writing and research, in order to improve my CV. After a few more years teaching experience, I may be able to get a job at a better university.

On the other hand, who knows how the course at Strathkelvin may develop? And, as I remarked earlier, I'll be there from the beginning. I can make it my own. I can't imagine that Ken Ramsay will prove much of a rival to any ambitions I might develop, though I shouldn't jump to conclusions until I know him better.

I see that I've been recounting the events of the day in reverse order. I've yet to report on our visit this morning to Mr Waddell, our new solicitor.

Mr Waddell's office is very handy, just off Byres Road. It is bright and modern and the staff, mostly young, seemed dynamic and friendly. Although we had an appointment for 10 am, we were kept in the waiting room for some time. There were several other people there, a couple of whom were seen before us. Some of those waiting seemed rather unhappy, but of course it's not always happy people who need to see a solicitor. At one point we could hear shouting in another room, and shortly afterwards a man who had been sitting with us earlier strode past, grim-faced, out of the office. Cathie reminded the receptionist of our presence and eventually, forty minutes after the time of our appointment, we were shown into Mr Waddell's room.

He quickly put our misgivings to rest. He is a man in his forties, immaculately dressed, with a confident manner. He apologised for keeping us waiting and our earlier suspicion that he had forgotten about our appointment faded a little. He took details about the flat and promised to submit an offer on our behalf later that day. He told us we should know the result by the end of the week.

He began to show us out of the office, but hearing the sound of an argument from the reception area, he made his excuses and retreated back to his room. In the outer office, a man was waving a piece of paper, apparently a bill, in the receptionist's face.

"I tell you I'm no' fuckin' payin' this. It's a fuckin' disgrace."

"You have to." The receptionist's professional composure was now a little dented.

"Do I fuck! A thousand quid? That cannae be right."

"I can assure you it's correct."

"If it is, it's the only fuckin' thing he's got right so far. You couldnae get mair cock-ups on a chicken farm." He turned to Cathie and me. "Don't put your business here, for Christ's sake. The man's a prime-size numpty."

"This is a fine time to tell us," said Cathie.

"You'll regret it," said the man, and turned his attention back to the receptionist.

There was an interested audience in the waiting room. Some looked uneasy, but others appeared unsurprised.

"Oh dear," I said as we left the office. "Have we done the right thing?"

"He's only submitting an offer. Surely not much can go wrong with that?"

But she sounded less sure of herself than usual.

Friday 4th September, 1992

I can't believe it. Choosing a solicitor at random from the Yellow Pages is certainly not a guarantee of getting the best lawyer in Glasgow, but it is really bad luck that we should have been landed with the worst.

We waited all week to hear whether our offer had been accepted, but heard nothing. This morning I telephoned Waddell & Co, but the receptionist said Mr Waddell was too busy to talk to me. Several other calls got the same result. Eventually, I managed to get through to Mr Waddell's secretary. She was away from the phone for a long time and when she came back she sounded a little harassed. She said she couldn't find any trace of our offer.

When Cathie returned from school we went up to the office together and asked to see Mr Waddell.

"You'll need to make an appointment," said the receptionist.

"I've been phoning all day," I said.

"We're not leaving until we've seen him," said Cathie. "Would you please tell him we're here?"

The girl complied. After speaking briefly on the phone, she said, "He says you'll need an appointment."

"We're not leaving until we see him," said Cathie.

"It's almost time to close the office. Can you come back on Monday?"

"No, we want to see him tonight."

"Please yourself. He won't see you."

But he did. Twenty minutes later, as he tried to make his escape for the weekend, Cathie barred his way, well ahead of two other contenders who had shared the waiting room with us. It wasn't clear whether Waddell recognised us or not; however, on seeing Cathie he looked like a man who has realised too late the folly of renting an office without a back door. She is a big woman, formidable in appearance when in a determined mood. Waddell made a token protest, but eventually retreated to his room with us in pursuit.

He asked us our names and made a show of opening a drawer of his filing cabinet and rifling through some files. Then he closed the drawer again and sat down behind his desk.

"When I spoke to your secretary on the phone, she said she couldn't find anything about it," I said.

"She's gone for the night," said Waddell. "Can you come back on Monday?"

"No," said Cathie.

"Right. What were your names again?"

"Mr Anderson and Miss Hyde."

"Right. Oh yes, I remember now. Your offer wasn't accepted. There's a letter to you in the post about it."

This sounded like an improvisation. We would find out in due course, should the letter fail to arrive. One way or another it came to the same thing. We hadn't got the flat. I felt a deep disappointment and just wanted to go away. Cathie seemed inclined to linger, as if she were contemplating some kind of violence against the lawyer.

Perhaps Waddell sensed this. At any rate, he had picked up a notebook from his desk and was quickly leafing through it, as though it contained some magical weapon of defence. "Ah yes, here we are," he said. "I've found my notes of our meeting. Downside Road, two-bedroom flat. Sounds like a nice place. I can understand your disappointment. But, as it happens, a client of mine is selling a very similar flat. In Oldberry Road, just round the corner from the one you wanted. You could probably view it tonight, if you're interested. I'll speak to my client on Monday and we can quickly do a deal."

"But if you're acting for the seller, we'll need to get another lawyer," I said.

"Not necessary. The same lawyer can act for both parties."

"Just the same, it might be better if we went elsewhere."

"It's up to you, but by the time you instruct someone else and get an offer in, I can't guarantee that the flat will still be on the market. A few surveyors have been sniffing around and I've already got two offers. But if you act quickly, you don't need to worry about them. If you catch my drift," he added, giving us a wink.

We did and perhaps should have left right then. But we exchanged looks and it was clear that we were thinking alike. We were curious about the other flat. While we hesitated, Waddell phoned his client and managed to catch him just home from his work. He agreed to show us round the flat right away.

The other flat is only a few minutes' walk from Waddell's office. As we made our way into the street, I said, "I don't like it. The other offers will be from different lawyers. Waddell can tell us how much we need to bid to beat them, and then he gets two fees instead of one. The man's a crook as well as an incompetent."

"Obviously," said Cathie. "Assuming that the other offers actually exist. But if it gets us a flat, why should we care? Anyway, it can't do any harm to go and have a look."

"We don't know for certain that the Downside Road flat's been sold. I'm sure he forgot to send our offer."

"You're probably right. We can check that out if we don't like the new one."

But we did. We liked it even more than the first one. Like the Downside Road flat, the building has been stone-cleaned, reroofed and generally refurbished. On one half of the ground floor there is a shop, and the other half is enclosed by a new parapet wall and railing with a wrought iron gate. The other buildings in the block lack this extra.

The flat is on the first floor. Inside, it is exactly what we want. Like the other, it is in walk-in condition. The owner and his wife look about two or three years older than us and have a young child. They told us that they are selling in order to move to a larger house in a more suburban area. The west end is great for single people, they said, but not the best place to bring up a family. They, or owners before them, have done much to improve the property: the large kitchen is divided between a modernised work area and a dining area, which utilises the large bed recess at the back; there is gas-fired central heating and all of the windows have been renewed, those at the front with double-glazing; the state of decoration is good and the carpets and curtains, which are to be included in the sale, reasonably conform to our taste and are a considerable improvement upon those supplied by Cathie's landlord. All of the modernisation has been done tastefully, in a way that harmonises with the building's nineteenth-century design.

"What are the neighbours like?" Cathie asked.

The man hesitated, and his wife didn't seem disposed to fill the gap. "Oh, they're all right," he said eventually.

"I noticed we were being spied on when we entered the building."

"Oh?"

"From the flat opposite."

He seemed relieved for some reason. "Oh, that's Henrietta Quayle. She's all right. A bit eccentric, but quite harmless. She probably thought you were burglars."

"Do we look like burglars?"

"Everyone looks like a burglar to her. You don't need a burglar alarm with her on watch."

He prattled on about the opposite neighbour and her eccentricities. Was this to keep us from asking about the other neighbours? Everything about the flat seemed so perfect that maybe we were looking too hard for a catch.

"What about the other neighbours?" Cathie asked.

"Well, below us there's Arthur Briggs. He's quite old, and you hardly see or hear him. The two flats above are on private lets, but they never cause any bother. And Gus Mackinnon lives on the top floor. He's a lawyer, but nobody's perfect."

We dutifully laughed along with them. By my reckoning, this left one flat unaccounted for, but the conversation seemed ready to move on. The owners gave us further details, including the price they are looking for. This almost brought the discussion to a halt, but Cathie and I calculated separately that it's just about within our budget. However, it's just as well that we wouldn't have to spend much on the place in the immediate future.

We told them that we were definitely interested and that we would be contacting Mr Waddell first thing on Monday.

On our way downstairs we met a man on his way up. He was coming from the back door of the building and was dressed in his house clothes. He was middle-aged and bald, and he stared at us in a hostile fashion.

"Good evening," said Cathie.

"Make sure you shut the front gate after you," he said.

"Leave the bloody thing open," said Cathie, as we emerged from the close. But I closed it carefully behind us. There's no point in antagonising the neighbours before we've even submitted an offer for the place.

"Well?" I said, as we began walking towards Byres Road.

"That's the place for us," said Cathie.

We stopped and turned to have a last look at the building. The sight of the man we'd met on the stairs, now glowering at us from a second-floor window, made only the faintest dent upon our enthusiasm.

Saturday 12th September 1992

What are we going to do? We are facing financial ruin. How could we have got into such a mess? How could we be so stupid? How could we …?

Stop. This panic is a little contrived. It is a fair representation of my reaction when we first heard the news, but since then the situation has improved. My emotion may not be recollected in tranquillity, but its hysterical edge has been blunted a little.

Cathie's emotion is of a different nature. It is not panic, but anger. A homicidal fury directed towards a certain Robert Waddell, sole partner of the legal firm, Waddell & Co. I've had to try and impose some restraint upon her. We will never get through this crisis if she is sent to jail and loses her job.

Let me pick up the threads from my last entry. We saw Mr Waddell last Monday and instructed him to submit an offer on our behalf to purchase the flat for £60,000. The sellers were asking for offers over £59,000, and we decided to submit an extra £1,000 to secure the deal. It is the absolute maximum we can afford, and Waddell appeared to agree that it would be sufficient.

After that we heard nothing all week. Then yesterday morning we received a letter from Waddell & Co. It said that the sellers had accepted our offer of £65,000 and that the flat was now ours.

After the news had registered and the panic had subsided just a trace, Cathie phoned her school to say that she was unwell and wouldn't be in. This wasn't entirely a lie. I had no urgent duties at either university, so we set out together for the office of Waddell & Co. We had already decided, without needing any discussion, that phoning would be a waste of time.

The usual secretarial barriers were in place, as well as a short queue of clients who had got there before us. This was no defence against Cathie, especially when in a temper. Only a double bolt on the door could have kept her out of Waddell's room. He is probably having one fitted now.

I tagged along behind her. Despite the worry, I was beginning to enjoy the drama.

Waddell appeared suitably rattled by the intrusion. "What's the meaning of this?" he said. "What do you think you're—?"

An old man, sitting in front of Waddell's desk, looked up at us in fear. Cathie made an effort and spoke to him nicely. "I'm sorry, would you mind giving us a minute or two? This is rather urgent." The man immediately got up and made for the door. "In fact, if I were you I'd find another lawyer. This one's a crook as well as a prize dumpling."

241

"How dare you!" said Waddell. "Get out of here immediately before I—"

"Shut the fuck up!" said Cathie, taking the seat vacated by the old man. Waddell did as he was told. I found another chair and brought it over to sit beside Cathie. For me, this was a very forward and daring action. However, I surmised that my rudeness was probably not top among Waddell's concerns.

Cathie brought out Waddell's letter and slapped it down on the desk. "What the hell do you mean by this?"

Waddell did his best to read it while keeping an eye on Cathie for indications of violence. Then he said, "But this is good news. What's your problem?"

"We asked you to put in an offer of £60,000, not £65,000."

"No you didn't."

"Yes we fucking well did."

"No you fucking well didn't."

"That's disgraceful language for a lawyer."

And for a teacher of young children, I thought. But I didn't say it. I know whose side I'm on.

"Fuck off," said Waddell.

"*You* fuck off," said Cathie. "But not just yet. First we want an explanation. We can't afford more than £60,000. Another £5,000 will ruin us."

"That's too bad," said Waddell. "You submitted a legally binding offer and it was accepted."

"No we didn't. We signed nothing."

"You authorised me to act as your agent. I submitted an offer on your behalf. That's just as binding as if you signed it yourself."

"Let me get this straight," said Cathie. "You're an agent for the Dunns as well. Does that mean you signed an offer on our behalf and then signed an acceptance for them? That sounds a bit dodgy to me. A kind of legal self-abuse. Something that I'm sure comes naturally to you."

"No, of course not," said Waddell. "That would have been most irregular. I signed an offer on your behalf and the Dunns signed the acceptance personally."

I'm sure that when we arrived Waddell had no idea who we were. But clearly his memory was being refreshed by the moment. He was now managing to summon up a few facts to supplement the improvisation.

"I bet they did," said Cathie. "An extra five grand? They must have taken a lot of persuading."

"You wanted the flat," said Waddell. "There were others interested in it. You wanted me to bid whatever it took."

"No we didn't."

"Yes you did."

"No we fucking well... Oh, what's the point? We intend to find ourselves a new lawyer. One who's honest and has some idea how to do his job. You'll be hearing from him soon."

"Please yourself. He'll tell you the same as me. You can't prove anything. It's my word against yours."

"We'll see what he says anyway. And you can forget about sending us a bill."

"You owe me for my time."

"So you can sue us. If you know how."

Waddell didn't seem inclined to argue further. Now that Cathie had shown an intention to leave he had no desire to detain her. We made our way out of the office, attracting some curious stares from the people in the waiting room. Possibly they had heard something of our exchange with Waddell. While we were with him we had left the door of his room open. An accident or an unconscious desire for an audience? Who knows?

"So what do we do now?" I asked as we made our way home.

"I don't know. We'll need another lawyer, but we'd better get a recommendation this time. Or we could speak to the Dunns and see what they have to say."

We needed some time to think. Cathie decided to go to work in the afternoon. They were expecting her to be off all day, so her unexpected appearance might mitigate any problems about her absence.

The world of higher education is more flexible. At Glasgow University, still my official employers, there was nothing for me to do at the moment. I am not yet on the payroll at Strathkelvin, but I decided to pop in and show my face.

Unfortunately, there was no one to show it to. Ken wasn't in, nor were many other members of the academic staff. Was this a pre-term lull, just a Friday afternoon thing, or a more normal occurrence? I would find out soon enough. I chatted to the departmental secretaries for a while, and then one of them offered to show me my new room.

"It's still to be fitted out," she told me.

My own room! My excitement, however, was a little short-lived. The room is tucked under the stairs leading to the floor above, and is more like a large cupboard, except that it has an outside window. A photocopier and several metal shelves piled with stationery take up most of the space. These would be removed, the secretary assured me, and relocated in the main secretarial office.

"It's a little small," I said.

"It's either that or put you in with a sociologist."

"I'm sure it'll be fine."

I lingered for a little longer then, as it was a nice day, decided to walk back to the west end. Cathie arrived home shortly after me and we discussed what to do next. We decided to speak to the Dunns. We could phone them, but an unexpected visit might catch them off guard and prove more fruitful. I would never have dared do such a thing on my own, but with Cathie by my side anything is possible. We had a meal and then, shortly before six o'clock, walked down to Oldberry Road. This should have given Mr Dunn time to return from work.

An opportunity, however, that he had not taken. Mrs Dunn was at home on her own, looking after their young son. She seemed surprised and a little flustered by our arrival. Her husband would be in The Centurion, she told us, having a quick drink on the way home. Apparently this was a regular occurrence and we had been lucky to find him in the previous week. Or unlucky perhaps.

On this occasion, he would be celebrating the sale of their flat. Prematurely, possibly.

We told Mrs Dunn the reason for our visit and her agitation increased. "I don't know anything about that. Mr Waddell told us everything was fine. You'll need to speak to Ray about it."

This was becoming clear to us. We knew The

Centurion, having visited it once or twice in the past. It is one of the few Byres Road pubs to have escaped the ubiquitous process of contemporary refurbishment and of having its doors flung open to the android hordes. It houses a fair cross-section of the local population. If the Western Infirmary possesses a psychiatric wing, The Centurion could easily pass as its day centre.

We found Ray Dunn sitting with two middle-aged men in business suits. We had only met once but he recognised us immediately. I have found that Cathie and I, as a couple, seem to be quite a memorable entity. Probably because I am rather slight in build and Cathie is not.

Dunn greeted us warmly and offered to buy us drinks, but we thought it better to get our own. When we sat down at his table, he said to his companions, "This is the couple who've bought our house," but without introducing us any further.

He became less affable when we explained our presence. In contrast to his wife, he became defiant. "Mr Waddell told us everything was in order. You'll need to speak to your lawyer."

"*He's* our lawyer. That's the problem."

"He was our lawyer first."

"Don't worry," said Cathie. "You're welcome to him. We'll be getting a new one."

"Good. I don't think we should discuss this any longer." He quickly finished the rest of his pint and left the bar.

His two companions had remained silent during our conversation, but had been following it with interest.

"Oh dear," one of them now said, "so you're the latest victims of the celebrated Bob Waddell."

"You know him?"

"Oh yes."

"You could say that."

"If you're friends of his…"

"Not friends."

"Acquaintances."

"Colleagues, you might say."

"We've both known him a long time."

"And nothing we've heard surprises us in the least. I'm Gus Mackinnon, by the way, and this is my friend Ernie Dunlop. If your purchase goes ahead, I'll be one of your neighbours. If you still want to wriggle out, I won't take it personally."

"It's a great flat. We want it, but we don't know if we can afford it at the new price."

"Yes, it's a good building, apart from Walter Bain." They both laughed.

"Who's he?"

They both laughed again. "An enviable state of innocence," said Gus. "Floor above you, other side."

"What's wrong with him?"

"Have you got all night?"

"No," said Cathie. "You said you were colleagues of Waddell's?"

"I'm a lawyer," said Gus, "and Ernie here —"

"Works in a lawyer's office," said his companion.

"And you're right, you do need another lawyer. I warned Ray Dunn against using Bob. Many times. But he wouldn't listen. He said Bob acted for him when he bought the flat and everything went well."

"A rare occurrence," said Ernie. "Unique, probably. Not the usual output from our Bob's legal mangle."

"He probably made two cock-ups that cancelled each other out," said Gus. "Anyway, we'll need to get you sorted out. I'd offer to help, but I'm not in private practice any more, I work for the council. Ernie, on the other hand..."

"I'm tempted," said Ernie, "but I'd better not. I'd never hear the last of it."

"You're probably right. Better to stab him in the back. We can tell him eventually, of course, when the time's ripe for a wind-up. Now, who can we send them to? Joe MacCormick maybe?"

"Or Marion McDade."

Gus chuckled. "Marion would sort him out all right."

After a little more discussion, they settled on a shortlist of three lawyers for us to consider, one in the west end and two in the city centre.

"Will we have to buy the house?" asked Cathie.

"Maybe, maybe not," said Gus. "Or you may get a price reduction. One way or another you should report him to the Law Society."

"Definitely," said Ernie.

"I thought you lot always stuck together."

"Not in his case," said Gus. "Cowboys like him affect the reputations of us all. It's time someone put his gas on a peep." He glanced at Cathie, as if he thought she might be the ideal candidate for this task. "I suspect the Law Society's already on his case."

"But for all we know," said Ernie, "they may not have had a complaint about Bob this week. They'll be wondering what's wrong."

We stayed on for a while and bought them both a drink, relieved to have a course of action at last. Gus went on to tell us about our prospective neighbour, Walter Bain. It almost gave us second thoughts about the flat, but we suspect he was exaggerating.

In any case, you don't decide against buying a flat just because of one neighbour. That's not a good enough reason. Is it?

Friday 18th September 1992

My last entry took so long to write that nearly a week has passed before I've found the time to continue. A lot has happened in the intervening period. Our situation has improved somewhat.

On Monday afternoon, after Cathie returned from school, we had a meeting with Marion McDade of Dodd & McDade, solicitors. She was first on our list. Gus Mackinnon had promised to phone her to pave the way for us, and apparently did so. Hence our early appointment.

Ms McDade's office is in the city centre, near George Square. She is a smart-looking woman in her forties, about the same age as Gus and Ernie, and Bob Waddell too for that matter. I believe they all knew each other from university. Cathie was particularly impressed and seems to regard her as a good female role model. We should remember, of course, that at first we were also favourably impressed by Bob Waddell. In Marion's case, however, we don't seem to have been deceived by appearances.

She listened to our story in silence, though I think she

had already heard the gist of it from Gus. Then she said, "So the famous Bob Waddell strikes again?"

"You believe us?"

"Oh yes. Many years of experience assure me that everything you've said is true. I'll phone him in a moment and see what we can sort out. But first we need to be clear about one thing. Do you want the flat or not?"

We looked at each other and nodded. "We want it," said Cathie.

"Then I'll try for a price reduction. We may have to compromise. If we try to go back down to £60,000, they may go for one of the other offers. Assuming they exist, of course. There's no way of knowing. Anything involving that man is a morass of deceit and incompetence."

"I'm not sure we can afford more than £60,000," said Cathie.

"We may be able to get your loan increased. What value did your building society's surveyor put on the flat?"

Cathie and I looked at each other, a little shamefacedly.

"You mean he didn't show you the surveyor's report? Or at least tell you about it? And he was acting for the sellers as well!" She shook her head. "This plumbs new depths, even for our Bob."

She asked her secretary to get Waddell on the phone and, within a very short time, they were being connected. Marion briefly put her hand over the mouthpiece. "I knew he'd speak to me," she told us. "We go back a long way." She took her hand away. "Hello, Bob … I'm fine, how are you? …. You may change your mind about that in a moment. I've got two former clients of yours sitting opposite me at the moment, a Mr Anderson and a Miss Hyde."

She held the receiver away from her ear during the angry tirade that followed. I couldn't quite make out what Waddell was saying, but I got the general drift.

"Now now, Bob," said Marion eventually. "I think Miss Hyde can hear what you're saying and she doesn't look very pleased … That's better … How did they come to me? I've no idea. From the Yellow Pages, I presume … What? I suppose it is a bit of a coincidence. A small world, isn't it? But never mind that. The point is, you've made another royal cock-up, haven't you Bob?"

She held the receiver away again, during a further abusive interlude. "Yes yes, of course it's only their word against yours. Except, as we both know, you've got a long line of angry clients who tell the same woeful story, or one very similar. In many cases, it's only their word against yours. But they constitute something of a trend, wouldn't you say? A corroborative trend. Remember the Moorov Doctrine … What's that? … Of course, silly of me. You know bugger all about the law, don't you? How you ever managed to pass any exams beats me. Never mind, I'm sure the Law Society will have heard of the Moorov Doctrine … Yes, I thought that might shut you up. Now listen, Bob, here's what we're going to do. You're going to fax the Missives to me right away. You know what the Missives are, don't you? The offer and acceptance for the flat … And the same to you with knobs on … Yes, I know it's nearly quitting time and the pubs beckon, but if there's any delay in sending me these documents, I'll assume that they're last-minute forgeries. If you don't know how to work the fax machine, you'll just have to pay one of your girls some overtime … Good, I see we understand one another."

Cathie was listening to all of this with open admiration. I think she has found a feminist icon.

A short while later we had a provisional deal. Waddell would recommend to his clients a price of £62,000. We would accept that, subject to a satisfactory survey report and a sufficient loan. Marion would not report Waddell to the Law Society.

"Of course," she said, after replacing the receiver, "what *you* choose to do is entirely your business. I won't have anything to do with it. I'll only tell you what to write and who to send it to."

"We may take you up on that," said Cathie. "By the way, what's the Moorov Doctrine? Was that a bluff?"

"No," said Marion. "Well, not entirely. It's a well-known case in the law of evidence, though we wouldn't expect our Bob to know anything about that. Mr Moorov was charged with a number of sexual attacks on women. In each separate case, it was only his word against the woman's, but all the attacks were so similar that they were considered to corroborate each other. The doctrine generally only applies in criminal cases, but we don't need to tell Bob that. He may not be guilty of sexual attacks, but he's been getting away with murder for years."

"Thanks for everything," said Cathie when we were taking our leave. "It can't be very pleasant, having to deal with a colleague like that."

"I rather enjoyed it," said Marion. "There's something I didn't tell you about Bob. When we were at university, we went out together for a while. But that was in another lifetime, and that particular wench is dead."

A lawyer with literary sensibilities! I was becoming as smitten as Cathie.

That was only a few days ago, but by this morning everything had been sorted out. The surveyor's report was satisfactory. The flat is ours for £62,000. The deposit we have had to pay is the same, but our loan is higher and our repayments marginally increased. Cathie says we will just have to live on pie and chips for a while. I hope she doesn't mean that literally. She knows it wouldn't be good for her diet.

"Are we still going to report Waddell to the Law Society?" I asked.

Now that everything has been sorted out, I would be inclined to drop the matter. I am not malicious by nature. But Cathie is less forgiving.

"Is John Major an android?" she said.

Sunday 11th October 1992

More than three weeks since my last entry! So much for the resolve to write up my diary daily. But now my new desk and chair have arrived in the flat, my computer is set up, and I've run out of excuses.

We got the keys to the flat just over a week ago and moved in on Friday. Since Cathie's bedsit was a furnished let, we've had to buy most of the furniture we need, putting us further in debt. At least we were able to save the cost of a removal with the help of a friend who has a small van,

253

which was able to handle our few belongings of any bulk. Cathie's rent is paid until the end of the month and the distance between our two homes is quite short, so we are gradually transporting the rest of our personal effects by foot, in suitcases.

We have now transported everything, except for most of my books. I should have remembered what it was like when I moved in with Cathie. She nearly sent me back to my own place when she saw how many there were.

Other things have been happening. I have now officially finished at Glasgow University and begun work at my new campus. For a week I was attending meetings in both institutions.

How should I narrate the events of my life over the last three weeks? Day by day, chronologically? That would be very boring. A broader approach is preferable.

In fact, there are two main developments that I have to report upon. The first is my initial impressions of Strathkelvin University. The second is our first encounters with our new neighbours, particularly Walter Bain. It may be that Gus Mackinnon's account of that man was not exaggerated after all.

My impressions of my new place of employment are necessarily a little scrappy, being based upon a limited amount of evidence. Overall, my enthusiasm has become a little more blunted and my reservations have increased. Several weeks ago, shortly after my last diary entry and some time prior to my official start, I attended a meeting which was held in order to consider the results of the resit examinations. The Dean, Professor William Trotwood, chaired the meeting, and also in attendance were a representative of the central administration and most of the Social Science School's academic staff. I was there merely in the capacity of an observer. It was my first opportunity to obtain a more complete view of my new working environment and my new colleagues. My whole life – at home, during my education, at work – has been spent among academics and nothing should have surprised me. Yet I was unprepared for the childishness, rudeness and aggression displayed by the people present at that meeting. Searching the memories of my brief life for a suitable comparison, I recall a childhood visit to Edinburgh Zoo where I witnessed a chimps' tea party. The general effect was very similar.

However, Professor Trotwood, whom I'd met only briefly before at my interview, seemed nothing like the communist ogre that Ken's account might have led me to expect. He is a polite, mild-mannered man, probably in his early forties, casually dressed, but well groomed. His accent reflects his public school and Oxbridge background, though his Scottish origins have not quite been obliterated. His educational background was one aspect that Ken had already prepared me for: "When he was at Cambridge he was appalled by the number of upper-class idiots who managed to get a degree there. He made it his mission in life to extend the same educational opportunities to working-class idiots."

I'm beginning to suspect that Ken's views may not be entirely impartial.

Professor Trotwood made a favourable impression upon me right from the start. Before the meeting, he introduced himself to me and welcomed me to the department. Once the meeting started, he repeated this introduction and welcome, and got everyone else round the table to introduce themselves and identify their discipline. Many of them nodded and smiled across at me. A few others looked a little suspicious, possibly because I was sitting beside Ken.

The first half-hour of the meeting was spent making the important political decision about the departmental coffee. (Not the coffee for the meeting, but for the informal coffee breaks which staff can enjoy at their desks, or communally within the department.) A new coffee maker was required, and there was endless discussion about which make to buy and which blend of coffee to use. A much quicker decision was made, on an egalitarian and non-sexist basis, that the actual making of the coffee should still be the responsibility of Gillian, the younger of the two school secretaries.

After that it took an interminable time to get through what looked initially like a simple sheet of results. This was because practically every name read out had accompanying documentation about extenuating circumstances to explain poor results: illness, accident, poverty, divorce, bereavement, unexpected pregnancy, inconvenient or oppressive work shifts, abortion, memory lapse regarding exam dates, misreading of exam timetables, even autumn holidays optimistically booked before the June results had been posted. I felt thankful that my own academic career has managed to progress to its present level so free of illness or other debilitating misfortune. There was a long debate (not for the first time, I suspected) about the definition of a valid medical certificate. There were even longer debates about the meaning of particular university regulations; this was pointless, because in cases where the meaning was clear but inconvenient, the regulation was ignored. A vote on each individual decision was taken by a show of hands.

Beside Professor Trotwood the harassed-looking administrative assistant, who had the responsibility of taking the minutes, scribbled furiously, as she continually struggled to pick out the matters of substance which needed to be recorded from all of the nonsense smothering them.

By the time another hour had passed we had barely got through a quarter of the names on the sheet. The meeting had started promptly at 1.30 pm, but I began to wonder if I would make it home that night. As it was a resit exam, the sheet was relatively short, and I wondered how long it could possibly have taken them to get through the first diet results in June. Presumably at that time there would have been more clear passes and fewer controversial results, allowing the decisions to be made more quickly. However, with this team nothing was certain.

Then, after the latest show of hands, someone said, "I hope the new man hasn't been voting. He's not entitled to. He didn't do any of the marking." The speaker was a thin, bespectacled, scholarly-looking man of indeterminate age, with a middle-class Scottish accent.

Suddenly everyone was looking at me. "I haven't voted," I said. A few people looked unsure. In the hubbub that attended every show of hands, I could probably have raised mine without anyone noticing.

"Dr Anderson is merely here as an observer," said Professor Trotwood.

"If he voted," said the objector, "then that invalidates all the decisions so far. We'll need to go back to the beginning."

There was an exasperated outbreak among the ranks. "Does that only apply to the exam results," one man asked, "or will we have to decide about the coffee again?" The new speaker was grinning broadly, obviously intent upon making mischief.

"I didn't vote," I repeated.

"Even if he didn't vote," persisted the objector, "it should have been made clear at the outset whether or not he's only an observer. If he's officially attending the meeting and formally abstained from the voting, then that still invalidates all of the votes."

The outcry round the table threatened to get out of control. Beside me, Ken bellowed, "For Christ's sake. I've been right beside George the whole time. He hasn't voted and he hasn't even spoken a word until now. He's only here as a fu– He's only here as an observer."

Professor Trotwood called for silence and the hubbub gradually died down. "I made it clear at the very beginning of the meeting," he said, "that Dr Anderson is merely observing proceedings. If I remember rightly, Simon" – looking across at the man who had started the fuss – "you arrived a little late, and may have missed my announcement. Anyway, in order to avoid any doubt whatsoever, I will now take chairman's action to validate every decision made so far. Including the one about the coffee, Adrian. Now can we get on?"

The meeting proceeded, passing slowly down the names on the sheet, the progress as interminable as before. Triumphantly, we would turn a page, then find ourselves returning to an earlier one in order to ensure that a proposed decision was consistent with one that had been made earlier. Finally, after another hour, we had got almost halfway through the sheet when Professor Trotwood called a ten-minute break. A trolley with two pots of coffee and several plates of biscuits had been delivered about twenty minutes earlier and had been slowly cooling at the side of the room.

During the break, several of those present came over to talk to me. They were generally friendly, including some who had been among the most vociferous and belligerent during the meeting. The man called Adrian, who had made the remark about the coffee decision, was particularly affable. "Hardly in the door and you're causing trouble already," he said jovially. He was probably in his late fifties, I reckoned, and was much better dressed than most of the people there, looking rather old-fashioned in a sports jacket and tie. "How do you do, I'm Adrian Armitage." He shook my hand. "I see we'll need to keep an eye on this one, Ken."

But Ken still hadn't completely calmed down. "What do you think of that bloody Simon Simpson? He's not real."

"Our Simon is certainly on prime form," said Adrian. "Ripe, as usual, for a spot of urine extraction."

"Is it always like this?" I asked.

"You've seen nothing yet. In June, we started first thing in the morning and it still took all day. Welcome to the monkey house."

The meeting finally finished just after 5.30. Towards the end, as everyone grew tired and even more irritable, the speed of decision making increased noticeably, and those present seemed less worried about the consistency of decisions. At the end, we were asked to consider the following statistics for the first year of the social science degree:

Pass: 89.3%
Voluntary withdrawal: 9.5%
Non-voluntary withdrawal: 1.2%

Voluntary withdrawal, apparently, refers to those students who had not submitted enough work and/or extenuating paperwork around which there could be constructed a pass; in many cases it would have been difficult to confirm that they still exist, without the help of a private detective. I asked Ken later what non-voluntary withdrawal meant.

"It means they failed," he said.

"Oh. That must have been quite difficult. How did they manage that?"

"They probably wrote their name on the script and nothing else," said Ken, "and spelled it wrong into the bargain. We're discussing the second-year results on Thursday. You don't need to come if you don't want to."

"I'll get my doctor to write a sick note," I said.

I left the meeting in a mental condition that made me unfit for any further work that day and with an overpowering desire to go for a drink. Perhaps this helps explain the lifestyle of some academics.

I phoned Cathie and arranged to meet her in The Centurion. By now it was six o'clock and she had been about to report me to the police as a missing person.

I started officially at Strathkelvin University on the first day of the month. It was a Thursday, and teaching was due to begin the following Monday, at the beginning of the semester.

I arrived at 9 am fresh, eager and anxious to begin my new duties. However, I still wasn't sure what these were. At our last meeting, Ken had been a bit vague about my teaching duties, and I hoped I wasn't expected to start these on Monday. Ken had said he'd be around, but hadn't given me a time. He wasn't in when I arrived and neither, so far as I could see, was anyone else, apart from the secretarial staff. They gave me a key to my room and directed me to the Finance Department, so that I could complete the formalities necessary to ensure I was on the payroll. That was my most important initial duty. To safeguard our first mortgage repayment.

My room, at any rate, provided a pleasant surprise. Gone were the photocopier and metal shelves. It has been redecorated in bright colours, fitted with a new carpet, and the window now has a blind to protect my eyes from the sun, should it ever appear. I have been allocated a bare minimum of furniture: a desk and two chairs, a bookcase and a filing cabinet. On the otherwise bare desk there is a computer and a telephone, by its side a metal waste bin. As a result of this minimalist approach, the place now seems a little more spacious: less like a cupboard and more like a small room, a womb into which I can retreat for embryonic therapy. A small window on the door provides a link to the rest of the department and some insurance against claustrophobia.

On the outside of the door a new plate bears my name: Dr George M. Anderson. My PhD is still recent and I haven't yet got used to my new title. It doesn't feel like me, but like some older, more impressive academic whose space I've intruded upon.

I returned to the main office, picked up some junk mail from my new pigeonhole, and went back to my room. Soon my new waste bin had begun to fill. The only matter of substance was a memo from Professor Trotwood inviting me to attend a departmental meeting that Wednesday afternoon. I put this appointment in my diary, filling one of the many blank spaces. I had disposed of another ten minutes. What next? A new development gave me another idea.

I made my way back down the corridor, having left the light on in my room. This is a trick I've learned from many years' association with academics. It announces that one may not be deskbound, but is nevertheless somewhere on the premises, presumably hard at work.

There are separate toilets for staff and students. I chose the latter. I like to mingle with the masses, keep my ear to the ground. As it happened the toilet was empty, but the principle is sound.

The graffiti on the walls of the cubicle was depressing. There was very little to distinguish it from contributions by members of the public in less specialist locations. At the universities of Edinburgh and Glasgow the obscenity and adolescent humour has at least attained a minimum standard of literacy, with the occasional creative spark. But not here.

I did, however, manage to pick out two contributions to remind me that I was in an academic institution:

Karl Marx said: To do is to be
Jean Paul Sartre said: To be is to do
Frank Sinatra said: To do be do be do be do

Were the Marx and Sartre quotations the right way round? Did I care?

Above the toilet roll holder, I read:

SOCIAL SCIENCE DEGREES. PLEASE TAKE ONE.

I readily obliged and acquired several. After my experience at the exam meeting, the message seemed entirely pertinent.

I spent the rest of the morning ferrying books and papers from home. Soon my bookcase was beginning to fill and the room generally to look a little more lived in. I reckoned that, even in our spacious new flat, every book and file located on campus and not at home would be an aid to domestic harmony.

By the end of my third trip, Ken had arrived and invited me to lunch. We ate in the staff dining room, which had reopened at the beginning of the semester. It adjoins the main dining room and allows the staff to eat separately from the students, enjoying the same food at higher prices, that being the cost of the privilege. Ken told me that some of our colleagues in the Social Science School eat in the main hall along with the students, in order to demonstrate their solidarity; whether or not the students appreciate this gesture, I'm not sure.

We were joined at our table by Adrian Armitage. "Good to see you again, George," he said. "Have you applied for a new job yet?"

"Not quite."

"We'll see how you feel after Wednesday."

"Fuck!" said Ken. "Don't remind me."

Any faint hopes I'd been nurturing that the exam meeting might prove untypical began to wane. But I would have to go. "Will I be allowed to vote this time?" I asked.

"If you really want to. You probably won't."

"Another afternoon of shite," said Ken. "It would drive you to drink."

"I thought you'd already reached that destination," said Adrian, "without any help from our Marxist friends."

"Fuck off!"

"I take it you're not one of them?" I said.

"Adrian sits on the fence," said Ken. "There's a long red line across his arse."

"I join in occasionally," said Adrian. "Just to stir things a bit. You need a bit of relief from the tedium."

"I suppose I'd better show up this time," said Ken. "I missed the last two and Trotters had a quiet word with me."

"I think you'd better," said Adrian. "Anyway, you'll need to be there to hold George's hand." I hoped he was speaking metaphorically.

I had been wondering what Adrian's discipline was. At the exam meeting he had introduced himself as a general factotum. I'm not sure whether he even has a degree, or any formal qualifications apart from a couple of teaching diplomas. I've learned that he and Ken are two of the longest-serving members of the Social Science School, both of them predating the Marxist coup in the 1970s. Ken must have been barely out of school at the time. I doubt if either of them would have been appointed by the current regime. Apparently Ken does have a degree, though only an ordinary MA. But I already knew how difficult it is to dislodge an academic with tenure, short of a conviction for gross moral turpitude, such as rape or murder. The present lot would probably have added voting Tory to the list, if it could have been proved. As it was, they'd had no option but to accept Adrian and Ken, and a few others besides, as sitting tenants. Moreover, they are destined to remain there indefinitely, as neither is well enough qualified to get even another college job these days, let alone another university post where the competition is even stiffer. Having become university lecturers by the back door, they have reached a dead end. Unless they make a determined effort to improve their CVs, which seems unlikely.

I also discovered that expulsion for gross moral turpitude is not the automatic consequence of a criminal conviction. Lesser offences are not only forgivable but can even be an asset. This emerged during the lunch conversation when I learned that Norrie Spence, the school's only law lecturer, is a former solicitor who has been struck from the roll of solicitors and has served a prison sentence for stealing his clients' money. I remembered Spence from the exam meeting, mainly because, like Adrian, he had been more conventionally dressed than most of the others. He had contributed very little to the discussion and, for a lawyer, had seemed remarkably uninterested in the hair-splitting, legalistic debates that had dominated the proceedings.

When his interesting pedigree was referred to in passing, I thought I must have heard wrongly and enquired further. But I hadn't misheard. Moreover, he had been appointed by Professor Trotwood himself, shortly after his arrival (though before the advent of the new Principal).

"But if he's been struck off," I protested, "surely he's no longer qualified?"

"He's not a solicitor any more," said Adrian. "But he's still got a law degree. And Billy Trotwood believes in rehabilitation, in giving people a second chance. He's been earmarked to teach the new Criminology module, for which our Billy thinks he's ideally qualified."

"The lefties think his spell in the joint gives him street cred," said Ken. "Would you fuckin' believe it?"

"Anyway, he's a pleasant enough fellow," said Adrian. "Whether he's demonstrated any genuine repentance is another matter. But a track record as a confidence trickster will serve him well in this place. He knows not to rock the boat."

We finished lunch and Ken and I went down to his room to discuss my teaching duties. This was the first time I'd been in his room. The contrast with my own was striking. It is substantially bigger than mine, but seems smaller because of the amount of clutter, which looks as if it has been accumulating throughout his twenty-odd years as an academic. There is paper everywhere, on his desk, on two tables, on the shelves of a shallow alcove beside the window, and all over the floor, apart from a network of paths leading to strategic parts of the room. The pile on his desk is particularly high, like a small haystack: the top half of his computer, its keyboard completely buried, protrudes from the top like an island; the telephone would have been completely invisible, except that the paper pile on the window sill has been shoved to one side to make room for it there.

I suspect that the computer has never been used. I don't think Ken has yet entered the digital age.

I said nothing, but my reaction must have been apparent. "I could probably throw most of this shite out," he said, a little apologetically. "But sorting out the stuff I need to keep would take bloody ages."

I nodded in sympathetic agreement, though in truth such a degree of disorganisation is alien to me. But I've been an academic long enough to be well schooled in hypocrisy. At his invitation, I transferred a stack of old exam scripts on to the floor from the chair opposite his desk and sat down.

"For the very first time we've got a first-year module all to ourselves in Semester One," he told me. "At the principal's insistence, it's got to be free of political content. Liberal fucking studies. With a small 'l'."

After shuffling about on his desk for a bit, he produced a copy of the syllabus and handed to me. It has clearly been cobbled together from the syllibi of various other universities: a Dickens novel (*Bleak House*), followed by a standard selection of writers from the first half of the twentieth century: Conrad (*The Secret Agent)*, Lawrence (*The Rainbow*), Joyce (*Dubliners* and *Portrait of the*

Artist), and a wide selection of poetry, with particular emphasis upon the war poets, as well as Yeats, Eliot and Dylan Thomas. All very unimaginative, but serviceable.

"I'm starting them off with *Bleak House* next week and then I'll move on to Lawrence. I've changed the book to *Women in Love*." He regarded me quizzically, as if seeking my approval.

"Fair enough," I said.

"Can you take over after that?" Again he looked at me a little uncertainly.

"Shouldn't be a problem. It's all very standard stuff. I'm familiar with most of it."

He looked relieved, and a little surprised. "Great. You can start your lectures in week three, after I've finished with Dickens and Lawrence."

"You're covering them in two weeks?"

"We've got a three-hour slot to fill. Two lectures and one tutorial. We've got a whole day to ourselves, with the tutorial slots carrying on into the afternoon. The students will get a tutorial once a fortnight, so that we can cover everyone."

"How many students are there?"

"Three fucking hundred," said Ken. "Every daft bugger in the Glasgow area now thinks he can get a university degree."

He is clearly unused to such numbers. I am not, but covering the classes with only two people is definitely a novelty. "How many tutorial slots are there?"

"Four a day. Eight over two weeks."

I did a quick calculation. "That's nearly 40 in a group!"

"Half the buggers won't turn up. Less than that by the

end of the semester. If there's a problem, we can give them a tutorial every three weeks. Though that's stretching it a bit."

"OK," I said, a little doubtfully.

"Do you really want any more teaching hours? I was hoping you could cover my Dickens and Lawrence tutorials as well. They don't start until week three, so that should give you time to prepare."

"All right," I said. "You've convinced me."

"By the way, I'll still have an input to modules in second and third year, part of the old degree that's working its way out. Just in case you thought I was going to be sitting on my arse doing nothing."

"I'd never think that," I said, with as much conviction as I could muster.

"I've also got stuff to cover in Semester Two," he said. "As well as my new module."

"The one on the detective novel?"

"Aye. But we can discuss all that later. I think you've got enough to be going on with."

I thought so too. The teaching hours were reasonable, but a great deal of preparation would be needed. And a lot of my time was going to be spent marking. My research would need to be put on hold for a while.

We talked for a bit longer, then Ken went off to the toilet, leaving me alone in the room. I passed the time by examining the contents of his two bookcases. They contained very few books, but the remaining space was filled with more bundles of paper, mostly scripts of exams and essays. I glanced through one of the essays. By now I should have been used to the modern generation's poor standards of literacy, but the contents still shocked me. It had been scribbled over in red ink (by Ken, I presume) and at the end he had written, "Absolute shite. 25%."

I might have expressed it differently, and I thought the mark a shade generous, but otherwise saw little to disagree with. I took a look at his small selection of books. Most of them were part of a series called *Ripley's Notes for English Students.* I had never heard of the series. They were well worn and, I saw, more than thirty years old. There were notes on Shakespeare plays, Dickens novels, and a selection of other standard nineteenth- and twentieth-century texts.

In my experience, the rooms of most academics contain bookcases crammed to capacity with books. In many cases they are seldom opened and mainly serve as window dressing for the benefit of colleagues and students, but Ken seemed to be uninterested in even this mild pretence.

I had time to sneak a quick look in his filing cabinets, which were crammed with even more paper, before I heard his footsteps in the corridor and quickly returned to my chair.

"I was having a look at your study notes," I said. "I haven't seen that series before."

"It's very good."

"Is it still available?"

"Christ no," he said. "We can't have the students knowing where I get my fuckin' notes from."

It occurred to me that having them on open display in his room might furnish visiting students with a clue. But maybe none of them are that observant.

I will try to spend a little less time describing the meeting that took place the following Wednesday. Its tone and its protracted length were similar to that of the exam meeting I attended earlier. It started with further discussion of the new coffee blend, which several people had expressed dissatisfaction with after sampling it for only a few days. I've been contenting myself with the machine swill and so had nothing to contribute. No consensus was reached, so it was decided to postpone a decision until the supply of the present blend was due to run out. Thankfully, this would be some time in the future, since (after purchasing the new coffee-making machine) Gillian had invested almost all that was left of her newly-collected funds on sufficient reserves of the new blend to last until the end of the semester.

Then minor administrative matters regarding the introduction of the new degree were subjected to a debate of quite unnecessary length. It resulted in a deadlock, which Professor Trotwood resolved with his casting vote. After that, small changes to the university regulations, proposed by the university management, were subjected to the usual hair-splitting, legalistic scrutiny, even though the school was only being sounded out for its views, which were likely to be overruled when the final decision was made centrally.

The most controversial item concerned a proposal by the sociologists to amend the assessment of their new module, 'Introduction to Sociology'. The agreed assessment was based upon a proportion of 60 per cent for coursework and 40 per cent for the final exam. This already constituted a greater emphasis upon coursework than any of the other modules. The new proposal was to dispense with the final exam altogether, or rather (which I suspect will amount to the same thing) to grant a complete exemption from the exam to all students achieving an overall average of more than 40 per cent for two short essays.

During the barney that followed, I became more aware of the political polarisation within the school, and identified a few more of the key players.

The far left still forms a majority, but there is a growing counter-revolution from the far right. One of the more outspoken of the latter is a middle-aged economist called Bradley Skinner, a long-standing member of the school whose appointment, like those of Ken and Adrian, pre-dates the Marxist dawn. Another (reputedly a product of the new principal's interventionist approach) is a youngish psychologist called Stanley Warburton. He was a recent external appointment to a vacant senior lecturer's post, a decision which continues to give rise to much controversy.

"We all know what's going to happen," said Bradley. "Anybody that half-remembers their lecture notes and toes the party line will get a free ride. You might as well award everyone a pass at enrolment."

"That's an absolutely disgraceful allegation," said Denny Merrigan, one of the sociologists. "Exams are outmoded and regressive. They cause unnecessary stress and can result in permanent psychological harm."

This provoked Ken into adding his own considered, academic opinion. "Ballocks!" he shouted.

Adrian turned to the minute secretary. "Do you know how to spell that, Marion?" he asked her.

"That's enough, Ken," said the professor. "And you, Adrian."

Stanley Warburton then embarked upon a psychological defence of the exam system. It seems that they are a useful test of character, of old-fashioned grit, a necessary preparation for the tribulations of adult life.

There were a few warnings about the dangers of plagiarism, which the exam element provides some defence against. From my own experience, this is the most persuasive argument against the change. Nevertheless, when it eventually went to a vote, the proposal was approved by a comfortable majority.

There was a final proposal that the number of departmental meetings should be reduced. This humanitarian suggestion met with general approval. However, by now everyone was too tired to discuss it further and was desperate to go home or to the pub. It was decided that another meeting would be needed in order to discuss the possibility of a reduction in the number of meetings. It took another fifteen minutes to settle upon a date: now that classes have begun, diary synchronisation is becoming more difficult. I found myself hoping fervently for an alternative, unbreakable appointment.

Writing the above has taken until almost three in the morning. Cathie is in danger of becoming a diary widow. I've still to report on our first real encounter with our neighbour Walter Bain, but I think doing that justice will need a new day and a new entry.

When Cathie had read the last entry, she asked, "Are there any women in your Social Science School, apart from your long-suffering secretaries? Who, by the way, have my heartfelt sympathy. You haven't mentioned any others."

"There are only two female lecturers. There's Daisy Chambers, a psychologist. She seems like a nice woman. She doesn't say much."

"I don't blame her."

"And there's Sonia Stevens. She's a real left-wing firebrand. The sort of feminist that gets the movement a bad name."

"Watch it!"

"Adrian Armitage calls her Sonia Bitch."

"I think your department badly needs a larger female contingent. A few sensible women to keep the little boys under control."

"Are you thinking of applying?"

"I'd rather have my fingernails pulled out one by one. I suspect that's the trouble. Anyone able to do the job will be too smart to want it."

But none of this is the purpose of the present entry. Last week our neighbour Walter Bain called a meeting of the building's owners, which needs to be recorded. I've spent too much time describing the academic lunacy at my place of work. There is even more lunacy right on our doorstep. Ten days ago the following note was put through our letterbox:

There will be a meetting of all close owners at 7.30 in flat 2/1 on Wedensday 7th Octobar 1992 to discuss close affairs and oblige. Mr MacDuff the factor will be pressent. The new securty door is on the agenda.
Walter Bain (Flat 2/1)

The note was handwritten in large, childish letters. Cathie said it looked like something written by one of her eight-year-olds, except that they have a better grasp of the English language.

"What do you think?" I asked.

"I think we should go. A security door is a good idea. And I want to have a proper look at this guy, after everything we've heard about him."

Most of what we'd heard had been from Gus MacKinnon. We ran into him the evening before the meeting, during a brief visit to The Centurion.

"Are you going to the meeting tomorrow night?" I asked him.

"What meeting?"

"Walter Bain's meeting."

"Am I fuck! Sorry, Cathie. That would be a criminal waste of good drinking time."

"We think a security door's a good idea," said Cathie.

"So do I. I said so in my note."

"You've submitted your apologies?"

"I sent him a note saying I wouldn't be there and agreeing to the door. I wouldn't apologise to that cunt for anything. I'm sorry, Cathie."

Cathie laughed. "So you should be. Your language is fucking disgraceful."

"Let's see what yours is like when you come out of the meeting," said Gus.

As we walked home, Cathie said, "Surely Bain can't be that bad?"

But he is.

I've given some thought about how best to describe the meeting we attended in the Bain flat. As it proceeded on its protracted way, it felt increasingly unreal, matching those of the Social Science School in length and tedium. Between work and home, I am beginning to feel like a character in a farce. When I mentioned this to Cathie, she suggested I should broaden my literary skills by writing it up in the form of a play. I think this is a great idea, and I've decided to follow her suggestion, though I think it may turn out more like a situation comedy. Maybe I can submit the result to BBC Scotland, whose headquarters are just up the road:

> *The living room of a Glasgow tenement. It is part of an old building, but the room has been modernised in extremely bad taste. The high, nineteenth-century fireplace has been replaced by a lower substitute of garish red tile, the old-fashioned, panelled doors by ones of smooth, brightly-painted hardboard, fitted with plastic handles. The pattern on the flock wallpaper has in places been relieved (if that is the right expression) by execrable prints of tearful children and cute animals. The furniture, dating from the 1960s and 1970s, seems to have had its brief life expectancy extended by careful maintenance. Nearly all available surfaces have*

been littered with cheap china ornaments, which only add to the general —

"Enough!" said Cathie, when she came to read this. "We're not all middle-class snobs from Edinburgh."

"You're not telling me that you liked it?"

"No, of course not. But you don't need to lay it on quite so thickly."[6]

The three-piece-suite has been supplemented by dining room chairs, in preparation for a meeting. Sitting on the settee are the Bains, Walter and Agnes, both middle-aged, slightly built and unsmiling. They might have been twins, except that he is bald and wears glasses. The room's only other occupant is a man in a business suit, also glum-faced and middle-aged.

A two-tone doorbell chimes and Walter Bain goes out of the room, leaving Mrs Bain and the other man to glower at each other in silence. Bain re-enters the room with Cathie Hyde, a tall, attractive woman of twenty-four —

"Flatterer!"

and George Anderson, a slightly built, scholarly-looking man of 25. They have barely sat down on

6   For any reader puzzled by the chronology of this I should explain that, thanks to the magic of word-processing, this section was added after Cathie had read my first draft. Please excuse the footnote, and take note of this revision possibility in order to save the flow of my prose from being interrupted by future footnotes.

two adjoining dining room chairs when the doorbell chimes again and Walter leaves the room. Mrs Bain makes no attempt to introduce the newcomers to the other man.

CATHIE: How do you do, I'm Cathie Hyde and this is my partner George Anderson. We haven't met yet. You must be Arthur Briggs from downstairs. (*The man opens his mouth to speak, but Cathie continues before he has a chance to say anything.*) We think getting a security door is a good idea.

THE OTHER MAN: Yes, I think so too. By the way, I'm —

CATHIE: I believe the factor's coming, for all the good that's likely to do. My father used to say that you only get three types of factor, bad factors, worse factors and absolutely bloody diabolical factors.

She turns to George Anderson and they both laugh. The other two make no response, their demeanour unchanged. Walter Bain re-enters the room, a grey-haired, terrified-looking woman trailing behind him.

WALTER: I see you've met Mr MacDuff, the factor.

CATHIE: But of course you can't generalise. There are always exceptions.

WALTER: I think you all know Miss Quayle.

He makes this introduction in a dismissive tone, as if he is casually referring to a person of no importance. The newcomers sit down and there is an awkward silence.

GEORGE: Who else is expected? Gus Mackinnon won't be coming. We spoke to him last night.

Bain glares at him. Admitting acquaintance with Gus appears to equate with confession to an unpardonable crime.

GEORGE: But he told us he's in favour of fitting a security door.
WALTER: Huh! Did he really?
GEORGE: But I believe he sent you a note?
WALTER: (*contemptuously*) Huh! Yes, he sent me a note.

There is another awkward silence.

CATHIE: (*with a shamefaced glance at the factor*) What about Mr Briggs? Will he be here?
WALTER: Mr Briggs never comes to meetings.
CATHIE: And Mr Singh?
WALTER: Mr Singh never comes to meetings. Anyway, the security door doesn't affect him. The entrance to his shop is on the street.
MR MACDUFF: And he has his own, direct access to the back court. But strictly speaking that doesn't matter. Under the title deeds, he's liable for an eighth of all common repairs.

WALTER: You mean he can be asked to pay for a share of the door?

MR MACDUFF: Yes.

Walter Bain smiles for the only time throughout the meeting.

MR MACDUFF: But since he won't be using the door, the other owners can agree to cover his share if they want.

GEORGE: That seems only fair.

WALTER: Oh no. It's in the deeds. We've got to do it legal. Mr Singh will have to pay a share.

CATHIE: But that's not right. Surely —

WALTER: We'll have a vote. All those in favour of making Mr Singh pay?

He thrusts up his hand, and glares at Miss Quayle, daring her to disagree with him. She shrinks back further in her seat and raises her hand.

MR MACDUFF: (*sighing*) Since I have a mandate to represent the two tenanted flats, I'd better vote on their behalf.

He raises his hand. Cathie and George look at him in surprise.

WALTER: Those against?

Cathie and George both raise their hands.

WALTER: You two only get one vote between you. So even if Mr Briggs and (*snarling*) Mr MacKinnon vote with you, we've still got a majority of four to three. Mr Singh can't get a vote on this. He has a vesting interest.

CATHIE: Well, anyway, we're in favour of getting a security door. So there doesn't seem to be anything to discuss. We can just get Mr MacDuff to —

WALTER: There's other things to talk about. I've wrote an agenda.

He hands each of them a sheet of notepaper. The agenda has been separately handwritten on each sheet, in large, childish letters:

MEETTING OF CLOSE OWNERS AT 7.30 ON WEDENSDAY 7th OCTOBAR 1992 AT FLAT 2/1, 13, OLDBERRY ROAD, GLASGOW G2.
AGENDA
1. Securty door.
2. Close dutys.
3. Noise nusance from Flat 3/1
4. Other compitant busness.
Walter Bain (Flat 2/1)

WALTER: I like to do things proper. Though I don't know why I bother, for all the thanks I get.

He glances round the room's occupants, as if daring any of them to contradict him.

WALTER: Has anybody got any items they'd like to add? *(no one has)* So if there's nothing else, number one on the agenda is the security door.

CATHIE: Fine, so if everyone's agreed, then we can —

WALTER: So for the benefit of the new owners, I thought I'd say a bit about all the changes I - we've - made over the years.

CATHIE: There's no need. I'm sure we —

WALTER: Yes, we've seen a lot of changes over the years. A lot of residents have come and gone. Yes, a lot of them have gone. Since I've been here the longest I try to keep an eye on things and make sure they're done right. Though I don't know why I bother, for all the thanks I get. But it's only right for everybody to get the benefit of my experience. We've had a lot done to the building in recent years: stone-cleaning, a new roof, lead pipes replaced ... you know, drinking water through lead pipes can damage your brain.

CATHIE: Really?

WALTER: Yes. So, as you can see, the whole building's been completely refurnished. We got the roof done first. That was in 1982. Or was it in 1983? No, it was in 1982. Then there was the stone-cleaning. What a business that was! The council wanted to give us a grant to get our building done on its own, but as I pointed out to them - quite a few times - we're on a main road, so we needed to get all the buildings done together, otherwise we'd have a line of piebald tenements. The council were really slow to see it my way, but I managed to talk them into it. Eventually. After that, it was the back wall. That was in 1983. Or was it…?

During all of this time the other people in the room have been sinking into a catatonic state, having given up all attempts to move things along. The ornamental clock on the mantelpiece shows the time to be 7.50.

The same room, some time later. The clock now shows the time as 8.30. The room's occupants seem frozen in the same positions as before.

WALTER: And that was in 1989. No, I tell a lie, it was in 1990. Anyway, as you can see the whole building's been completely refurnished. It's added a lot to the value of the houses.
CATHIE: So we noticed.
WALTER: So the main thing still needing done is to fit a security door.

The room's other occupants return partially to life.

CATHIE: Good, so now we can —
WALTER: But first I need to tell you about the bus stop.
CATHIE: The bus stop?
WALTER: You'll have noticed that the bus stop is in front of the next close, Number 11. It was

originally in front of ours. This meant that men who'd been indulging in one of the public houses in Byres Road would, while waiting for a bus – I hope the ladies will pardon me – come into our close to relieve themselves. We couldn't have that. This is a family building.

CATHIE: So we need a security door. Right, so we —

WALTER: The council wouldn't give us a grant for a security door. We'd have had to pay for it ourselves. So I pointed out to them that the distance between the bus stop and the stop to the east was 343 yards 4 inches, whereas the distance to the stop on the west was only 305 yards 7 inches. However, if the stop was moved eastwards to the front of Number 11, this would make it virtually equi – equi – right in the middle.

CATHIE: (*incredulously*) And the council agreed to that?

WALTER: Yes. (*a pause*) Eventually. After a few letters. And a few phone calls. And one or two visits. Have you met the council's Director of Administration? He can be a bit excitable, but I got him to come round eventually. Anyway, after they moved the stop, the men in the bus queue began to relieve themselves in the close next door instead. Then Number 11 got a security door and they all started using our close again. So we'll need to get a door, despite the expense. We need to keep these drunkards out. This is a family building. Is everybody agreed?

CATHIE and GEORGE: (*in unison*) *Yes!*

Miss Quayle vigorously nods her head.

WALTER: Mr MacDuff, can you get estimates? Would ten be enough?
MR MACDUFF: We usually only get three or four.
CATHIE: I think we should leave it to Mr MacDuff's discretion.
WALTER: No, I think we should get at least ten. Better make it twelve.
CATHIE: Is that really necessary?
MR MACDUFF: (*sighing*) It's all right. I'll get a dozen estimates.

He hurries to agree, as if afraid that the number will go up again.

CATHIE: (*rising to her feet*) Right, I'm glad that's sorted. Thanks for organising the meeting. We'd better —
WALTER: That was just the first item on the agenda. The next one is close duties.

Cathie sighs and sits down again.

WALTER: By close duties I mean washing the stairs, putting out the wheelie bins, and a few other things.
CATHIE: We've been doing that. We've washed the stairs twice since we arrived.

GEORGE: You mean I washed them.

CATHIE: You've got more time off than I have.

WALTER: Did you polish the banister? And dust the banister railings?

GEORGE: Uh, well…

WALTER: The railings really trap the dust. And the landing window needs to be washed regularly. And we all need to take a turn of the close. Mr Briggs is supposed to do it, but he's not very regular.

GEORGE: Well, I don't mind taking a turn. The close gets the most traffic. And I believe Mr Briggs is quite old.

WALTER: What's his age got to do with it? But he's not the worst. That drunkard on the top floor never does anything at all. Quite apart from the stairs, the windows in his house are a scandal.

CATHIE: I haven't noticed. You can't see them very well from the street.

WALTER: They're filthy. I don't think they've ever been washed.

GEORGE: What about the other top floor flat? Do they take a turn of the stairs?

WALTER: Sometimes. But they're students, what do you expect? I send them notes, reminding them. I send everybody notes, for all the good it does. For all the thanks I get.

CATHIE: Can't we club together and pay someone to do all these things?

WALTER: (*astonished*) But that would cost money.

CATHIE: No! Surely not!

WALTER: (*regarding her suspiciously*) Yes it would. We can't have that. We can all take our turn. It's not too much to ask. But what I wanted to ask you, Miss Hyde – I believe you're a teacher.

CATHIE: (*looking a little taken aback by the apparent non-sequitur*) Yes, that's right.

WALTER: By the way, I see you don't use your married name, Miss Hyde.

CATHIE: We're not married.

WALTER: You mean you're living in sin?

CATHIE: (*angrily*) If that's how you choose to describe it. Though I don't think it's any of your business.

WALTER: (*muttering*) This is a family building. (*But he seems taken aback by Cathie's aggressive response and is clearly in retreat.*) Anyway, I've had to write a lot of notes. I thought there might be a better way. I've wrote out a list of close duties to circulate to everybody.

He picks up some sheets of notepaper and hands them to Cathie. She and George look at them together, a little dismayed as they leaf through the many sheets.

WALTER: I sometimes get my spelling and grammar a bit wrong. Here and there. Or so the wife always tells me.

He looks over at Mrs Bain, who remains impassive.

287

CATHIE: Really? I'd never have thought it.

WALTER: (*looking a little uncertain about her response*) Anyway, since you're a teacher, I thought maybe you could have a look over it for me.

CATHIE: I teach all subjects, not just English. To primary kids. But George here is a specialist. He's an English lecturer. I'm sure he can have a look at it for you. (*turning to George, with a sweet smile*) And you could type it up on your computer and run off enough copies for everyone.

GEORGE: Uh, well…

WALTER: That's a good idea. Can you do it soon? And let me see it when it's ready.

George reluctantly takes charge of the sheets of paper, and Bain presses on, not waiting for a reply or making any attempt to thank them.

WALTER: The next item is noise nuisance from Flat 3/1. The security door should take care of the drunks from the street. But that still leaves us with the drunk on the top floor. It's high time something was done about him.

CATHIE: (*innocently*) Who are you talking about?

WALTER: (*once again uncertain how to react*) Mackinnon, of course. The man's a degenerant. An absolute disgrace! A blot on our close. Playing his radiogram at all hours.

CATHIE: Yes, I think I've heard it. In the distance. He plays some lovely classical music, doesn't he George?

GEORGE: Yes, he's got really good musical taste.

WALTER: Huh! You wouldn't say that if you were right below him, listening to it at two in the morning. I've tried everything. I send him notes. I knock on the ceiling. But all I get is insolence, or he doesn't reply at all. I've phoned the police, but he just asks them in and offers them a drink. The council won't do anything. Or the factor. (*glaring at Mr MacDuff*)

MR. MACDUFF: I've written to him. More than once.

WALTER: For all the good that's done. There must be something else you can do.

MR. MACDUFF: What?

WALTER: I don't know. You're the factor. You tell me.

MR MACDUFF: I don't have any powers that would help.

WALTER: Who does?

MR. MACDUFF: The council. The police. (*Walter snorts*) Or you could hire a lawyer and sue him.

WALTER: But that would cost money.

MR MACDUFF: Yes. Maybe you could club together with some of your neighbours.

CATHIE: He isn't causing us a nuisance.

WALTER: Huh! Just wait till you've been here a bit longer. The noise is only the start of it. He never washes the stairs. He never washes the landing window. He doesn't take out his wheelie bin. And goodness knows what the inside of his house must be like. If his windows are any guide,

289

the place must be overrun by vermin. I'm telling you…

The room's other occupants have relapsed into their catatonic state. The time on the clock is 9 o'clock.

The same room, some time later. The same people, in the same positions. The clock reads 9.30.

WALTER: So that's the position. Something needs to be done about that man. It's an absolute scandal. Has no one got any ideas about what we can do?
CATHIE: (*looking at her watch and rising to her feet*) We'll probably run into him in the pub. We can have a word. (*For once Walter is at a loss for a reply*) Well, if that's it we'd better be on our way.
WALTER: We've still to deal with any other business.
CATHIE: We don't have anything else. Does anyone? Good, then we can —
WALTER: There's a couple more things I want to discuss.

Defeated, Cathie sits down again.

Thursday 15th October 1992

We finally managed to get out of Bain's house at ten o'clock. We said goodnight to Miss Quayle, and Mr MacDuff accompanied us down the stairs. By tacit consent we passed our front door and carried on down to the street.

"Bloody hell," said Cathie. "Is he always like that?"

"No," said MacDuff. "He's usually worse. That man's going to drive me to an early grave."

"I'm not surprised. Did the owners of the tenanted flats really give you a mandate?"

"I've got their general authorisation to act on their behalf. And if I hadn't used it the way Bain wanted, he'd just have gone directly to the owners and harassed them until they agreed with him."

"We're beginning to get the picture," I said.

"You're not going home, I see?"

"Correct. We need a drink."

"I'm tempted to join you. But I'd better get home before the wife phones the police."

He got into his car, while Cathie and I carried on to The Centurion. Gus Mackinnon was already there, sitting beside his friend Ernie Dunlop. We bought drinks and joined them.

"How did it go?" asked Gus.

"Unbelievable," said Cathie. "We should have been here an hour ago, but we spent half the evening listening to him rant on about you."

"Don't tell me. I don't do my turn of the stairs. I invite degenerates back to my house."

"Degenerants."

"Yes, of course. And I play loud music late at night. And I keep a dirty house."

"Something like that. And you don't take out your wheelie bin."

"Yes I do. Regularly, every bloody week. OK, there was a time a while back when I might have missed it once or twice. I went through a bad patch a few years ago when I was out of work. I did have people back a little too often. But when you have someone who complains about absolutely everything, eventually you just decide that you might as well give them something to really complain about."

"So we gathered," said Cathie.

"But I'm working now. I go to bed early. Maybe, at the weekend, I sometimes have people back. Once in a while. And as for the stairs, the top flight doesn't get much traffic. The girls across the landing give it a clean from time to time. They don't mind. But you can't appease Bain, no matter what you do. Once you've transgressed there's no going back. 'Redemption' isn't in his vocabulary."

"Not many words are," I said. "Anyway, we're not complaining."

"Only about the loss of drinking time," said Cathie. "We also spent an age listening, in great detail, to all the things he's done to improve the building."

"Typical," said Gus. "*I* organised most of that, back when I was still in private practice. In conjunction with the factor and the council. We did our best to keep Bain out of the loop, to make sure he didn't scupper everything by his interference."

"Did you enjoy your extra drinking time while we were at the meeting?" asked Cathie.

"I got in just before you," he said. "This is my first drink. While you were enjoying the delights of Bain hospitality I was having a pleasant evening at home, listening to music."

"We didn't hear anything."

"I listened on my earphones. I wasn't going to give that bugger any ammunition in front of witnesses."

Cathie and I both laughed. I took Bain's manifesto of tenement duties from my pocket and showed it to our companions. "Thanks to Cathie, I've been given a job to do. To employ my professional skills translating this into English."

"Alternatively," said Cathie, "I could give it to my Primary 5 class. Even they could make a better job of it than Bain."

"Oh dear," said Gus, "it looks as if you've been earmarked as his new right hand men. You have my heartfelt sympathy. He'll quickly make your lives a complete misery. Nothing ever satisfies him. I know from experience. I fell into that trap when I first arrived. Believe me, it's much better to be his enemy than his friend. It makes life simpler and takes a great weight off your shoulders. You can even get some fun out of it from time to time."

Gus and Ernie read the pages together, chortling frequently. "I understand he works for an insurance company," I said. "How on earth can he hold down a clerical job when he can hardly string two words together?"

"They must have a good secretarial staff," said Gus. "Anyway, I believe he works as a credit controller. If a client owes them money, they set Bain on him to harry him relentlessly until he pays up. I imagine it's quite a cost effective method. It would have to be, considering the phone bill he must run up, and not just for business calls."

"It begins to make a bit more sense," I said, as I took Bain's draft back from him. "When I've finished rewriting it I've got to type it out and circulate it to everyone."

"Excellent. Make sure you use nice soft paper. Something a bit easier on my arse than that cheap stuff he uses for his wee notes. It's really abrasive."

"Maybe I can print it out on toilet paper," I said.

"Good idea," said Gus. "And *Close Duties* is a really boring title. Why not change it to *The Andrex Chronicles*?"

We all laughed heartily at this and I felt myself begin to unwind. "By the way," I said, "I've been meaning to ask you if you know one of my colleagues at Strathkelvin. A law lecturer called Norrie Spence."

The two lawyers fell silent. "Oh yes," said Gus eventually.

"We know him," said Ernie.

"He used to come in here quite a lot," said Gus. "Not so much recently."

"I understand he used to be a solicitor, but he's been struck off."

"In the madhouse where George works," said Cathie, "that seems to be a positive qualification."

There was a further pause. "What Gus is too tactful to mention," said Ernie, "is that I too used to be a solicitor and that I also got struck off."

"Oh," I said, feeling my face grow red. "I'm sorry. I didn't know… I didn't realise…"

"You weren't to know," said Gus. "And what Ernie is too *modest* to tell you is that his case was completely different from that of Norrie Spence. He didn't steal anybody's money, he didn't end up in jail. He just forgot to listen at school when the teacher was trying to teach the class arithmetic."

"It's true," said Ernie. "I learned the hard way that it's a false economy to save money by not hiring an accountant."

"So how is our old friend Norrie settling into academic life?" asked Gus.

"All right. My Marxist boss and his team seem to think that his past is an advantage. He's been earmarked to teach a new module in Criminology."

Both Gus and Ernie howled with laughter, almost choking on their pints. Eventually, Gus recovered somewhat and rose to his feet. "That's the best laugh I've had all week," he said. "You deserve a drink. What'll it be?"

Friday 16th October 1992

This morning I received a note from Walter Bain:

"Have you tiped the close dutys yet?"

I suppose I'd better get on with it, just to get the man off my back. I have more to report in my diary, but it'll need to wait until tomorrow.

I'm also re-reading *Bleak House*, in preparation for my first tutorials, but that is a much more pleasant task.

Saturday 17th October 1992

The day after the Bain meeting, I received several interesting communications, two at work and one at home. The first was an e-mail from Rhoda, the more senior of the two school secretaries:

> Professor Trotwood would like to have a meeting with you. Please speak to me to arrange a suitable time.

The second one was less easy to decipher. It was pencil-written, in block letters, on a page from a small memo pad:

> UP IFC EL2 TEL PA

It arrived in my pigeonhole inside an envelope, which bore my name written in a different hand. After asking around, I was able to effect a translation. UP = University Principal, IFC = inter-facial confrontation, EL2 = English Lecturer No 2 (i.e., me). Having got that far, I was able to work out the rest. The principal wanted me to telephone his secretary to arrange a meeting with him. It seems that, like many others, he has not yet adjusted to the new age of e mail correspondence, but has a long-term habit of saving his valuable time by using this shorthand method of communication. Here the few seconds he had saved had cost half an hour of my time, but I know my place in the pecking order. And the fact that the university principal actually wanted to meet with a humble lecturer like me was an unprecedented honour, so I had no grounds for complaint.

I arrived home to a note from Henrietta Quayle:

Thank you for agreeing to help Mr Bain with his epistle, but you should really try not to provoke him.
HQ (Flat 1/1)

We decided to ask her across to our flat for a cup of tea and a chat. We reckoned that she might be more communicative when separated from the man upstairs. This proved to be the case.

She arrived just after 7.30. At the previous evening's meeting we had noticed that, as well as being terrified into silence, she had a habit of constantly fidgeting. We had attributed this to the intimidating presence of Bain, but it seems to be constant. She appears to be permanently in a highly nervous state. However, we did our best to put her at her ease and she became more communicative.

"Thank you for agreeing to help Mr. Bain," she said.

"No problem," said Cathie.

"Not for you," I said.

"It'll be a dawdle for a man with your talents."

"That's true of course."

"I notice Mr Bain doesn't seem inclined to thank us himself," said Cathie.

"Oh no, that isn't his style."

"So I gather."

"You shouldn't provoke him," she said. "He doesn't

like it. Gus Mackinnon used to provoke him, but he doesn't talk to him at all now."

"So he told us."

"You've spoken to him?"

"Oh yes, we sometimes run into him in the pub."

She sighed. "Gus drinks too much. But he's not nearly as bad as Mr Bain makes out. He was a big help when he first arrived. He was the one who organised all the refurbishment of the building with the factor and the council."

"Not the impression you getting talking to Bain," I said.

"No. I think Mr Bain pushed him too far and he eventually gave up."

"Gus was a great help to us when we bought the flat," said Cathie. "He sorted us out with a much better lawyer. The first one was a disaster."

"Yes, his heart's in the right place. And he's been a lot better since he got his job in the council. But Mr Bain still hasn't forgiven him for the time before that."

She began to relax a bit, though the fidgeting never quite stopped. She told us something about her history. She had arrived in the building even before Bain. The flat had originally been rented by her father, but after his death her mother had used the proceeds of his life insurance to buy it from the owner, at a time when house prices had been much more affordable. Bain had arrived shortly after that, but for some unfathomable reason her mother had got on well with him. By the time her mother had died, any resolve to break free of Bain's tyranny seems to have faded.

We had a feeling that this was not the full story. We suspected that much more must have happened between her and Bain to fully account for the present situation.

It seems that she works in a charity shop a couple of days a week, but otherwise seldom leaves the house. She is wary of having friends back in case it annoys Bain. This is of course ridiculous, but such is the degree of his power over her.

She was formerly a school teacher and enjoyed chatting with Cathie about this for some time. She is also paranoid about burglars and has an exhaustive knowledge of all such activity in the area, gleaned from the media and from gossip with friends. She has been keen to get a security door for some time, but previously had been up against Bain's initial resistance to any further expense. Another constant worry is her dread of a gas leak within the building. One or more of these various obsessions seem to be forever present in her mind.

I think she is a rather lonely person and is glad of our friendship.

Sunday 18th October 1992

Yesterday morning I put my first draft of the close manifesto through Bain's letterbox. Barely half an hour later I got it back, my beautiful narrative scarred by illiterate alterations and additions. After several further attempts, and most of the morning gone, I finally got his reluctant agreement to run off copies.

When I'd finished I took the bundle to Bain's door and rang the bell. He took one copy from me and said, "Now you can deliver them to the other flats."

He closed the door again before I could reply. I remained standing on his doorstep for a moment and took a deep breath. I was tempted to take the remaining copies straight down to the back court and dump them in our wheelie bin. Instead I distributed copies to all the neighbours. It only took a few minutes.

I'm fast appreciating the wisdom of Gus's advice. To his copy, I added a short note of my own: "I hope the paper is soft enough. Sorry there are no perforations."

Wednesday 21st October 1992

On Monday afternoon I had my meeting with Professor Trotwood, and this morning my meeting with the Principal.

Professor Trotwood's room, which is on the same floor as Ken's, mine and the rest of the school, is not particularly ostentatious. It is a little bigger than Ken's, but is so clean and tidy that it appears even more so. The two large bookcases are filled with actual books, and the relatively few documents sitting on top are arranged into neat bundles. On the wall opposite his desk a large portrait of Karl Marx confirms his known allegiance, but a number of other art prints (possibly inherited from his predecessor) are less indicative. The computer on his desk was switched on, though in screen-saver mode.

It is a nice bright room, thanks to two large windows, both unimpeded by rubbish. A second door, on a side wall, gives direct access to an anteroom housing the two secretaries, Rhoda and Gillian.

"Come in George," he said. "Have a seat." I sat down opposite his desk. "I just wanted to have a chat to see how you're settling in."

"Fine. No problems."

"Is your room OK?"

"Great."

"It's a little small, but I think you have the basics."

"I've been able to transfer a few books and papers from home, which keeps my girlfriend happy."

He laughed. "I'm sure she and my wife could find some common ground on that score. Have you started teaching yet?"

"This Thursday. Ken took the first two weeks, to give me time to prepare."

"Very good of him." It wasn't clear whether or not this was meant ironically. "You're teaching the new first-year English module?"

"Yes. I'm lecturing on Joseph Conrad. But this week's tutorials are a follow-up to Ken's lectures on *Bleak House*."

"That's Charles Dickens?"

"Yes"

"I know of these writers, of course, though I can't claim to be particularly familiar with their work. Difficult of course not to know something about Dickens, from film and TV adaptations."

"They tend to focus on his earlier works, like *Oliver Twist* or *Nicholas Nickleby*. His later works – with the odd exception like *Great Expectations* or *A Tale of Two Cities* – tend to be less well known. Yet they contain critiques of society and the political system that are much more cohesive. Bernard Shaw described *Little Dorrit* as more seditious than *Das Capital*."

"Really? Why was that?"

"It's a biting satire of civil service nepotism and bureaucracy, as well as an attack on investment capitalism and the banking system. Also, one of the principal characters is permanently resident in a debtors' prison, which becomes a pervasive metaphor for the imprisonment of the various characters by their environment and their position in society."

"Well, well," he said. "Who'd have thought it?" I was detecting a slight change in his mood, which made me a little uncomfortable. It was still friendly, but tinged with amusement. "But this book…"

"*Little Dorrit*."

"Yes. That isn't the one on the syllabus?"

"No. That's *Bleak House*. It considers some of the same issues, but is mainly an attack on the law and the legal system."

"And do you think we can rely on our Ken to have brought out all these nuances?"

"Uh, I'm not sure."

"Nor am I," he said thoughtfully. "Never mind, I'm sure you'll keep them on the right track in your tutorials. So old Charles was a red-hot revolutionary? Maybe I should get a picture of him to put up beside Karl. Or should I replace Karl altogether?"

I was becoming less and less sure of his mood by the moment. "Uh, I didn't…"

He burst out laughing. "George, I don't know what you've been hearing about me from some of our colleagues. Though I can hazard a guess. I asked you here to get to know you a bit better on a personal level, not so that you could regale me with what you think I want to hear. You come here well recommended, not just by virtue of your qualifications and your references, but I have a few contacts at Glasgow and Edinburgh universities and I asked around about you. I have every confidence in you and I'm sure you'll do a good job."

I had gradually been feeling my face grow red, but I said nothing.

"The new module is intended to contribute to an element of liberal studies, an essential part of our development from technical college to university. I expect you to do your job to the best of your ability, drawing upon your education and your own honest views. I don't expect you to toe any particular party line. We already have more than enough of that. As part of this development we needed to have an English lecturer, and that's your role."

"But Ken's already been here a while?"

"Yes, he has, hasn't he?" He seemed inclined to say more, but stopped himself. "How do you get on with Ken?"

"All right. I don't know him all that well yet. But I think we can rub along well enough on a personal level."

"On a *personal* level. What about professionally?"

"I'm sure we have our own individual styles."

"I'm sure you have. So do you think you can introduce a fresh approach without treading on each other's toes?"

"Yes, I think so."

"Good. Then I think we understand each other."

We chatted on for a few minutes more before he brought the meeting to an end. "Well, thanks for looking in, George. Remember, if there's ever anything else you need to see me about my door's always open. Just check with Rhoda for a suitable time."

"Yes, I will. Thanks." I started to make for the door. "Oh, I meant to say earlier. The Principal also wants to meet with me."

"Really? You're honoured. Never mind, just be honest with him. As you were with me. Eventually."

I felt my face grow red again as I made my way to the corridor. But he was still smiling.

Despite my gaffe, I think my meeting with Professor Trotwood was a success. It confirmed my growing respect for the man, and I've decided to make up my own mind about him rather than be influenced too much by the opinion of Ken and others. Of my meeting with the Principal, however, I am less sure. I still don't quite know how to interpret our encounter. I'm fast coming to the conclusion that he is a very peculiar man.

At my interview for the post he had chaired the interview panel. At the time it had seemed a little odd that he should have bothered to get involved in such a routine task, but I had been too nervous to dwell on this. However, I did think then that some of his questions had been a little strange, and I had been rather unsure how to answer them. It had left me uncertain about how well I'd done and I'd been pleasantly surprised when I heard that I'd got the job.

Based on what I've subsequently learned, I think he was sounding me out about my political beliefs, but in such an oblique and roundabout way that I was left merely baffled. I think he was doing something similar at our latest meeting, though it's still difficult to be sure. He doesn't seem the type to tackle a subject head on.

His room is on the top floor of the building and is large and luxurious. The windows face to the west no doubt, on a good day, affording the rumoured view of the River Kelvin in the far distance. The floor is covered by a thick fitted carpet, in contrast to the utilitarian covering found elsewhere in the building. His wide desk is bare apart from a telephone and a small notepad and pencil, presumably the source of cryptic messages like the one that had summoned me there. Several expensive-looking chairs with padded seats sit in front of his desk and, nearer the wall, a luxurious, leather-covered three piece suite is arranged around a long coffee table. A number of art prints on the walls look as if they came from the same job lot as those in Professor Trotwood's room, though they are somewhat larger, in keeping with the status of the room's occupant. There are no bookcases and, apart from the fittings already described, the room is completely paper-free and equally bereft of any stamp of individuality. It was difficult to work out what he could possibly be doing when there was no one else in the room, as it didn't contain the slightest indication of any activity. Maybe, like my computer, he relapses into screen-saver mode until the arrival of his next visitor.

The temperature in the room was almost unbearably high, and I noticed that the central heating was being boosted by two small electric convectors.

When his secretary (or rather his PA) showed me into his room from her adjoining anteroom, he stood up and held out his hand. "Good morning, Dr Anderson, do have a seat." He is softly spoken, his Scottish origin barely detectable within his Anglified diction. His age is difficult to determine: I believe he is in his late fifties but, as if he has been permanently dehydrated by years of excessive heat, his features are so wrinkled that he seems much older. He is thin, bald, wears rimless glasses and, though reasonably tall, he has a permanent stoop that makes him appear shorter.

When Cathie read this description, she remarked that he sounds like a Bond villain. As to whether or not he constitutes as big a threat to the civilised world, the jury is still out. "Maybe you should buy him a fluffy wee cat," Cathie suggested. "That should get you into his good books."

At first he seemed to be following a similar script to that of Professor Trotwood. "Thank you for dropping in," he said. "I wanted to see how you were settling in."

"Very well, thank you. I was delighted to get the job and see it as a valuable opportunity." I recalled Professor Trotwood's advice and decided to rein in the sycophancy a little. But Principal Robert Gray seemed less averse to being fed what he wanted to hear.

"Yes indeed," he said. "As a university, we need to be less narrowly vocational and to develop the Arts. An appreciation of English literature by our students is an important ingredient. Appointing an English lecturer is a major step forward."

"We already had an English lecturer of course."

"What? Oh yes, of course." He sounded unsure. I experienced a moment of panic. Had he not known about Ken's existence? Would my new job be suddenly snatched away, as an unnecessary duplication of scarce resources? Then I remembered my "EL2" designation and relaxed a little. "How are you getting on with Professor Trotwood?" he asked.

"Very well." I decided to leave it there. Lavishing my Professor with praise might be counter-productive. "We had a short meeting on Monday."

"Good. Did he give you any ... encouragement?"

"Oh yes, he was very supportive."

"I mean, did he offer you any ... ah ... guidance as to the path you should take."

I was detecting his trend. "Not really. He wants me to be free to draw on my educational background and develop my own style. To further the element of liberal studies."

"Does he indeed?" He sounded suspicious. I think I may now be irretrievably associated with the Marxist conspiracy. "What's your background again? What is it your parents do?"

"They're both academics like me. My father is Professor of Medieval History at Edinburgh University and my mother is a Senior Lecturer in Philosophy at the University of Stirling."

"I see." This was surely an innocuous enough pedigree, an unlikely breeding ground for a communist rebellion, but he sounded unconvinced. "I think it's important for our students to be given a balanced outlook." In other words, not to be fed left-wing propaganda, but he stopped

307

short of actually saying this. "I'm sure you'll be a valuable addition to our team, Dr Anderson." He rose to his feet. It seemed that our meeting was over.

It was now almost lunch time and, after a short spell back in my room, I went upstairs to the staff dining room. There was no one there I knew. I bought my lunch and sat at an empty table, but a minute or two later I was joined by Adrian Armitage.

"How goes it, George?" he said. "Back on duty, keen as ever, eh?"

I told him about my meetings with Professor Trotwood and the Principal. "I don't care what you guys say, I rather like our Professor. The Principal I'm less sure about."

"Oh, Trotters is all right. I've seen a lot worse in my time. You shouldn't run away with the idea that I agree with Ken about everything."

"Right." I decided not to expand on this. I still didn't know either of them all that well.

"Trotters' views are no secret. He does what it says on the tin. He's something of an idealist, but he's not stupid."

"I've gathered that. He put me in my place. Nicely, but firmly."

"Did he really? But you're right, the Principal is a different matter. I haven't had much contact with him, but I reckon that there's definitely something dodgy about him. He's barely been here a year, but during that time virtually every senior post that's fallen vacant seems to have gone to one of his pals. People that he's worked with either at his last institution or at some other time in the past. A whole clutch of posts that could have been filled internally were briefly advertised early in the summer, when everyone's eye was off the ball. Then we all returned in the autumn, refreshed from our break, to find that they'd been mysteriously filled by Gray acolytes. I'm convinced the proper procedures weren't all followed, but from our humble perspective it's difficult to be sure."

"I hope you don't think I'm one of these appointments."

"No offence, George. But your job isn't high enough in the pecking order. I think you're in the clear."

The internal politics of my place of employment were becoming more interesting by the moment. "I think they're intended as a kind of anti-Marxist league," Adrian continued, "a bastion against the creeping enemy within. From what I've seen so far, I don't think many of them have been appointed on merit. If I'm right, it's a ridiculous over-reaction. The problem, if it is a problem, is confined to the Social Science School.

"I hope our new university status isn't going to ruin this place," he went on. "For the life of me, I can't understand the rationale behind turning perfectly good colleges into second-rate universities. You shouldn't be fooled by the cynical talk you hear from some of us. Woodside was a damn good college. It provided – still provides – some excellent vocational courses. It's strong on civil and mechanical engineering, it has a good surveying course, it's well ahead in the growing field of information technology, the Business School has a reasonable success rate. The Social Science School is atypical. You'll have gathered from the toilet graffiti, if nowhere else, that we have something of a reputation among the other schools. But even we provide courses for social workers, nurses and the like. We help people into jobs."

He paused to eat for a moment or two. "Sorry, George," he said eventually. "I seem to have got on to my soapbox. I just don't understand the point of trying to beat the old universities at their own game and coming off a poor second. We should stick to what we're good at."

"Rather than teach airy-fairy subjects like English?"

He laughed. "Nothing personal. We need an English lecturer. We've always had an English lecturer."

"But now we've got two."

"Well, yes, but don't run away with the idea that they're trying to develop an Arts degree just yet. They didn't want two English lecturers. They just wanted an English lecturer who isn't Ken. But they can't get rid of him, so now they have two of you as part of the package."

"Oh." I wondered what the source was of all Adrian's information. He seems very well informed for someone at his level. However, it all sounded very convincing. I remembered that he has been there a long time and probably has many contacts all over the campus. Compared to some universities, it is a fairly small community.

"How are you getting on with Ken?"

"All right." I decided to be careful what I said. I was quickly realising that Adrian is a quite different creature from Ken, despite their common vintage, but I still wasn't sure how close friends they were. "I've never met an English lecturer quite like him before."

Adrian chuckled. "I'm sure you haven't. But if you don't bother him too much, he won't bother you. He's too lazy to do anything else. If he doesn't see you as a threat, he'll leave you free to get on with your own thing."

"That suits me. I don't want any trouble. I just want to do my job."

"That's the best way. I've been here a long time. It's always been a shambles of one kind or another. The smart thing to do is avoid getting involved in school politics. Just keep your head down and do your job as well as you can. The students will appreciate it if no one else does."

I think this is very good advice. From the outset, I've rather liked Adrian Armitage, and now I find I have a growing respect for him as well.

The opposite is true of my neighbour Walter Bain. He is fast becoming a real nuisance. More of that in a future entry.

Friday 23rd October 1992

Last Monday evening (the day after I distributed the close instructions) we returned home to the following note:

> Have you spoke to Makinon about his noise. He playd his radiogram after 11 last night I nocked on the ceeling but it did no good the man is a mennis.
> Walter Bain (Flat 2/1)

I sent him a short note, simply saying that I had mentioned his complaint to Gus. On Tuesday evening, another note was waiting for us:

> Your wheely was in the street all day yesterday it shuold be took back as soon as posible bins in the

street detrack from the close appearance. What
did Makinon say to you about his noise.
Walter Bain (Flat 2/1)

I wrote back that, as Cathie and I had both been at work all day on Monday, we hadn't had a chance to return our wheelie bins earlier. After some thought, I decided to say nothing about Gus. Giving a true account of his response might have proved counter-productive.

We got a new note every day for the rest of the week. He asked us if any of the neighbours had spoken to us about the instructions, complained that we hadn't taken our turn of cleaning the close (in fact we had, but it gets a lot of traffic), accused us of forgetting to shut the front gate, and made further complaints and enquiries about Gus.

"What should we do?" I asked Cathie.

"*I'm* doing nothing. I suggest you do the same. Gus has the right idea. Ignore the bugger."

"He'll just keep bothering us if I don't reply."

"He'll just keep bothering us if you do."

I think this may be the best idea. So far he has avoided a face-to-face confrontation. I think he may be afraid of Cathie. A lot of people are. This can be very useful.

However, the most memorable event of the week happened yesterday, when I gave my first lecture. This deserves to be reported at some length, so I'll take my time over it at the weekend. I'm not in danger of forgetting any of the details.

Sunday 25th October 1992

The first-year English lectures take place on Thursday mornings, between nine and eleven. As agreed, Ken had lectured for the first two weeks. I had been due to take over this two-hour slot last Thursday, but Ken asked if he could have the first hour, as he had overrun a little. I was glad to agree. Since I would have the class for the rest of the semester, I had enough flexibility to make up the lost hour. Also, preparing for my first classes had kept me fully occupied. I had finished re-reading *Bleak House* in readiness for that week's tutorials. I had also re-read *The Secret Agent* in order to prepare for my first lecture, and had still to get through *Women in Love* in time for the following week's tutorials. Fortunately, I'm a fast reader and I've read them all before, though it was some time ago. I borrowed Ken's copies of *Ripley's Notes* for the Dickens and the Lawrence. Provided that I didn't find too much in them to object to (which I didn't) I reasoned that it would be better for Ken and I not to contradict each other. This would also save me much time and I could always add a few thoughts of my own. However, my lectures on *The Secret Agent* were taking more time to prepare and being able to spread them over two weeks would be a great help.

Our first-year intake of 300 students, attracted by our new university status, had put a strain on the existing campus accommodation. None of our classrooms, in the main building or the adjoining annexes, were big enough to accommodate a class of that size (or even what was left of it after two weeks of Ken). As a result the university had rented a church hall conveniently located across the road from the back of the campus. In these heathen times, maintaining this hall along with a listed nineteenth-century church building was proving something of a strain upon the dwindling congregation, and a financial input from their academic neighbour was timely. The main church building was earmarked to accommodate the new university's first graduations the following year; in view of this elevated status, graduation photographs in a setting of nineteenth-century neo-Gothic architecture now seemed more appropriate. Meanwhile, their large hall would be used for lectures and exams.

As part of the deal with the church, some of the government funds provided to facilitate Woodside College's transformation into a university had been expended on refurbishing the church hall. Among other things, it had been repainted, refloored and provided with a new central heating system. The day before, I had inspected the hall while it was empty. I was a little nervous, having never lectured to such a large class before, and wanted to be as well prepared as possible. It is a large hall, and even has a small balcony: any lecturers inclined to play to the gallery would be able to indulge in this practice literally. When the church had first been built, the minister must have been able to thunder his sermons, not just here but in the main church building, using only the power of his lungs. For modern users, academic and churchgoing alike, who might be less well-endowed vocally, an amplification system had been installed. I had a chance to try this out during my exploratory visit with the help of the resident janitor. A small radio microphone could be attached to the lapel, thereby conferring the freedom to walk about while lecturing, in case this should suit the speaker's oratorical style.

I arrived at the hall at five to ten to find several students standing around outside the front door, smoking and chatting. It looked as if Ken's lecture had already finished. Inside, there were more students in the corridor, making their way to and from the toilets, queuing for drinks and snacks at the newly-installed vending machines. Outside the door of the hall Ken stood chatting to Bradley Skinner. In addition to the main hall the building contained several smaller rooms which were used for tutorials. Presumably Bradley was teaching in one of these.

"Here he comes," said Bradley. "A lamb to the slaughter."

"Not that bad, surely," I said. I was still rather nervous and this didn't help. "Have you finished off your part?" I asked Ken.

"All done," he said. "They're all yours. And the best of fuckin' luck to you."

"Thanks," I said dubiously. "I'd better get on with it then."

There was a ten-minute break between the two lecture slots, but I wanted to get everything set up. A large proportion of the students were still in their seats and others were coming in and out of the room. They were all talking amongst themselves and the background noise was considerable.

I tested the overhead projector, arranged my slides on the desk in front of me, and checked that they were all in the right order. I put up the first slide and adjusted the projector's focus. During my visit the previous evening I had made sure that the lettering was large enough to be read anywhere in the hall. The slide contained a key extract from Conrad's book, and a number of students began to write it down. This is an established device designed to help them focus on the impending lecture. It was only partially successful and the level of background noise was still high.

I arranged my notes and skimmed quickly through them, though I already knew them fairly well. I became subliminally aware of a different background sound, distinct from the chatter in the room, but couldn't identify what it was. I looked at my watch. Apart from a few strays, the influx of students had died down and most of them were in their seats. It was nearly five past ten. I held up my hands for silence. "Right," I said. "Let's get started."

This had little or no effect, apart from reminding me how ineffectual my voice was in this large room when trying to be heard above such a hubbub. It was only then I remembered that I hadn't clipped on the radio mike. I looked around for it and for the small transmitter that fitted in the pocket, but they were nowhere to be seen. Where were they? A minute or two later the answer became obvious.

I called for silence again, more loudly this time, and rapped on my desk with the whiteboard duster. The noise died down a bit, not entirely, but enough for me to begin making out the background sound that had been teasing the back of my mind. The students were beginning to notice it as well, and this finally grabbed their attention much more effectively than I'd been able to. They were quickly reduced to silence.

Ken's voice could now be clearly heard, issuing from the various loudspeakers scattered about the room. "The cunts have been drifting away over the last two weeks," he was saying. "They seem to have come back for George, but I don't suppose it'll last."

Bradley's reply was from further away, and what he said couldn't be made out. Then Ken went on, "I'm telling you Bradley, I don't know where they dug this lot up from. Any bugger with a 'C' in woodwork seems to have been given a place. We're already handing out degrees like fuckin' sweeties, so Christ knows what it's going to be like now."

The noise in the room was beginning to grow again. Some students were laughing, but there was also outrage. I was so taken aback that I was slow to react. Then I realised what I had to do and made for the door. But by the time I got there the voices had stopped, and when I looked out into the corridor Ken and Bradley had disappeared.

I returned to the hall, unsure what to do. Maybe Ken would remember about the mike and come back. Or maybe I'd have to make do with my own, unamplified voice.

The noise had risen again and for a moment or two I struggled to regain the class's attention. I had only been partially successful when more sounds from the loudspeakers completed the job more effectively and the students fell silent again. Ken was no longer speaking, but instead we heard much grunting and heavy breathing, followed by a deep, satisfied sigh. From further off came the sound of a splash, and a few farts, also distant but unmistakeable. This time the class's reaction was almost entirely laughter.

I recovered from my paralysis and headed for the door. As I entered the corridor, I could hear further laughter from the class, followed by hushing sounds from others who were intent upon hearing every detail of Ken's bowel movement. I quickly made my way to the male toilet, which was only a few yards along the corridor. The room appeared empty, but one of the cubicles was occupied.

"Are you there Ken?" I asked, keeping my voice low, hoping I was too far away for it to be picked up by the microphone.

"George? What are you —?"

"You're broadcasting," I said. "Your mike's still on."

"What? Oh fu –" He broke off, and presently I heard the rustle of toilet paper followed by the cistern flushing. Ken emerged from the cubicle in a panic. "Oh Jesus Christ!" he said. "Could you hear me in the classroom?" I put my finger to my lips. "It's all right," he said, "I've switched it off. Could you hear me through there?"

"I'm afraid so. Not just your – uh – visit here, but your conversation with Bradley. I looked for you earlier, but I'd no idea where you'd gone until —"

"Oh fuck," he said. "Fuck, fuck, fuck!" He washed and dried his hands and handed the mike and transmitter over to me. The red light on the transmitter, which indicated a live broadcast, was now out. "Why didn't you ask me for it before the lecture?"

"I forgot. I've never used it before. Anyway, I'd better get back."

He was too demoralised to argue further and I saw his shoulders slump as he made his way to the front door.

After that, my lecture was something of an anticlimax. I re-entered the hall to another burst of laughter and a few of them gave a round of applause. "Spoilsport!" said a man in the front row. He looked a little older than the rest, a mature student.

How could I possibly follow such an introduction? I gradually managed to get them quietened down, and my now amplified voice rose easily above the sound of the restless few who remained. I put up another slide.

They quietened down as they copied out the new slide. My limited teaching experience had already taught me that there's no point in speaking immediately after putting up a slide, as you'll be talking to yourself until they have finished writing down every word. On the other hand, it can be counter-productive to give them too long, as some will deliberately write slowly in order to postpone the resumption of your lecture. When a few started chatting again, I left the rest to catch up and began to talk.

"Right," I said. "Joseph Conrad. I trust you've all finished reading *The Secret Agent*?"

I hadn't intended this as a joke but they reacted as if I had. "I'll take that as a 'yes' then." Further laughter. "Or maybe you haven't quite finished reading *Bleak House* and *Women in Love*?"

I seemed, unexpectedly, to have acquired a new skill as a comedian. This last question evoked further jollity. I sighed and began taking them through the bullet points in my slide. I talked at a reasonable speed, repeated the most important points, and they responded by settling down and writing diligently. If they weren't going to read the books, they would need good notes.

In this fashion, I managed to get through my lecture and finished up shortly before five to eleven. I hung about at the front of the room to see if any of them wanted to consult me individually. Most of them walked on past, out of the door. Then a girl approached me. I gave her a welcoming smile, anxious to discover how I could further enlighten her on the work of Joseph Conrad. "Yes?"

"Will that be coming up in the exam?"

I tried not to make my disappointment too apparent. "I don't know. I haven't written the paper yet. Anything on the syllabus is fair game."

"Oh."

"Have you read *The Secret Agent* yet?"

"No. Are we supposed to read it?"

"That's the general idea. It's very good. You might actually enjoy it."

She seemed unconvinced. "Oh. I took down everything you said. I think I've got good notes. Better than the ones I got from Mr Ramsay."

"Right. Good. It wouldn't do any harm to read the book as well, if you can find the time. We'll be discussing it at the tutorials in a couple of weeks."

"Right." I could see that I still hadn't quite won her over. She took her leave and left the room, an unsatisfied customer.

It was now almost eleven and I quickly gathered up my papers and made my way back to the campus for my first tutorial. I was initially gratified to find the room full, until I counted them and discovered that a little more than half of them were there. Ken's prediction had been accurate. What would I have done if they had all turned up? Apparently this was a possibility that the administrators responsible for arranging the accommodation hadn't taken into account. I passed around a sheet of paper for them to sign, so that these more conscientious ones would at least get some credit.

I waited a moment or two for late arrivals, but no one else came. "Right," I said. "Let's get started."

"What did you think about Mr Ramsay?" one of the boys asked.

"What about him?"

"He doesn't seem to like us very much. Do you agree with him?"

"I don't know you yet," I said. "It'll depend on how you behave. But that's not what we're here to talk about. We're here to discuss *Bleak House*."

Silence. "How many of you have read it?" No one had. "Have any of you started reading it?" None of them.

"It's an awful long book," a girl said. That was true. My Penguin copy has a thousand pages.

"So you at least bought a copy?" I asked.

"No. I looked at it in the shop."

I sighed. This was becoming a habit today. "OK. I presume you all attended Mr Ramsay's lecture?" As *Bleak House* had been the subject of his first lecture, before they all started drifting away, it seemed like a safe bet. There was a murmur of agreement. "Right. What can anyone tell me about it?"

No response. "I presume you copied down his slides? What was on them?"

"He didn't use any slides," someone said.

"Right." I made a mental note to prepare some slides on *Women in Love* for the following week's tutorials. Meanwhile, it looked as if an improvised lecture would be required. Normally this is something I frown upon: if they aren't prepared to work for a tutorial, I don't see why I should do the work for them. But it looked as if Ken's input might need some remedial work done on it. I could take a stricter line with those parts of the course for which I was fully responsible.

I quickly provided them with an outline of the book's plot. I wrote the names of the main characters on the whiteboard, in block capitals. At least they might now be able to spell them correctly. Then I went through the main points from *Ripley's Notes*. This ought to corroborate what they'd heard from Ken, but since none of them seemed to remember what that was maybe it didn't matter.

During my talk they all wrote steadily in their notebooks. When I'd finished, one of the boys said, "I think I know that story. Was it on the telly?"

I remembered that the BBC had broadcast a dramatization of *Bleak House* a few years before. It had starred Diana Rigg and Denholm Elliot and a host of other well-known British actors. It had spanned a number of weeks and had done the book reasonable justice. "Yes that's right," I said. "Did anyone else see it?"

A couple of people thought they might have. "Well, I suppose that's something," I said. "Right, if you can possibly have a go at *Women in Love* for next week that would be a great help."

No one said anything, but their response was not encouraging. I was taking it for granted that none of them had yet read it, but no one said otherwise. I stopped short of following up my suggestion with an enthusiastic recommendation. I love Dickens, but I don't care all that much for Lawrence. They didn't need to know that but I wasn't prepared to lie to them. If they skipped him and went straight on to Conrad maybe it would be for the best. There would be a choice in their exam. Reading some of the texts would be better than reading none of them. Maybe next year we can change the Dickens text to one of his shorter books, like *Hard Times.*

Despite everything, I'm still an optimist.

Monday 26th October 1992

I haven't quite finished my account of last Thursday, but writing the last entry used up far too much of my weekend. Cathie quickly forgave me for this when she read my account of Ken's mishap. In order to maximise its effect, I had postponed telling her about the incident. My plan worked and I don't think I've seen her laugh so much since I've known her.

She'd been forewarned that something interesting might be on the way after we both ran into Ken late on Thursday evening. Meeting him before reading my account, she told me later, really helped bring it to life.

We paid a late visit to The Centurion just after 9.30, a bad habit we seem to be slipping into. Looking round the bar, the only people I recognised were a couple of sociologists from the Social Science School, but they were in other company. The faces of some of their companions were familiar, and I believe they are sociologists at Glasgow University. I didn't want to intrude, nor was I in the mood for a lecture on Marxism, so I briefly spoke to them and introduced them to Cathie before we left for a table on our own. As we were leaving, Denny Merrigan said, "I hear your pal Ken had a wee accident this morning."

Everyone at the table laughed. They all seemed to have heard the story. Either Ken had indiscreetly confided in one or more of our colleagues or the student bush telegraph was working well. I felt a little sorry for Ken. Soon it could be round the entire academic community in Glasgow and beyond. It could become a new urban folk tale: in 20 years' time people could be telling of someone they knew to whom it had happened the previous week.

"What was that, then?" I asked innocently.

"Come off it, George," said Tom Masterton, the other sociologist from our school. "We know you were there. You were an ear witness, so to speak. The students have always told us that Ken's lectures are crap, but we never realised they meant it quite so literally before."

Further hilarity from everyone at the table. "I don't know what you're talking about," I said.

"Such loyalty!" said Denny as Cathie and I went off to find a table of our own.

"What on earth was all that about?" asked Cathie.

"I'm saving it for my diary. You'll enjoy it, it's a great story."

"What happened, for God's sake?"

"You'll find out. What do you want to drink?"

"You should bloody well know by now." She let me go off to the bar, but made several more unsuccessful attempts to get the story out of me when I returned. I was enjoying building up the suspense too much and I managed to resist giving in to her interrogation.

Shortly afterwards, the arrival of Ken himself further added to the intrigue. Cathie had heard a lot about him from reading my diary, but hadn't met him before. It was clear even from a distance that The Centurion was not his first port of call. He looked blearily around the bar, saw the sociologists and then noticed Cathie and me. I wasn't particularly surprised when he headed for our table.

"Hullo Ken," I said. "Have a seat. This is my girlfriend Cathie. Ken Ramsay."

"Pleased to meet you," said Ken, shaking hands with her and sitting down. His voice was slurred and he looked even more dishevelled than usual, a difficult feat but he'd managed to pull it off.

"Would you like a drink?" I asked.

"Aye, thanks. I'll have a half."

"Lager or beer?"

"For God's sake!" said Cathie. "How long have you been living in Glasgow now? The man wants a whisky, don't you?" Ken nodded. "See these Edinburgh folk!" she said to him.

"You want beer as well?" I asked.

"No. The whisky'll do. Add a couple blocks of ice and a wee dribble of water. Don't drown it."

I didn't feel disposed to press him further and returned to the bar. When I got back he and Cathie were chatting about generalities. She hadn't got round to asking him about what had happened that day, but I was sure she'd do so soon enough.

"I suppose you told her what happened this morning?" said Ken.

"No," said Cathie. "Whatever it is, I can't get it out of him."

But obviously she knew that something had happened. "I haven't said anything," I said. "But I'm afraid it's got about. Denny and Tom were talking about it earlier."

"Bastards!" said Ken. "The fuckin' students must have blabbed to them. At least you'll have them for the rest of the year and I can keep out their road. Maybe they'll have forgotten about it by the time they get to second year, if any of them make it that far."

"From what I've seen so far, I wouldn't bank on it," I said, though I doubted if any of the survivors would forget.

"Anyway, what on earth happened?" asked Cathie.

"I don't want to talk about it," said Ken. "It was a fuckin' disaster. Sorry. I'm sure George will tell you later. He might as well, everyone else seems to fuckin' know. Sorry." He looked at me gratefully, clearly amazed at my discretion. I didn't tell him that I was merely saving the story for my diary, where it would be a highlight, and I felt guilty.

"I've had a wee bit to drink," he said. "I've been on a bit of a pub crawl. The wife'll kill me when I get home."

I think we'd already worked out most of this. It seemed he'd been drinking since early evening. I knew that he'd had a second-year class late in the afternoon, otherwise he'd probably have started before lunch.

"Where do you live?" Cathie asked.

"Vinicombe Street."

That was quite near. It is off Byres Road, a few hundred yards further up. I already knew that Ken and I were almost neighbours, but this was the first time we'd run into each other. I rather hope we can keep it that way. I think we can probably tolerate each other as colleagues, but I don't particularly want him as part of my social circle. I think Cathie feels the same. Ken rambled on drunkenly for a while, apologising to Cathie every time he swore, which was often. Then he offered to buy us a drink.

"What a horrible wee man!" said Cathie, when Ken had departed for the bar. "I thought your description of him was a bit exaggerated, but he's even worse in real life."

"I think we'll get along all right, as long as we keep out of each other's way as much as possible."

"I hope he doesn't start coming in here now."

"The sociologists are in here quite often. That might keep him at a distance. There's no love lost between them."

Ken came back with our drinks and the conversation continued along the same lines as before. Then Ken said, "Would you like to come back to my place for a coffee?"

I was unsure whether this was a genuine offer of hospitality or whether he just needed protection from marital homicide. "Thanks," I said, "but we just came in for a quick one. We'd better get back."

"Go on," said Ken. "You don't have a class tomorrow morning." Neither did he, which was just as well.

"I'm only a school teacher," said Cathie. "My class'll be waiting at nine o'clock as usual. But you go if you want. Just don't be too late."

I could hardly reply that I didn't want to go, so it was agreed. I would be his escort home and his shield against spousal violence. At closing time, Ken went off to the toilet and I said to Cathie. "Thanks a bundle for that. I don't want to go back to his bloody house."

"Don't be like that," she said. "This is your chance for a bit of professional bonding. And he's too pissed to be careful about what he says, so you might find out something useful."

I doubted that, but she proved to be right.

As we saw Ken returning, she fired her parting shot. "I'll look forward to reading about it in your diary."

Was this her revenge for keeping her waiting about that morning's incident?

As we parted company in the street, Ken said to Cathie. "George is a great guy."

"I think so," she said. "That's why I put up with him."

"He's one of the best. We're going to become great pals. It was nice meeting you, Cathie. I'll see you again soon."

"Yes," said Cathie, clearly trying hard to disguise her lack of enthusiasm at this prospect. "Right, I'll be on my way. Don't keep him too late."

"A great girl that," said Ken as Cathie walked off.

"I think so," I said.

We made our way up Byres Road. It should have been a five-minute walk but it took a little longer. At one point I had to stand by while Ken was sick in the gutter. As usual, the streets were busy and passers-by gave us a wide berth.

I hoped that none of them knew me. Eventually we turned right into Vinicombe Street, a short street mainly lined with tenements. We stopped at one about halfway up and I waited again while Ken fumbled about for his key to the security door. We went up to the first floor and then there was a further pause while he laboriously sorted through his keys. Like our own flat, Ken's flat has two doors, an inner, glass-panelled one and a storm door. The storm door was closed, which wasn't a good sign.

We were met in the hall by a large, grim-faced woman. She wasn't actually armed with a rolling-pin, frying pan or any other weapon, but her general demeanour gave a similar impression. What frightened me most was that she resembled an older, nightmare version of Cathie. But I am nothing like Ken, I quickly told myself. My Cathie will have no reason to develop into maturity along a similar route.

"Where the fuck have —?" She broke off when she noticed me.

"This is George Anderson, the new English lecturer at the college. At the university. My wife Wilma."

"Pleased to meet you," she said, though she didn't look pleased and made no effort to shake hands.

"I've asked him back for a coffee."

"Fine. You'll need to make it yourself. I'm off to bed." She went into a room on the left, banging the door behind her. She probably assumed I would be as drunk as Ken and didn't feel inclined to hang about in order to make sure.

We made our way down the hall to the living room. It was a fairly nondescript room. None of the furniture or fittings looked particularly new, but it seemed well looked-after and the place was reasonably clean and tidy. This, I suspected, would be due to the efforts of Mrs Ramsay rather than her husband. The walls were papered with floral wallpaper, but bore few other decorations: a large print of a highland scene, a calendar, a mirror, a wall clock. An undistinguished décor, but at least lacking the obtrusive bad taste of Walter Bain's household.

I sat down at Ken's invitation and he said, "Do you want coffee or would you prefer a drink? I think I've got some whisky."

"A whisky would be fine," I said. Anything to get the visit over as quickly as possible.

He went off and came back with a half-full bottle of whisky, two glasses and a small jug of water. The glasses were in one hand, jammed together between thumb and forefinger, the jug in the other hand, the whisky bottle tucked under one arm. The scrambling about outside the door that I'd heard must have been his efforts to open it while bearing these encumbrances. Nevertheless, he managed to convey them all safely to the small coffee table. A lifetime's drinking had clearly equipped him with some skills.

The glass he offered me looked clean and I tried to forget that his grubby thumb had been inside it. "I don't have any ice," he said.

"That's OK." I managed to stop him from pouring me too generous a measure and topped up my drink with water.

He sat down opposite me. "Cheers," he said, taking a large sip.

"Cheers."

"I'm really glad you joined the team, George," he said.

"Thanks. So am I." This was sincere enough. As I said in an earlier entry, lecturing jobs are hard to come by.

"For a while it looked as if I'd be doing that new module all on my own. It would have been a fuckin' nightmare." For him, I thought, preparing all that new material probably would have been. I already knew that the choice of syllabus hadn't been entirely his, so he would have been outside his comfort zone, prevented from simply rehashing material that he'd used before. "But then Trotters decided to push for a new English lecturer. I'm still not quite sure why. I can see you're not one of these fuckin' lefties, but thank God they decided to appoint you anyway. Cheers."

"Cheers." It looked as if Adrian had tactfully refrained from sharing his theory with his friend. I told Ken about my meetings with Professor Trotwood and the Principal, which I hadn't had a chance to mention earlier. "I think the Principal was trying to sound me out about my political views. He's a strange man."

"I've never met him," he said. "But what about Trotters? Did he try to tell you what to put in your lectures? Are you supposed to toe the party line?"

"No. Quite the opposite. I wouldn't have done that anyway, but he seems to want me to be free to develop my own approach."

"That'll be fuckin' right. He's a devious bastard. But anyway, I'm glad you've joined us. Cheers."

"Cheers."

"Must go a place." He abruptly got up and left the room. Whether this was to urinate or be sick again I wasn't sure. Possibly both. Since he was no longer wearing a wire, it would have to remain a mystery.

As usual, I took advantage of his absence to indulge my curiosity. I got up and inspected the two small bookcases that sat against opposite walls of the room. The first was filled with paperbacks of popular fiction, the choice of Mrs Ramsay, I suspected. The other contained several rows of VHS videotapes, divided about half in half between commercially-produced tapes and home-made ones recorded from TV. The former were mainly films reflecting, I suspected, Mrs Ramsay's taste, but then one in particular caught my eye. It was Ken Russell's 1969 film of *Women in Love*. An unkind theory began to form in my mind.

I switched my attention to the home recordings. The titles were handwritten on labels stuck to the spines, so this took a little longer. Most, in an unfamiliar hand which I presumed to be Mrs Ramsay's, were of drama, mixed with some wildlife documentaries. Then I noticed two four-hour tapes inscribed with Ken's scrawl: "*Bleak House* 1" and "*Bleak House* 2". Presumably it was the BBC adaptation I referred to in my previous entry. My theory grew in strength.

I returned to my seat, anxious not to be caught by Ken on his return. I needn't have worried. He was gone so long that I was about to go out looking for him when he finally returned. He was staggering under the weight of a large cardboard box which he dumped on the floor between our two seats.

He slumped in his chair and recovered his breath. Then he said, "This is my pride and joy."

"Right," I said uncertainly.

"I think I can trust you, can't I, George?"

"What? Yes of course."

"Not a word to anyone else about this. Especially not to any of our colleagues. Especially not to Trotters or any of his fuckin' crew."

"Definitely not," I said, though I mentally made an exception of my diary and its single reader.

"Go on, have a look," he said.

I began to look through the contents of the box. It was filled with what these days are euphemistically described as graphic novels, but are better known to the general public as comics. The front pages mainly consisted of a cover illustration, over which was printed the title and author of the individual issue, but at the top of each there was a rectangular yellow box upon which the generic title of the series was printed in black letters: "Classic Comics" and, later in the series, "Classics Illustrated". They were all adaptations of well-known classics, in comic form. Many were of popular titles – *Tom Brown's Schooldays*, *Black Beauty*, *The Call of the Wild* – but many others were of books that regularly appear in English syllabi in both schools and universities. They included Shakespeare (*Hamlet*, *Macbeth*, *Julius Caesar*, *A Midsummer Night's Dream*) and Dickens (*A Tale of Two Cities*, *Oliver Twist*, *A Christmas Carol*, *David Copperfield*, *Great Expectations*), as well as a number of other key texts such as *Moby Dick*, *Huckleberry Finn*, *Wuthering Heights*, *Crime and Punishment*, *Silas Marner* and others. Conrad was represented by *Lord Jim*, and I remembered Ken mentioning that he had wanted this title on the syllabus but had been overruled.

I browsed through the contents of some of them. In *Hamlet* there were speech balloons containing soliloquies that occupied as much space as the drawings. I wondered how they'd managed to reduce *David Copperfield* to a forty-eight-page comic. They must have been very selective in their choice of material.

"I've got almost a full collection," said Ken. "There's another box in the hall cupboard. I've been collecting them since I was at school. They stopped doing new ones in the early 1970s, but you could still get them for a while after that."

Ken tried to give the impression that he had read all of the books at one time or another and merely used the comics as a useful *aide memoire*. But I'm not sure whether to believe him. Was it possible that he had waffled his way through an English degree on a diet of lecture notes and comics? Maybe he had. I already knew that he hadn't proceeded to honours, and I doubted whether his grades had ever earned him any class prizes.

We talked on for a while and he again swore me to silence. He offered me another drink, but I declined it and managed to make my way out, amid further vows of friendship and professional solidarity within our hostile working environment.

As I walked home, I reflected that Cathie had been right in her surmise that I might learn something useful from a drunken Ken. I now know that he definitely doesn't see me as a threat, which he might well have done, but that he wants to be friends. He had trusted me with information that could be dangerous to him, and I'd received further corroboration of his academic approach from the contents of his bookcase. If I wanted to make trouble for him I now had excellent ammunition. But that isn't my intention. If he's happy to let me follow my own path, then I'm content to let him continue with his.

Friday 30th October 1992

I'm afraid that my diary entries are likely to be shorter and less frequent in the immediate future. I've found recording my life to be an extremely enjoyable practice, which will continue, but it's very time-consuming. Preparing my lectures and tutorials for the rest of the semester involves a mountain of work, for which I'll reap the benefit in future years, but meanwhile it's practically a full-time job just to keep ahead of the students from week to week. Also, Cathie expects us to have a social life, a perfectly reasonable ambition which I'll do my best to fulfil.

Meanwhile, I'll continue to keep notes of anything interesting, pending more formal entries later.

Walter Bain continues to be a pest. I now answer very few of his appalling notes. However, unlike Gus, I haven't consigned them to the dustbin (or to the toilet). I am collecting them in an archive for future use. An album of ignorance. To be used in future, perhaps, as a counter-argument against any who may dispute the value of education.

Sunday 6th December 1992

Tomorrow is the submission date for my first-year coursework, up to 300 essays on the subject of the war poets.

I'm not sure what to expect, but will report my findings in due course. Meanwhile, this may be my last chance for some time to fill the month-plus gap since my last entry.

First of all, I must report on events on the home front. Over the last month my feelings about Walter Bain have developed from finding him a minor annoyance to one of being consumed by an overpowering hatred for the man. It has become an obsession. Cathie simply pretends that he doesn't exist, and I know that she's right, but I don't have this facility. Unfortunately, Bain seems to have worked this out. He is wary of Cathie and goes out of his way to catch me without her. At first this was when I failed to reply to his notes, which remain constant, but now he tries to catch me whether I reply or not. If I'm washing the stairs or the close, he will appear. If I take rubbish down to the bins, he follows me out. If he sees me approaching the building from his window, he meets me on the stairs. If he sees Cathie go out on her own, he will even knock on our front door. On days when I have no university commitments I have the option of working at home which would allow me make these appearances while he is away during the day. However, I greatly prefer to do most of my work on campus, to keep my home and place of work as separate as possible. Cathie is a little unsympathetic about my Bain obsession, as she doesn't understand why there's a problem at all, but at least she's agreed to take out the rubbish, which helps a bit.

This ability to ignore Bain seems to be a general tactic among the neighbours (apart, of course, from Henrietta Quayle, for whom my sympathy has grown). I already knew that it was Gus's policy, and shortly after my last diary entry I met our downstairs neighbour Arthur Briggs for the first time. He came out of his house while I was washing the close and we got talking. He is quite old and leads a reclusive life, but was friendly enough.

"I see Walter Bain has got you well trained," he said.

"I don't mind taking my turn," I said. "I'd do it with or without him."

"Don't let that man run your life," he said. "He'll do that if he can."

"I've noticed. My girlfriend says I should just ignore him, and so does Gus Mackinnon."

"You've met Gus, have you? Is he keeping sober these days?"

"Reasonably."

"That's very good advice from both of them. I've been completely ignoring Bain for nearly thirty years. It's the only way."

"Miss Quayle says —"

He interrupted me, laughing. "Don't listen to Henrietta. She's not the most reliable source. She and Bain have a history."

I wondered what he meant by this, but he didn't elaborate. "Anyway, it was nice meeting you," he said. "See you later." He locked his front door behind him and made his way out of the building.

There is no end to the subjects about which Bain pesters me. He complains about the neighbours, particularly Gus, he complains about the factor, he complains about any contractors sent to the building. He is infuriatingly repetitive on all of these subjects and others. The progress towards the installation of the security door has been a particular obsession. He has constantly pestered the factor about it and keeps trying to recruit my help in this. I tried to appease him by writing a polite letter to the factor and by making a couple of apologetic phone calls to Mr MacDuff, who is being driven mad by the man, but nothing seems to satisfy Bain.

I am anything but a violent man, but for the first time in my life I find myself entertaining fantasies about committing homicide. I would like to murder Walter Bain. I want to repeatedly batter him over the head with a blunt instrument until his stupid face and his stupid glasses and his stupid bald head are broken and bleeding and his brains – if you can call them that – are leaking out over the stairs, which I'll be happy to wash afterwards. I want to see his stupid knitted cardigan soaked in his blood and his stupid toes pointing to the sky. I want his endless flow of illiterate notes to be stopped forever, his insistent, repetitive, whining voice silenced for eternity.

Being sent to prison for life would be a small price to pay. The idea even has some attractions, as I would be able to get on with my writing in peace. I would miss Cathie, though. I wonder if she would stand by me.

The legal work for our acquisition of the flat was successfully completed by Marion McDade shortly after we took entry, confirming her to have been an excellent choice of lawyer. Under her guidance, Cathie wrote a letter of complaint to the Law Society about Bob Waddell. They replied, asking for more detail, which she supplied, but we've heard nothing further.

On campus, the semester has continued along the lines mapped out in my earlier entries. I proceeded with my first-year classes and have now finished most of my preparation. Numbers have fallen away slightly, but not quite as much as I feared. I've even discovered one or two students, still a minority, who actually seem to be interested in what I have to say. Some of them even began to read the texts, particularly once we got on to poetry, the lesser bulk of which made it easier for them to find a niche among the many other demands upon their time, both social and academic. I had cause for cautious optimism, which would now be put to the test when I read their coursework.

There have been further departmental meetings, equally lengthy, contentious, infuriating and inconclusive, but my earlier reports tell all that needs to be known about them. It was tedious enough having to sit through them, without boring the reader as well. Relations with Ken remain friendly, but our paths don't have to cross very often, which I'm happy about. He has made no further mention of our conversation in his house, and I suspect he may now regret the extent to which he made himself vulnerable by taking me into his confidence. Or maybe he doesn't remember any of it. We haven't met him in The Centurion again, though our visits there have been less frequent lately. I have got to know more of my colleagues, and learned more about my academic environment, from different perspectives.

A phenomenon that has been confirmed by many colleagues, and from my own observation, is the growth in new appointments engineered by the Principal. Many of them filled existing vacancies, some (like Stanley Warburton in our school) in academic posts, but more typically at management level. However, the incidence of vacancies doesn't seem to be frequent enough to accommodate the burgeoning management team and new jobs are also being created, generally creating an extra level of bureaucracy within the existing administration. The dubious rationale for this is that our new university status requires it. As a matter of procedure many of these jobs, particularly the existing posts, were advertised internally, but virtually all of them have gone to outsiders.

The crown prince of this new dynasty is a former colleague of principal Robert Gray called Ernest Goodfellow – a less appropriate name is difficult to imagine – who took up a new post of Vice Principal (Administration) at the beginning of this session. Since his arrival the incidence of new committees to be filled, forms to be completed, boxes to be ticked, and reports to be written, filed and forgotten has grown exponentially. Such is the bureaucratic dust cloud stirred up by this new broom that the university's communication paths, both paper and electronic, have almost choked to death. Much of this had a familiar feel, which prompted me to look out my copy of *Little Dorrit* and reacquaint myself with that paradigm of management science, the Circumlocution Office. Almost a century and a half ago Dickens had the measure of such people, but little seems to have changed.

A particular characteristic of our new Vice-Principal is his mastery of the acronym. Like many others who hold the English language sacred, the acronym is a pet hatred of mine. I know of no other device that can so quickly reduce a serviceable piece of prose into gibberish. Very few of those appearing in Vice-Principal Goodfellow's regular circulars are familiar to me. I suspect that he has invented many of them. The following is a recent example:

TRANSITIONAL IMPLEMENTATION OF
MANAGEMENT ENDS (TIME)

The Academic Progress and Enterprise Symposium (APES) has identified the following Interim Institutional Objectives (IIOs):

- Accelerated pathways to SCL
- Systemised and progressive depletion of SDRs
- External Monitoring to facilitate Effective Teaching In Classes (EMETIC)
- Portfolio Review And Taxonomy (PRAT)
- Incremental CNAA disengagement
- Research And Teaching Synchronisation (RATS)
- SHEFC and DELNI sensitive routes to RAE 96
- Pan-campus adoption of SMART targets

The ORGAN of TIME will be balanced as a reciprocal and logistical concept, as a function of HENRI but not of TOAD.

EG, VP(A)

3/11/92

I understood very little of this communication, but the third bullet point seems a little sinister. Could it be that Ken is about to be administered a purgative?

I was at first unable to make up my mind about the level of self-awareness experienced by the perpetrators of such communications. However, the abbreviated title of the body responsible for the above abomination, along with several of the bullet points that followed, have finally convinced me that these people have no sense of the absurd.

There is a story in academic circles that there was once a Professor of English at Glasgow University, or maybe it was Edinburgh, or maybe Aberdeen, or maybe somewhere else, whose name was Frederick Bacon, and who so lacked the sensitivity to the nuances of language expected from someone of his calling that he quite innocently named his only son Roland. I once thought this to be an urban folk tale, but now I'm less sure. Such people exist.

I wonder if this new language devised by the Vice-Principal is used orally as well as in writing. If so, secretaries or anyone else within earshot of an exchange between the Principal and his deputy must think that they are listening to a couple of aliens from *Star Trek* conversing in Klingon.

It is of course tempting to completely ignore these communications, to treat them merely as an annoying background static to be tuned out while focusing on the real work, but this leaves a residual worry that some of them may require action. Fortunately, Billy Trotwood, bless him, has come to the rescue. He has sifted through the Vice-Principal's edicts, picked out any few that need to be taken further, and translated them into comprehensible instructions for his staff. My admiration for the man continues to grow. He has not yet converted me to Marxism, nor is he ever likely to, but in any confrontation between him and the university management I know whose side I'm on.

Saturday 11th December 1992

Bob Waddell has been struck from the roll of solicitors by the Law Society. Gus thought (correctly) that we would be interested in this news and dropped in to tell us over a cup of tea and a chat: these days we're all visiting the pub less often and our paths haven't crossed there for some time. I felt a little guilty when I heard about it – I'm not vindictive by nature and was happy just to be free of the man – but Cathie is unrepentant. In any case, Gus assures us that we were just one of many complainants, the main surprise being that it has not happened years before. Unlike Ernie Dunlop, Bob Waddell had employed a book-keeper, mainly to ensure that his bills went out on time and were paid promptly, but it had the added benefit of keeping him free of the financial misappropriation which the Law Society can always be relied upon to treat promptly and severely. However, the overwhelming evidence of other professional misconduct had finally become too much for them to ignore.

Shortly after receiving this news, I got talking to Norrie Spence during a coffee break at work. I hadn't had much contact with him before then, as he doesn't mix much with colleagues, but he is friendly enough in a reserved way. He is a man in his forties – I already knew him to have been a contemporary of Gus, Ernie, Marion McDade and Bob Waddell – and is generally more conservatively dressed than most of his current colleagues. He still has the smooth manner of the successful lawyer, or of the successful fraudster. Wondering if I was venturing into delicate territory, I mentioned that I knew Gus and Ernie. But he responded positively.

"How are they?" he asked. "I haven't seen either of them for ages." *Occupying a prison cell can have that effect on your social life,* I thought. Surely he knew that I would be aware of his history? If so, he gave no indication of it. "I must pop into The Centurion one of these days," he continued. "It's long overdue. I hear Gus has got a job at the council. Is he keeping sober these days?"

"Most of the time. He did my girlfriend and me a big favour when we bought our flat."

I realised too late where this might be leading. And it did. Soon, the name of Bob Waddell came up. Had he heard the news? It seemed that he had.

"I hear the Law Society has finally caught up with our Bob," he said. "Not before time. It's been on the cards for ages."

A well-known saying about pots and kettles came to mind, but I tactfully refrained from commenting. We chatted for a few minutes more before I returned to my room and my essay marking.

Between home and work, I seem to be growing increasingly acquainted with the underbelly of the legal profession. At least Gus is still in practice, despite his bad patch a few years ago.

Wednesday 16 December 1992

Another cryptic message from the acronym king:

> Senate has decided that all academic staff should conform to TALOS at all times, while maintaining CAM and employing maximum use of VAAAS.
>
> Anyone not addressed by this should respond for remedy.
>
> EG, VP(A)
>
> 15/12/92

I have no idea what the first part of this means – he seems to have completely given up providing the full version for at least some of his abbreviations – but the last part seems to be saying, "If you didn't receive this, let me know and I'll send it to you."

Adrian tells me that, a few years back, there was a move to rename Woodside College. He claims that he nearly got approval for his proposal of Scottish Higher Institute of Technological Education before anyone caught on. I don't think I believe him, but why spoil a good story with an unwelcome infusion of the truth?

This has prompted me to amuse myself by thinking up some plausible sounding titles that have rude acronyms. They can even be assembled into sentences that almost make sense, for example: "The Central Union of National Technologies has decided to merge the Federal And Regional Training Scheme with the Joint Organisation for British-Born Youth." Cathie tells me that I'm being infantile, but this is simply a product of the mental state created by a day of marking first-year essays. Anyway, it hasn't stopped her from having a good laugh at my efforts.

Saturday 19th December 1992

The persistent dulling of the brain induced by student assessment – now thankfully almost complete – continues to make me find solace in my imagination. I have often given thought to the subject of my first novel. I have considered venturing into science fiction, which I believe to be the most interesting of the recognised genres and the one that offers the most literary potential.

The takeover of the university management by Principal Gray and his android army reminds me of the paranoid fantasies of the 1950s, when the fear of communist invasion was at its most virulent. The most famous example is the film *The Invasion of the Body Snatchers*, but this is only one of many films and books that imagined the gradual infiltration of society by extraterrestrials in human form.

It occurs to me that this could provide an excellent metaphor for a satire of academia. I've even come up with a title:

Arseholes from Outer Space.

These aliens do not attack us with laser cannons or by commanding hordes of flesh-eating zombies. Instead they enslave the human race by employing that most deadly and fearsome weapon of all: bureaucracy.

346

Continue watching this spot! Soon things will begin to happen!

Thank goodness my marking is almost finished. I've promised the students their marks before Christmas.

Tuesday 29th December 1992

It is the festive season and we are both enjoying a break from work. Semester One has finished apart, of course, from the unpleasant task of invigilating and marking the January exams. And that seems trivial compared with the prospect of sitting through the day-long departmental meeting that will in due course review and, I hope, approve the results.

But that is the only shadow to be cast upon my sunny outlook for the new year and the new semester. The enormous task of preparing my materials for the first year module is now complete. I will review them next year, of course, and make adjustments, but all the hard work is done. In Semester Two I'll be taking over much of Ken's second- and third-year input, to give him space to develop his new module on the detective novel. He has offered to lend me his notes to work from. I thanked him, but suspect that I'll have to begin from scratch. However, I'll have much more free time and should at last be able to pay some attention to my research, maybe even give further thought to my first novel.

I was curious about Ken's crime novel project and asked him about it. He tells me that he'll be focusing upon the Inspector Wexford novels by Ruth Rendell. I made other suggestions for him to consider, but he is fixed upon

Ruth Rendell. I have no quarrel with this as Rendell is a very interesting writer who, like Georges Simenon before her, has divided her output between police procedurals and much darker, psychological novels. With the latter in particular, she has developed far beyond the genre limitations of her early work. However, I doubt if these considerations influenced Ken's choice. Thanks to my earlier insight into his academic methods, I have formed an alternative theory. For several years now many of the Wexford novels have been dramatised on ITV, starring George Baker. I am convinced that a further inspection of Ken's bookcase at home would reveal a number of home-made recordings of these broadcasts. But I am in no hurry to arrange a return visit in order to confirm my theory.

I have mixed feelings about the first-year essays, now all marked and returned. The best I can say is that it could have been very much worse. Of a possible 300 submissions I received just under 230. A few of these were up to a week late, but the Social Science School seems to be tolerant of missed deadlines, so I decided to go along with this. Those I marked included a handful that were very good, saving me from complete despair, but the majority were either mediocre or absolutely awful. Many fell well below the recommended word length. There was much rehashing of my lectures, which some had recorded more accurately than others, though many had in fact read and tried to understand some of the poetry. But as a result of my provisional marking – I recorded my initial marks on a separate sheet – only about half managed to attain the pass mark of 40 per cent. Bearing in mind that many would be relying upon a good coursework mark to compensate for a poor exam performance, this did not bode well. I wanted to be honest, but I could be in danger of ruining the social science degree's reputation as a rival to the campus toilet paper.

I decided to consult Ken and showed him a few of the essays, which he skimmed through. "I think your marking's quite fair," he said finally, "but if you try to put these results through they'll have your balls for breakfast. The exam meeting will take a whole fuckin' week." As neither of these prospects particularly appealed to me, I took his advice and raised all my marks by 10 per cent. Then I changed a few more marginal fails into marginal passes. Finally, I further boosted the marks of some of the better ones, raising the class average a little more. This only left about a quarter of those submitted with a fail mark, and Ken assured me that these would be further depleted by resubmissions over the summer. When the deluge of medical certificates and other excuses has also been taken into account, the fail rate will be reduced further. We could avoid crucifixion, while maintaining some pretence of academic rigour.

This, of course, still left the seventy or so who hadn't submitted an essay at all. Virtually none of them had ever attended my tutorials. Most of them had probably dropped out, and this would be confirmed if they failed to show up for any of the exams.

Nevertheless, I had ended up being shamefully tolerant in my marking. Only a few months in the job, and I'm already compromising my principles. But I'm not a rebel by nature. I am a coward. That's why Cathie is so good for me. Together we have some backbone.

But that doesn't help me at university. I tell myself that my influence upon the few good students will make it all worthwhile. That with experience and good teaching I will be able to raise standards and have to compromise less. That in a few years' time I'll be well enough qualified to get a job at a better university, should I decide to take that path. That having a base upon which I can develop my research and my writing will allow my influence upon the world to be a positive one.

Do I really believe all this? I'm not sure. There is a breed of lecturer, of which many examples (including Ken) can be found at Strathkelvin University but also elsewhere, who have got away with doing a poor job for so long that they genuinely believe they're performing well. The academic community is an ideal environment for nurturing self-deception. This is particularly prevalent among those, the vast majority, who have never had to hold down a job in the outside world.

This of course includes me. But I'm determined not to become one of these deadbeats. I'm not by nature prone to self-deception: if anything, I am too self-critical. And there are many good academics, even at Strathkelvin University, who have not fallen into this trap. Adrian Armitage is one of them. My first-year results would have been much worse if the students hadn't attended his induction module, where they were taught essay writing, basic research methods and many other useful academic skills. I never discuss other staff members with students – I believe this to be very bad form – but they have a habit of volunteering information unbidden. They don't regard Ken very highly, for reasons recounted earlier, but their opinion of Adrian is much more positive. It seems that he is witty and entertaining, always helpful, and always approachable. They regard him as one of the good guys. All this, of course, merely confirms my own impression of the man.

All in all I am optimistic about my academic future at Strathkelvin University. I can do good work there, I have already met like-minded colleagues, and I have made friends. We will prevail, despite the onslaught from Vice-Principal Goodfellow and his band of APES, RATS and PRATS, as they try to bury us in paper, truss us up with every colour of tape, force-feed us EMETICS, and suffocate us in a toxic cloud of gobbledegook.

The prevailing issue on the home front has been the Bain problem. When I'm at work, I can almost cast him from my mind and reduce him to a distant shadow, which unfortunately grows into monstrous proportions as I approach home. I see him in every twitch of a curtain, hear him in every sound of an opening front door, every click of the letterbox, every ring of the phone. And more often than not these fears are justified, as his harassment has continued unabated. He has reduced me to a completely demoralised state in my own home.

Cathie had become seriously concerned about me. "This is completely ridiculous," she told me. "You need to sort out that idiot, once and for all. I can't do it for you."

"I don't want you to. I have some pride. But if you're going to tell me I need to man up, I'm going to get really annoyed."

"No dear," she said, giving me a hug. "You're already man enough for me. But for your own sake you need to deal with this. You're letting the man drive you mad. It can't be all that difficult to deal with him. He doesn't bother me, he no longer bothers Gus, he doesn't trouble Arthur Briggs or anyone else."

"Apart from Henrietta."

"Apart from her."

"And Mr MacDuff."

"And him. But he's our agent, he doesn't have a choice. And she's mad. What's your excuse?"

I didn't have one. She was right as usual. But, also typically, I prevaricated.

Then, last Wednesday, the day before Christmas Eve, it finally reached a climax. I had completed my marking marathon, the marks had been adjusted and returned to the students, and I returned home exhausted, intent upon a quiet evening. I was hardly in the door when I heard the sound of the letterbox. As I feared, it was the latest note from Bain.

I won't bother my reader(s) with a transcript. The style and content have been well documented already. It was his longest note yet, a full two pages from his cheap notebook, repeating *ad nauseam* all his obsessions about the factor, the security door, the contractors, our neighbours, Gus, all of the stuff I'd heard a dozen or more times before. It ended with, "I am dissapointed by your lack of progres. You must deel with it imediatley and oblige."

I became filled with rage. "The fucking bastard!" I shouted.

Cathie looked alarmed. Such a reaction and such language was untypical of me. I showed her the note. "What do you think of that?"

"You know what I think."

"That's it," I said. "I've had enough."

I brought out my red biro, which still had a small amount of ink left. I went through his note word for word, covering it with red scrawls, correcting every single piece of misspelling and bad grammar. At the end I wrote: "1/10. More effort required."

I showed it to Cathie. "Attaboy," she said. "Go with it."

We put on our coats and left the flat. I tiptoed upstairs, pushed the corrected note through Bain's letterbox, then we both hurried out of the building.

We hadn't eaten, and had a meal at a restaurant on Byres Road, emerging just after eight o'clock. I didn't feel like going home right away, though Cathie assured me that I'd have no more trouble from Bain. I can't believe that it's as simple as that, but she's usually right. In any case, he would never bother me when Cathie was with me. But Cathie didn't particularly want to go home either, so we went to The Centurion. We hadn't been there for a while, it was almost Christmas and we were on holiday.

As it happens, it will be a while before we go back there. But let me narrate the events in their right order.

Gus was there, sitting at a table with Ernie Dunlop and Norrie Spence, who had obviously carried out his resolve to look up his old friends. We went over to them, as I was anxious to tell Gus about my solution to the Bain problem, which I knew he'd appreciate. I introduced Norrie to Cathie and we chatted for a moment or two. However, I noticed a certain degree of reserve among them. I gained the impression that we weren't entirely welcome. Had we intruded upon some confidential legal discussion? At any rate, there was only one free seat at the table, so we decided to go off and find a table of our own.

But before we could leave, we discovered that the vacant seat at the table was in fact taken. The trio of (mostly) defunct lawyers became a quartet as Bob Waddell returned from the bar. He had been buying himself a drink, though whether this was his normal practice or a consequence of his recent unemployment was unclear. He saw Cathie and me and became filled with rage.

"How do you know these bastards?" he demanded of his friends. He had clearly been drinking for some time.

"They're my neighbours," said Gus. "Why, what's the matter?"

"They're the bastards who reported me to the Law Society."

"I don't think we were the only ones," said Cathie. "It seems to have been a habit among your clients. I can't really say I blame them."

"So you fucking admit it?"

"Certainly. Why deny it? We performed a useful public service."

"Somebody must have put you up to it. Who was it?" He glared around the group of his supposed friends.

"Don't look at me," said Gus innocently. "We just live in the same building."

"No one put us up to it," said Cathie. "We managed it entirely on our own. And we'd do it again. You were a bloody menace. A crook as well as an idiot."

"Fucking cunts!" yelled Waddell. His face had gone purple. He looked about to get violent, but that was something even drunks hesitated about when confronted with Cathie. "Fuck off! You're not wanted here."

"Don't worry," said Cathie. "We're particular about who we drink with."

We began to walk away. Then Waddell shouted after us, "You two are like a cartoon from the *Sunday Post!*"

I've never seen Cathie so angry. She strode back to their table and struck Waddell on the chin with a right hook, so powerfully that his chair toppled over and he sprawled on the floor, amid a shower of spilled drinks and smashed glasses.

The incident was witnessed by the pub's owner Richard Aitken and several of his bar staff, and soon Cathie was being escorted to the door, barred from the premises for the foreseeable future. Technically, I am still allowed in, but I followed her of course.

Next morning we met Gus in the street. "That's some woman you've got there, George," he said. "You'd better keep on the right side of her."

"Don't worry," said Cathie. "I'm very selective in my choice of opponent. My George has nothing to fear."

"I'm relieved to hear it." He told us that he and the others had managed to talk Waddell out of having Cathie charged with assault. They had felt that an appeal to his better nature would be a waste of time, so they'd emphasised the embarrassment of having to admit that he'd been floored by a woman in such a humiliating way. Once again we have good reason to be grateful to Gus.

I told him about my response to Bain's latest note. He had a good laugh. "Nice one," he said. "He won't bother you again." I hope he's right.

After we left The Centurion the previous evening we crossed the road to The Aragon. We found a place in a quiet corner and I bought drinks.

"Sorry about that," said Cathie when I returned to my seat. "But the bugger asked for it."

"Don't apologise," I said. "You were wonderful. Will you marry me?"

She was taken completely by surprise, but recovered quickly and accepted my proposal.

Tomorrow we're off to choose her engagement ring.

9. OUR DUMP

September 1988
Gus Mackinnon, Flat 3/1

"Take a look around you," said Ernie. "What do you see?"

"Is this a trick question? I'm not in the mood, Ernie."

"You're remarkably sober for the time of day. That's as near to the right mood as you'll ever be. Go on, what do you see?"

Gus lifted his eyes from the table and the half-full pint in front of him. Some might have described it as half-empty but, for no reason he could have defended, he was still an optimist. Especially when there was still time for several replacements before closing time. He was feeling pleased with himself because it was nearly nine o'clock and he'd still to have a whisky. He decided to indulge Ernie for a little while.

"I see the usual crowd of drunken punters."

"Not the people, the place."

"The *place*? It's a dump."

"I think that sums it up quite succinctly," said Ernie. "To be more specific, I would say that it's probably a 1930s dump. Not the Art Deco frivolity of the well-to-do, but a basic spit-and-sawdust utility where low-paid workers and the unemployed could match the mood of the Depression in depressing surroundings. The building's older, of course – late nineteenth century – but I reckon it was originally a shop unit or, more probably, several shop units which were knocked together. I suspect those bare iron pillars are a replacement for load-bearing walls."

"I didn't come in here for a lecture on architectural history, Ernie. I know you miss your days in court, winding up your local sheriff. But is this going anywhere?"

"That was cruel. But bear with me. We have established that the place is a dump. A God-awful, depressing dump. The sawdust and its solvents may be gone (if they were ever here in an actual sense) but bare, worn-out linoleum creates something of the same effect. The seats may now be padded, but almost everywhere the padding is making a bid for freedom. The dull-yellow décor of the walls and ceiling has been darkened even further by decades of tobacco smoke. Though it's more than ten years since the Sex Discrimination Act, there is still no Ladies' loo in the bar. The women have to join the queue for the single cubicle in the lounge, or nip across the road to The Aragon under the modest pretence that they feel like a brief change of scene. Since my wife's still talking to me, I'm a party to these secrets."

"OK, I'm sorry about the court jibe. You were boring me. Now you've got your own back."

"Sorry. It's just that Susan's been great. I don't know what I'd have done if she hadn't stuck by me."

"Your sins weren't of the Norrie Spence variety. They were a little more forgivable."

"Maybe."

Earlier that year, Ernie had suffered the same fate as Norrie Spence and had become the second of Gus's friends and contemporaries to have been struck from the roll of solicitors. Unlike Norrie, there had been no dishonesty and there had been no criminal charges. He had been more likely to forget to charge his clients than to steal their money. He had run a one-man firm and had thought that he would be saving money by not employing a book-keeper. But all his energies went into practising law and looking after his clients' interests. The result: an unprecedented degree of financial mismanagement and, eventually, bankruptcy. Since they had given several warnings that went unheeded, the Law Society felt compelled to strike him off.

He was now working as an unqualified assistant for another firm of solicitors, doing the work he loved (apart from appearing in court) without any financial responsibility. He was earning substantially less than the salary a qualified solicitor could command; however, Gus suspected that the amount of money he had actually taken home from the financial anarchy of his doomed business might not have been very much more.

Gus also suspected, now that the distasteful part was over, that Ernie was quite happy. Unlike Norrie, who had not reappeared since being released from prison, Ernie had not left the west end.

Nevertheless, it annoyed Gus to see someone like Ernie come to grief when Bob Waddell, whose attributes were exactly the opposite of Ernie's – meticulous finances and no regard for clients – was still successfully bludgeoning his way through legal practice.

"Anyway," said Ernie, "you agree something could usefully be done to this place?"

"Yes. Anything would be an improvement. Say a modest application of paint to brighten the yellow. New seat covers. Give the cleaners and bar staff a bonus, as an incentive in their fight against grime. Maybe a new floor or a Ladies' loo, though that's probably too much to expect from a miserable bastard like Aitken. Does he come from Paisley by any chance?"

"I've no idea. Why do you ask?"

"It doesn't matter. What's all this about?"

"You say that almost anything would be an improvement. How about a jukebox, playing loud pop music?"

"For God's sake! Anything *except* that."

"Really? How about two new fruit machines, flashier, noisier, no longer tucked away in a corner. Noxious designer drinks to attract young yuppies. Since you'll need to leave room in the glass for the expensive mixers, spirit measures would be down from a quarter to a fifth of a gill."

"*What*? I hope this is just your sick fantasy, Dunlop."

"Unfortunately not. It's all from a reliable source."

"Who?"

"Brian Martin. Aitken told him all about it."

"Martin? I don't talk to that bastard."

"Of course not. You think Aitken would have confided in anyone who talked to you? Unfortunately, he overlooked me as a middleman. I've made some enquiries of my own. It's all true."

"Christ!"

"And there's more. Meals."

"Meals?"

"Served all day from an extensive menu."

"But they already do pie and beans. Maybe they could add toasties, but…"

"Not everyone shares your simple tastes, Gus. Times change. Byres Road is moving up market, even the lower part. Aitken has his ear to the ground, and he hears the growing rumble of a bandwagon."

"You mean we'd have to sit beside people who've come here to *eat*?"

"No. I haven't finished. As part of the general plan, the place will be gutted, down to its bare shell. The bar and lounge will become one. This will create enough extra space for a kitchen. A new, colourfully-tiled and pristine Gents' bog will arise from the ruins of the old one, and the site of both lounge toilets will combine to make room for a state-of-the-art Ladies' facility."

"I don't grudge them that. But we don't want to mix with those people from the lounge. They're from a different planet."

"You won't have to. You're very slow today, Gus. Aitken doesn't want them. He doesn't want us. He wants an entirely new clientele."

Gus was reduced to silence. He took a large gulp from his pint. The thought of adding a quarter-gill of Grouse, now that it was an endangered species, was becoming compulsive. "But where would we go?" he said eventually. "This is the last outpost of civilisation in the whole damn area."

"You're asking the wrong question, Gus. It's not 'Where would we go?' it's 'What are we going to do about it?'"

"What can we?"

"We have two sharp legal brains between us. One and a half, anyway. I suppose we could write to the Secretary of State, urging him to add these premises to his list of buildings of special architectural or historic interest. Try to convince him that the interior deserves to be preserved as a prime example of a 1930s spit and sawdust dump. Though I can imagine what his reply might be."

"Fuck off?"

"Essentially. Couched, of course, in terms more suitable to the Civil Service. Though you can never be sure what those wankers in the Scottish Office might decide needs preservation. Maybe manky depression-era dunnies are the latest flavour, their spartan functionalism an interesting contrast to Art Deco elegance and a successor to the Mackintosh school. Though I rather doubt it. We can always try listing, if only to give the inspectors a laugh. But we'll also need an alternative tactic, a number of alternative tactics."

"We will, will we?"

"Oh yes. You're our key man, Gus. Unlike some of your unfortunate friends, you're still on the roll of solicitors. You've got a first-class brain, when you're not dousing it in drink. And, if I may say so, since you retired from your firm, you need something to give you an interest, something to get you out of bed in the morning."

"Oh I do, do I?"

"Yes," said Ernie. "You do."

Ernie was right. Since he had retired from the firm of Murray & Mackinnon (now Murray & Forbes) almost a year before, Gus had done little he could call constructive. From the initial sum he had received for his share of the business, he had paid off his mortgage, settled some money on his children, and had now almost finished drinking the balance. A further instalment was due in a month's time, but that was no reason to carry on in the same way. He had previously attributed his drinking to the stress caused by his work. What was his excuse now?

In the past year his activities had basically been reduced to two: drinking and Bain-baiting. And lately the latter, his most enduring hobby, had reduced in scope. He and his downstairs neighbour were no longer on speaking terms, their only communications the occasional abusive and illiterate note, and the banging on the ceiling whenever Gus dared to turn his hi-fi above a minimal level. He didn't even do that very often these days, not out of consideration to Walter Bain, but because his interest in music, along with everything else, had waned as alcohol took over. When was the last time he had bought a new record? He didn't even have a CD deck. To buy one compatible with his system would have cost at least £200 of drinking money.

He had given much thought to these things recently, usually in the morning during his prolonged long lie, in between dozing off to the music on his clock radio. Eventually he would get up and have a light breakfast, if he had anything in. Usually there would be fruit juice – an essential morning remedy – and some instant coffee, but little more. Then he would watch TV until he could summon up enough energy to go out for a curer.

There was one basic discipline that he had managed to hang on to. He never kept alcohol in the house. And he never went out without washing, shaving, and ironing a clean shirt to wear. He was still a lawyer, there were certain standards he had to maintain. He therefore presented himself with a daily dilemma: balancing his need for a drink against the lassitude that prevented him from going through the ritual that was necessary before he could obtain one.

Sometimes it was almost evening before he had his first drink. Usually he would have it in a pub other than The Centurion, where he was less likely to get into company that would detain him. Then he would visit the University Café for a plate of soup and a fry-up, before going up to The Centurion for the main evening session.

Lately he had been playing another game, trying to confine his drinking to beer. He would attempt to cut out spirits altogether, or reserve his whisky as a final nightcap, in response to the call for last orders.

It was pathetic. He fully appreciated this every morning during his guilt-infused hangovers. The cycle could only get worse unless he could find a way of breaking it.

Occasionally he would get out early enough for a pub lunch, though that was liable to start him drinking too early. He had no objection to pub lunches, only to the prospect of having them in The Centurion. The Centurion was a specialist pub. It was a drinking den. That was its sole function, its essential nature, the reason for its existence. It was a place where one could consume the maximum amount of drink together with the minimum of amenity, in accordance with the long-standing west of Scotland tradition; a retreat where those brought up in Calvinist or Catholic guilt could indulge this sensation by means of dipsomania in appropriately depressing surroundings. People who wanted to eat, sometimes including him, were well catered for nearby.

The more he thought about it, the more Ernie's idea appealed to Gus. Here was a project that would be close to his heart, one that might well provide the stimulus he was looking for. The Centurion's virtues, he now realised, were mainly negative ones. It was only when presented with a nightmare alternative that you appreciated how considerable they were.

And now that Bain-baiting was on the wane, Gus could think of no better substitute for his attentions than Dick Aitken, the owner of the pub. The man whose very name denoted his character as a self-abuser. Some might look upon the proposed undertaking as biting the hand that refreshed him, but few of them would be people who knew the man. The contempt in which most of his customers held Aitken was only matched by his feelings for them. If there had ever been any doubt about this, his plans for the transformation of the pub had proved it.

Infected by Ernie's enthusiasm, and less debilitated than usual by the evening session, Gus arose early next morning. He added to his usual toilet routine by polishing his black shoes and looking out his best suit. Fortunately, he had hung it away carefully during some moment of passing sobriety and it didn't need pressing. He did check that the trouser zip had not fossilised from disuse. The smart, lawyerly image he was trying to re-create would not be helped by a burst fly.

The unusual sound of his storm door being closed and locked at ten in the morning – now that he no longer had any need to avoid Walter Bain, he had taken to using the big key again – provoked a response from downstairs. He had expected some kind of reaction from the Bain household. Not from the man himself – he would be at his work, harassing the factor or some other victim with phone calls at his employer's expense – but from Mrs Bain as his proxy. Never a direct confrontation, but perhaps the slight opening of a front door, an indication that the Bain surveillance system remained in operation during the man's absence. A sign of Bain solidarity in the face of universal opposition. However, now that he thought about it, there had been less evidence of this recently. Gus reflected that, even although she had been his neighbour for as long as her husband, he knew hardly anything about Mrs Bain. She remained a shadow, a ghost, an enigmatic figure.

He passed the closed and silent Bain residence and found Henrietta Quayle waiting for him on the next landing. An early burglar had probably seemed a likelier prospect than an early Gus, and her relief was obvious when she saw him. Her perpetual background anxiety had suddenly peaked, but was now temporarily on the wane. Her storm door had barely been open, ready to be slammed shut if necessary, and she now opened it fully.

"Morning, Henrietta."

"Good morning. You're out early this morning."

"Yes, I suppose I am."

"Are you working again?"

Gus had not told his neighbours about his retirement from legal practice. He would never on principle have given any personal information to Bain, even if they had been on speaking terms, and he knew that nothing he said to Henrietta would have remained confidential for long under Bain's interrogation techniques. But his recent unemployment would not have been difficult for them to deduce.

"Not quite. I'm going down to the City Chambers. I'm looking into a small legal matter for some friends."

"I didn't mean to be… I hope you don't think…"

"It's OK, Henrietta. I haven't seen you much lately, but I hope we're still friends."

"Oh. Yes. Would… I mean, would you like to come in for a coffee?" She was now speaking in a stage whisper, her usual way of countering the stairwell's amplifying effect.

Gus humoured her by replying in a like manner. Besides, he had no desire to supply the Bains with any gratuitous information, however trivial. "I'm sorry, Henrietta, I'll need to get on my way. Maybe another time soon, if you can catch me some other morning before the pubs open."

"Oh." She seemed uncertain how to reply. She was never sure when he was joking. Gus was about to take his leave, but detected that there was something else she wanted to say, something she was finding difficult to get out.

"What is it, Henrietta?"

"I'm sorry. I don't…"

"Go on. Tell me."

Her voice was now barely audible. "Mr Bain doesn't like it when you leave the front gate open at night." She shrank back, afraid of his response.

Gus laughed. "Is that all? I knew that gate would be more trouble than it was worth." He had raised his voice a little, but lowered it again on seeing her terrified reaction. "What's it defending us from? A wee Jack Russell could jump over the damn thing. It certainly won't keep out many burglars. Even the most stupid of them could figure out how to open the latch."

He saw that this reminder of her obsession was not improving matters. She shrank back further. "It annoys Mr Bain when the gate's left open."

"I know. I've received a few ungrammatical notes to that effect. I've put them in my album."

"You shouldn't annoy Mr Bain."

"Yes I should. It's practically the only fun I get nowadays."

"Oh Mr Mackinnon!"

"Gus."

"Gus. You're a terrible man." Other feelings competed with her terror and she managed a small laugh. "You know, he doesn't appreciate all the work you did getting the building improved. It's not fair."

"He doesn't do appreciation. Don't worry, I can handle his rejection."

"Oh dear. It's just that he keeps going on and on about the gate. He talks to me as if it was my fault. Sometimes I go downstairs and close it after you."

"You shouldn't do that, Henrietta. It's well past your bedtime when I get back. All right, I'll try to remember to shut it from now on. Just for you, mind, definitely not for him."

"Thanks, Gus. I'm sorry if…"

"It's all right, Henrietta. It's not a problem. Look, I'll need to get going. I'll see you again soon."

"Oh. Yes. Goodbye."

"'Bye."

Gus made his way out of the building. It was a while since he'd had to run the stair gauntlet. He'd got off fairly lightly.

It was a nice morning. Even though it was now well after ten, there was still a freshness in the air which he he'd recently missed out on during his mornings in bed. He was even tempted to walk into the city centre. But the morning was already slipping by and he had business to conduct.

He took the subway from Hillhead to Buchanan Street and walked round to George Square. At its far end, the Victorian opulence of the City Chambers reminded downtrodden Glaswegians that the city had once known better days, that it had formerly occupied an important position at the centre of the British Empire. The whole square looked good. The last few years' refurbishment had included commercial and public buildings as well as houses, and the city centre was looking better than it had done for years. This all helped to enhance Gus's buoyant mood.

He walked past the City Chambers and down George Street. Council buildings extended for some way down the street. A few hundred yards along, he entered a door and went upstairs to the first floor.

The reception area of the Planning Department was designed exactly for the purpose of Gus's visit. Opposite the enquiries window, there was an open area with a large wooden table and chairs. Gus made his request at the window, and soon afterwards he sat down at the table with a copy of Aitken's planning application. He examined it carefully and took detailed notes. Then he returned the papers and made his way to the Building Control office, where he saw more plans and made further notes.

Ernie had been right. It was all there. The council didn't concern itself with jukeboxes or fruit machines, or other such symptoms of decadent modern taste, or with whether pubs chose to honour the Scottish tradition of serving spirits in a quarter-gill measure. In Gus's view these were all legitimate matters of public concern. But there was enough. The gutting of the interior, the construction of the new kitchen, the new toilets, the proposed addition of a restaurant use, all were documented.

Moreover, there was still time to lodge objections.

When he arrived back in George Square it was almost 1 pm. What next? The day's task had been achieved. He was meeting Ernie that evening to discuss the project further. It wouldn't be a very fruitful meeting if he spent the afternoon drinking.

He found a Chinese restaurant and went in for a business lunch – a pub lunch would have been too dangerous – then went to the cinema. It seemed like too nice a day to spend in a dark hall, but he knew what the result would be if he decided to enjoy the sunshine. The streets of Glasgow were filled with pubs. He would never manage to walk past all of them.

It was the first time he'd gone to a film for years. It was called *The Dead Pool* and starred Clint Eastwood, reprising his role as the San Francisco detective Dirty Harry. As with the film's predecessors, he couldn't really approve of its violent and simplistic approach to law enforcement, but took a guilty pleasure in it just the same. He had been a regular cinema-goer as a young man, but family life, then work, then drink had progressively got in the way. He enjoyed the film and decided he should go to the cinema more often. It would be a good way of getting out of the house without ending up in the pub, or at least beginning the day there.

When he came out he spent some time browsing round a record shop. They didn't sell vinyl LPs any more: he would really need to see about getting a CD deck. He walked down Sauchiehall Street, up to Charing Cross. Now that the west end was in his sights, he was walking past the open pub doors easily, as if he'd been doing it all his life. Eventually he was skirting Kelvingrove Park and approaching the art gallery. Was there time to reacquaint himself with the Rembrandts and the French Impressionists? Maybe on another occasion. He had done enough for one day.

He had a snack in the University Café, then went up to The Centurion. Ernie arrived at eight o'clock.

When Ernie arrived, Gus excused himself from the company he was with, and they retreated to a corner. Aitken wasn't in – he avoided evenings as often as he could – but it was as well to keep out of earshot while hatching a conspiracy.

"You're looking well," said Ernie.

"For God's sake, you saw me only last night."

"I mean, you seem amazingly sober."

"This is my second pint of the day."

"My scheme's working then?"

"Fuck off. Anyway, I've seen the planning and building applications. It's all as you said. The deadline for lodging objections is next Friday."

"That's a bit tight."

"They'll probably accept them later than that. But what's our interest to lodge objections? Byres Road Alcoholics? Not the most impressive pressure group."

"*We* won't lodge the objections," said Ernie. "We don't want it to look as if everything's coming from the same source. Think about it. This place occupies the ground floor of two tenement blocks. Above us are – how many? – at least six flats. The same number again immediately adjoining. Already they put up with disgusting drunks like you hanging about the streets at all hours. Now, when they want some fresh air in the house, they'll get cooking smells: fish and chips, steak pie, scampi, the whole of Aitken's gourmet menu, floating in, all day, every day."

"*I'd* object to that. Maybe some of them already have. They should all have been notified of the application."

"Probably, but there's no harm in giving them a little nudge."

"What do you suggest? Knocking on all their doors?"

"There's no need. I know at least a couple of them who drink in here. We can have a wee word, get them to talk to their neighbours, offer to anyone who wants it the benefit of our free advice."

"Good thinking."

"And that's not all. I received this from Meadowbank House today." Ernie brought a copy of a legal deed from his pocket and handed it to Gus.

"What is it?"

"Aitken's lease. It could be our trump card."

"How'd you get on to that?

"I still work in a law office. I have contacts."

Gus examined the lease and Ernie explained what he'd found out. Much of it was familiar, from stories Gus had heard before but never had any reason to take an interest in. Until now. It seemed that Aitken didn't own the pub. At one time he had, but a number of years back it had been compulsorily acquired by the council, which had intended to demolish the whole block. Aitken had stayed on as the council's tenant, under a succession of yearly leases, until such time as the council would be ready to proceed with their plans. With eviction hanging over him, Aitken had had no incentive to spend money on improvements. The run-down condition of the pub was not just a result of his meanness, though that had undoubtedly played a part.

But then refurbishment fever had gripped the city and the council had changed its plans. Environmental and repair grants had replaced the bulldozer. Like Gus's own building, the row of tenements that housed The Centurion had been pinned back together, pointed, reroofed and stone-cleaned. Only the previous year, the council had granted Aitken a new, 25-year lease. Once more he had a capital asset to exploit. The old Centurion was a carbuncle on the backside of this brave new block. Radical cosmetic surgery was needed and (Aitken obviously reckoned) was likely to be profitable.

"He can't go ahead without his landlord's consent," said Ernie. "It's what you'd expect but, as you can see, it's all there in the lease. So the council's involved here in several capacities. They're wearing their landlord's hat as well as all the others. Aitken needs to get his plans approved, not only by the Planning Committee and Building Control, but by the council's Property Committee as well. It's their own property he wants to muck about with. Maybe someone should point that out to them. The stupid bastards may not have noticed."

"Absolutely," said Gus. "So we petition their Property Committee as well. On what grounds? Our sacrosanct drinking habits?"

"I don't think so. We'll think of something. Social reasons maybe? Will the new Centurion, or whatever trendy shite of a title they give it, cater for senior citizens?" Ernie pointed over to Death Row, where the Brigadier, the Brothers Grimm and two of their pals sat in a line, clutching their quarter-gills as they glowered at the customers passing in and out of the Gents' toilet.

"I doubt it," said Gus. "You know, I think we're making progress. It's thirsty work, hatching conspiracies. What you for?"

"Same again."

Gus went up to the bar and returned with two pints.

"I'd heard about the compulsory purchase before," he said, "but I'd forgotten about it. So the bugger's sitting on a nice compensation payment from the council. I wondered where he was getting the money from."

"That was more than ten years ago," said Ernie. "I don't know how much of it he has left. Maybe he's a secret gambler, or maybe he had it all invested in the stock market at the time of last year's crash. I certainly hope so. Whatever's the case, he's not paying for all of it himself. I happen to know that he's applied for a loan from one of the brewers."

"Damn it."

"Quite."

It had seemed to Gus that Aitken's plans already promised the worst imaginable scenario. But further deterioration was indeed possible. One of The Centurion's virtues, hitherto taken for granted, was being a free house. But brewers didn't grant loans as simple financial transactions. There would be strings. All of the main companies owned or were affiliated to distilleries. If Aitken acted according to his well-known form, his gantry would still include bottles labelled as Grouse, Bells and White & Mackay, but they would now be filled with cheap house whisky. When the labels became dowdy, there were plenty of local artists who could be cheaply commissioned to touch them up.

"You know," said Gus. "The brewers won't want to back Aitken's scheme unless they think it's a good investment."

"That goes without saying."

"But is it? Think about it. On paper it probably looks like a good plan. Knocking the bar and lounge together has worked well elsewhere. Your traditional Glasgow pub had a male-only public bar. The lounge was where the same guys took their womenfolk on weekends and special occasions. But that doesn't cater for women's liberation and a growing band of female alcoholics. So instead you get one big unisex bar with all those little extras that women tend to go for."

"Like food?"

"Exactly. But The Centurion's different. It was originally designed in the same mould, but that's not how it's used any more. In Byres Road women were liberated earlier, ahead of the infrastructure. Just as many women come into this place as men. It may be hard on their bladders, but they're still here. The lounge has a completely separate clientele. Think of it. Aitken effectively has two pubs under one roof. He wants to spend a fortune, throw out two sets of customers and replace them with… what? A crowd of young trendies who're already well catered for throughout the area. Can he compete with Bonhams or The Ubiquitous Chip? Does his plan sound viable to you?"

"You mean," said Ernie, "if we stop him we'll be doing him a favour?"

"For Christ's sake don't say that," said Gus. "You'll rob me of all motivation."

Over the next few days their project took off on several fronts. Gus wrote most of the letters (a speciality of his) and Ernie had them typed out at his office. Gus found that he was enjoying himself and managed to keep his drinking to a minimum.

Ernie spoke to the flat residents, who spoke to their neighbours, and eventually a dozen sets of objections were sent to the council. They found out which brewer Aitken had applied to and a letter was sent, casting doubt upon the financial wisdom of the plans. They even wrote to the Scottish Office, proposing the building as a candidate for listing, though they knew that was a long shot.

They also organised a petition. It would not do if their protest merely seemed like a petulant complaint from two drunken former lawyers. It had to come from all of The Centurion's customers, regular and occasional, or as many of them as could be reached within the short time available. In less than three weeks the council's Property Committee was due to meet and Aitken's plans were on the agenda.

The petition was addressed to Aitken. They didn't want it to seem as if they were going behind his back, though they didn't expect him to act upon it. The copies they would send to the council and make available to the media were more likely to be effective. They took some care over the wording:

We, the undersigned, the regular customers of The Centurion bar and lounge, want to express our concern about the development proposals submitted to Glasgow Council. We feel that these are likely to destroy the unique character and atmosphere of the pub. Because of these virtues, most of us have been coming here for many years in preference to other Byres Road pubs. We hope that the number of signatures below will assure you that there is a substantial market for the pub in its present form, and we look forward to continuing our patronage for many years in the future.

They felt that this contained nothing that Aitken could reasonably take objection to. He *would* take objection to it, of course, but it was the appearance that mattered.

They made a number of copies and distributed them among volunteers for circulation. They insisted that the petition wording should head every sheet of signatures; they could not afford any accusations that the signatories had thought they were signing something else. The petition was circulated nightly round the customers in the bar and the lounge. It was taken round the other Byres Road pubs, whose customers sometimes frequented The Centurion. It was taken by Glasgow University lecturers to their colleagues and by students to the students' unions. It was passed round at parties, at people's workplaces, to any place where there might lurk a Centurion customer, or someone who might pass muster as one.

Both Gus and Ernie were taken aback at the response. Soon they were running off extra copies of the petition on a daily basis. Everyone who drank in The Centurion, or knew of it (it was a well-known pub in a well-known area) gave enthusiastic support. In less than a fortnight they had collected almost a thousand signatures.

Such was the groundswell of genuine support, that they subjected the signed sheets to a rigorous editing process. Inevitably, many people had signed when drunk. It would take only a few obviously fake signatures to discredit the whole undertaking. Isolated offenders were obliterated by the application of correction fluid; if there were too many on one page, the page was scrapped and as many as possible of the genuine signatures obtained again. In this way they eliminated those who had signed twice by mistake, those with addresses too far off to possibly pass for regulars, those known to be barred from The Centurion, and many others whose authenticity was dubious.

This last category included Fred Quimby, Sir Osis O'Liver, Ivor Biggin, Menzies Biggar, Donald Duck, Wee Alec, Big Betty, Richard Cranium, Elf, Johnny Rubber, Walter Bain – who signed *his* name? – Dick Pullar, Willie Player, Ruby Cube, Woy Jenkins, Margaret Thatcher, Ronald Reagan, Michael Gorbachev, Mary Hill, Bella Houston, Kelvin Hall, Albert Square, Hal E.L. Ooyah, Sam Handwich, Ella Salmon, Ted R. Hoof, Charlie Chappin (Dominoes Captain), Isa Barr (Weatherwoman), Monty Python, Basil Fawlty, Derek Trotter, Barbara Carthorse, Julie Kipper, Paddy Whacker (Hired Assassin), Helena Handcart, Mel O'Drama (c/o BBC Scotland), Europa Gumtree, James T. Kirk, Darth Vader, Luke Skywalker, Clark Kent, Lois Lane, Lex Luthor, Annie Hooten, Mick Jagger, Hen Broon, Sid Vicious, Penny Tray, Daisy Pusher (Deceased), Heidi High, Ann O'Rak, Johnny Walker, Jack Daniel, Julie Piece, Stanley Tool, Armand A. Legge, Aaron G. String, Jack McCarrup (Mechanic), Phil McCarrup (Petrol Station Attendant), Attila McCunn, Art Deco, Al Fresco, Millie O'Nair, Ailsa Craig, Isla White, Carrie Out, Ethel Alcohol, Millie Litre, Annie Seed, Rhoda Dendron, Rosetta Stone, Grannie Smith, Orson Parsley, Titus A Newt, Olive Twister, Lance Boyle, Wally Dugg, Matt Emulsion, Dickie Brickie, Dougie Woogie, Stevie Stovie, Phyllis Stein, Doris Decker, Patrick Thistle etc.

Some of these were easy to spot. The Centurion didn't have a dominoes team. No major politicians had ever been seen there, not even the Right Honourable Roy Jenkins, either before or after losing his seat at the previous year's election. And although the captain of the Starship Enterprise had also autographed the wall of the Gents' toilet, that too was believed to be a forgery. One or two other signatures of dubious provenance were only picked up after further readings by different people.

A genuine Winston Churchill – born to patriotic parents soon after World War Two – complained about being removed, but they explained to him why it was for the best.

Many different types of people frequented The Centurion, of all ages and from all backgrounds, reflecting its position at the centre of the Byres Road melting-pot. There were many that either Gus or Ernie knew to speak to, but many more whom they only knew by sight. Now the disparate groups became united, their common dislike of Aitken finding focus in their opposition to his plans. A loose collection of familiar and less familiar faces was turning into a community. Danny Boyd – who, now that he was working, had swapped situations with Gus – proved a useful bridge to many regulars whom Gus had hardly known before. They even became on speaking terms with the lounge customers.

Aitken's few confidants, those whom he favoured as a pretext for ignoring the bulk of his customers, were also happy to sign the petition. "They don't like him any more than the rest of us," said Ernie. "They're just arselickers by nature. They'll go to any length to secure a free half at New Year."

"They'd better support us then. Otherwise, next year it's going to be a fifth of a gill."

It was inevitable that Aitken would find out what was going on, though it took him several days. Then one evening he made a point of taking Gus's order at the bar, something that had not happened for a number of years.

As he handed Gus his pint and took his money, he said, "What's this I hear about a petition?"

Gus had a few moments to think of a reply while Aitken was fetching his change. His first impulse was to deny any knowledge – Aitken's involvement could only complicate things – but he quickly realised that wouldn't do. Aitken clearly knew Gus was behind the petition: he would not have spoken to him otherwise. How much did he know apart from that? Better to tell him as little as possible.

"The regulars are unhappy about your plans for this place. They're signing a petition about it."

"What plans are these?"

Gus was now glad he hadn't denied it. That type of dishonesty was more appropriate to someone like Aitken.

"The plans you've lodged with the council. In the Planning Department and with Building Control."

"Oh yes. You're a *lawyer* aren't you?" Aitken was pretending to be friendly, but the sneer was apparent. He'd probably noticed that Gus had been down on his luck lately.

"That's right."

"They're paying you a fee, are they?"

"No, it's a labour of love. Call it my hobby."

"Really?" Aitken didn't seem sure how to respond. He knew Gus much less well than Gus knew him. In Aitken's case there was much less to know. If he had any hidden virtues, or other complexities of character, they were very well hidden.

Maybe Aitken's uncertainty of him could be used to advantage. At the very least, he might as well have some fun at the bastard's expense. "You've got a first-class pub here, Mr Aitken. It's got a great atmosphere, a unique mix of customers. It's easily the best pub in Byres Road. It has all the traditional features that seem to be disappearing everywhere else."

Like lack of hygiene, poor amenities and general indifference to the customers. But if the times were bad enough, failure to move with them was a virtue in itself. The Centurion had many good qualities, though they had all come about by accident; for none of them was Aitken due any credit. But there was no point in telling him that.

"You really think so?" Aitken still seemed uncertain. He was clearly flattered by the praise of his establishment, but even he must have realised that it had most of the traditional features of a rubbish tip.

"Absolutely. Look at the people who drink here: lawyers, professors, doctors, architects, even the students are mostly postgrad, doing PhDs. They like a place where they can get some peace and quiet, indulge in the art of drunken conversation. They don't want invasions of androids from Bonhams or the Chip."

Gus had convinced himself, never mind Aitken. It was mostly true, of course. Did Aitken know that the generally casual appearance of his customers concealed people of such distinction? Possibly not. Maybe he should try to convince Aitken that half of them were eccentric millionaires. No, that would just encourage him to put up his prices.

It wouldn't make any difference, of course. Aitken, the guardian of traditional values, would not win out over Aitken the money-grubbing entrepreneur.

"So do I get to see this petition?"

"Of course. It's addressed to you. As soon as we've finished collecting signatures, we'll hand it over."

"I'll look forward to it."

Was Aitken conceited enough – or stupid enough – to think that they had gone to so much trouble just to appeal to his good nature? That it hadn't occurred to them to send a copy of the petition to the council, or to contact the media? Surely not. But there was no harm in keeping that information to themselves for the time being. Aitken would see the rest of their hand soon enough.

When they had collected a thousand genuine signatures they handed a copy of the petition to Aitken and sent another copy to the council; they had already warned the latter in advance and requested a hearing at the Property Committee's meeting.

Several journalists had signed the petition and had offered to help. Articles appeared in the *Glasgow Herald*, the *Daily Express* and the *Evening Times*. A debate began in the letters column of the *Herald*, the main contributors being Centurion regulars whom Gus and Ernie had put up to it. Gus was interviewed on TV and on the radio. A TV crew tried to film inside the pub, but were refused access by Aitken. This was probably a mistake on his part. The features of The Centurion the petitioners were so keen to preserve would not easily be picked up by a camera. More probably the place the campaigners were praising so highly would have been exposed on everyone's screens as an undistinguished fleapit, full of scruffy people.

In all of these outlets the same themes were repeated: the need to preserve a traditional pub that catered for all ages and social groups; the nuisance that would be caused by cooking smells in a building full of flats; the superfluity of such a development in an area packed with restaurants, takeaways and pubs that already served food.

When Gus appeared in The Centurion after his TV interview, he was greeted with a round of applause. Aitken was behind the bar, but didn't join in.

Most of the coverage had been sympathetic to the protest, drawing heavily upon the details of the petitioners' case. The backlash came in a local Sunday tabloid, *The Sunday Scoop*:

SAVE OUR LOCAL CESSPIT

We've been hearing a lot lately about the campaign by the regulars of west end pub The Centurion to stop the owner from giving his establishment a long-overdue facelift.

Curious, we sent a *Scoop* reporter to investigate. Instead of the much-vaunted "haven of traditional pub culture" our stunned scribe found:

- A dingy bar that has not seen a lick of paint for years.
- Stuffing sprouting from the seats.
- A filthy toilet without soap, hot water, towels,

or a lock on the cubicle door, but with obscene graffiti going back for years.

- A barman who ignored new arrivals while chatting to a customer.
- Pints of beer being topped up from the slop trays.
- A clientele of scruffy drunks.

It's long been known that the west end of Glasgow is full of people who are a few tiles short of a bathroom suite. Now we know where they all drink.

We applaud the long-overdue plans of owner Richard Aitken to gut and fumigate his hell-hole.

Get on with it, Mr Aitken, we say. Ignore this incredible campaign.

You'd be as well giving pigs democratic control over their pigsty.

"They say all publicity is good publicity," said Ernie.

"To hell with them," said Gus. "Who's going to pay any attention to a rag like the *Sunday Scoop*?"

"About three-quarters of the population of Glasgow. Including the town councillors."

"Their bloody reporter didn't even realise that the barman ignoring him was the owner himself. And Aitken's the only one who ever serves slops. The other barmen never do it unless he's watching them."

"It doesn't matter," said Ernie. "The main point was to catch the headlines, and we've done that. We've certainly drummed up extra business for the bugger."

It was true that the publicity had brought in many new customers. Most of them had seemed to agree with the

Sunday Scoop's assessment and had not been seen again. But Aitken's takings must have been up substantially.

"You'd think he would be grateful," said Gus.

"Do you really?"

"No, I suppose not."

They had limited their agenda to goals they had thought realistic. Gratitude from Dick Aitken was not among them.

The only remaining part of their campaign was Gus's appearance before the council's Property Committee. Once again he was at the City Chambers, this time in the main building. The money of local taxpayers had not been spared, he noticed, in refurbishing the interior to the same high standard as the George Square frontage outside. This was already apparent in the broad, high-ceilinged corridor, with its intricate cornicing, in which he sat while waiting to be admitted to the committee room.

For some reason he found he was extremely nervous, much more so than during his TV interview. He'd had to summon much will power in order to make his way to the City Chambers and announce himself at the enquiries desk. His dominant impulse was to run away to the nearest pub. Only the knowledge of how many people he would be letting down kept him going, that and the fact that it was not yet opening time.

He was eventually admitted to a large room that matched the style of the corridor outside. He was asked to take a seat at the end of a large table, round which there sat about eight or nine councillors and a secretary.

The man at the opposite end of the table introduced

himself as the chairman, Councillor Grant. "I understand you're here to speak for the petitioners, the ones who object to the proposed changes to The Centurion pub?"

"That's right."

"You're their lawyer, are you?"

"Not officially. I am a lawyer, but I'm also one of the petitioners."

"I see. We've circulated your letter. You put forward an impressive argument. Would you like to speak briefly to it?"

Gus did so. He was glad the committee had his case in writing before them, as his nervousness made him less fluent than usual. When he had finished, Councillor Grant said:

"Thank you, Mr Mackinnon. One thing bothers me. Why have you brought your objections here, rather than the council's Planning Committee?"

"I believe residents of the adjacent flats have lodged planning objections."

"And you had nothing to do with that?"

"Not directly."

The chairman smiled, but didn't comment.

"Our objections go far beyond the jurisdiction of the Planning Committee," said Gus. "We think there are other issues that the council should consider, as landlords of the pub. Social ones mainly."

"Thank you, Mr Mackinnon. Does anyone else have anything to say? Councillor Todd?"

"Aye," said a small, grey-haired man who sat to Gus's left. He wore a badly fitting suit and his tie seemed to be in the process of throttling him. "I would just like tae ask ye, Mr Mackenzie, what right you think you have to tell a man what tae dae wi' his own property?"

For God's sake, Gus thought. "But it's not his own property," he said. "It belongs to the council."

"What dae ye mean?"

Gus thought carefully. How could he explain things to this man, in simple terms, without seeming to patronise the others? "The pub is council property. You're Mr Aitken's landlords. He needs your approval to carry out his plans."

"How dae you know that?"

Because I'm a lawyer, you stupid old bastard. "It's in his lease. I've read it."

"But that's outrageous! That's a private document! You've got nae right!"

"The lease is registered in the Land Register. Anybody can get a copy, for a fee."

"That's a bloody scandal! It should be confidential."

A man sitting next to the chairman whispered to him briefly. Gus had thought he looked familiar. He wasn't a councillor, but one of the council's lawyers.

The chairman nodded. "I think this is a bit of a red herring, Councillor Todd. I'm told that Mr Mackinnon is completely within his rights in obtaining a copy of the lease. In any case, as a council we're publicly accountable. That's why we're all here."

"I still think it's ridiculous."

"Your view's noted. Are there any other comments?"

"Yes," said another councillor, who was introduced as Councillor Sharp. He was younger than his predecessor and sounded a little better educated. As he spoke, Gus quickly realised that he would be a much more formidable opponent. "Did you see the article in last week's *Sunday Scoop*?"

"I'm afraid so."

"I paid your pub a visit the other day. I didn't put the drinks on my expense account." There was a ripple of laughter round the table. Gus was now more relaxed, but remained on his guard. "I have to say, I largely agree with them."

"There was also an article in the *Herald*. And it —"

"I read that too," said Councillor Sharp. "And while I wouldn't normally rate the opinions of the tabloid press over our illustrious local broadsheet, I think the *Herald* swallowed your propaganda a little uncritically. I think the *Scoop* has a point. Out of the mouths of babes and sucklings…"

Gus sensed a little unease among the other councillors. They had seemed a little embarrassed by Councillor Todd, but probably liked a smartarse even less.

Councillor Sharp seemed to sense this too. "I mean," he said, "we're not exactly talking about The Horseshoe Bar. The Centurion's a bit of a dump, isn't it? Why should the council want to stop Mr Aitken cleaning it up a bit?"

"They shouldn't," said Gus. "We don't. We would be delighted if the place were redecorated. And the seats recovered. A Ladies' toilet is badly needed." He suddenly realised that quoting the *Sunday Scoop* couldn't be regarded as defamatory. "And nobody would be more pleased than us if Mr Aitken stopped serving slops and paid more attention to hygiene. Soap and hot water would be most welcome, as well as a lock on the door of the toilet cubicle. Not everybody has got legs as long as mine."

There were a couple of sniggers, but more blank faces. Gus decided not to get carried away. "What I mean is, we want the place to be cleaned up. We just don't want it transformed out of all recognition."

"I think you've made your point, Mr Mackinnon," said the chairman. "Are there any other comments?"

There were a few more questions, but Gus was able to handle them. Finally, the chairman said, "Thank you, Mr Mackinnon. We'll certainly take your views into account."

Soon, Gus was back outside, feeling a considerable sense of anticlimax. The campaign was now over, it was out of his hands. All he had to do was report back to Ernie and the other regulars that evening. In the meantime, he would need to stay reasonably sober.

Unfortunately, he was desperate for a drink. He had felt the same when emerging into the sunlight after his previous visit to the council offices. This time the day was overcast and there was rain in the air, but it made no difference. The weather, he admitted to himself, was irrelevant to his craving.

He compromised by going to The Horseshoe Bar for a pub lunch. It was just after midday and the normally busy pub was still reasonably quiet. He sat at the back of the large, oval counter that gave the pub its name, bought a pint, and ordered a meal that was delivered by a dumbwaiter from the restaurant above.

As he looked around, he realised the force of Councillor Sharp's comment. Campaigning for a shithole like The Centurion seemed ludicrous when you compared it with a place like this. The pub belonged to the same era as the City Chambers and had recently been refurbished to a similar standard. The Horseshoe was centrally located, in a side street round the corner from Central Station, and the brewers who owned it rightly regarded it as one of their flagship properties. The walls had been painted, the varnish on the old woodwork restored, a new tile floor laid. The antique mirrors and paintings had been cleaned and managed to gleam in the dim lighting. Nothing had been changed, except to make the place look like new. If it weren't for the TV sets, you could imagine going out the front door and finding yourself back in Victorian Glasgow.

The pub gradually got busier as more office workers came in for lunch. Gus finished his meal, had a second pint, and then the growing crowds made it easier for him to break off and take his leave. His earlier nervousness, combined with his lunch, made it necessary for him first to seek out the cubicle in the Gents' toilet.

He found that the brewers, having spent tens of thousands of pounds on refurbishment, had stinted on the small outlay of replacing a broken lock on the cubicle door. The WC was set well back from the door, and even Gus's legs were not long enough to ensure privacy; this was inconvenient, but somehow it cheered him up a little.

He took the subway back to the west end and went straight home. He changed out of his good suit and snoozed in front of the TV for the rest of the afternoon.

After that things moved fairly quickly. The Planning Committee recommended that the council should grant planning permission, but made the consent subject to so many conditions – including a restriction allowing microwave cooking only – that Aitken's restaurant plans were rendered effectively unviable. The Property Committee, following the Planning Committee's lead, decided that the council, as landlords, could not agree to many of the proposed alterations. And the brewers, alarmed by the publicity and the stance of the council, withdrew their offer of a loan. Gus received notification of the first two of these; the last was only a rumour, but he believed it. Finally, a short article appeared in the *Herald*, to the effect that the plans for The Centurion had been abandoned, though some redecoration and other minor improvements would be made. Richard Aitken, the pub's owner, was quoted as saying: "I have many regular and loyal customers whom I value very highly. Clearly they were unhappy with my plans, and the customer is always right."

That evening Gus arrived in The Centurion just before eight o'clock. He was in a good mood, not just because of the *Herald* article, but also because this would be almost his first drink of the day.

Aitken was behind the bar for the first time that week. On seeing Gus arrive, he put down his cigarette and hastened to attend him, beating the other barman with uncharacteristic alacrity.

Gus was not flattered for long. "I'm sorry," said Aitken. "I'm afraid you're barred."

"What?"

"You're barred. I don't want you drinking in here any more."

"But why? I haven't done anything."

"I think you've done quite enough. Anyway, it's my pub. I can bar anyone I want to."

Gus was too taken by surprise to think of a suitable reply. Later in the evening he might have said much more, but he was still sober. He settled for a dignified retreat.

Across the road in The Aragon, he met Ernie, who had been barred before him. Not long afterwards, they were joined by Danny Boyd.

"Fucking bastard," said Danny. "I told him to stick his pub up his arse."

"An interesting approach to his redecoration plans," said Ernie. "But appropriate in the circumstances."

In the course of the evening the community of Centurion exiles continued to grow as other campaign executives arrived. Some of them were accompanied by sympathetic friends.

"Deep down, he knows we did him a favour," said Gus. "It's just bloody spite."

"He'll have us back eventually," said Ernie. "He needs us. Think how much money we all spend in there."

One of Danny's Marxist friends suggested they form a regular picket line outside The Centurion, but that didn't get general support.

"He can keep his pub," said Danny. "I don't give a fuck."

But he did. And, despite their general assent, so did the others. Just when their community was at its strongest, they had been banished from it. The victorious leaders had been cut off from their followers, and it hurt.

10. HOW TO MURDER YOUR NEIGHBOUR

Autumn 1978
Henrietta Quayle Flat 1/1

Extract from *Secrets of the Psychiatrist's Couch: 15 Intriguing Case Studies* by Philomena Warner (2005).

The following passage is taken from a book by the eminent psychiatrist Dr Philomena Warner, which tells the stories of patients whose cases she found particularly memorable during a long career spanning more than 35 years. It is more of a memoir than a textbook, and is therefore cast in a form that may fit in better here than an academic paper might have done.

Chapter Four: Matilda Jones, the quiet tenement dweller who dreamed of murder

As with other patients discussed in this book, Matilda Jones is a pseudonym adopted to protect the patient's identity. I have done the same with the other people who appear in her story. In particular, although the two neighbours who play a major role are both now deceased, they have living relatives, and in any case revealing their names could lead to the identification of Matilda herself. As with the other subjects who are still alive, Matilda has given me permission to include her story, on condition that this anonymity is preserved.

Matilda first became my patient in 1978 when I was employed as a consultant psychiatrist at Gartnavel Royal Hospital in Glasgow. She was admitted in a condition of complete nervous collapse, after locking herself in her first-floor flat for more than a week. The alarm was raised by a ground-floor neighbour, Mr Morris, who noticed that she was failing to pay her daily visit to the small grocer's shop, also on the ground floor of the building, where she bought a newspaper, milk and rolls every morning. This absence was confirmed by the shop's owner. Mr Morris finally became sufficiently alarmed to call the police when Matilda failed to take her turn of washing the stairs and landing leading to her flat. This was so uncharacteristic that he was now certain something must be wrong.

When repeated knocking and ringing of the doorbell failed to raise her, the police gained access through a front window, using a ladder and by removing a pane of glass. They had been advised by Mr Morris that access via the front door could only have been achieved with much difficulty and by causing a great deal of damage. This was later confirmed when it was discovered that the entrance to the flat was barricaded by a storm door and inner door, each secured by three locks and two large bolts, and that metal bars had been fitted behind the glass panel on the inner door.

Matilda was found crouching in terror on her bed in the back bedroom, and was only marginally reassured by the sight of the police uniforms. An ambulance was called and she was taken to hospital.

Matilda had run out of food several days earlier, after which she had consumed nothing but tap water. She was otherwise physically unharmed. She was initially uncommunicative, but after she had eaten and rested she began to talk to me and I gradually won her confidence.

One of the first things she said was, "I haven't washed the stairs. Mr Wilson will be furious."

I asked her who Mr Wilson was and she immediately relapsed into a state of terrified silence. I eventually learned that Mr Wilson was the neighbour who lived in the flat immediately above her. It soon emerged that Mr Wilson was a leading character in her story, one who figured prominently in her problems.

Patient Overview

At the time of her admission to hospital Matilda was forty-five years old and had been employed for the past twenty-two years as a history teacher at a secondary school in Glasgow. She had lived for most of her life in her current flat, which was originally rented by her parents, but purchased from the owner by Matilda's mother after her father's death. Following the death of her mother the year before, the flat was now owned by Matilda. Her psychological problems seem to have begun in childhood, particularly after the death of her father when Matilda was ten, though until fairly recently they had not been severe enough to prevent her from functioning almost normally, both at home and at work. They seem to have taken a notable turn for the worse after the death of her mother, evidenced by erratic behaviour at work, including frequent late-coming and unexplained absences, as well as increasingly strange behaviour observed by the neighbours who occupied other flats within the building.

Symptoms The observed behaviour seems to have resulted from a number of severe and morbid obsessions. An extreme fear of being burgled and of being attacked in her own home had resulted in excessive security precautions, which included fitting the multiple locks and bolts on her front doors. She had also developed a habit of returning back home several times after leaving for work to make sure that her flat was properly lock-fast. In addition, she had acquired the practice of keeping watch at her front window and waiting until her upstairs neighbour Mr Wilson had left for his work in the morning so as to avoid any possibility of encountering him on the way out. She exhibited severe hypochondria, causing her to stay at home on many days suffering from, largely imaginary, illnesses. She also claimed that she regularly smelled gas, which was supplied to other flats in the building, though not hers, and she was terrified of a gas leak. Another obsession was with cleanliness, observed by her neighbours in the form of frequent brushing and washing of the stairs and landing leading to her flat, far in excess of her fortnightly turn. Immediately before her prolonged withdrawal within her flat, she was cleaning the stairs and landing virtually on a daily basis, sometimes even more often.

However, her most severe obsession was a pathological fear and hatred of her upstairs neighbour Mr Wilson. Outwardly, this took the form of avoiding him as much as possible and going to excessive lengths not to annoy him in any way. Inwardly, she harboured fantasies of murdering the man, by increasingly violent and bizarre means.

At one point, when discussing her fear of burglary and the extensive security precautions she had taken, I asked her why she had not taken the obvious step of installing a burglar alarm.

"Oh, I couldn't possibly do that," she said.

"Why not?"

"Alarms are always going off by accident. That would infuriate Mr Wilson."

Apparently the fear of her upstairs neighbour trumped all of the others.

Diagnosis and treatment I diagnosed Matilda's condition as a severe example of generalised anxiety disorder coupled with obsessive-compulsive disorder. There was no evidence of delusions, hallucinations or any other signs of a psychotic break with reality. Her condition was purely neurotic in nature, though in an extreme form. Over the years that followed, I had no reason until recently to doubt this diagnosis.

My recommended treatment was twofold: medication with an anti-depressant drug (Clomiparine) along with Cognitive Behaviour Therapy (CBT) in the form of Exposure and Response Prevention. This has been confirmed many times since as a successful treatment for patients with similar conditions, including a number of other patients in my care. The drug merely attacks the symptoms, not the cause, of the condition, but substantially modifies their severity, allowing the patient to function more successfully. The CBT involves a self-imposed regime by the patient of deliberately refraining from the compulsive actions that characterise her condition, including the excessive house cleaning, the stair washing (apart from her allotted turn), and the repeated checking that her house is lock-fast, the iron switched off, etc. The patient knows that these repeated actions are irrational, and when stopping them has no dire consequences her state of anxiety generally lessens. This part of the treatment at least seems to have been almost entirely successful. The patient remained a good housekeeper and continued to perform her communal duties within the building, but her excessive repetition of the associated actions virtually disappeared.

I also had some success in tackling her obsessions during our discussions. Matilda is an intelligent woman, and I tried to get her to confront the irrationality of her obsessions, particularly the hypochondria and the fear of burglary, by using *reductio ad absurdum* arguments (more of which later).

The one obsession which I was unable to dislodge, or even make much impact upon, was her fear and hatred of her neighbour Mr Wilson, and her fantasies about murdering him.

After two weeks in hospital Matilda was well enough

to return home, but continued to see me as an outpatient for some time afterwards, initially at weekly intervals and later less frequently. After six months I left her in the care of her GP in order to continue her medication and general care, but with instructions to report back to me through her GP should further therapy be required in the future. After that I never saw her again until I contacted her regarding her inclusion in this book.

I therefore regarded Matilda as a partial success. I left her able to function on a daily basis provided that she continued with her medication. However, I eventually came to the conclusion that she was not well enough to return to work and, on the basis of my diagnosis, she was given early retirement from her job on medical grounds, with a modest pension to live on. Her continuing murderous thoughts about Mr Wilson remained a worry, but I was reassured by the fact that irrational obsessions involving violence to other people are very common in people with an obsessive-compulsive disorder. These fantasies are never acted upon, but merely add to the patient's anxiety burden, convincing the patient that he or she must be a bad person and lowering further their feelings of self-worth. My only lingering reservation was that a typical preoccupation in such cases is of doing violence to a child or family member or someone else that the patient truly loves. It is obvious to the patient that this is completely irrational, even although the unwanted thoughts may persist. In Mr Wilson's case, however, Matilda's obsession, though undoubtedly greatly exaggerated, was not completely irrational. During my investigations I briefly met Mr Wilson and found him to be a very annoying person. It would not have surprised me if a desire to murder him were to arise, purely based upon merit, in the mind of a completely rational person.

And then, late in 2000, I heard in the news that Mr Wilson had in fact been murdered. This gave me a considerable shock. It vividly brought back memories of Matilda's case, which I had never completely forgotten, even after the details of many subsequent cases had faded with the passage of time. Could I have been mistaken in my diagnosis? Had I been fatally wrong in my judgement that Matilda's obsession about Mr Wilson had been harmful to no one but herself? Could her long-internalised, bottled-up fixation have finally boiled over into direct action?

Gathering the facts

In the days following upon Matilda's admission to hospital I had a number of meetings with her and acquired much information about her and her family background. I learned about her upbringing, particularly her relationship with her mother, about her relationship (if it can be called that) with her upstairs neighbour Mr Wilson, about her work, and about much else. However, so much of what she told me, particularly about Mr Wilson, seemed so exaggerated that I felt some corroboration was required. I decided, with Matilda's consent, to visit her flat and find out as much as I could for myself. Matilda agreed to this because a constant worry since her admission to hospital was that her house had not been left lock-fast and would be raided by burglars during her absence. In fact she was convinced that this would already have happened, and urged me to notify the police when I confirmed it. I readily agreed, feeling sure that it would not be necessary.

Normally, this is the wrong way to deal with a patient suffering from an obsessive-compulsive disorder. This is because offering reassurance has the effect of condoning the compulsive actions instead of helping the patient to break free of them. However, it suited my own purposes to make the visit, and so I made it clear I would visit her flat once and once only. I would make absolutely sure that the flat was left lock-fast and that the front window had been replaced, and that would be the last time anyone entered her flat until she was able to return to it herself. I asked her if there was a neighbour she trusted, someone who could keep an eye on her flat and contact me if there was any problem.

"Not Mr Wilson! Don't make it Mr Wilson!"

"I won't. Who else would you suggest?"

She initially couldn't think of anyone until I mentioned Mr Morris, the downstairs neighbour who had raised the alarm. "That would be all right," she said, a little reluctantly. "We're not exactly friends, but he's a nice man. It was good of him to be worried about me. And he doesn't like Mr Wilson."

"Why not?"

"Nobody likes Mr Wilson."

"Not even his family?"

"I'm not sure about that. I often wonder."

"Your mother seems to have liked him."

"Yes," she said, but added nothing further and I left it

at that. Then she said that I would have to visit her flat on a weekday, during the day. I asked her why.

"You don't want Mr Wilson to see you."

I wasn't worried about meeting Mr Wilson – in fact I was quite keen on having a look at the man – but I initially agreed. However, when I telephoned Mr Morris to arrange a visit, it turned out that he would be absent at work at the same time as Mr Wilson. We therefore agreed to meet the following Saturday morning.

Matilda was unhappy about this but didn't oppose me. "I'll avoid Mr Wilson," I told her.

"You won't be able to," she said. "He'll see you."

In this she proved to be right.

I arrived at Matilda's building at ten o'clock on Saturday morning. It was a typical vintage Glasgow tenement, dating probably from the late nineteenth century. It was beginning to show its age, but was otherwise in reasonably good condition. I identified Matilda's flat as the one immediately above the shop and saw that the missing window pane had been replaced. I wondered who had arranged that.

I entered the close and reached the first floor without meeting anyone. I brought out Matilda's large bunch of keys from my coat pocket – I'd had to jam them down with tissues to avoid clanging like a bell as I walked down the street – and stood on the landing sorting them out. There were two yales, three mortices and a large, old-fashioned iron key that was several times the size of the others. I surmised that it was the original door key dating from the time of the building's erection. It clearly was meant for the large keyhole on the storm door, and so it proved. As

I turned it in the lock it sent a loud, echoing signal up the stairwell. I regretted not having tried the mortice lock first. I began to try the mortice keys one by one and finally found the one for the storm door on the third attempt. I was trying out the yales when I heard a door open and shut again on the landing above and a man came down the stairs. He was bald, and wore old-fashioned, horn-rimmed glasses and a knitted cardigan, all of which made him look older than I believed him to be. If I was indeed in the presence of the notorious Mr Wilson then he was barely forty. He was what a friend of mine would have described as "a young fogie".

He glared at me in a hostile manner. "That's Miss Jones's flat," he said.

"I know."

"Who are you? What are you doing here?"

"I'm a friend of Miss Jones. She asked me to check her flat."

"Miss Jones doesn't have any friends. I think I should phone the police."

"There's no need for that." I was facing a dilemma. My instinct was to tell this man as little as possible: quite apart from any question of doctor–patient confidentiality, that was my own strong inclination. On the other hand, if he carried out his threat, which I suspected he would, I would have to identify myself anyway. And it must be common knowledge within the building, possibly even witnessed by Wilson himself, that the police had been called out and Matilda removed in an ambulance. I reluctantly produced a business card and handed it to Wilson. "I'm Miss Jones's doctor. She hasn't been well."

"What's wrong with her?"

"I can't discuss that."

"You're a psychiatrist," he said, after reading the card. "The woman's mad. I've always known it."

"That's not a term I recognise. As I said, I can't discuss it with you."

"Why not?"

"It's confidential," I said. "Now, if you'll excuse me—"

"She's missed her turn of the stairs for two weeks running. We can't have that. We have standards here. This is a family building."

"She's not well enough."

"When will she be back?"

"I can't say for sure."

"That's not good enough."

"I can't do anything about that. She'll be back when she's better, and I've no doubt she'll resume her communal duties then. I'm sure the building will survive."

"But that's not good enough. If there's a lunatic living below me I need to know about it. This is a family building."

As we were talking, I had finished unlocking the storm door and had gradually backed into the flat. "I'll need to go now," I said, shutting the storm door in his face. A provocative act, but my professional composure was quickly slipping away and losing my temper would have been even worse.

I stood in the small vestibule between the outer and inner doors and took several deep breaths, trying to calm down. After a short while I heard Wilson return upstairs, followed by the slamming of a door. I sorted out the remaining keys and opened the inner door. Then I turned back to pick up the scattering of mail lying between the doors.

It included several handwritten notes from Wilson. The following is one which I kept in my file for reference:

> You have now faled your turn of the stares a second time this is unnaceptible. You must make up your mind wether you are a flybynite tennant or an owner with owners responsibilitys your mother would be ashamed of you. This is a family building.
>
> WW (Flat 2/1)

I reread this and several others in a similar vein with complete disbelief. Nowadays the extremes of human behaviour hold fewer surprises for me, but this was much earlier in my career. It was beginning to seem as if Matilda's description of Wilson was much less exaggerated than I had thought. I put the notes and the rest of the mail into my briefcase and began to explore Matilda's flat.

It was old-fashioned in appearance but in very good condition. Apart from the thin layer of dust that had accumulated since Matilda's departure, cleanliness and tidiness were paramount. Everything was in its place, with nothing lying about. All of the flat's original features – panelled wooden doors, intricate cornicing etc. – had been preserved, with no attempt at modernisation. The furniture was old and solid but well looked after. The walls were papered with floral wallpaper and the carpets, now a little threadbare but very clean, were free-standing with a linoleum surround. In the living room there was a very old black-and-white TV with a 14-inch screen.

All of the flat was in a similar style reflecting, I assumed, the taste of her mother. The sole exception was the back bedroom, the smaller of the two, which was the only room in the house where Matilda's individual personality had made its mark. Here there was crammed, along with the single bed, a compact wardrobe in a more modern style, a small dressing table, a large bookcase – the only one in the house – and a writing desk. The books were mainly a mixture of history texts and classic novels, the only exception being a large, well-used medical encyclopaedia. On top of the small bedside cabinet there was a portable transistor radio, and on the walls there were several art prints, also the only ones in the house. I picked out two books that Matilda has asked me to collect for her and put them in my briefcase.

I learned from Matilda later that she only ever listened to the radio in her bedroom, which was immediately below the room least used by Mr Wilson in the flat above. Here, listening with the volume kept low, she hoped that the radio would not be overheard, which would have annoyed Mr Wilson. This had conformed to her mother's wishes as well.

It seemed that, a year after her death, the ghost of Matilda's mother still lingered. Her double bed was still in the front bedroom and her clothes were still in the large wardrobe and chest of drawers. The whole flat was a shrine to her, apart from Matilda's small bolt-hole at the back.

I left the flat after making sure that all six of the keys

had been turned in their locks, and that the house was once more as secure as a bank vault. I heard Wilson's door open again upstairs but this time he didn't come down. He had kept my business card and by this time I reckoned he would have phoned the hospital to check me out. I went downstairs and waited in the close until I heard his door shut again before going back and ringing the doorbell of Mr Morris's ground floor flat. If possible, I wanted to keep Wilson from knowing that I had visited Mr Morris. I suspected that this would be futile. He was probably already stationed at the front window waiting to confirm that I had left the building.

Mr Morris looked like a man in his fifties, though his dress and demeanour made him seem younger than his upstairs neighbour.

He greeted me warmly. "Come in, Dr Warner," he said. "It's nice to meet you."

I followed him through the hall and into the living room. His flat also reflected a traditional outlook, but was a little more modern-looking than Matilda's. A large-screened colour TV faced the leather three-piece suite. On one of the armchairs a fair-haired youth of about fifteen sat with his nose buried in an American comic.

"This is my nephew Johnny," said Morris. "He's staying with me over the weekend while his parents are away." ("Johnny" is also a pseudonym. Mr Morris's nephew inherited his uncle's flat and moved into it after his uncle's death a few years ago.) The boy looked up briefly to shake hands before returning to his comic. I was near enough to read the title on the lurid front cover: *Binky Brown meets the Holy Virgin Mary*. I thought at first that I must have misread it and took a second look. I had got it right first time. I noticed that the comic was in good condition, though it had lost its new appearance, as if it had been re-read a number of times. I reflected briefly that the creators of such products must be subjects ripe for psychoanalysis.

Mr Morris noticed my interest and chuckled. "Looking for new business, are you doctor?" he said. "Don't worry about my nephew, he just has rather peculiar tastes." The boy glanced up again and smiled a little sheepishly. "But have a seat," Morris continued, "and tell me how Matilda's doing. I've been worried about her for a while."

"I think she's making progress," I said, sitting down on the other armchair.

"Good. Tell me all about it and how I can help. Would you like a cup of tea or coffee?"

"Tea would be nice."

He went through to the kitchen, leaving me alone with the boy. There was an awkward silence, awkward on my part that is. The boy barely noticed that his uncle had left the room and remained absorbed in his comic, so I left him to it.

Mr Morris returned with a tray of tea and biscuits, and set them down on a coffee table in front of the sofa, where he sat down himself. He handed me a teacup and took one himself. There was a third cup on the tray. "Tea, Johnny," he said. The boy nodded, but carried on reading. His uncle shook his head.

"So you think Matilda will be OK? Will she be able to return home soon?"

"I hope so. She's responding to treatment. You'll

appreciate that I can't tell you too much about her condition?"

"Of course not. I understand. I want to help if I can."

"That's good of you. Are you friends?"

"Not really. She's a very private person. But we've been neighbours for many years and we're on good enough terms. She's always been a bit eccentric, but since her mother died last year she seems to be having real problems."

"You knew her mother then?"

"Oh yes. She was a right old bitch. I'm sure most of Matilda's problems stem from her. I thought having her out of the way might have been good for Matilda, but it seems to have had the opposite effect."

"If you could tell me what you know about her family background, that would be a big help. I've heard all about it from her, of course, but a different perspective would be very useful. And I'd also like to know what you can tell me about the man upstairs."

"You mean that bugger Wilson? He makes Matilda's life a misery. He and Matilda's mother were great pals while she was alive, and they both bullied Matilda relentlessly. He's been carrying on the tradition since the old cow croaked. If you ask me, the man's off his head, but you're the expert."

"I met him briefly when I was up at Matilda's flat. I didn't seek him out, but he found me."

"That figures. What did you make of him?"

"Let's just say, I wasn't too favourably impressed."

"He's the one who should be seeing a shrink, not Matilda. You should be getting your men in white coats to take *him* away. This area is full of nutters, as I'm sure you know, but they don't all frequent the Byres Road pubs."

"The word 'nutter' isn't part of my vocabulary. Though maybe I could make an exception in Wilson's case."

"He's a bloody menace. He suffers from the delusion that he owns the entire building. The whole tenement is his castle, which he guards jealously. I completely ignore him, it's the only way, but Matilda doesn't seem to be capable of that."

I got him to tell me everything he knew about Matilda's mother, about Wilson and about Matilda's relationship with them both. I wondered briefly if the boy should be a party to this, but I don't think he heard a word we were saying and Morris didn't seem to be worried about it. Everything he told me was consistent with what I had heard from Matilda herself. It was all very useful.

He was also able to confirm the circumstances surrounding the death of Matilda's mother. This was another incredible part of Matilda's account that I'd had to check out.

"Who replaced the glass in the front window?" I asked as I was taking my leave.

"Oh, I arranged that. I couldn't leave it like that."

"That was good of you. She was convinced the place would be overrun by burglars as soon as she left."

Morris laughed. "That's Matilda all right. You'll be able to set her mind at rest."

"That'll take a bit longer. But it'll be a big help. Thanks for doing that."

"No problem. Matilda will reimburse me when she gets back. That's the least of my worries."

As I reached the front door on the way out, I turned and said, "I don't need to tell you that I'd rather you kept all of this to yourself. You'll probably be interrogated by the man upstairs."

"Without a doubt. Don't worry, I'll tell him nothing. It'll give me great pleasure to stonewall him."

"Good." I left him my card, in case of emergency, and took my leave. I went out the back door, as there was something I wanted to check at the rear of the building, then returned to the close and made my exit. When I reached the pavement I turned and looked up at Wilson's window. As I had predicted he was there. On a whim I stopped where I was and stared back at him, and we glared at each other for a moment or two. Then I walked back to my car.

My site visit at Matilda's building had been very fruitful, but there were a couple of other meetings that would help with my investigations. The first was with the head teacher of Matilda's school whom I'd made an appointment to see the following Monday. As the new school term was due to begin that day, I had already forwarded a medical certificate and notified them that Matilda would be unfit to return to work for some time. However, I wanted to complete my picture of how Matilda had been before her illness. I needed to know how she had functioned away from her home environment, among her professional colleagues, when she was interacting with children. She knew that her performance over the past year had been unsatisfactory and she had continually been brooding about this over the summer break. This had added even further to the burden of worry and guilt that already filled her mind to overflowing, as she panicked over whether she would be able to cope at work, as she tortured herself over what her colleagues must think of her. Her dread of the approaching term had provided the final catalyst that caused the complete withdrawal within her flat.

Matilda's head teacher Mr Melrose (another pseudonym) was a pleasant man in his forties who made me welcome. He had been at the school for more than ten years, as a teacher before becoming head teacher, and he knew Matilda well. Like Mr Morris he showed a genuine concern for her welfare and was anxious to hear about her progress. Like Morris, he and most of Matilda's colleagues had been worried about her erratic behaviour over the past year. Apparently, although considered rather eccentric (in my experience not an unusual characteristic among school teachers), she was well liked by both staff and pupils and was considered to be a good teacher. She had never had any serious problems with discipline, something that surprised me a little, reminding me that that it could be misleading to make assumptions about a patient's condition before becoming ill. She apparently had an infectious enthusiasm for her subject and a talent for making it accessible to her pupils. History was apparently not at all a dry subject in her hands.

However, in the past year, since the death of her mother, all of Matilda's colleagues had noticed a marked difference. Apart from the late-coming and absences, she had become withdrawn and uncommunicative with the other staff, had seemed to be continually on edge, had been unable to carry out routine tasks without constant rechecking, and had found it difficult to face her classes. The pupils had picked up on this and discipline had deteriorated. On more than one occasion another teacher had discovered her in tears in the staff toilet, something that had embarrassed Matilda considerably.

Apart from the fact that Matilda had lived with her mother who had died the year before, her colleagues knew nothing about her personal life and her home background. Like Morris, they had found her to be a very private person.

All of this was very useful and gave me much to work on. As I had suspected, Matilda's extreme feelings of low self-esteem were not at all justified. This was a valuable confirmation.

The other meeting was with the police (more of which later).

Home background

There has been much debate in psychiatric circles about the extent to which neurotic disorders, including obsessive-compulsive disorder, result from genetic or from environmental factors. Matilda's case tends to confirm the view that they can result from a combination of both. Genetically, Matilda seems to have been cursed with a legacy from both of her parents. Her high level of anxiety and obsessive-compulsive behaviour were apparently traits shared by her father, though in his case the symptoms had been much milder. However, they had been enough to invoke constant criticism from his wife, a dominant figure in his life as well as that of his daughter. Matilda appears to have been close to him, and his death from a heart attack when Matilda was ten had undoubtedly affected her badly.

On the other hand, some of Matilda's obsessions, notably her hypochondria, her fear of gas and her dread of burglary had been inherited from her mother. It was her mother who had insisted on having the front door locks, bolts and bars fitted, though Matilda had become so infected with her mother's paranoia that she also now regarded all of these precautions as essential. In a similar way, she had succumbed to her mother's hypochondria: apart from a succession of increasingly exasperated general practitioners, Matilda had for years been the sole confidant on the subject of her mother's countless illusory diseases and their phantom symptoms. What had originally been a mild tendency on her mother's part, common to millions of normally functioning people, had been amplified beyond reason by the sudden and unexpected death of her husband, reducing her to the condition of a near-invalid. Also rendered susceptible by her father's death, Matilda had been an easy prey to her mother's fixation.

Matilda's mother had originally been a strong woman, physically as well as mentally, but her imagined frailty had kept her virtually housebound for many years prior to her death. Matilda had become her slave, browbeaten into cleaning the flat to an impossible standard, fetching medicines, both prescribed and unprescribed, being in constant attendance to her mother's needs and wishes. Her only escape was to her work, and even that absence was resented by her mother, despite it being the household's only source of income.

Matilda's only successful act of rebellion had been to fulfil her ambition of going to university and qualifying as a teacher. Her mother had eventually gone along with this, however reluctantly, on the basis that the earning potential of her sole breadwinner would eventually be enhanced. The level of income earned by schoolteachers had been a disappointment, which Matilda had never been allowed to forget. Despite this, Matilda had managed to resist her mother's pressure to look for a better-paid job, such was the strength of her teaching vocation.

Nothing Matilda ever did satisfied her mother, who constantly berated her and fanned the flames of her low self-esteem. As well as her earning capacity, everything Matilda did was constantly criticised: her housekeeping, her cooking, her appearance, her speech. She had also convinced Matilda that she was unattractive to men and would never get a husband.

I would not claim to be an expert on the subject of what men find attractive in women (or, for that matter, what women find attractive in men). This remains a mystery to psychologists of both sexes, so many variations are there from any supposed norms. But I have no doubt at all that Matilda and her mother were mistaken, and that she could have made much more of herself. She had a rounded figure, even in middle age, and features that might have been appealing if not permanently clouded by anxiety and terror. A less dowdy mode of dress, a new hairstyle, a discreet use of makeup, and above all reclaiming some of the self-confidence eroded by a lifetime of her mother's malign influence, could have brought about a transformation.

A particularly intriguing feature of Matilda's past was her mother's relationship with her upstairs neighbour Mr Wilson. Mrs Jones seemed almost to regard Wilson as a substitute child, exhibiting all of the qualities lacking in her own offspring, a role-model for Matilda that she had permanently failed to live up to. Wilson was a frequent visitor to their flat and on the few occasions when Matilda's mother had left the house it had generally been to visit her upstairs neighbour. I wondered where Mrs Wilson featured in all of this. Had she accompanied her husband on these visits?

"No," said Matilda, "he always came alone."

"What's Mrs Wilson like?"

"I don't really know her very well. She never says much."

Although Wilson's wife had also been Matilda's neighbour for many years, Matilda seemed to know very little about her. Her husband was clearly a dominant influence in her life, but Matilda was unable to tell me much beyond that.

What had been the reason for this bond between Mrs Jones and her neighbour? They clearly had much in common. They were both bullies. To use a popular modern expression, they were both "control freaks". A layman might have described them as monsters, who had deserved each other. This is not the language generally used by people with a scientific approach to the mysteries of the human psyche. But finding language

417

that *is* appropriate is more difficult. There was much justice in Mr Morris's comment that Wilson would have been a better subject for psychiatric analysis than Matilda. But he was not my patient, Matilda was. And her mother, another worthy subject, was now out of my reach. I could only speculate about the motivation of these people.

Another thing they had in common was their similar backgrounds. Both Wilson and Mrs Jones were of working-class origin, and both were the first of their generation to venture into home ownership. In each of their cases a natural pride of property had been exaggerated to a perverse degree. Matilda and her mother were the building's residents of longest standing, the flat originally having been rented by Matilda's father. After his death, Matilda's mother had used the proceeds of her husband's life insurance to buy the flat from the building's owner, at a fraction of the price that such a property would command nowadays. The owners with the next-longest tenure were Wilson and Morris, who had both arrived in the 1960s.

One aspect of Matilda's home background was beyond doubt. For very understandable reasons Matilda had hated her mother. After Wilson's arrival on the scene, he and Matilda's mother had become the joint recipients of this sentiment, which had now been inherited by Wilson on his own.

Mrs Jones, who also shared with her upstairs neighbour an almost complete insensitivity to the feelings of others, seemed nevertheless to have sensed some of this hatred. Despite her daughter's subservient nature, some of her feelings seem to have leaked out. This had combined with Mrs Jones's hypochondria to convince her that Matilda was repeatedly trying to poison her. As well as constantly accusing her daughter of this, she had confided her suspicions to Wilson.

As a result, when Matilda's mother died of natural causes after a stroke, Wilson had accused her of murdering her mother and had reported Matilda to the police. The police had investigated his complaint and a post-mortem had been carried out upon Mrs Jones. Matilda was exonerated, but was left traumatised by the incident, which had been a major cause of her breakdown. The murderous fantasies which she now entertained against Wilson had originally been directed at her mother. When her mother finally obliged her by dying, Matilda had been left feeling as guilty as if she had actually carried out the deed.

These feelings might have faded with time, except that Wilson had been unconvinced by the police findings and had continued with his accusations for some time, regularly harassing both Matilda herself and also the police. Matilda had held on to Wilson's notes from that time, the following being one of them:

The incompitant authoritys may be happy but I know the truth. You murderd your poor mother who gave you nothing but love I will keep reminding the police until they do something about it.
WW (Flat 2/1)

I had little doubt that this was nonsense, Matilda's own account being consistent with that of Mr Morris, though Matilda's feelings of guilt and Wilson's continued accusations had almost convinced her that she might indeed have been responsible. She knew that she hadn't deliberately poisoned her mother, but could she have done so accidentally? I doubted it, but decided to seek confirmation by finding out what the police had to say about it. I met with a Detective Sergeant MacDermott, who had handled the case and was most cooperative when I showed him my credentials and explained the situation.

"The man's talking nonsense," he declared. "The old woman died of a strokc. She was in her mid-seventies, she was overweight and she had been housebound for years. Her GP was in no doubt – he'd been a regular visitor to their flat for years – and though there had been little wrong with her except in her mind, her inactivity, weight and elevated blood pressure meant that she was a stroke waiting to happen. A PM wouldn't have been thought necessary, except that we were driven into it by that bugger Wilson who wouldn't let the matter rest. But it confirmed the GP's findings without any doubt whatsoever."

"I've met Mr Wilson," I said. "I think I've got the picture."

"The man's a bloody menace. He's always pestering us about one thing or another. If you ask me, he's off his head. *He's* the one who should be your patient, not poor Matilda Jones."

"Funnily enough, you're not the first person to say that to me."

"What do you think?"

"I'm thinking that Matilda's the one who *is* my patient. But what you've told me has been very helpful. It confirms my own opinion."

"I'm glad to be assistance. Good luck with Matilda. I feel sorry for the woman."

The reasons for Matilda's mental deterioration since her mother's death were now becoming clear.

Homicidal burglars round every corner

Matilda has a vivid imagination. When she was teaching, I'm sure it played a great part in bringing the past alive for the benefit of her pupils. However, at home it tended to be put to a less constructive use. Nowhere was this more evident than in the way she had populated the west end of Glasgow with hundreds of thieves, united in their determination to force themselves into her house, rob her of all her modest possessions, and murder her while they were about it. She kept a regular watch at the front window and any stranger entering the building immediately fell under suspicion. When a new postman took over from the regular one, he was immediately identified as a robber in disguise. Visitors falling under this general umbrella of suspicion could be of either sex and any age, united only by their implausibility in the role of homicidal criminals. I attempted to appeal to Matilda's intelligence by a *reductio ad absurdum* argument.

"But surely you can always recognise burglars? You know what they'll look like?"

"What do you mean?"

"They all wear a mask and a striped jersey and carry a bag marked 'Swag'. At least that's what they always looked like in the *Beano*."

Matilda looked hurt. "I think you're making fun of me, Dr Warner."

"No," I said, "I'm just trying to appeal to your common sense. Your fear isn't rational. What would be the motivation of these burglars? Your flat is nice, but what do you have that they would want to steal? Your books? Your little radio? Your antique TV set? Believe me, there are much better pickings in just about every other home."

"They don't know that."

"And why would they want to murder you? It doesn't make sense."

"To get their revenge when they find out there's nothing worth stealing."

"Then get some new things that might make it worth their while. A new colour TV maybe. A record player, some records. Other portable consumer goods that would be worth selling. Make sure everything's covered by insurance. Leave some money lying about."

But she still wasn't convinced. She liked music, but would be reluctant to play it, because it would annoy Mr Wilson. So would the sound of a TV. And they still might murder her. They were criminals. They were bad people. That's the sort of thing these people did.

"But how would they get in? You've got so many locks."

A burglar could climb up a drain pipe on the back

wall, she told me, and get in by her bedroom window. Then he would murder her in her bed before going on to ransack the house. But I was prepared for that argument.

"I checked that out when I visited your flat. There isn't a drain pipe near enough to any of your windows."

"Some of these cat burglars are really athletic."

"But most burglars are opportunistic. They go for easy targets. They're more likely to pick a ground-floor flat, or break into a top floor one by climbing into the loft and cutting through the ceiling. First- and second-floor flats are the safest. They'll also look for houses with fewer locks than yours."

But she couldn't be convinced. A determined burglar could always find a way in. Why he would be so determined in her case was a mystery to me. As far as I knew, she didn't have any enemies.

Apart from Mr Wilson. I was beginning to think him capable of a great deal. But climbing in Matilda's bedroom window to take bloody vengeance for the murder of her mother was not a role I could easily visualise for him.

The thousand natural shocks that flesh is heir to

Matilda's imagination was equally active in conjuring up a plethora of fatal illnesses that constantly threatened her life. Ever since the sudden death of her father, every minor chest pain had heralded a heart attack both for her mother and for Matilda. After her mother's death, Matilda's every passing headache had been a stroke. Or possibly a brain tumour. Or maybe both. The slightest head cold was sure to develop into pneumonia or pleurisy. Every cough meant tuberculosis or lung cancer, every pain in the stomach or gut a tumour of the bowel. Any tingling sensation or numbness, any slight trembling of the hand, no matter how transitory, signalled the onset of multiple sclerosis or Parkinson's disease. And she regularly brooded over each known type of cancer, particularly those difficult or impossible to treat, and had even pioneered a few new ones, previously unknown to medical science. She did exclude testicular and prostate cancers but only with some reluctance. She had a collector's zeal for completing the set.

And these were only the more common ailments. The well-scrutinised medical encyclopaedia which I had seen in her flat had been her reference list for obscure diseases, all as nasty as they were rare, and to all of which she had succumbed at one time or another. They included (in alphabetical order) Buerger's Disease, Chorea, Dismenorrohoea, Erysipelas, Hyperthyroidism, Intertrigo, Mitral Stenosis, Myalgia, Nephritis, Pyelitis, Spondylosis, Tietze's Syndrome, Trigeminal Neuralgia, Wens, Xanthelasma and many others. Many of these tended to be fatal, but there were also other, less life-threatening conditions, which she worried about on good days.

For many years such reference books have nurtured hypochondria and have been the bane of doctors. Nowadays this phenomenon has become much worse with the arrival of the internet. Amateur hypochondriacs have attained professional status by having access, via a few mouse-clicks, to a worldwide community of quacks.

Any medical professional will tell you that the ubiquitous Mr Google has much to answer for.

There was one notable difference between Matilda's hypochondria and that of her mother. Unlike her mother, Matilda had kept all of her worries to herself. She had never bothered her doctor with them. She had never confided in anyone else about her health fears, not even her mother. She knew that Mrs Jones would never have accepted her as a serious rival contender in the health stakes, so she had not even tried to become one. Her reasons for not consulting her doctor were partly diffidence – she didn't want to be a nuisance, particularly when her mother was such a colossal one – and partly fear of what a proper medical examination might reveal. Instead she had bottled up her worries, creating a level of stress that in turn had brought about the headaches and other symptoms giving rise to these fears in the first place.

At first Matilda didn't even mention her health preoccupations to me and they only gradually came out during discussions about other things. When I realised their full extent, I talked them through with her at some length. Once again I tried *reductio ad absurdum* arguments.

"You shouldn't worry about the same disease all the time," I told her. "It could become psychosomatic, a self-fulfilling prophecy. You should use your medical encyclopaedia to make a long list and then worry about a different one every week. That should keep you safe."

"You're making fun of me again, Dr Warner."

"No," I said. "Just trying to get your fears into perspective. Have you ever read Jerome K. Jerome's *Three Men in a Boat*?"

"I've heard of it, but I've never read it."

"Let me show you my favourite passage. You might find the narrator's problems a little familiar."

I picked out my treasured copy of the book from the shelf where it sat among the medical texts. I showed her the relevant part, near the beginning of the first chapter. Worried about a minor complaint, the narrator visits the British Museum to consult a reference book. He begins to browse, and is appalled to discover that he has all the symptoms of a much more serious complaint:

> I sat for a while frozen with horror; and then in the listlessness of despair, I again turned over the pages. I came to typhoid fever - read the symptoms - discovered that I had typhoid fever, must have had it for months without knowing it - wondered what else I had got; turned up St Vitus's Dance - found, as I expected, that I had that too - began to get interested in my case, and determined to sift it to the bottom, and so started alphabetically - read up ague and learnt that I was sickening for it, and that the acute stage would commence in another fortnight. Bright's disease, I was relieved to find, I had only in a modified form, and, so far as that was concerned, I might live for years. Cholera I had, with severe complications; and diphtheria I seemed to have been born with ... Gout, in its most malignant stage, it would appear, had seized me without my being aware of it; and zymosis I had evidently been suffering with from boyhood. There were no more diseases after zymosis, so I

concluded there was nothing else the matter with me.

Jerome K. Jerome *Three Men in a Boat* (1889)
Chapter 1

Having gone through the entire alphabet, Jerome's hero discovers that the only ailment he is completely free of is housemaid's knee, and he feels slightly aggrieved by this unfair omission. He finally concludes:

I had walked into that reading-room a happy, healthy man. I crawled out a decrepit wreck.

Jerome's narrator has a sensible doctor who quickly sorts him out. Matilda, I feared, would be more of a challenge. She understood what I was trying to do by showing her this passage, but I don't think she was entirely convinced. In fact I think I left her beginning to worry about housemaid's knee. At least that is not life-threatening, so maybe I could record a partial success.

Though I was sure that none of Matilda's ailments were real, I was aware that she had not previously sought medical attention. If I ignored her worries and one or more of them turned out to be justified then I would be guilty of negligence. I therefore arranged, in conjunction with her GP, for her to have a thorough medical examination and a series of tests. They confirmed that there was nothing physically wrong with her. I hoped that Matilda would be reassured, though, unsurprisingly, she was not entirely won over. At least I had protected myself.

When I had finished treating Matilda her

hypochondria, like her gas and her burglary obsessions, was much reduced. In both cases I was uncertain of the extent to which this was brought about by the psychotherapy or by a combination of her medication and the cognitive behaviour therapy. Obsessive-compulsive disorder and hypochondria are related and the treatment for one of them can also be effective with the other. At any rate, I left Matilda much improved if not entirely cured.

How to murder your neighbour

Planning the demise of her upstairs neighbour was a constant preoccupation with Matilda, to which all of her other obsessions took second place. None of her scenarios involved poison, the method by which she had been suspected of killing her mother. As illustrated by the small selection of them noted below, their common element was extreme violence. Only that seemed capable of satisfying her:

> *Mr Wilson, like all conscientious residents of the building, is taking his turn of washing the stairs leading to his house. Matilda waits until he has finished with the landing and is about to start on the first flight of steps. Then she goes up to him on the pretext of discussing some trivial piece of communal business. Before long, in his usual rude fashion, he becomes tired of her presence and turns his back on her to continue with his task. With all the force she can muster – her strong motivation*

has conjured up unexpected reserves – she shoves him on the back with both hands, propelling him headlong down the stairs. Before he can recover, she tips the water out of his metal bucket and follows him down. As he struggles to rise to his feet, she swings the bucket over her head and catches him on the face, smashing his glasses and stunning him. She swings the bucket again and again, cracking open his bald pate with its metal edge until he lies inert and lifeless, his piggy eyes staring.

Quickly, she wipes the handle of the bucket with her handkerchief and hurries down to the safety of her flat before any witnesses can appear.

"Does Mr Wilson usually wash the stairs himself?" I asked her.

"What do you mean?"

"Does he wash them himself or does he get his wife to do it?"

"Mrs Wilson usually does it."

"That rather spoils your plan, doesn't it?"

"He does them occasionally. She may take ill. Anyway, that isn't my only plan."

Punctually at 8.20, as he does every weekday morning, Mr Wilson leaves for work. He walks down to Byres Road and along to Hillhead Underground Station. Matilda follows him, far enough behind to remain unobserved. He buys a ticket, goes through the barrier and down to the platform. Matilda follows. Rush hour has begun, half of the west end's population is on its way to work and the platform is crowded. Matilda creeps up, unobserved, behind her target and waits for the arrival of a train. At just the right moment she pushes her neighbour from the platform into its track. His terrified scream echoes through the station before being abruptly cut short by the force of the impact. Too late, the driver applies his brakes as Wilson's body is mangled under the wheels of the carriage.

By this time, Matilda has sunk back, anonymous, into the crowd.

"I thought the underground was closed just now. They're modernising it."

"It'll be open again soon."

"But how can you be certain nobody will see you do it?"

"The platform will be too crowded."

"How can you be sure? What time is rush hour? There could be a witness."

"What if there is? It would worth going to jail just to be rid of the man. I'd be performing a public service. A good lawyer might even get me off. All he needs to do is get all of the other neighbours to testify. They all hate him."

"There must be a safer plan."

"Oh, I have plenty of others."

It is Saturday morning and Mr Wilson has decided to wash the windows of his flat. In a family building like his, it is essential that the spotless glass should sparkle, unblemished, in the morning sunlight. Especially on the front windows, which face on to a busy road.

From the bay window of her own flat, Matilda is able to keep watch until her neighbour has started on the outside panes of the window above her. As usual, he is sitting outside on the window ledge, his back to the street. His legs are tucked safely through the gap beneath the raised window frame and his heels are jammed against the inside wall, anchoring him in place.

Matilda rings his doorbell and when the door is opened by Mrs Wilson, she quickly pushes her inside the flat, jamming her chloroform-soaked cloth against the other woman's face until she falls unconscious. She hurries through to the living room, over to the window, pulls the frame further up, and grabs Wilson's feet, pushing his legs out until he topples over the sill. She hears the loud crack as his bald head hits the concrete in front of the shop. She looks out and sees his inert body, a growing pool of blood surrounding his head.

She hurries back to her flat while Mrs Wilson remains unconscious.

"But that doesn't make sense. Mrs Wilson will be able to identify you."

"I could wear a mask."

"Right. You could also put on a striped jersey and carry a bag marked 'Swag'. That would really throw her off the scent."

"Don't be silly. Anyway I told you. I don't care if I get caught."

"But his flat's only on the second floor. The fall might not kill him."

"If it didn't, he'd probably be disabled for life. In constant, chronic pain. I could live with that."

"Your ideas are very imaginative, but not very practical. Maybe you need something simpler."

"How about this one?"

Again it is Saturday morning, and Mrs Wilson has gone out shopping. Mr Wilson is alone in his flat. Matilda rings his doorbell on the pretext of wanting to discuss a recent letter from the factor. Wilson invites her in and they go through to his living room. She waits for her chance until he obliges her by bending over to pick up some papers from a coffee table. Quickly, she darts across to the fireplace, grabs the ornamental poker, and smashes it over Wilson's head with all the force she can command. As he falls to the floor, she repeats the blows again and again until his body has stopped moving and his blood and brains are spread over his new fitted carpet.

She hurries back to her flat before the body can be discovered.

This scenario was indeed less fanciful and I had to work harder in order to find reasons to pour scorn upon it. However, I did my best. And although Matilda purported to be absolutely serious about her plans, and denied that they were just a fantasy safety-valve, I couldn't believe that she would ever actually try to carry any of them out. Her pattern of appeasement and of keeping Wilson at the safest possible distance seemed too ingrained to make room for any other approach. When Matilda was otherwise well enough to return home, these fantasies remained as vivid as before, but I couldn't believe they presented any real danger.

That remained the case for more than twenty years, until I read of Wilson's murder in the paper and noticed that he had been killed in a way very similar to that final scenario.

Rehabilitation

I started Matilda on anti-depressant medication shortly after her admission to hospital. She was initially extremely resistant to the idea of taking drugs – to someone with her old-fashioned upbringing this was an admission of failure – but I persisted with my arguments and she was finally persuaded to give it a try. After a couple of weeks the drug had sufficiently reduced the severity of her symptoms for me to recommend her discharge. The next part of her treatment was the cognitive behaviour therapy in the form of exposure and response prevention. This was a self-imposed regime of disciplining herself to give up her compulsive behaviour – the repeated cleaning, stair washing, checking of locks etc. – which was initially very difficult for her, but which got easier with time. During her regular follow-up visits as an outpatient she reported her progress with this procedure. It was remarkably successful. There were a few lapses, and I had to talk her out of the resulting despair, but in the end the CBT made a significant contribution to her improvement.

A major obstacle she had to endure on her return home was the resumption of harassment by Wilson. My meeting with him had not slowed down the arrival of his notes and these continued after her return. While she was in hospital Wilson had repeatedly tried to telephone me but I refused to take his calls. Then he wrote to me:

> You have rudly refused to speak to me on the phone I must know when a madwoman is coming back to the building and of the pearl to me and my family. This is a matter of grate urgency so kindley write fourthwith and oblige.

I wrote back, as politely as I could manage under such provocation, to the effect that Matilda presented no danger to him or anyone else and that, apart from that, the state of her health was none of his business. I said nothing about when she would be returning home, but she was discharged the day after my letter was sent.

I was unsurprised to hear later that Wilson had complained about me to the hospital management. I was called to a meeting with the hospital's general manager, but had little trouble in persuading him that the complaint was unfounded. The style and content of Wilson's letter had not predisposed him in the man's favour, and my account, supplemented by a few more of

Wilson's missives, was more than enough to satisfy him that my behaviour had been completely professional.

Wilson didn't stop there and went on to report me to the police. I know this because Detective Sergeant MacDermott was good enough to telephone me and reassure me that ignoring Wilson was now standard police procedure. I thanked him and confirmed that Matilda did not present a danger to the public, which he readily accepted. The remote possibility that she might be a danger to Wilson himself wasn't something that seemed to worry the sergeant unduly.

I initially hoped that Matilda would recover sufficiently to resume her work as a teacher. However, as the weeks passed it became clear to me that this would not be possible and I recommended her early retirement. She accepted this, a little reluctantly, as she had loved being a teacher, but she never quite conquered her fear of returning to work and agreed that there was no alternative.

Her retirement therefore posed another problem which we had to face together. An important part of the recovery process for patients suffering from disorders like hers is the presence of supportive family members. This was something that Matilda lacked entirely. And she had few, if any friends. A natural shyness and her mother's tyrannical rule had seen to that. Leaving her job would condemn her to complete social isolation, a sure recipe for a relapse. I made a number of suggestions about how she could combat this, and one proposal which appealed to her was to work as a volunteer in one of the charity shops in her area. She managed to obtain a job in such a shop, began working there once a week and, by the time her outpatient visits came to an end, this had increased to two days. I hoped that this might help to overcome her shyness and help her to develop a social life.

I also encouraged her to begin exorcising her mother's ghost from her flat. In the weeks following her discharge from hospital, I got her to dispose of her mother's clothes and any other small effects that would have served as a reminder of her parent. It would have been impractical for her to completely replace the furniture in the flat but, at my suggestion, she moved some of her belongings, including the writing bureau and bookcase, and most of her art prints, into the living room. Also at my suggestion, she managed to summon the courage to ask her downstairs neighbour Mr Morris to help her move some of the heavier items, which he was pleased to do. She even rented a new colour television. She decided on this after finding out that she could avoid annoying Mr Wilson by utilising the subtitle service provided by the BBC and other channels. It would have been much preferable if she had been able to directly confront this problem, but I suppose it was still an improvement.

There was of course another, more radical avoidance technique, that could have disposed of her problem entirely. She could have sold her flat and bought another one, far away from her upstairs neighbour's little domain. When I finally accepted that confrontation with Wilson, by far the best approach, remained beyond her, I recommended this alternative solution. But she was completely resistant to it. She had lived in the flat almost all of her life, moving elsewhere would be a hassle, she might need a mortgage, which would be impossible after she left work, etc., etc. I eventually gave up, but hoped that she might reconsider this in the future. But she didn't. I eventually learned that she was still there at the time of Wilson's death.

Matilda's dreams come true

Wilson's murder was reported in all of the local newspapers and on TV. The initial reports were very brief, only to the effect that he had been found by his wife on his living room carpet, battered to death by repeated blows to the head. One account mentioned a poker as the suspected weapon. I noticed in passing that my old friend Detective Sergeant MacDermott, now a Chief Inspector, was in charge of the police investigation.

My time with Matilda had been many years before and at first I wondered – or rather hoped – that my memory was deceiving me. I immediately looked out my file on Matilda to refresh my memory. On reading it I was overcome by panic. Had I been fatally mistaken in my assessment of her condition? Was I guilty of negligence? Would I shortly find myself in the witness box, testifying at a murder trial?

In the days that followed, I scrutinised the news minutely for further information about the case, desperately hoping that my fears would prove to be unfounded.

NOTE: The rest of Dr Warner's chapter has been omitted. Whether or not Henrietta Quayle murdered Walter Bain will be revealed later.

11. LIKE FATHER, LIKE SON

November 1998
Gus Mackinnon, Flat 3/1

"What time will you be back?" Gus asked.

"I'm not sure," said his son. "It depends how things go. We're meeting in the Beer Bar. They may want to go on somewhere else afterwards. I may go with them, maybe not."

"Andrea won't be with you?"

"I told you. It's a stag do."

"In my day they had dances in the Union on Fridays. We'd spend the evening in the Beer Bar and then go up to the dance at closing time. We generally got knocked back for being too pissed."

"Times have changed, Dad. We're more civilized now. They actually admit women into the Beer Bar these days. But I'm not looking to get off with anyone. Andrea would skin me alive."

"Quite right too. Just be careful. Don't overdo it. I'm sure that den of iniquity hasn't changed all that much."

"Just let me get this right? *You're* actually giving *me* a lecture about drinking too much? That's really rich. I can't wait to tell Mum about that one. That should give her a good laugh."

"Less of your lip," said Gus. "I just want you to benefit from my bitter experience. And I'm a reformed character, you know that."

"Point taken. So you'll be staying in all night? You'll be here when I get back?"

"It's Friday night. I'll probably pop down to The Centurion later. I still like to keep in touch with my friends occasionally. Have you got your keys?"

Callum patted his jacket pocket. A reassuring jangle could be heard. "I'll see you later, Dad."

"See you later, son."

As his son left the flat, Gus reflected again about how well he had turned out. He was tall and good-looking, a younger version of Gus himself, before the ravages of life had taken their toll. But there was no reason why he should go down a similar disastrous path to that of his father, even though, like him, he had chosen the law as a career. Maybe, with Gus's help, he could avoid some of the pitfalls that had tripped up his father. He had just entered his final year of a law degree at Glasgow University. So far his grades gave hope for a good honours classification and he had ambitions to go to the bar.

His younger sister was also doing well. She had just finished school and had entered the first year of a medical degree. Gus had good reason to be proud of both of his children. They must have borne some scars as a result of being from a broken home, but these seemed to be minimal. Even during his worst periods, Gus had always seen his children regularly and had done his best to prevent them from witnessing the full extent of his drinking. And all that was now firmly behind him. He wasn't teetotal –

that would have been difficult, considering his social circle – but had somehow managed to rein in his worst excesses and become an occasional social drinker.

The transformation had begun after the successful campaign to rescue The Centurion ten years earlier. He had been invigorated by the campaign and made a determined effort to continue keeping his drinking in check, helped by the fact that he remained barred from the pub for some months before Aitken relented, his initial resentment tempered by the desire to hold on to some of his best customers. During that period Gus applied regularly for jobs and finally landed one as a solicitor with Glasgow Council. He still had a good reputation in legal circles and knew some of the other solicitors who worked there. Also, the solicitor attending the meeting of the Property Committee at which Gus had spoken in favour of The Centurion petition had been impressed by his performance and had put in a good word.

The job was suiting him well. Despite the belief of many private practice practitioners, it was not a sinecure. He had plenty of work, much of it interesting. It had its own bureaucratic frustrations from time to time, but didn't subject him to the intense stress he had experienced in private practice. In particular, he was now part of a large team and no longer had to carry a privileged senior partner almost single-handedly on his back. He earned less than he had done in private practice, but the mortgage over his flat was paid off and his overheads were low. He had been able to contribute to the cost of his children's education and had even managed to put some money by.

He'd had a few relationships with women over the years, though none had so far led to remarriage.

His children still lived with their mother and stepfather in the south side of the city, but occasionally stayed overnight with Gus. This was particularly the case with Callum since he had been attending university. Gus's flat was easier to get back to after late nights, and he had Gus's past to hold over his father's head after any occasional cases of overindulgence. However, there weren't many of these, certainly not enough to ring alarm bells. Callum had been going steady with the same girl for nearly two years and that had provided a moderating influence upon his behaviour that Gus had lacked at the same age.

What next? How would he pass the time until it was safe to go down to the pub? He had enjoyed having Callum there and now felt alone in the empty flat. He could listen to music. He had now added a CD deck to his system and bought a few CDs, though he still had a preference for vinyl LPs. Instead he switched on the TV and settled down in front of it. He watched the end of the news, then switched channels to catch a repeat of *LA Law*. That was always good for a laugh. Anything less like his own experience of working in a legal office was difficult to imagine. In the glamorous City of Angels you never saw anyone ploughing through a routine conveyancing transaction, or settling into the mind-numbing tedium of gathering in the assets in a deceased person's estate. The high-octane courtroom dramas bore little resemblance to the chaos, incompetence and spontaneous comedy witnessed daily in Glasgow Sheriff Court. The old episode of *Columbo*, even less realistic, that he switched across to afterwards was equally entertaining.

By the time the scruffy police lieutenant had successfully concluded his cat-and-mouse game and brought low yet another rich and influential offender – an exercise that must regularly gratify millions of underprivileged people across the world – it was nearly nine o'clock and Gus felt that he had earned a drink.

Norrie and Bob were already in The Centurion and Ernie joined them shortly afterwards. Ernie and Norrie were sober – like Gus, they were both employed again and confined their drinking to weekends and occasional passing visits – but Bob seemed to have been there for a while. It was now six years since he had been struck off and, not for the first time, Gus wondered where he was getting his money from. He must have put quite a lot by during his years as a legal brigand. Gus had also seen him consorting with the alcoholic gangsters from time to time, and he suspected that some unsavoury deals, which he was better not knowing about, might have been going on.

George Anderson was also there – it must have been Cathie's turn on babysitting duty – but the presence of Bob Waddell had as usual caused him to sit at another table, where he was drinking with Danny Boyd and a couple of sociologists from the university where he worked. As far as Gus knew, he was still managing to resist the Marxist propaganda.

Gus took a couple of sips from his pint, then put down his glass. "Damn it!"

"What?"

"I've used the big key!"

"You've used what?"

Gus produced the large iron key from his jacket pocket. "The key for the original lock on my storm door. I usually just leave it on the mortice, but there have been burglaries in the area recently. Henrietta Quayle is going frantic, but this time it's not entirely in her head. It's best to be safe, so I've been using the original lock for extra security. It's pretty solid."

"So what's the problem?" asked Ernie. "You're not making any sense."

"Callum's staying with me tonight. I don't have a spare copy of the big key to give him. I've locked him out."

"Where is he?" asked Norrie.

"He's at a stag night in the Beer Bar. I'd better nip back to the flat and unlock it. It'll be OK on the mortice for one night."

"Don't be daft," said Ernie. "You'll be back home long before him. You know what that place is like."

"He could get back early. The others might move on to a night club or something. He won't join them. He's got a steady girlfriend."

"He won't be back before you," said Norrie. "Would you have been at his age?"

"Probably not."

"And in the extremely unlikely event that he does get back early, he knows where to find you, doesn't he? Just round the corner. You're not exactly unpredictable."

"I suppose not."

"And it's your round next," said Ernie. "We're not letting you out of our sight."

So that was it settled.

The prediction of Gus's friends would normally have proved to be accurate, but on this occasion a number of factors combined to make things different. As Gus had speculated, the main crowd had decided to move on elsewhere and Callum had decided not to join them, though not for the reason, or not entirely for the reason, that Gus had assumed. Also, the decision that he should retire early was as much that of his friends as it was his. Quite uncharacteristically, he had somehow managed to get very drunk very early on in the evening. There were a number of reasons for this. Partly as a reaction against the dubious example of his father, he was not normally a heavy drinker, and his capacity was not nearly as great as that of his friends. His stomach was almost empty; his father had made him an evening meal, but at that time he hadn't been hungry and hadn't eaten much of it. Also it was a stag night – one of his friends was getting married the following week – and excess had seemed obligatory. The rounds were coming far too regularly, and when Callum tried to sit some of them out, he was met with derision. Eventually, as the alcohol went to his head, he began to acquire more bravado, and his friends found this untypical behaviour a great source of amusement. Like the others, he had been drinking nothing but beer, but then one misguided member of the company thought it would be amusing to surreptitiously slip a double vodka into his pint. Such was Callum's condition by then that he drank it up without noticing.

Shortly after nine o'clock, while Gus was still having his first drink, Callum was almost unconscious, and the others were ready to move on.

"Where we going?"

"The Inferno's the nearest."

"That'll do. You coming with us Callum?"

"You joking? Look at the state of him. He'd get us all barred."

"Better phone him a taxi."

"Where does he live?"

"Somewhere on the south side."

"No, he's staying with his father tonight. Just off Byres Road."

"Hey, Callum, man, you want a taxi?"

"What?" Callum shook his head. "No, it's all right. I'm just… just…"

"What's he saying?"

"I think he's saying he's just going round the corner."

"You mean just over the hill?" Laughter. "I suppose that's about right."

"I don't think we should leave him. How'd he manage to get as bad as that?"

"I slipped him a Micky Finn."

"You stupid bastard. That's not funny. Somebody had better see him up the road."

"Don't be daft. If we leave it too late we won't get in. Hey Callum, you OK to get back on your own? What's that? He says he just needs a seat for a minute. Let's go."

They left Callum sitting on a wall outside the Union, and crossed the road to Ashton Way, which cut through the middle of Kelvingrove Park and led them quickly to their destination.

Normally it would have been a quick ten-minute walk for Callum to return to his father's flat. However, the greater part of this journey consisted of ascending University Avenue to the highest point in Hillhead, before continuing on down to Byres Road. Callum sat on the wall for an indeterminate time before starting on his way up the hill. Normally, he would barely notice that it existed, but now it seemed to be an impossible obstacle. Several times he stumbled and fell, attracting the concern of passers-by, who moved on when they saw how drunk he was. Drunken students were not an unusual sight in this area, particularly on a Friday night. He made it past the end of the Union building and across a side street. Halfway up he stopped opposite the neoclassical frontage of Wellington Church with its ancient Graecian columns, which he appreciated even less than usual, except that it was fronted by an iron railing against which he could lean and have a rest. More people passed by, after a quick check of his condition. Eventually, he was able to carry on again, zig-zagging back and forth across the pavement, several times almost staggering on to the road, before finally making it almost to the top of the hill and in front of the Reading Room, a circular, two-storey building which was an annexe to the University Library. Then he stopped again, this time to be sick.

He managed to make it to the top of the hill, then found another wall to sit on. After a while, he began the slightly easier journey down the other side of the hill.

His next major obstacle was Byres Road, where the traffic was almost as thick as it had been at rush hour. Somehow he managed to summon enough residual good sense to wait at a pedestrian crossing until the appearance of the green man. Even so, he had only managed to stagger three-quarters of the way across the road before the lights changed and he stumbled on to the pavement amid a chorus of car horns.

After that it was a relatively uneventful journey to his father's building. He couldn't remember which of the keys was the one for the security door and had tried all of them before realising that he was at the door of Number 11, the building adjoining that of his father. He walked round to the correct door and then, after dropping the keys and having to pick them up again, finally found the one that admitted him to the close.

Now climbing the stairs to the top floor seemed as great a task as the ascent of University Avenue. After stumbling and falling several times on the way he made it to the second floor, the one below his father's flat.

There is a phenomenon well known to those with a drink habit, familiar to Gus Mackinnon, though not to his son. You can undertake quite a long walk home, even taking much longer than usual, without being in the least aware of any pressure upon your bladder. Then, with only one or two doors left to unlock between you and your toilet, the need to urinate suddenly becomes irresistible.

This sudden compulsion appeared without warning while he was grappling with the security door. It quickly grew in strength as he climbed the stairs with as much urgency as his rubbery legs could manage, but by the second-floor landing he finally lost control. He felt a warm, wet sensation flow down his leg and a puddle formed on the landing. It was right outside a storm door brightly painted in garish lilac. An ornate plastic nameplate read: "BAIN".

The name struck a chord in the recesses of his befogged memory and a realisation slowly formed. He began to laugh. Wait until he told his father about this! He would find it hilarious.

He finally made it to the top floor, where the last barrier proved insuperable. He had two mortice keys, and the second one he tried turned easily in the lock. But the door wouldn't open. He locked and unlocked it again, with the same result. He grabbed the metal handle and shook it ineffectually. He put his shoulder to the door with the same result. It wasn't just jammed, it was still locked and the lock was solid.

It took him a while to realise what was wrong. There was a second lock on the door, accessed by a large keyhole, a foot and a half below the mortice. There was only one copy of the big iron key, which his father hardly ever used, and never when his son was staying with him. The old bugger must have forgotten. He had said something about burglaries in the area recently. At least he knew where to find him, and it wasn't far.

It was still very annoying to have to retrace his steps after getting so close. It was with some impatience that he tried to hurry back down the stairs, an unwise move in his present condition. He descended the first of the two flights of steps between the third and second floors, and rounded the corner to the top of the second flight. Then he stumbled again and plunged headlong down the stairs. He landed back in front of Walter Bain's door, his head striking the stone landing with some force. He lay in the puddle of his own urine, a smaller puddle of blood forming under his head. Vomit began to trickle from his mouth.

Walter Bain and his wife heard the noise on the landing outside. Walter went out to investigate, his wife close behind him.

A young man lay outside his door. He appeared to be unconscious. He had made a disgusting mess on the landing, one that was gradually growing in size. Walter bent down and shook the body. "Hey, you! You can't lie there. Get up!"

The boy stirred and muttered something, then lay still again. Walter kicked him and shook him again. "I said, get up. You can't stay there. Who are you? What are you doing here?"

"It's that boy from upstairs," said his wife. "Mr Mackinnon's son. He stays here quite often."

"Huh! I should have known. You'd better phone his father. Let it ring a while. He's probably lying drunk up there."

Mrs Bain went off, and shortly afterwards there could be heard the faint sound of a telephone ringing upstairs. As instructed, she let it ring for a long time, but there was no reply.

"I don't think he's in."

"Of course not. He'll be in the pub." Walter gave the body a final kick, but with no success. "I'll need to phone the police."

"You should phone an ambulance. I think he's hurt."

"Nonsense, he's just drunk. What else can you expect? Like father, like son."

"But he's unconscious. He's bleeding. I think he fell down the stairs. He might be injured."

Walter shook the body again. "Hey you! Wake up."

Callum stirred and managed to raise his head a little. "Wha'?"

"Are you all right? Are you hurt?"

"Wha'? Sorry, I've had a wee bit too much to…" He slumped unconscious again.

"I told you. He's drunk. I'm phoning the police."

"I still think we should phone for an ambulance."

"Don't be stupid. The police can check him out. We just need to get him off the landing."

An essential difference between the two emergency services was that the ambulance service had never heard of Walter Bain and the police had. An ambulance could probably have arrived quite quickly from the Western Infirmary, which was only a quarter of a mile away. On the other hand, for many years now Walter Bain had occupied the number one spot on the police's top ten list of nuisance callers. Their Walter Bain policy was well established. You persistently ignored his calls in the hope that they would go away, and only when you got worn down by the brain damage from the incessant further calls did it become less tiresome to send someone to his flat. And so almost forty minutes had passed before a couple of officers who happened to be passing drew the short straw and looked in to see what the bloody man was on about now. During all this time, Callum lay on the landing, unconscious and bleeding. Everyone else in the building was either in for the night or had gone out but not returned, and no one else had found him.

As soon as the two policemen saw Callum, they realised what had to be done. They managed to get him to his feet, semi-conscious, but unable to support himself. They began to slowly help him down the stairs and had just passed the first floor when they met George Anderson on his way back from the pub.

"Good God!" said George. "What happened?"

"He's drunk," said one of the policemen. "But he may also be hurt. Do you know who he is?"

"He's Callum Mackinnon. His father lives on the top floor. I've just left him in The Centurion. I'll go back there and let him know. Are you taking him to the police station?"

"No. We'd better get him checked out. Tell his father we're taking him to the casualty department at the Western."

"OK. Who phoned you?"

"Who do you think? He should have phoned an ambulance, but he just phoned us. I'm sure you know what the man's like. We don't exactly treat his calls as a matter of priority."

"What do you mean? How long had the boy been lying there?"

The two policemen looked at each other shamefacedly, hesitating. "Maybe half an hour? Possibly longer."

"That bastard Bain!"

"Quite. We'd better get on our way."

"Yes, yes, on you go. I'll just have a quick word with the wife, then I'll go and get his father."

George quickly went up to his flat. The kids were long in bed and Cathie was in the living room watching TV. He told her what had happened.

"I never heard anything," she said. "I was in here all the time. The living room door was shut and the TV was on. You say Bain just left him lying there?"

"Yes."

"The bastard!"

"Yes."

"You'd better get right back to The Centurion and tell Gus. I hope the boy's all right. Maybe this time Gus will finally do us all a favour and top Bain."

"Absolutely. I'm sure a good lawyer would get him off. I'll be back shortly."

George went out again and hurried back in the direction of Byres Road.

A couple of hours later Gus returned to his flat. His shoulders were slumped and he appeared to be in shock. He walked slowly upstairs, but when he saw the mess of blood, urine and vomit on the second-floor landing he shuddered and hesitated for a moment before carrying on up the stairs. Then, when he opened the storm door, he found a handwritten note on cheap notepaper lying in the vestibule. He picked it up and looked at it. For a moment or two he stood transfixed, as if he could not quite believe what he was reading. Then he hurried back downstairs, leaving the storm door lying open.

George and Cathie had gone to bed, but were roused by the commotion on the floor above. George put on his dressing gown and slippers and went out to investigate. He found Gus pounding and kicking Walter Bain's front door and yelling at the top of his voice. "Bain, you murdering bastard! Come out here! I'm going to kill you!" And so on, with minor variations, again and again.

George grabbed Gus's shoulders and tried to pull him away from Bain's door. "Come on Gus, get back from there." But Gus was twice his size, his strength augmented by fury, and George was unable to budge him. Then Cathie arrived to lend a hand and together they finally managed to haul him back from the door.

They heard Walter Bain's voice, high and frightened, from behind the storm door. "Go away! I've phoned the police!"

"Then bloody well unphone them!" shouted Cathie. "You've already done more than enough! We'll deal with this! Come on, Gus," she said to the big man. "Come downstairs with us and tell us what happened."

Gus finally stopped resisting, his lethargy returned, and he allowed them to lead him down to the floor below, Bain's note still grasped in his hand. They took him into their flat, through to the living room, sat him down on an armchair. "What's the matter?" asked Cathie. "How's Callum?"

"Is that one of Bain's notes?" George asked. Gus said nothing, but handed the note to George.

George read it quickly. "Bloody hell!" he said, handing the note to Cathie.

She, too, found it difficult to believe what she read. "The bastard!"

The note was in Walter Bain's usual childish scrawl:

You're sons a drunkin disgrase like father like son. You must clean up the mess on my landing right away or the police will be back. This is a family building youre son left the front gate open your a menis to all desent people and oblige.
Walter Bain (flat 2/1)

"What happened?" Cathie asked again. "How's Callum?"

Gus made no reply but burst into tears, sobbing uncontrollably, on and on. Cathie walked over and put her arms around him.

The living room door opened tentatively. George and Cathie's children stood in the doorway, Eddie standing in front of his sister. Both of them looked terrified.

George quickly walked over to them. "It's all right. There's nothing to worry about. We're just helping Mr Mackinnon with something."

"Everything's all right," said Cathie. "Go back to bed. I'll be through shortly."

George took them back to their bedroom and settled them down again. When he returned, Gus was still sobbing and Cathie was still comforting him. George went through to the kitchen and came back with a bottle of whisky and a glass. He poured a drink for Gus, which he drank quickly. George refilled his glass.

Eventually he calmed down sufficiently to tell his story. He had arrived in the casualty department to find Callum sitting in the middle of a long queue, much of it consisting of noisy drunks. He was conscious, the cut on his head had stopped bleeding, but he was still obviously drunk and Gus could get little sense from him. When they had been sitting together for half an hour, the queue only slightly shorter, Callum had collapsed. Gus summoned immediate help and Callum was taken off on a stretcher.

Gus had another hour to wait before a doctor brought him the news. Callum's fall had caused a brain haemorrhage, which had grown slowly, its effects initially

454

concealed by his drunkenness. When it was finally revealed in a CT scan, he had been rushed off for an emergency operation, but it was too late and he had died on the operating table.

Gus began to sob again. "What will I tell his mother? What will I tell his sister?"

"Haven't you contacted them?"

"I can't get hold of them. They're away for the weekend. What am I going to tell them?" Cathie continued to comfort him as his grief continued unabated.

There were many factors that had contributed to the disaster, most of them unpredictable. A number of people could have been blamed. There was the idiot who had thought it was funny to spike Callum's drink; there were the rest of his so-called friends, who had been more interested in their night out than in making sure that Callum got home safely. But Gus knew nothing about them. In his view, two people were responsible.

The first was the self-styled "family man", who had left his boy dying outside his front door, to whom his son was just another piece of rubbish littering the stairway. Would the prompt arrival of an ambulance have been enough to save Callum? It was impossible to know for certain, but his chances would surely have been better.

The second person Gus blamed was himself. If only he had made Callum eat more before leaving the house, if only he had been more insistent in his warnings, if only he hadn't stupidly locked the storm door with the big key, if only he had taken five minutes to go back home and remedy the situation instead of listening to his friends...

He gulped down the rest of his whisky and George poured him another.

This proved to be prophetic and before long Gus's normal reaction to trauma had reasserted itself. His drinking became as bad as it had ever been. Within six months the council had forced him into early retirement, on the tiny pension that his ten years' service had earned.

12. THE GREATEST PARTY EVER HELD

Spring 2000
Tony Miller, Flat 2/2

> "I think it cannot be said that a house is properly built if it will not resist an exceptional row or dance." Sheriff William Guthrie in *Harbison v Robb* (1878), in which a tenant was injured by a falling ceiling, allegedly caused by a party in the flat above.

When Tony Miller first saw the flat at 13 Oldberry Road he knew it was the one for him. A spacious, nicely-furnished apartment, in a refurbished tenement, right in the middle of the west end. That was the only place to live, so everyone told him. If the adventure that had so far eluded him during his young life was ever going to happen, it would happen in the west end. That was what they all said.

His first experience of disillusionment came when he heard what the rent was. "That's more than my take-home pay," he said to the letting agent.

"How much do you earn?" He told her. "Is that for a month or a year?"

"A year."

"I see what you mean. Where do you work?"

"Sunlight Insurance."

"I gather they're as generous as ever."

"Did you work there?"

"Not in that one, but they're all the same. Well, I could get you a nice bedsit, but that would still take a large chunk out of your salary if you were paying it on your own. Or you could take the Oldberry Road flat and find two others to share with. We're not supposed to lease it to more than two people, but who's to know if you sublet? The settee in the living room is actually a sofabed, but I never told you that."

"I don't know. It's a lot of money."

"Well, it's up to you, but flats like this don't come on the market every day. It just so happens that all of the previous tenants moved out at the same time. They had a row with one of the neighbours."

"What about?"

"I've no idea. These things happen."

"But what if I can't find any flatmates?"

"You're joking, aren't you? We're talking about the west end. I'll send two flatmates your way, no bother at all."

"That's very good of you."

"If you don't get your flatmates, we don't get our rent. Oh, and you'll need to invite me to the flat warming."

"But I don't—"

"I'm only joking. So what do you think?"

It was a measure of Tony's naïvety that he ended up not only signing the lease as sole tenant but also paying over most of his savings for the deposit and first month's rent. But he really wanted the flat. And the letting agent was a nice girl, very attractive, who had seemed genuinely to like him and want to help.

As it happened, she didn't let him down, and by the time he moved in at the beginning of April she had found him two flatmates who would be moving in later that month.

At first all went well. He liked having the flat to himself and wished he could afford to have it that way all the time. He enjoyed the extra time in bed, now that he no longer had a long train journey every morning from his parents' house in Kilwinning. He still didn't know anyone in the area, apart from George Mooney, a fellow insurance clerk who lived with his parents in Hyndland. Tony was a little shy by nature and didn't make friends easily, but he was sure all that would change when his flatmates came on board.

On the day he moved in he began to receive communications from some of the neighbours. They included a long document from the man across the landing, a Walter Bain, giving a detailed account of his communal duties as the occupier of Flat 2/2. It seemed a little officious, and he resented the implication that tenants were likely to be less dedicated to these tasks than the owner-occupiers. But he wanted to be a good neighbour and not cause any trouble, and it was useful to have the means of achieving this so clearly laid out. He decided to do something about it right away and that same day, which was a Saturday, he went to Woolworths and bought a brush, shovel, mop, bucket, detergent and a bottle of pine disinfectant. Anxious to demonstrate his goodwill, he went out early on Monday evening and thoroughly cleaned the landings and stairs, wiping down the tile surrounds, polishing the wooden banister and dusting its metal support. While he was working on the lower of the two flights of stairs, he heard the door of the opposite flat open, and he waited for Walter Bain to appear and catch him in the act of vindicating the honour of the tenants. But no one came and a moment or two later he heard the door close again.

When he had finished the stairway was filled with the smell of disinfectant, advertising his neighbourly virtue to all who would pass that way within the next few hours. He returned to the house and made himself a cup of tea. About ten minutes later a note came through the letterbox:

> It was also your turn to wash the landing window and you overdone the pine a bit we usually do the stares on Fridays and oblige.
> Walter Bain (Flat 2/1)

Did this mean that he had cleaned the stairs four days early, or that he should have done them the day before he moved in? He would find out when Bain's turn came. It was now too dark to wash the landing window, but he could manage it the following evening as soon as he got home from work. He wondered if he should knock on Bain's door and tell him that, but such direct confrontation seemed to be against the rules, so he wrote Bain a note instead. He got no reply and presumed that his proposal was acceptable.

Before going to bed, he went out to the back court and pushed his wheelie bin through the building and out to the street. He took it back on his way home from work the following evening, but this was already too late and a note was waiting for him:

It looks bad if a wheely is out front all day this is a family building.
WB (2/1)

Jim McKelvie, the first of his flatmates, moved in ten days after Tony. Jim was a first-year engineering student, a year younger than Tony. Until now, he had continued to live with his parents but had wanted a place of his own in order to study for his exams, which were only a couple of weeks away.

"Won't you want to go back home for the summer?" Tony asked him.

"Back to Nitshill when I've got a pad in the west end? You're jokin', man."

When he first viewed the flat, Jim had said:

"This would be a great place for a party."

Tony had made no response at the time, but Jim had barely moved in before he repeated the observation.

"Do you think so?" Tony asked.

"Definitely. We'll get it organised as soon as Freddie arrives."

Freddie Barr, the other flatmate, was a management trainee in a large department store. When he moved in, a week after Jim, practically the first thing he said was:

"When we havin' the party?"

In fact, several people at Tony's work, including George Mooney, had been continually asking the same question. It looked as if a party was becoming inevitable. It was just that he had never held a party before – he hadn't even *been* to all that many – and it was unknown territory. But no doubt the others would keep him right. He had wanted to meet people hadn't he, to get into the swing of west end life? So the party was probably a good idea.

All the same, Tony wondered about the probable attitude of Walter Bain to the event. He mentioned this to Jim.

"He's not above or below us," said Jim. "He won't hear anything."

"I'm not so sure."

"If he doesn't like it, he can fuck off."

Tony also raised the subject with Freddie.

"What's it got to do with him?" said Freddie. "He can fuck off."

Tony had showed both of them the various notes he'd received from Bain and they'd both agreed, though without much enthusiasm, to share the housekeeping chores, both internal and external. Though Tony was beginning to wonder how much either of them could be relied upon for stair cleaning or wheelie bin duties.

They fixed on the last Saturday of the month for the party, which was just over a week after Freddie had moved in and Jim's exams had finished. Tony wondered if they would be able to assemble a sufficient number of guests at such short notice.

"I wouldn't worry about that," said Freddie. "The

main thing is to make sure there are plenty of women. We don't want it to be all guys."

"Absolutely," said Jim.

"I'll ask my girlfriend to bring some of her pals," said Freddie.

"Good," said Jim. "Tell her she can come too. And I'll get my sister to do the same."

"What's your sister like?" asked Freddie.

"She's got some nice-looking pals."

They turned to Tony, who had neither a girlfriend nor a sister. "Have you asked the people at your work?" asked Freddie.

"They've all invited themselves already."

"Including the women?"

"I think so."

"Do you know any other women?"

Tony cast his mind around the barren corners of his sheltered life, and remembered the letting agent.

"What's she like?"

"Very nice."

"Great. Phone her up."

This was something Tony would never have done on his own, but under the joint pressure from his flatmates, he eventually did. She said she would be delighted to come. "Tell her to bring her friends," they said to him. So he did.

"Good," said Freddie. "That should give us some leverage with the landlord, just in case."

"Just in case what?"

"Don't worry about it. It's just a bit of insurance. That's your line, isn't it?"

Tony also wondered what preparations they should make, what they should get in by way of supplies.

"Spend money?" said Jim. "Don't be daft."

"That's right," said Freddie. "We supply the premises, they bring the drink."

"What about food?"

"I like your sense of humour, Tony."

"We'll get some crisps and nuts."

Eventually, they got in a couple of bottles of spirits and two dozen cans of beer, splitting the cost three ways. Jim and Freddie decided that Tony's stereo was adequate, though not his records, but they managed to remedy that from their own collections and from friends.

As far as Jim and Freddie were concerned, the preparations were complete. Tony went to the supermarket at the top of Byres Road and, at his own expense, bought several large bags of crisps and nuts and some paper cups. He also cleared up and thoroughly cleaned the flat, which had become quite untidy since the arrival of his flatmates.

On the day before the party, he took particular care with his turn of the stairs. Insurance was his line, after all.

At 9 pm on the night of the party, Tony was sitting alone in the house. Guests were invited from eight o'clock onwards, but so far no one had turned up. Freddie had arranged to meet his girlfriend at the Queen Margaret Union and would be along later. Jim had hung about impatiently until twenty past eight, then decided to go down to the other students' union to look for business, leaving Tony in charge. "I'll spread the word in the Beer Bar," he said. "That should liven things up."

At 9.15 Tony was still on his own. He put on the TV to pass the time.

At 9.35 the doorbell rang. Tony got up and quickly went into the hall. How had they got into the building? Had the security door been left open? Never mind.

When he opened the front door there was no one there, but a note had been put through the letterbox. By now the handwriting was completely familiar:

Tell your logers to shut the front gate after them and oblige the gate was not got at great trouble from the counsel to be left swung open.
WB (Flat 2/1)

Tony experienced further forebodings about Bain's probable reaction to the party. On the other hand, maybe he was worrying unnecessarily. Maybe no one would turn up.

At ten o'clock George Mooney arrived with his girlfriend Liz. Tony had asked them to come early.

They sipped their drinks and stared at each other across the empty room. "This is a nice flat," said Liz.

"Thanks."

"Is anyone else coming?"

"I hope so."

"Wait till the pubs come out," said George.

"This is Saturday," said Liz. "There are places open all night."

"It's cheaper to come to a party. Don't worry, they'll show."

Sure enough, a few minutes later the door entry system buzzed.

"Is this where Eddie lives?" A girl's voice. Things were looking up.

"You mean Freddie?"

"Is this where the party is? Eddie invited us."

"Come on up."

The girls introduced themselves as Leanne and Sylvia. They each brought a bottle of wine. Tony served them drinks and they joined the silent circle.

"We met Eddie in the QM," said Leanne. "He said we had to come here." She looked around her. "I'm not quite sure why."

"Don't worry," said George. "The place'll soon be buzzin'."

Right on cue, the entry system obliged.

From then on the rate of arrivals steadily increased. The party spread out into the hall and kitchen. The music was turned up and dancing began. Just as the flat was beginning to look full, Jim arrived with an army, shortly followed by Freddie with another one.

Tony could no longer always hear the door buzzer. However, there was always someone nearby in the hall to answer it and indiscriminately admit whoever was there.

At one point, a small group of youngsters appeared on the landing, supporting a large, semi-conscious figure.

"We found this old guy lying in the close. He says he lives here."

"I don't think so."

"Hey pal, is this where you live? What's that? … He says he lives on the top floor."

"Fuck that. I'm no' carryin' him up another flight of stairs. You want to come to a party, mate?"

"Christ, he's a dead weight. Where will we put him?"

"Just sit him down in the hall."

"That's it. There we are. Right, where's the kitchen?"

Around midnight the phone rang. Before Tony could reach it, a drunk had answered it.

"Who was that?"

"Some guy called Kane, complaining about the noise. I told him to fuck off."

At about the same time, Charlie Clark and his team, having drunk all their money, emerged from the Bluebell Bar in Partick.

"Right, where'd that cunt say the party was?"

"Oldberry Road."

"Where's that?"

"Off Byres Road."

"We'll need a carry-out."

"Will we fuck."

"Aye we will. Fair's fair. Here's one comin'."

A young man, carrying a plastic bag, was walking along Dumbarton Road towards them. Charlie went up to him and towered over.

"Give us your carry-out, pal."

"But —"

"Did you hear what I said? Give us your fuckin' carry-out. I don't want to hit a man wi' specs."

467

The man handed over his bag and ran away.

"Right, what's in it?"

"For fuck's sake!"

"What's the matter?"

"It's a bag a messages. There's an all-night grocer down the road. He musta been there."

"You mean he was gettin' in his messages? At this time on a Saturday night? Fuckin' poof."

"Throw it away."

"Naw don't. It looks like a carry-out. It'll get us in the door."

"Here's another one comin'."

Charlie repeated his technique and they acquired another bag, this time containing drink. They set off for Byres Road.

Terry, Joan and the rest of their crowd were out party surfing. Their method was simple. From midnight onwards on a Saturday night, armed with several carry-outs (real or fake, depending upon the current financial situation) you toured the streets off Byres Road listening for the sound of a party you could bluff your way into.

At first they had no luck. They found several parties, but none was at a sufficiently advanced stage for gatecrashers to be admitted undetected. "We're friends of John", the usual announcement at the security door, did not work. Either (defying the laws of probability) there was no John at the party, or the host demanded a surname. At one place they were admitted to the building by an unwary guest and had almost made it to the top floor when a large, angry dog chased them back down again.

Their fortunes changed when they reached Oldberry Road. They could hear the party from the far end of the street. The buttons on the door entry system showed names but no flat numbers, so they pressed each of them in turn.

"See that old guy at the window? In the flat opposite the party?"

"You mean the baldy one with the phone?"

"Aye. When I press this button, his head twitches. See, he did it again."

"Never mind him. Which one's the party?"

"I doubt if they can hear the buzzer."

"Hey, the door's open. We don't need to bother."

"Great. Let's go."

In the back bedroom, through a haze of smoke, Tony could see a group of older men sitting round the edge of the bed.

"What's going on here?"

"Who the fuck are you?"

"Steady on, Danny, he's our host."

"Sorry man. It's OK. We're just havin' a wee blaw."

"But you can't! It's not —"

"Calm doon, man. It's only a wee bit dope. If I was you, I'd be mair bothered about thae folk in the kitchen drinkin' a' the water."

"I noticed that. What's going on there?"

"You serious, man? Where d'you come from?"

"Kilwinning."

"Aye it shows. If I was you I'd worry about them. Or about that cunt that was shootin' up in your toilet."

"*What*?"

"Why d'you think everybody had tae go ootside for a pish?"

Not long after Bain's phone call, Tony was again summoned to the hall, where a large, furious-looking woman met him.

"For Christ's sake, Tony, what are you playing at? You've wakened my kids, not to mention half the neighbourhood."

"I'm sorry, Mrs Anderson, I'm really sorry. I don't know where these people came from."

"What do you mean? They're your guests, for God's sake!"

"I don't know who they are. I don't know where they came from. It's a nightmare." Cathie Anderson's intimidating presence was finally too much for him and he burst into tears.

Cathie's attitude softened. She had begun to understand the situation. "Come on downstairs, son. Have a cup of tea. Have a wee rest from the fray and get your strength back."

He followed her down to the flat below, pushing through the overflow from the party that littered the stairs. In her flat the din seemed only marginally less, since so much of it was coming from the stairwell.

Cathie's husband George was there and their two young children. The children were wide awake, but well behaved. Cathie Anderson was not the sort of woman you argued with, whether she was your neighbour or your mother.

Cathie made tea and the Andersons listened sympathetically as Tony poured out his story. Tony had met both of them before, they had already made a fairly accurate assessment of his character, and so they had no difficulty believing him. They also knew what the west end was like, something Tony himself was just fully grasping for the first time.

"You'd better not wait too long," said George, "if you want to be there when the police arrive."

"Or you can hide from them down here if you want," said Cathie. "Let your flatmates face the music. From what you say, most of this is their fault."

Tony began to panic again. "Have you phoned the police?"

"No of course not," said Cathie.

"But you can be sure you-know-who has," said George.

"Probably about a dozen times by now," said Cathie.

Tony was tempted to take up their offer and hide out through the storm. But he was the tenant. It was his responsibility. "I'd better go back up," he said. "In a minute or two."

When the two policemen were admitted, one girl gave a scream of delight. "I never knew it was fancy dress!"

Tony was still downstairs, but Freddie met them in the hall. "How can I help you, officers?"

"I like your sense of humour, son. We've had complaints about the noise. About twenty from a Mr Bain next door."

"That obnoxious bastard."

"I couldn't possibly comment, sir."

"How many complaints did you say?"

"We haven't been able to log them all. Twenty at a rough estimate. Or maybe one big long one, depending on how you look at it."

"I'm sorry. I'll turn the stereo down."

"Is your stereo on?"

"I think so. Apart from that, I could ask them all to leave, but I don't think they'd listen."

"I see what you mean. We could give you a hand, but we might need backup."

"Anyway, since you're here, why don't you have a wee drink?"

"Since we're here, that sounds like a good idea."

"Hey that's my carry-out," said Charlie.

In Glasgow, stealing a carry-out is a capital offence, even when it's one you originally stole yourself.

The other man was much smaller than Charlie, but stood his ground well. "Steady on, pal, there's plenty of drink here."

"I'm no' your fuckin' pal, pal. If there's plenty of drink, you don't need my carry-out."

"What's the difference?" The man took a drink out of the can. That was a mistake. Charlie grabbed it from his hand. "Hey, steady on."

Tam and Willie had now joined them. "What's the problem, Charlie?"

"This cunt stole my carry-out."

"I never, I —"

"Fuckin' bastard. Saw the cunt earlier, never liked the looka him. See you, Jimmy, you a Catholic or a Protestant?"

"What's it got to do with you?"

"What's it got tae do wi' us? Just give us the answer and I'll fuckin' tell you. Are you a Catholic or a Protestant?"

"I'm an atheist."

"Are you deaf or just daft? Are you a Catholic atheist or a Proddy atheist?"

"Neither. I'm Jewish."

"Jesus Christ!"

"Aye, so was he. Jewish, I mean. Not an atheist."

"Thinks he's a funny cunt. For the last time, pal, are you a fuckin' Catholic Jewish atheist or a fuckin' Proddy Jewish atheist?"

"Fuck off."

"He's a Tim! Get the cunt!"

"I'm goany kill that bastard!"

"What's the matter, Bob?"

"He's chattin' up my bird."

"You only met her tonight."

"What difference does that make? I'm goany burst the four-eyed bastard!"

Several men with glasses looked worried. Many others, who were more than a few feet away, were fortunately out of earshot.

"Help us hold him back. He's goany murder that guy."

"Hold on, Bob. No use. He's too bloody strong."

"C'mere ya bastard." Bob jumped on the other man and they fell over together.

"Fucksake, they've smashed the stereo."

"It's bloody hot in here."

"I know, I'm sweltered. Why don't we open a window?"

"I already tried. It won't open."

"Is the catch off?"

"Aye, of course. It seems to be jammed."

"Take an end each. Right. Pull."

"No good. Try again."

"Here we go. Heave! Oh fuck!"

"Christ, that's done it."

"You OK?"

"Aye. We'd better take out the rest of the glass in case somebody gets cut."

At the police station, the switchboard was jammed with calls, mostly from Walter Bain. He'd also monopolised the emergency services. He'd even tried to get hold of his MP, but with no success.

"How can one man make so many calls?"

"He's using two mobiles as well as his land line. I think one of them's set to keep dialling 999, over and over and over."

"Have Dave and Frank reported back?"

"They asked for backup."

"I thought we sent Al and Sheila."

"They've asked for backup too."

"That's it. Send everybody. It's happy hour for the Glasgow criminals till we've cleared out that party."

"At least it's quiet elsewhere. For a Saturday night, that is."

"That's because everybody's at that fucking party."

For what seemed like an eternity, Tony looked on helplessly, as every room in the house filled to capacity and beyond, as the party spread out on to the landing, up the stairs, down the stairs, into the back court. Every time the house seemed about to burst, there came a new wave of arrivals, who squeezed in somehow. When the army of police arrived at 3 am, he felt nothing but profound relief.

He was escorted downstairs, along with a random selection of guests, through a mess of empty cans and bottles, intact and broken, half-full ones spilling their contents, as well as cigarette ends, vomit, urine, and much much more.

"Hey Tony," called one of his guests, one of the many strangers. "I hope it's no' your turn of the stairs this week."

The policemen laughed. They were enjoying themselves. This was much better than chasing criminals. There had been a few at the party, of course, but they'd been the first to make their escape.

Tony and the others were released early next morning. He didn't feel like going back to Oldberry Road, but had nowhere else to go. Any hopes that the building's condition might be less bad than he remembered disappeared as soon as he pushed open the broken security door.

A number of people still lay around the flat. They had been too drunk to make their escape when the police arrived, but had somehow managed to escape arrest. Probably the police had been reluctant to take anyone who was unable to walk unsupported. They included Jim and Freddie, though it was not clear whether they had been there all along, or had made their escape and returned later. Gus Mackinnon, the man from upstairs, was also still there; he seemed as lifeless as he had been all night, though he had somehow managed to move from the hall to the living room.

After checking that they were all still alive, Tony then spent two hours thoroughly cleaning the stairs and landing, from the top floor to the end of the close, and out to the front path, which he swept down, lifting all the litter from the front garden and the pavement, carefully closing the front gate behind him. He then went out to the back court (noting in passing that the back door lock was also broken) and cleaned it up as best he could; he wasn't quite sure how best to tackle the vomit on the drying green, but liberally splashing it with water seemed to help.

All of this time he was afraid of an encounter with Walter Bain. When he was cleaning the landing below his flat, he heard Bain's door open, but it closed again without the man making an appearance. He also glimpsed his face at the window when working both at the front and at the back. However, there was no direct confrontation. This didn't surprise Tony. That was not the man's style.

Tony suspected that Bain's displeasure would be shown in some other way. He was right.

When he had finished he wrote notes of apology, including a promise to pay for all damage, and put one through the letterbox of each of his neighbours; he left out Gus Mackinnon, who was still in Tony's flat, though now showing some signs of recovery.

After that, he found he had no stomach to get started on the interior mess; that could wait until the guests had all departed and Jim and Freddie had sufficiently recovered to be conscripted into assistance. Fortunately, it was a nice day outside, and the draught from the broken window was bearable, almost pleasant.

The only point at which he regretted this postponement was when the reporter arrived at the door.

When he eventually cleared up, there were some surprises waiting for him. Several records had been added to their collection, mostly ones which the owners had probably wanted to get rid of; however, this was academic, as Tony's sound system had been reduced to firewood. There was a chair in the kitchen which no one could remember having seen in the flat before. There were also many dummy carry-outs which had been brought (probably unnecessarily) in order to gain admission. They included a bag of empty cans, upside down, with a brick at the bottom for ballast, wine bottles variously filled with water, urine, bleach and other, less easily identifiable fluids, and a whisky bottle filled with weak tea.

The purpose of all of these was clear. The only enduring mystery was a plastic bag containing a loaf, a tub of Flora spread, a jar of marmalade, a bottle of semi-skimmed milk, a carton of Weetabix, a packet of bacon, and a tin of kidney beans that had been opened, partly consumed, then replaced in the bag.

As Tony had feared, a newspaper story appeared the following day:

WEST END PARTY "GOT A LITTLE OUT OF HAND"
25 ARRESTED

25 people were arrested at a party in Glasgow's west end early on Sunday morning, some of them for drug offences. It is believed that several hundred people attended the spree in a two-bedroom flat at 13 Oldberry Road, near Byres Road.

The flat's tenant, Tony Miller (19), who was charged with breach of the peace, claimed that most of the guests were unknown to him. "They just kept coming and coming," he said. "I couldn't stop them."

A police spokesman said they had received innumerable complaints from neighbours, though most of them were from one person. Walter Bain (62), owner of the flat opposite, denounced the party as "absolutely outrageous". "This is a family building," he said, "that I have lived in with my family for 35 years. This tenant is evil. He will have to go."

Another neighbour, Gus Mackinnon (56) took a more philosophical view. "It is a tribute to the great architects and builders of the nineteenth century that our sturdy little tenement should have escaped relatively unscathed after accommodating so many visitors. I could name a few modern builders whose structures would have collapsed under a fraction of that number."

However, after the initial embarrassment and trauma had begun to fade, Tony began to feel that he might survive the incident. The party was known about at his work (many of his colleagues had been there) but there was no indication that the management of Sunlight Insurance knew about the criminal charge or the newspaper report or, if they did, that they intended to take any action about it.

Tony's landlord also proved supportive at first. Since he had bought the flat five years earlier, complaints about his tenants from Walter Bain had been almost a daily occurrence. In a way, he was almost glad to have given the man something substantial to complain about at last. He told Tony that the cost of much of the damage could be recovered by insurance and that he could have time to pay the rest. This, plus the fact that the bill would be split three ways, made it affordable to Tony and his flatmates. Economies would be required, but it looked as if they would be able to keep the flat on.

But things were to change as soon as the Bain campaign began to take effect. None of the other neighbours seemed to bear a grudge, but Bain made up for them a hundredfold. Everyone who could possibly be instrumental in getting Tony and his flatmates removed from 13 Oldberry Road – Tony's employers, his landlord, the factors – were subjected to a continuous assault of incoherent phone calls and ungrammatical correspondence, until they felt compelled to take the easy way out. Sunlight Insurance, who now, thanks to Bain, had seen the newspaper stories and knew about the criminal charge, dismissed Tony from their employment. His landlord, after his initial resistance, gave in when he saw another flat for sale that looked like a good Bain-free letting prospect: he submitted an offer for it which was accepted, put the Oldberry Road flat on the market in order to raise the money, and sent a notice to quit to Tony and his flatmates.

And so it came about, on the last night of their tenancy, a few hours before Walter Bain would be found murdered, Tony and Jim were sitting in the flat feeling sorry for themselves. Freddie had left the day before. They were due to move out in the morning. Tony, humiliated, jobless and in debt, his youthful dreams shattered, would be returning to his parents' home in Kilwinning.

"It's all Bain's fault," said Tony.

"I know," said Jim. "The party was a bad scene, but we'd have got away with it, apart from him."

This had been the theme all evening. Tony had never been much of a drinker – a little more alcohol on the night of the party might have eased his pain a little – but on this special occasion he and Jim had spent their last west end evening in a succession of local pubs. They had run into a few people who had been at the party – a statistical certainty – and several had bought them drinks after hearing their story. The unaccustomed amount of alcohol had an unexpected effect upon Tony's personality. It broke through his normally introverted and inhibited nature and released a tendency towards aggression.

"That man's ruined my life," he said. "I'm going to do the world a favour and kill him."

Jim had been hearing this all evening. "Aye, so you should," he said. "Anyway, that's the carry-out finished. I'm off to bed."

"I'll just finish my drink first," said Tony. "Then I'm going to nip across the landing and murder the bastard."

EPILOGUE: WHO DONE IT

September 2000

When Bob Waddell had staggered out the front door, Cathie took her leave from the table where she had been sitting and walked over to the one vacated by Bob. "Mind if I join you?"

"Certainly," said Ernie. "I mean, of course we don't mind. He won't be back. You're quite safe."

"I didn't feel unsafe."

"Quite," said Norrie. "Anyway, Aitken isn't in tonight. You have our permission to thump Bob again if you want. We could do with a laugh."

"Absolutely," said Ernie. "Just don't tell him we said so."

"Where would the world be," said Cathie, "without such hypocrisy to oil the wheels? But I wouldn't waste my strength on the likes of him. I wanted to have a word with you about Gus."

"Good idea," said Ernie. "We were thinking the same."

"George's turn to hold the fort, is it?" asked Norrie.

"Yes, but he's quite happy. He's got the kids watching a video while he sits at his laptop working on his *magnum opus*."

"What's it called again?"

"*Caledonian Visions: A History of Scottish Speculative Fiction from Hogg to Gray.*"

"If it's all the same," said Ernie, "I think I'll wait until the movie comes out."

"To tell you the truth," said Cathie, "I may do the same myself. But if you ever breathe a word of that to George, I'll have to kill you."

"Duly warned."

Cathie lifted the drink she had brought over from the other table. "At least he's got a publishing contract for this one. Unlike the case with his novel."

"Still no luck with that?" asked Ernie.

"Not a nibble."

"Maybe it's just as well," said Norrie. "From what he's told us it would probably get him the sack."

"Just think," said Ernie. "He would become a house husband and you'd have to go back to teaching full time."

"I wouldn't mind that at all," said Cathie. "In fact it's quite an attractive prospect. Unfortunately, we need the money. For some reason, society rewards working in an academic madhouse more highly than teaching in a primary school. I've never quite understood that. Speaking of which, I needed a break from the revolutionary cell over there. Dennie and Ted are OK, but it can get a bit tiresome."

"Let me guess," said Norrie. "'Tory' Blair is a traitor to the cause. He's just as bad as Thatcher."

"Something like that."

"George and I have to listen to it every day," said Norrie. "Mind you, the far right opposition is just as bad.

Being stuck between them is like being the ball in a squash court."

"I take it George hasn't been converted?" asked Ernie.

"He's got more sense. Anyway, I wouldn't let him. I should really take offence," she continued. "I think Blair's doing a good job. I voted for him."

"So did I," said Ernie.

"So did I," said Norrie.

"Really?" said Ernie. "Maybe Dennie and Ted have a point after all."

"Fuck off."

"I mean," said Cathie. "He introduced the minimum wage, he's putting money into schools and hospitals, the Good Friday Agreement has done more to bring peace to Northern Ireland than anything else for decades. But I didn't come over for another political discussion. I want to talk about Gus."

"So do we," said Ernie. "But it wasn't easy while Bob was still here. Empathy isn't exactly his strong point, even when he's sober."

"Where's he gone off to?"

"God knows," said Norrie. "Probably down to Partick to meet some of his crooked pals. We're better not knowing."

"So how's it been at Number 13?" asked Ernie. "What's it like living in a Bain-free environment?"

"You wouldn't believe it. It's as if the building had been shrouded in a black cloud that's now been lifted, and that the sun's come out. It's bizarre. It doesn't seem right. That a man's death could have that effect. Mind you, I don't want to speak ill of the departed…"

"Oh yes you do."

"Well, OK, if anyone's worth making an exception for... It's unbelievable. Everyone has a new spring in their step. It's just a pity that someone had to be held accountable."

"That's the law."

"I know, but just about everyone else in the building wanted to do the same thing. I can't help feeling sorry for her."

"She must have been the last person that anyone suspected. Why did she do it?"

"Who knows?" said Cathie. "She's had to put up with him for all these years. It can't have been easy. It must finally have been too much for her."

"Were there no signs?" asked Ernie.

"Possibly, but it's always easier with hindsight. It came as a complete surprise to everyone."

"She must have hated him as much as the rest of you."

"Obviously. But to tell you the truth, she's always been something of a mystery. She never said very much. We had no idea what she was thinking."

"Of course, when you think of it, she's had to suffer the man far longer than anyone else."

"That's true. In the early days the two of them always seemed solid, like twins. But, thinking back, I did detect a few cracks more recently, just odd signs. After Callum died, she stopped me on the stairs and told me that she had wanted Bain to phone an ambulance, but he wouldn't listen. I was quite surprised."

"They never had any kids, did they?"

"No," said Cathie. "It's ironic, considering the way he kept banging on about it being a family building. I don't know why they never had a family. It may have been a sore point with her."

It was now a week since Walter Bain's death and the mystery had been solved for almost as long. Mrs Bain had confessed to it the very next day. Her fingerprints had been the only ones on the poker and, as soon as this was drawn to her attention, her resistance had broken down.

Getting an explanation from her proved more difficult. They had been wakened in the middle of the night by someone repeatedly ringing their doorbell and banging on the front door. When Walter had challenged the caller from behind the safety of the storm door, there had been no reply. It still wasn't known who was responsible. The suspects were Gus, Archie MacDuff, Joe Robinson, Angela Murray and Tony Miller. But Tony had now gone and none of the others could remember.

All the police could get from Agnes Bain was, "I just wanted to go back to bed, but he wouldn't stop. He went on and on and on and on and on about it. He wouldn't stop. I couldn't stand it any longer."

"Anyway, about Gus," said Cathie. "You know what his drinking's been like since Callum died. He can't go on like that."

"You're right," said Norrie. "He's got a strong constitution. Otherwise he could never have survived the abuse he's heaped on his body over the years. But he can't do it forever."

"It's a horrible thing to say," said Cathie. "But maybe Bain's death may provide him with some closure. He still blames himself for what happened. But that bloody man also had a lot to answer for."

"He's certainly brightened up over the past week," said Ernie. "Though I haven't noticed him drinking any less. He says he's celebrating."

"So where is he tonight?"

"Who knows? I expect he's continuing his celebrations with a pub crawl. I've no doubt he'll appear shortly."

Right on cue, Gus entered the bar. However, he was sober. The others tried to hide their surprise as he sat down beside them.

"Where have you been?" asked Norrie.

"At home," said Gus. "Listening to music. Wagner, Tchaikovsky, Shostakovich. The loudest pieces in my collection, at full volume. There's no one downstairs any more to bang on the ceiling."

"We've just been talking about you," said Ernie. "We were about to stage an intervention. We think it's high time you cut down drastically on the drink, before your long-suffering liver finally calls it a day."

"Your intervention won't be necessary," said Gus. "I've already come to the same conclusion. I don't have any choice. My pension's rubbish and my savings have almost run out. I'll need to get my act together and find a job."

He looked round the company, smiling. "But that's enough of that. I'm dying of thirst. Whose round is it?"

ACKNOWLEDGEMENT

I would like to thank The National Trust for Scotland for kindly granting permission for me to quote the extract from their guidebook The Tenement House, which neatly sums up the traditional image of Scottish tenement life, as well as explaining a few terms that may be unfamiliar to readers outside Scotland.

The Tenement House is a flat, part of the tenement building at 145 Buccleuch Street, Glasgow, and maintained by the Trust as a fascinating time capsule. It was occupied for more than 50 years in the first half of the twentieth century by a shorthand typist Miss Agnes Toward, and her furniture and many of her effects have been preserved in the flat, providing a valuable insight into Glasgow tenement life at that time.

This book presents a, slightly different, picture of tenement life in the second half of the same century.

Angus McAllister

THE KRUGG SYNDROME

Angus McAllister

One day Arthur Montrose, 18, woke up from a fainting fit, and realised that he was the vanguard of the Krugg invasion force.

The Krugg were a race of alien trees destined to destroy puny Earthling culture and enslave this miserable planet for their own ends.

But as Arthur struggled against the crippling loss of his telepathic powers and fought to apply the mighty Krugg intellect to the affairs of the law firm of Salamander and Smail, his mission suffered its first major setback.

He was unable to contact any fellow Kruggs. The trees here were even more stupid than the humans – and meanwhile the twin vices of sex and alcohol shone before him like beacons of Earthly knowledge…

Published by Grafton Books in 1988. Copies are available online.

"… a rollicking, good-spirited read, that's guaranteed to give you a lift." Glasgow *Evening Times*.

"Set against a well-drawn background of seedy bedsits and a decaying solicitor's office, THE KRUGG SYNDROME combines a send-up of the 'alien invaders' genre with a convincing picture of Glasgow in the 1960s. Entertaining." *Paperback Inferno*

"… McAllister plays adroitly for giggles and produces an engaging effect of seediness… Any alien scourge whose most cogent effort consists of writing THE KRUGG ARE COMING on toilet walls is OK by me." David Langford in *White Dwarf*.

"Scottish comic novels are rare, and good ones about lawyers rarer still, so I was delighted to find that Angus McAllister's marvellous The Krugg Syndrome, about a young law clerk in the west of Scotland who believes himself to be a vegetable from outer space, can be obtained through Amazon. It is much funnier than the same author's Scottish Law of Leases, which is, of course, a good book too." Sheriff Andrew Lothian *The Journal of the Law Society of Scotland*.

THE CANONGATE STRANGLER

Angus McAllister

The Canongate Strangler is a psychological thriller with supernatural overtones set in Edinburgh: the wynds and closes of the Old town, the Georgian facades of the new; the pubs; the Castle; Arthur's Seat… Edward Middleton, a respectable lawyer, finds himself strangely involved in a series of murders. Horrified, he at first tries to explain, then to prevent, their headlong progress – but who is the man the press are calling 'The Canongate Strangler'?

Published by Dog & Bone in 1990. Copies are available online.

"A gripping and highly original psychological thriller."
Glasgow *Evening Times*

"McAllister generates a vivid sense of one consciousness battling to stop itself splitting in two and uses his Edinburgh – old alleys, steep stairs, modern discos and pubs – to great effect … Give the book half an hour in a shadowy room on a winter's night and the hair will soon start to prickle at the back of your neck." *The Guardian*

"… an enjoyable, compelling thriller. An added distinction is McAllister's handling of the setting – and what better setting for such a story than schizophrenic Edinburgh?" Brian McCabe *The Scotsman*

"… a very fine first novel of acute originality … the superb, laconic, comic and grotesque closing sequences live up to the novel's great models." Professor Douglas Gifford *Books in Scotland*

"The unveiling of this mystery is gripping, and the city itself and its layers of society is well captured as Middleton – or is it he? – sinks into a morass of supernatural terror." Edinburgh *Evening News*

"Angus McAllister … goes right to the heart of the Scottish *doppelganger* tradition with *The Canongate Strangler*, a tale of murder in Auld Reekie which invokes comparisons with Stevenson and, in that it shares with *The Justified Sinner* a climactic scene on Arthur's Seat, James Hogg. Unreservedly recommended." *The Journal of the Law Society of Scotland*

THE CYBER PUPPETS

Angus McAllister

Prime time science fiction satire.

The Lairds of Glendoune are rich and powerful, their wealth based on the family whisky. Their constant crises keep the lawyers and hospitals in Primeburgh in business, the eldest son Wilson Laird tried to frame his father for murder (but his parents forgave him after his near-fatal accident) and no-one notices when the family patriarch Hector Laird comes back from Europe with a new head. Add all this to his memory lapses and complete absence of free will and Hector's son-in-law Scott Maxwell slowly becomes convinced that this can't be right ... and then the reality around him collapses altogether, plunging him into a devastated world of the future.

Back in the real world, the Earth is dying; the environment is poisoned and human society itself is on the downward plunge. What has all this to do with a twentieth century American soap opera?

Published in 2012 as an e book by Brain in a Jar Books, available from Amazon Kindle.

"Enjoyed reading this book, set in a very Dallas/ Dynasty like soap world, where one character starts to realise how false it all is and questions the nature of what is happening around – while lots of ridiculous soap opera antics keep the story moving forward ... a very entertaining science fiction yarn that had me laughing." Amazon reader

"The Cyber Puppets is part Sci-Fi, part comedy, part thriller and part social commentary ... Ben Elton collides with Iain M Banks ... it will have you laughing and scratching your head as the plot twists." Amazon reader

ABOUT THE AUTHOR

Angus McAllister worked as a solicitor and university professor and is now retired. He has written several legal textbooks and a number of legal articles, as well as fiction. Angus's earlier novels include *The Krugg Syndrome*, *The Canongate Strangler* and *The Cyber Puppets*.